Beyond the Horizon

Carol Prescott

Published by Carol Prescott, 2024.

BEYOND THE HORIZON

First edition. October 8, 2024.

Copyright © 2024 Carol Prescott.

ISBN: 979-8227966933

Written by Carol Prescott.

Chapter 1: The Diagnosis

The beeping of the monitor melds into a rhythm I never wanted to learn. I sit propped up against the crisp sheets, the stark white of the hospital room bleeding into the confines of my mind. With each beep, the doctor's voice echoes in my ears, a relentless metronome keeping time to my spiraling thoughts. "Leukemia." The word hangs in the air, a specter I can't shake off. It lingers, casting shadows over every vibrant memory I cling to, memories that seem so fragile now.

Outside, the sun surrenders to the horizon, its fiery orange glow a stark reminder of the life I had just a breath ago. I think back to the last time I felt the grass beneath my bare feet, the wind in my hair as I sprinted through the fields of Willow Creek, laughter bubbling up like a stream. My friends, their faces painted in hues of joy and mischief, always so sure of the future that awaited us. We had plans—dreams bursting at the seams of our teenage hearts. But now, the tangible world beyond the hospital window feels like a fading postcard, the colors leeching away with every passing moment.

I catch sight of my reflection in the glass. My normally sun-kissed skin looks pale, almost ghostly, and the dark circles under my eyes are the only reminder of the nights spent tossing and turning, my thoughts colliding in a frenzy. My auburn hair, usually cascading in unruly waves, is tied up in a haphazard bun, strands escaping like they're trying to flee the reality I can't escape.

The door creaks open, and in walks my mom, her eyes puffy and red-rimmed, a warrior draped in the armor of love and worry. She's been here, steadfast like a lighthouse, guiding me through this storm. She carries a half-eaten donut from the cafeteria, the sugary glaze smudged on her fingers. "I thought you might like a treat," she says, her voice light but wavering, as if it might crack under the weight of her worry.

I manage a smile, though it feels more like a grimace. "A donut? You shouldn't have. I'm on a strict diet of hospital food and despair," I tease, trying to lighten the atmosphere, but the joke falls flat, swallowed by the gravity of the moment.

"Don't be like that," she replies, a hint of laughter breaking through her somber expression. "You need your strength for the fight ahead." She plops down in the chair beside my bed, her presence both a comfort and a reminder of the burden I now carry.

"What fight?" I scoff, even though I know there's truth in her words. The reality of it is a heavy cloak draped around my shoulders. "It's just... me against my own body. It's not exactly a fair match."

She reaches for my hand, her grip firm, and I can feel the warmth seeping into my cold skin. "You are stronger than you think, Ava. You'll surprise yourself." Her optimism is infectious, but I can't help but feel a swell of anger bubble beneath the surface.

"Yeah, well, maybe I just want to be a normal seventeen-year-old for once. I didn't sign up for this," I snap, my voice sharper than I intended. A moment of silence stretches between us, thick and heavy. I know it's not fair to lash out at her. She's navigating this storm, too, just trying to keep us afloat.

"I know you didn't, honey," she whispers, her eyes glistening with unshed tears. "But you're not alone in this. You have me, and we'll get through it together."

I nod, though the weight of her words settles uncomfortably in my stomach. The thought of sharing this burden feels suffocating. I want to scream, to rage against the unfairness of it all, but instead, I look away, staring into the dusky sky.

As the sun fades into twilight, the room seems to fill with shadows. I close my eyes, wishing I could shut out the world, but the sounds of the hospital seep through—people murmuring in the halls, the faint clatter of carts, and the distant wails of someone else's struggle. I open my eyes, taking a shaky breath.

"Can we talk about something else?" I ask, desperate for a distraction. "Something not involving blood tests or medications?"

Mom smiles softly, her eyes brightening. "Of course! Did I tell you that Jess sent you a message?"

"Jess? The one with the ridiculously big curls and even bigger dreams?" I chuckle, picturing my best friend. Jess was the kind of person who could make any day feel like an adventure, her laughter infectious.

"She said she's planning a surprise for you when you get out of here. Something about a scavenger hunt through the town," Mom says, a glint of mischief dancing in her eyes.

I can't help but laugh. "A scavenger hunt? She must have lost her mind."

"She might be a little bonkers, but that's why we love her, right?"

The corners of my mouth lift, and for a fleeting moment, I forget the beeping machines, the needles, the loneliness that clings like a second skin. I think of the ridiculous clues Jess would concoct, the way she'd probably make it all sound far more dramatic than it actually was, her voice a lively melody that could pull anyone from the depths of despair.

"Maybe I'll be well enough to participate," I say, feeling a spark of hope ignite within me.

Mom squeezes my hand tighter, as if grounding me in the moment. "You will be, Ava. One step at a time."

As we sit together, the fading light of the day begins to weave itself into a tapestry of shared moments. The weight of my diagnosis doesn't lift, but for now, amidst the scent of antiseptic and the rhythm of machines, I can feel the warmth of love wrapping around me like a comforting blanket.

The next morning dawns, insipid and gray, as if the sky itself mourns the loss of color in my life. The sunlight that should have poured through my window instead shies away, leaving me cocooned in this sterile realm of pale walls and the persistent hum of fluorescent lights. The scent of antiseptic now feels like a second skin, clinging to me and invading my thoughts. I sit up slowly, feeling like a marionette whose strings have been tangled in a cosmic joke.

The steady rhythm of beeping returns, a reminder that I'm still tethered to this place, and just beyond the thin walls, lives are being lived in vibrant color—laughter, joy, and love, all the things I want to reach for but can't quite grasp. I shift in bed, the cotton sheets crinkling around me, and watch as a nurse enters, her cheerful demeanor almost startling against the backdrop of my gloom.

"Good morning, Ava! How are we feeling today?" she chirps, adjusting her scrubs, which are patterned with bright cartoon characters.

"Like a pancake that's been flipped too many times," I reply, trying to inject a hint of humor into the morning's lethargy. "You know, flat and slightly burnt."

She laughs, a genuine sound that cuts through the monotony. "Well, let's see if we can flip you back into something resembling a fluffy soufflé." She checks my vitals with the precision of a seasoned chef, her movements efficient but gentle.

"Are soufflés supposed to have an expiration date?" I ask, my tone half-serious, half-playful. "Because if I'm going to be one, I'd like to have a good run."

The nurse smiles, her eyes crinkling at the corners. "You're in luck! You've got plenty of time left in the oven. Just hang tight while I get the doctor."

As she leaves, the room falls back into a silence that feels almost oppressive. I let my gaze wander around, landing on the bulletin board plastered with colorful drawings from children who've stayed here. A crayon-rendered sun beams at me from one corner, while a stick-figure family holds hands beneath it. A pang of longing pierces through me. I used to think of the future in shades of gold and bright blue. Now it feels like I'm lost in a fog, every step forward shrouded in uncertainty.

The doctor enters, a whirlwind of white coat and serious expression. He glances at my chart, his brow furrowing slightly, as if the numbers and notes held some secret I was too young to understand.

"Good morning, Ava. How are we doing?" he asks, his voice steady but edged with the familiarity of clinical detachment.

"Like a pancake," I say again, hoping the levity cuts through the medical jargon.

He chuckles softly, a sound that doesn't quite reach his eyes. "Well, that's an interesting metaphor. I'd say you're more of a soufflé in the making."

I raise an eyebrow, the corners of my mouth twitching in amusement. "I suppose it depends on how you define fluffiness, Doctor."

With a brief smile, he launches into the details of my treatment plan. It's a haze of medical terminology, words like "chemotherapy" and "side effects" swirling around me like leaves caught in a whirlwind. I nod at all the right moments, but my mind drifts elsewhere—toward the conversations I won't have, the plans that will remain unmade.

"So, in layman's terms," I say, cutting through his detailed explanation, "when do I get to be me again?"

He pauses, a flicker of something—sympathy, perhaps?—crossing his features. "That depends on how your body responds to treatment. We will be monitoring you closely."

"Monitoring sounds a lot like babysitting," I quip, "and I don't need a babysitter."

His expression lightens, though the gravity of the situation lingers in the air. "We'll aim for a combination of freedom and support. You'll still get to be you; it just might take a little longer than you hoped."

"Great, so I'm on the long path to adulthood," I reply, my sarcasm buoyed by a hint of desperation. "Can I at least get a trophy for enduring all this?"

He smirks. "I'll see what I can do about that. Maybe a sticker on your chart?"

As he leaves, I let out a breath I didn't know I was holding, and the silence of the room wraps around me like a familiar blanket. I pull out my phone, scrolling through a feed filled with snapshots of friends living their lives—gatherings, adventures, and laughter. My thumb hovers over a message from Jess, the ever-enthusiastic cheerleader who could make even the most mundane events feel like an epic saga.

"Can't wait for your scavenger hunt! I've got the clues all planned out. Are you ready for an adventure?"

I let out a soft laugh, envisioning her wild hair bouncing as she rattles off ridiculous ideas. "Scavenger hunt? I'll be more like the trophy you find buried under the couch cushions," I type back, the corners of my mouth lifting. "But sure, let's make it interesting."

Just as I hit send, the door creaks open again, and in steps my dad, his presence as grounding as an oak tree in the middle of a storm. He's holding a lopsided smile, the kind that's meant to convey warmth but has a hint of worry lurking in the corners.

"Hey, pancake. How's the soufflé?" he asks, his voice soft but teasing.

"Lumpy and in need of some serious whisking," I reply, throwing him a grin that feels almost genuine.

"Can't have you flopping around like that," he says, taking a seat beside me. "I brought your favorite—peppermint tea from that little café down the street." He holds up a steaming cup, and the familiar scent wafts through the air, momentarily replacing the sterile smell of the hospital.

"You're a lifesaver," I murmur, accepting the cup with both hands. It feels comforting, the warmth seeping into my skin. "At least something from outside still tastes like home."

He watches me carefully, a mix of concern and pride in his gaze. "You know, you're the bravest person I know. Not everyone could handle this with so much humor."

"Dad, I'm just trying to cope. You know how hard it is to sit here, listening to the adult world go on without me."

"I do. But you're not alone in this."

Our eyes lock, and for a moment, it feels like we're both balancing on a tightrope stretched over a canyon of fear and uncertainty. Then the moment shatters, a loud crash echoing from the hallway, breaking the fragile tension.

"What was that?" I ask, my heart racing as the sound reverberates through the walls.

"I'm not sure, but it sounds like some serious chaos out there," Dad says, glancing toward the door.

"Just another day in the hospital, right?" I mutter, trying to mask my sudden surge of anxiety with humor.

As if on cue, the door swings open, and in bounds a wild-eyed intern, clutching a clipboard that looks like it has seen better days. "Uh, sorry to interrupt, but we're experiencing a slight... mishap with one of the machines down the hall. Nothing to worry about! Just a minor meltdown."

A chuckle escapes me, and I shoot my dad a sidelong glance. "You know, this place is starting to feel like a reality show."

He laughs, a rich sound that makes the atmosphere feel lighter, just for a moment. "You should pitch that idea. 'Survivor: Hospital Edition.'"

We share a smile, both aware of the uncertain road ahead. I sip my tea, letting its warmth settle into my bones, even as the reality of my situation looms like a shadow in the corner of the room. Today may have started in gray, but amid the chaos and worry, I can feel a flicker of resilience beginning to glow within me, a tiny flame against the darkness.

The day drags on, the clock's ticking almost mocking in its insistence that time marches forward while I feel frozen in a moment I can't escape. The tea has long cooled beside me, but I clutch the cup like a lifeline, my fingers wrapped around the warmth. It's familiar, grounding me even as the sterile smell of antiseptic seeps deeper into my senses, threatening to overwhelm me.

Nurses come and go, their chatter an unending background hum, while the distant beeping of machines forms a bizarre symphony that accompanies the parade of medical professionals. They float in and out of my consciousness like characters in a play, their faces blurring into a montage of concern and efficiency. It's as if I'm in a bubble, peering out at a world that has not been shaken by the earth-shattering news that has cracked my own foundation.

As the afternoon sun begins its descent, a knock breaks the rhythm of my thoughts. Jess bursts into the room, a whirlwind of energy in her oversized sweater, her hair bouncing with every step. "Surprise! The scavenger hunt planning committee has arrived!" she announces, brandishing a clipboard like a trophy.

"Planning committee?" I chuckle, appreciating her effort to inject some normalcy into this chaos. "I thought that was a one-person job."

"Not when that one person is me," she grins, plopping down onto the edge of my bed. "I need your input, oh wise one. We can't have you flopping around without a proper adventure, now can we?"

I shake my head, still trying to wrap my mind around the fact that she's here. "You know, I'd rather not get lost in a hospital. I think I'm already familiar with all the nooks and crannies."

"Exactly! That's the fun part! You'll have the entire hospital as your playground. It's practically a maze. Think of it as a 'Survivor' challenge, but instead of voting someone off the island, you just take a detour to the gift shop."

I can't help but smile at her enthusiasm, her excitement a balm against the weight of my reality. "What's on the itinerary for this scavenger hunt? Searching for the best saltine cracker? Finding the hidden stash of ginger ale?"

"Even better," she says, her eyes sparkling with mischief. "We're going to collect mementos. Each clue leads to a place, and each place has a memory attached. It's going to be epic. You in?"

"Sure, why not? I'll be the intrepid explorer," I reply, leaning into the idea, allowing myself to imagine the thrill of the hunt. "Just promise me there are no needles involved."

"Deal!" she says, shaking my hand as if sealing a sacred pact. "Now, let's start planning this thing. First clue... hmm, how about the cafeteria? I hear they have a very special dish today—mystery meat surprise!"

I laugh, a sound that feels foreign yet refreshing. "Oh, nothing says 'adventure' quite like a game of 'guess that meat.'"

Jess flips her hair back, a dramatic flair I've always admired. "It's all part of the challenge. Plus, you'll need sustenance to fuel your epic quest."

Our laughter fills the room, and for the first time, I feel a flicker of hope threading through my fears. We dive into planning, Jess flipping through her notes, jotting down ideas with an enthusiasm that seems boundless. As she rattles off locations—the garden, the rooftop, the little coffee stand down the hall—I imagine each stop filled with memories we could share, the mundane transformed into extraordinary.

Then the door swings open again, and a doctor I don't recognize steps in, his expression a mixture of seriousness and a hint of urgency. "Ava, we need to talk," he says, glancing at Jess, who suddenly goes quiet, sensing the shift in the air.

My heart races. "Is something wrong?"

He hesitates, and my stomach drops. "There have been some unexpected results from your latest tests. I need to discuss them with you."

"What kind of results?" I ask, my voice trembling slightly as Jess's hand squeezes mine, grounding me in a moment that suddenly feels fraught with tension.

The doctor pulls a chair closer, his demeanor professional yet somehow heavy with the weight of what's to come. "It's best if we go over everything in detail. I'll try to be as clear as possible."

"Just say it," I insist, a mix of impatience and dread swirling within me. "I'm not a child; I can handle it."

"Ava, the treatment plan we discussed—there's been a complication. The leukemia is more aggressive than we initially thought. We need to adjust your approach immediately."

My world tilts again, a fresh wave of panic crashing over me like a tide. "More aggressive? What does that mean?"

He runs a hand through his hair, taking a moment before answering. "It means we'll need to start a more intensive treatment regimen. We want to ensure we're addressing it as effectively as possible, but it may involve some side effects that could be more challenging."

The room spins, the vibrant plans I had for our scavenger hunt suddenly dimmed by the stark reality of his words. Jess's hand tightens around mine, her silent support a tether in this storm.

"What kind of side effects?" I manage to ask, my voice barely above a whisper.

"Fatigue, nausea, possible hair loss. We'll also need to increase your hospital visits," he explains, his tone as measured as it is clinical. "I know this isn't what you wanted to hear."

I nod, fighting back tears, an internal battle raging between the urge to scream and the desperate desire to be strong. "So... I won't get to go home anytime soon?"

He meets my gaze, compassion mingling with professionalism. "Not for a while. But we'll be here for you, and we'll do everything we can to help you through this."

The weight of his words sinks in, heavy and suffocating. I feel as if I'm being pulled under water, gasping for air. Jess's presence beside me is my only buoy in this swelling sea of uncertainty.

"Can you give us a moment?" Jess asks, her voice steady as she tries to shield me from the weight of the news.

The doctor nods and steps out, the door closing behind him with a soft click that reverberates in the silence that follows.

"Hey," Jess whispers, her expression fierce and determined. "You're not alone in this, okay? We'll fight together. I promise."

I want to believe her, but the chasm between reality and hope feels too wide to bridge. "What if I'm not strong enough?" I admit, my voice cracking under the strain of vulnerability.

"You are. And if you need me to be your strength, I'll do it. We'll make it through, one ridiculous scavenger hunt at a time."

As her words wrap around me like a comforting blanket, the room feels both stifling and strangely safe. But then, as I look out the window to the horizon where the sun has completely disappeared, a commotion erupts in the hallway. Shouts rise and fall, a cacophony that disrupts the fragile peace we've carved out.

"What's happening?" I ask, panic rising again, a prickly sensation creeping down my spine.

Jess stands, peering through the glass window, her face paling as she squints at the scene unfolding outside. "I think... I think something is going wrong. They're calling for security."

My heart thunders in my chest as dread coils tighter around me. "What do you mean? What's going on?"

Before Jess can answer, the door bursts open again, this time with more urgency, and in walks a nurse, her face drawn and serious. "Ava, we need you to stay calm. There's been a situation on your floor, and we need to evacuate some patients."

The air in the room goes cold, and I exchange a terrified glance with Jess. "What kind of situation?"

"Just stay with me," the nurse instructs, her voice soothing yet firm. "We're going to take care of you, but we need to move quickly."

I grab Jess's hand tightly, my mind racing as panic begins to swirl once more. "What's happening?"

"Stay close," the nurse says, and as she begins to guide us toward the door, I can't shake the feeling that everything is about to change in ways I never saw coming. My heart pounds like a war drum, and in that moment, I realize that this fight is far from over.

Chapter 2: Meeting Nate

I hadn't anticipated the dull hum of hospital machinery would become a part of my everyday soundtrack. The sterile walls of the ward, once an unwelcome prison, began to feel oddly familiar, even cozy in an unsettling way. The scent of antiseptic hung in the air like an unwelcome guest, but it was here, amid the rhythm of beeping monitors and distant footsteps, that my world would take an unexpected turn. I was still grappling with my diagnosis, the words "you have cancer" echoing in my mind like a broken record, when a new patient shuffled into my life.

Nate entered the cafeteria like a gust of wind through a stuffy room, his dark hair tousled in a way that suggested he'd fought a losing battle with a comb. He radiated a kind of reckless charm, his blue eyes sparkling with mischief, despite the hospital gown hanging loosely around his frame. I was nursing a limp sandwich that tasted like cardboard, each bite a reminder of the culinary abyss that was cafeteria food. I looked up just as he plopped into the seat across from me, his smile infectious, as if he carried a pocketful of sunshine with him.

"Is that a sandwich or a sad excuse for a meal?" he quipped, raising an eyebrow as he gestured toward my plate.

"It's definitely sad," I replied, unable to suppress a smile. "I think they call it 'hospital cuisine.'"

"Ah, the infamous H.C.," he declared dramatically, placing a hand over his heart as if he were recounting a great tragedy. "Legend has it, no one has ever actually enjoyed it."

We shared a laugh that floated through the cafeteria, a momentary reprieve from the heavy air of illness that usually weighed down our conversations. I had almost forgotten how to laugh, how to feel anything other than the creeping dread that had settled in my chest since my diagnosis. Nate had a way of easing that tension, a magnetic presence that pulled me into his orbit.

"What's your poison?" he asked, nodding toward the array of food options that seemed to conspire against our taste buds. "I'll trade you my jello cup for your sandwich. I hear it's a real delicacy."

"Is that really the best you can do?" I shot back, my tone playful, testing the waters of our budding friendship. "How about a side of sympathy instead?"

"Sympathy? Boring! I'd rather barter in jello, thank you very much," he retorted, leaning back in his chair, his confidence palpable. "Besides, sympathy doesn't come with a cherry on top."

As our banter continued, I learned that Nate had been in and out of this place for as long as he could remember. He had a knack for storytelling, weaving tales about the mischief he had caused before he got tangled up in this battle. There was something liberating in his words, a reckless abandon that made me want to step out of my own shadow and join him in whatever world he inhabited, if only for a moment.

"Did you ever think you'd end up here?" I asked, curiosity piquing as I leaned forward, resting my chin on my hand.

He chuckled, the sound warm and inviting. "Not exactly. I had dreams of being a world-renowned chef. You know, the kind who flips omelets with flair and has a signature dish named after him. Instead, I'm just trying to survive the culinary apocalypse they call 'hospital food.'"

I laughed, the sound bubbling up like soda fizz, and it felt so good, so real. For the first time since this nightmare began, I could see a sliver of normalcy in my life, like sunlight breaking through the clouds. Nate and I traded stories like kids swapping baseball cards, each revelation forging a connection that felt more profound than the fluorescent lights above us could illuminate.

"Before all this," I said, my voice quieter, "I was planning to travel to Paris. I wanted to see the Eiffel Tower, sip coffee in little cafes, and pretend to be a sophisticated adult."

Nate leaned in, his expression serious for a moment. "You will. I mean, not now, but someday. We both will."

"Is that a promise?" I teased, feeling bold as the warmth of his gaze enveloped me.

"Absolutely. Just think of me as your personal tour guide," he declared, puffing out his chest like a cartoon character. "I'll teach you all the best places to get a croissant. And if you're lucky, I might even whip one up myself."

Our laughter echoed off the tiled walls, reverberating in a way that made the sterile surroundings feel a little more alive, a little less suffocating. The more we talked, the more I discovered about Nate—the dreams he had before this place took hold of him, the hopes he clung to like a life raft in stormy seas. It was comforting to know I wasn't alone in this struggle. Nate's laughter was a lifeline, pulling me closer to the surface, and for the first time, I felt hope nudging at the edges of my reality.

As the sun dipped lower outside, casting a golden hue across the cafeteria, I realized that I had forgotten the reason I was here. The incessant beeping of machines and the whispers of nurses faded into the background as Nate and I crafted our own world, filled with possibility and laughter, where illness was just a backdrop to the vibrant colors of our lives. In that moment, I felt a flicker of something I thought I had lost—a sense of freedom, a sense of belonging.

The days passed in a blur, each moment punctuated by laughter and banter with Nate, my unexpected companion in this strange chapter of my life. The hospital, once a place of dread, transformed into a backdrop for our evolving friendship, the sterile walls becoming witnesses to our whispered secrets and shared dreams. I found myself looking forward to the rhythms of the day: the soft rustle of the curtain as he'd swing by my room, that familiar cheeky grin plastered on his face as he'd rattle off some ridiculous story about his latest escapade in the ward.

"Today, I conducted a highly scientific experiment with the jello," he announced one afternoon, plopping down on the edge of my bed. "Turns out, if you mix the green and red, you get—"

"Ew, don't say it," I interrupted, holding up a hand dramatically. "I'm not prepared to hear about your culinary crimes against hospital food."

"Pfft, you're just jealous you didn't think of it first." He leaned back, feigning indifference while his eyes twinkled with mischief. "Anyway, I call it 'The Abomination.' Sounds appetizing, right?"

I burst out laughing, a sound that felt foreign yet exhilarating. "You should probably stick to flipping jello cups instead of omelets. Your talents are clearly wasted in the kitchen."

Our playful exchanges wove a tapestry of camaraderie, each thread pulling us closer together. On particularly slow days, we would concoct absurd plans for escaping the hospital. Nate insisted we could fashion a hot air balloon out of discarded bed sheets and helium tanks—though I often pointed out that we'd never get past the first floor without being stopped.

"It's the thrill of the chase," he countered, his eyes alight with excitement. "And besides, we could always distract them with an elaborate dance-off."

"Right, because nothing screams 'escape plan' like synchronized dance moves," I replied, grinning.

We built a world between us, one that floated high above the sterile confines of the ward, filled with ridiculous dreams and half-baked schemes. There were moments, though, when the laughter would fade, and the weight of our realities would creep in. It was during one of these pauses that I caught a glimpse of the vulnerability beneath Nate's bravado.

One afternoon, after a particularly grueling round of treatment for him, I found him staring out the window, his expression thoughtful, almost wistful. The late afternoon sun cast a golden glow across his features, and for a moment, the playful boy I knew seemed distant, lost in thoughts I couldn't touch.

"Hey," I said softly, not wanting to disturb the fragile air between us. "You okay?"

He turned, flashing a quick smile that didn't quite reach his eyes. "Yeah, just contemplating the universe, you know. Wondering if there's a secret to life hidden in this boring view."

"Or maybe just the mystery of the pigeons," I suggested, trying to lighten the mood. "Those little beasts have their own agenda."

Nate chuckled, but it was a hollow sound. "Sometimes it feels like they're the lucky ones, flying around, not a care in the world. Just... free."

There was a heaviness in his words that settled around us like a fog. I didn't want to pry, but my heart ached to know more. "Do you ever think about what comes next?"

He shifted, the hint of a shadow crossing his face. "Every day, Ava. Every single day. But I try not to dwell on it. I mean, what's the point, right?"

"Right," I replied, though the unease gnawed at my insides. The reality of our situations loomed over us, the specter of uncertainty. We were both fighting battles, and though laughter could lift the weight for a while, it couldn't banish it entirely.

Days turned into weeks, and our friendship deepened, layered with shared hopes and fears. Nate became my anchor, the one person who understood that the days were not just about surviving, but also about living. Together, we crafted our moments, turning the ordinary into extraordinary with our ridiculous dreams.

One evening, as the sun dipped below the horizon, painting the sky in hues of orange and pink, Nate suggested we hold a 'Hospital Olympics.' I raised an eyebrow, curious. "What's on the agenda? Bedpan racing?"

"Exactly! And we can also have a 'who can eat the most jello in under a minute' contest. Gold medals for everyone!"

"Gold medals made of foil, of course," I added, playing along. "Because nothing screams 'champion' like foil around your neck."

As we planned our ridiculous events, I realized how much Nate had become a part of my life, a vital thread in the fabric of my days. But just as our laughter rose to a crescendo, a nurse stepped in with news that would ripple through our fragile bubble.

"Nate, your doctor wants to see you," she said, her tone professional yet laced with a note of concern that made my heart skip a beat.

"Do I need to bring my bedpan?" he joked, but the laughter didn't quite reach his eyes this time.

"I'll come with you," I offered, rising from my chair, a sudden surge of anxiety coursing through me.

"No, it's okay," he said, waving his hand dismissively. "I can handle it."

But I didn't want him to handle it alone. There was something unspoken in the air, a feeling that churned in my stomach. "Nate, please."

He hesitated, eyes flickering between my expression and the door. "Okay, fine. But if I end up having to do jello shots for the rest of my life, I'm blaming you."

As we walked toward the doctor's office, a silence enveloped us, thick with tension. I could sense Nate's anxiety brewing beneath his carefree facade. Every step echoed with unspoken fears, the gravity of our realities weighing heavy in the air.

When we reached the office, Nate paused, turning to me with an uncertain smile. "Thanks for being my distraction," he murmured.

"Anytime. Just remember, you're not alone in this."

And as he stepped inside, leaving me standing in the sterile hallway, I felt a crack in the vibrant world we had built together. Would laughter still bloom in the cracks of uncertainty? Would our dreams hold strong against the weight of reality? I was about to find out, and I wasn't ready for the answers.

The doctor's office felt like an icebox, the air heavy with uncertainty and a hint of antiseptic. I stood just outside the door, my heart pounding with each tick of the wall clock. The walls were painted a dreary shade of pale blue, perhaps meant to evoke calm, but all it did was heighten the tension curling in my stomach. I could hear Nate's voice, a low murmur mingling with the soft rustle of paper—his usual bravado seemed to dissolve into something more serious.

I shifted from foot to foot, restless and anxious. I wanted to be there for him, to hold his hand and remind him that he wasn't alone, but I was also terrified of what might be said behind those closed doors. The minutes dragged on, each one stretching longer than the last, filled with the echo of my heartbeat and the muffled sounds of hushed conversation.

Finally, the door swung open, and Nate emerged, his expression a tapestry of emotions—relief, uncertainty, and something else that made my heart sink. "Hey," he said, attempting a grin that didn't quite reach his eyes.

"What did the doctor say?" I asked, stepping closer, my heart racing in tandem with the anxious thoughts spiraling in my mind.

"Nothing I couldn't handle," he replied, but there was a tremor in his voice that sent a chill down my spine. "Just some routine stuff."

"Routine stuff? Nate, you look like you just saw a ghost."

He hesitated, glancing down the hallway as if the walls might provide a way out. "Let's grab some jello. It'll make everything better, right?"

"Right, because jello is the cure-all for every ailment," I shot back, trying to inject some levity into the moment, but the tension lingered like an uninvited guest.

As we made our way back to the cafeteria, I tried to coax the truth from him. "Nate, if something's wrong—"

"I'm fine! I just need a moment to process everything, okay?" he interrupted, his voice sharper than usual. "Why does everyone always think they can just dig around in my head like it's an open book?"

I took a step back, startled. "I wasn't trying to dig! I just... care. That's all."

He looked at me, the playful spark in his blue eyes dimmed, replaced by something more vulnerable. "I know. I'm sorry. It's just hard sometimes."

We arrived at the cafeteria, the aroma of bland food swirling around us, and I grabbed a couple of jello cups in a bid to lighten the mood. "See? This stuff is practically gourmet," I said, handing him one with an exaggerated flourish.

Nate took it, but instead of eating, he stared at it as if it held the answers to life's mysteries. "You ever think about what life was like before all of this?"

"Constantly," I admitted. "I miss the little things, like going to the movies without worrying about germs."

"Or eating ice cream without guilt," he added with a smirk. "I could go for a double scoop of mint chocolate chip right about now."

"Not if I get there first!"

The momentary banter brought a flicker of light back to his eyes, but it didn't last. As we sat down at a table by the window, I noticed the distant look creeping back in. The sun had set, casting a shadowy glow across the cafeteria, and it felt as if the walls were closing in on us.

"What did the doctor really say?" I asked again, my voice softer this time, but firm with determination.

He took a deep breath, his fingers tapping nervously against the table. "I... I might need to start a new treatment plan. It's more intensive."

A wave of fear crashed over me, threatening to pull me under. "More intensive?" I repeated, struggling to process his words. "What does that mean? Is it serious?"

"Nah, it's just... it could mean longer hospital stays, more side effects. You know how it goes," he said, trying to shrug it off, but I could see the tension in his jaw, the way his hands trembled slightly.

I reached across the table, covering his hand with mine, wanting to anchor him in that moment. "You don't have to pretend everything is okay, Nate. It's okay to be scared."

He looked up at me, his blue eyes shimmering with unshed emotions. "Sometimes I wish I could just hit pause on everything. You know? Take a break from the whole thing and just... be."

A comfortable silence enveloped us, a shared understanding that transcended words. In that moment, I realized how deeply I cared for him, how much I wanted him to be okay. But there was something in the way he spoke, a resignation that made my heart ache.

"We'll figure it out," I said firmly, hoping my voice would convey the strength I felt inside. "You're not alone in this, remember? I'm here. We can tackle the Hospital Olympics together."

His lips quirked up at the corners. "Yeah, we could win gold in jello consumption."

"Exactly! And if all else fails, we can always bribe the staff with dance moves."

Just then, a commotion erupted at the other end of the cafeteria. A group of nurses burst in, their expressions a mix of concern and urgency. "We need to clear the area! Code Blue!"

The words struck like a bolt of lightning, and my heart lurched. I exchanged a panicked look with Nate. "What's happening?" I whispered, my heart racing.

"I don't know," he replied, his brow furrowed as he stood, instinctively scanning the room for danger.

As the nurses hurried past us, shuffling patients and visitors away from the commotion, my gut twisted with dread. We both moved instinctively toward the noise, the gravity of the situation pulling us closer.

Just then, a nurse rushed by, her face pale. "We need more hands in Room 203!"

"Nate," I breathed, urgency clawing at my throat. "What if—"

"Let's check it out. We can't just sit here," he said, determination igniting in his eyes.

We pushed through the cafeteria doors, hearts pounding in sync as we raced down the hallway. The closer we got, the more the air thickened with tension and fear.

Just as we reached the door to Room 203, a doctor emerged, his face lined with worry. "We need everyone out of the hallway. It's serious!"

My pulse quickened. Nate and I exchanged a glance, both of us feeling the weight of the unknown pressing down on us.

"Is it someone we know?" Nate asked, his voice barely above a whisper, a tremor of anxiety underlying his question.

The doctor shook his head, his expression somber. "I can't disclose any information. Please, move back!"

Panic surged through me as the realization hit—whatever was happening inside that room was beyond our control. But as we stood there, locked in uncertainty, something in Nate shifted.

"I can't just stand here," he said, his voice steady, determination flaring in his eyes. "I need to know what's going on."

Before I could stop him, he pushed through the door, leaving me standing in the hallway, heart racing and breath caught in my throat. "Nate!" I called after him, but the door swung shut behind him, sealing him away from my reach.

The tension crackled in the air like static electricity, and as I stood there, a terrible sense of foreboding washed over me. What awaited us on the other side? I felt the ground shift beneath me, and in that moment, I realized we were no longer just two kids navigating a hospital together; we were caught in a storm that could change everything.

Chapter 3: The Escape

The afternoon sun poured through the hospital windows, casting stripes of light across the sterile, white walls of my room. The scent of antiseptic hung in the air, mixing with the faint floral notes from the bouquet someone had left by my bedside, its vibrant colors a sharp contrast to my muted surroundings. It was a Wednesday, a day that felt like any other, until Nate's familiar silhouette slipped through the door, his presence a burst of color against the gray of my reality.

"Hey, Ava," he said, a mischievous glint in his eyes. "Wanna break out of here?"

I raised an eyebrow, half-expecting this to be a dream brought on by the heavy sedation that had become my constant companion. "Are you serious? Where would we even go?"

He leaned against the door frame, his grin infectious, and I couldn't help but smile back. "There's this abandoned train yard just outside town. It'll be like our own secret adventure—just you and me. Plus, I can't stand the hospital food for another minute."

My heart raced at the thought, a mix of fear and exhilaration swelling within me. Breaking rules was not something I was accustomed to. I'd spent so much time following the strict regimen dictated by doctors and nurses, each day a predictable cycle of tests, treatments, and the looming specter of illness. But Nate had a way of nudging me out of my comfort zone, of reminding me that there was still a world outside these walls. "Fine," I said, my voice barely above a whisper. "Let's do it."

The plan unfolded with the kind of stealth usually reserved for secret missions in movies. Nate and I navigated the sterile corridors, hearts pounding with a mix of anticipation and mischief. The sounds of bustling nurses and distant chatter faded behind us as we slipped out a side door, escaping the confines of the hospital like two children sneaking out to play after dark.

The outside world greeted us with a rush of fresh air, the tang of grass and distant blooms wafting in on a light breeze. The sun hung low in the sky, painting everything with golden hues, casting a warm glow on the path ahead. Nate took my hand, and I felt a thrill race through me—this was a freedom I hadn't tasted in far too long.

As we walked, the hum of the town faded, replaced by the gentle rustling of leaves and the distant clatter of metal. The train yard loomed ahead, a relic of the past, its rusted cars standing like sentinels guarding forgotten stories. The overgrown weeds tangled around the tracks, and wildflowers bloomed defiantly in the cracks, a vivid reminder that beauty can flourish in the most unexpected places.

"Welcome to our kingdom," Nate declared, gesturing grandly as we stepped into the yard. His voice echoed slightly, and I couldn't help but laugh, the sound breaking the tension that had built in my chest.

We wandered among the abandoned train cars, each one a piece of history, layered with peeling paint and faded graffiti, telling tales of long-gone journeys. The air was thick with the scent of rust and nostalgia, evoking a time when these metal giants were alive with purpose. I ran my fingers along the jagged edges, feeling the textures beneath my skin, marveling at how something so weathered could hold so much life.

"This place is incredible," I breathed, my heart swelling with a mixture of joy and disbelief. I was outside, really outside, laughing in the sunlight, and for the first time in what felt like ages, I wasn't defined by my illness. I was simply Ava, a girl discovering hidden treasures with her best friend.

"Just wait," Nate said, his eyes sparkling with excitement as he beckoned me to follow. We climbed aboard a car that had been turned into a makeshift art installation, colorful murals splashed across its sides. The vibrant hues were a celebration of life, each brushstroke a testament to creativity in a world that often forgot to breathe.

"This is amazing!" I exclaimed, stepping inside the darkened interior, where sunlight streamed through shattered windows, illuminating the dust motes swirling in the air. "It feels alive in here."

Nate grinned and leaned against the wall, crossing his arms. "It's a canvas waiting for us. What should we add?"

His playful challenge ignited a spark of inspiration. "How about a giant sunflower? One that reaches for the sky?" I began to sketch the idea in the dust with my finger, my imagination racing.

"A sunflower, huh?" Nate tilted his head, pretending to ponder my suggestion. "Only if it has a pair of sunglasses on, like a true sunflower superstar."

I giggled, and as I looked up, our eyes locked, the laughter fading into something deeper. The playful banter hung in the air, replaced by a charged silence that enveloped us. For a moment, I forgot about the sterile confines of the hospital, the weight of my diagnosis. Here, amidst the rust and the weeds, everything felt possible.

Then, in that suspended moment, Nate stepped closer, his expression shifting as he brushed a loose strand of hair behind my ear. The world around us faded, leaving only the sound of our breaths mingling in the quiet. And then, as if pulled by an invisible thread, our lips met—a tentative exploration that held the promise of something more.

The kiss was sweet and electric, sending ripples of warmth coursing through me, a reminder that amidst the chaos, life could still offer these breathtaking moments. My heart raced as I melted into the softness of the encounter, the fear that had clung to me slipping away like sand through my fingers. In that fleeting instant, I understood—hope wasn't lost; it was simply waiting for us to discover it, one kiss at a time.

The kiss lingered in the air like the fading notes of a song, electric and unnerving, as if the world around us had paused to take a breath. Nate pulled away first, his cheeks flushed, and I could see the uncertainty flicker in his blue eyes, an echo of my own feelings swirling inside me. "So...that just happened," he said, his voice a mix of disbelief and delight. He scratched the back of his head, looking sheepish but undeniably pleased with himself.

"Uh, yeah," I replied, a laugh bubbling up to fill the space. "I guess it did." My heart raced, each beat thumping with an exhilarating thrill I hadn't allowed myself to feel in what felt like forever.

As if to shake off the heaviness of the moment, Nate stepped back, his trademark grin returning. "Right, now that we've established we have chemistry, let's find something else to do before we get arrested for trespassing or worse—get caught by your doctors."

"Right. I'm sure they'll drag me back to my room, shaking their heads like I've committed a cardinal sin or something," I replied, matching his teasing tone. The idea of being carted back to the hospital felt far less appealing now that I was tasting a different kind of freedom.

We ambled deeper into the yard, passing under the rusty arches of a derelict freight car, its sides adorned with layers of graffiti that screamed stories of the people who had come before us. "You know," Nate said, kicking a small stone along the ground, "the last time I was here, I found a whole stash of old vinyl records hidden in one of these cars. They were in terrible condition, but I managed to salvage a few."

"Seriously? How did you even get in?" I asked, curiosity piquing my interest. I could almost picture Nate as a daring treasure hunter, unearthing hidden gems in forgotten places.

"Let's just say I have my ways," he replied, the corners of his mouth twitching upwards. "You should have seen me, sneaking around like a raccoon on a midnight snack run." He made a goofy face that made me snort, and I could feel the tension from moments before dissipate into the air, replaced by lightheartedness.

"Okay, raccoon boy, show me your stash," I said, nudging him playfully with my shoulder. He turned on his heel, leading me to another car that seemed particularly ominous, the door hanging open like a gaping mouth ready to swallow us whole.

Inside, shadows danced, and the scent of must and memories enveloped us. The light that filtered through the cracks illuminated piles of discarded furniture, broken glass, and, yes, a few vinyl records scattered haphazardly across the floor like fallen soldiers in a forgotten war. Nate began to sift through them, carefully inspecting each one, and I marveled at his enthusiasm.

"Check this out," he said, holding up a record as if it were the Holy Grail. "'The Beatles'—Abbey Road, baby!" His eyes sparkled with a childlike excitement, and I couldn't help but smile at his delight.

"Didn't that band break up ages ago?" I teased, leaning closer to examine the battered cover. "What's next, are you going to tell me that cassette tapes are making a comeback?"

"Actually, they are," he shot back, a smirk plastered on his face. "Vintage is in, and I have the perfect mixtape I've been working on. You'll be the first to hear it."

"I'd be honored," I said, rolling my eyes dramatically. "Just remember, if it involves a lot of ballads and questionable lyrics, I'm leaving."

"Ballads are classics, Ava! You'll see!" He laughed, tossing the record aside as if it were an artifact of the past, and we continued our exploration, venturing from car to car, unveiling forgotten relics of lives once lived.

As we dug through the remnants of yesterday, the sun began its descent, casting an amber glow across the yard that felt almost magical. I felt a weightlessness, as though the shackles of the hospital were being peeled away with each discovery we made. Every laugh shared, every secret exchanged felt like a building block, a way to fortify this newfound connection we were weaving between us.

"You know," I said, plopping down on an old, rusted step, "this feels like a scene out of a movie. Two misfits wandering through an abandoned place, finding their way back to themselves, one stolen kiss at a time."

Nate settled next to me, tilting his head back to gaze at the sky, now painted with hues of pink and orange. "Yeah, but every movie has a twist, right? The main characters can't just have fun forever without a catch."

"Stop it! You're ruining the moment!" I playfully punched him in the arm, though his words held an unsettling truth. We were both acutely aware of the fragility of our adventure, the clock ticking down to when we would have to return to the confines of reality.

"Okay, okay, let's not think about that," he said, his expression sobering slightly as he turned to me. "Let's focus on what we have right now. Just... promise me something?"

"Depends on what it is," I replied, raising an eyebrow in mock suspicion.

He hesitated for a moment, as if weighing his words carefully. "Promise me that no matter what happens next, you'll keep this memory close. This day, this feeling—don't let it fade away."

I felt my heart thud in my chest, a rush of emotion catching me off guard. "I promise," I said, my voice steady. "This moment is ours, Nate. I'll hold onto it."

With the sun slipping beneath the horizon, the world around us transformed, the colors bleeding into a deep navy, sprinkled with the first stars peeking through. I found myself leaning against Nate, our shoulders brushing, the warmth radiating between us a tangible comfort.

It felt safe. It felt real. And in the fading light, as I stole glances at him, I recognized something I hadn't allowed myself to consider before—a connection that ran deeper than friendship, an uncharted territory I was both excited and terrified to explore. Each second stretched, filled with unspoken words and possibilities, creating a tapestry of anticipation that wrapped around us like a blanket.

As darkness settled in, the abandoned train yard transformed from a place of decay into a sanctuary—a secret world where the weight of illness, time, and expectations fell away, leaving only the two of us, adrift in a sea of laughter and uncharted dreams.

As the darkness deepened around us, the train yard transformed into a stage set for a secret play, with shadows dancing like actors in a whimsical production. I leaned against the cold metal of the train car, soaking in the crisp night air, feeling more alive than I had in months. Nate, still buzzing with adrenaline, paced nearby, tossing pebbles into the gnarled weeds that whispered secrets in the night.

"Isn't this where the misfit characters meet their fate?" he asked, glancing back at me with a playful arch of his brow. "You know, right before the dramatic plot twist?"

I crossed my arms, feigning annoyance. "Stop ruining the ambiance, Nate. This is our moment! No tragic twists allowed."

He stopped and faced me, his expression softening, the moonlight casting a silver halo around his messy hair. "You're right. We're not letting anything ruin this night. Not even bad movie clichés." He shrugged, his smile transforming the weight of the world into something light, something we could both float on for a while longer.

"I've been meaning to ask," I said, suddenly serious, my curiosity outweighing my desire to keep the mood light. "Why do you come to the hospital so often? I mean, you could be out with your friends, living a normal life."

His gaze turned distant for a moment, and I could almost see the gears turning behind those bright eyes. "Because you're here," he replied, his voice steady. "It's hard to explain. I guess it feels right. I've seen what happens when you don't care about someone, when you just walk away. I won't let that happen with you."

His sincerity wrapped around me, warming me in the cool night air. I could feel the vulnerability swirling between us, a quiet promise that hinted at a bond deeper than friendship. "That's... really sweet, Nate," I whispered, the gravity of his words settling in my chest like an anchor.

"Yeah, well, don't get used to it," he shot back, mischief returning to his tone. "I have a reputation to uphold."

I laughed, grateful for the lightness that came so easily with him. "Right, the reputation of a notorious troublemaker." I stepped closer, our laughter mingling like a soft melody that played just for us.

In the distance, the clock tower chimed, the sound resonating through the night, and reality began to creep in around the edges. I frowned, the weight of time pulling me back to the hospital's grim inevitability. "We should probably think about heading back," I said reluctantly, feeling the excitement of our adventure start to fade.

Nate's expression darkened, and he shook his head. "Not yet. Not when we've barely scratched the surface of this place." He gestured toward an old train engine half-hidden in the shadows. "Come on, let's check that out."

Without waiting for my response, he bounded ahead, and I followed, curiosity pushing my feet forward despite the gnawing sense of urgency. The engine stood proudly, albeit in a state of decay, the paint flaking and the wheels sunk into the earth. I marveled at how it once symbolized strength and speed, now a mere ghost of its former self.

As we approached, I noticed a small door ajar on the side, inviting and slightly foreboding. "Are we really going inside?" I asked, hesitating at the threshold.

"Only if you're up for it," he teased, nudging my shoulder. "What's a little adventure without a bit of risk?"

I took a deep breath, feeling the mix of excitement and trepidation swirl within me. "Fine, but if we get stuck in there, I'm blaming you," I warned, stepping inside the dimly lit cabin.

The air was musty, filled with the scent of rust and forgotten dreams. Sunlight filtered through the grimy windows, casting thin beams of light that danced on the wooden floor, illuminating dust motes floating like tiny stars. Nate moved ahead, peering into nooks and crannies, while I stayed close, my senses heightened in this strange, alluring space.

"This is incredible," I whispered, brushing my fingers along the controls, imagining the powerful engine roaring to life beneath my touch. "It feels like we're stepping back in time."

"Exactly! We're time travelers in an alternate universe," Nate declared dramatically, and I couldn't help but chuckle at his flair. "So, what's our mission? Save the world or just salvage some records?"

"Can't we do both?" I suggested playfully, glancing around. "But I'd settle for just not getting caught first."

Just as Nate laughed, the sound echoed strangely in the silence. Suddenly, the tranquility of the moment shattered as a loud clang resonated from outside, sending a shiver down my spine. We froze, eyes wide, instinctively stepping closer together.

"What was that?" I whispered, the lighthearted atmosphere swiftly dissolving into something far more ominous. Nate held a finger to his lips, signaling for silence, and we stood there, hearts pounding in the stillness.

"I don't know," he murmured, tension tightening his features. "But we should check it out."

"I don't think that's a good idea," I protested, but he was already moving toward the door, curiosity leading him like a moth to a flame.

We peered outside, hearts racing in unison, and saw a figure lurking in the shadows, shrouded in darkness, just beyond the flickering streetlights. I could barely make out the outline, but something in my gut twisted—a primal instinct screaming that we shouldn't be here, that something wasn't right.

"Do you see that?" Nate whispered, his voice barely audible.

"Yeah, and I don't like it," I replied, a chill running down my spine. "We should go back inside."

Before we could retreat, the figure stepped into the light, revealing a familiar face. My heart dropped as recognition crashed over me like a wave. It was a nurse from the hospital, her expression hard and unforgiving, and she was looking straight at us.

"What are you two doing here?" she demanded, her voice slicing through the night, filled with an authority that made me feel as small as a child caught sneaking cookies.

Panic surged through me, and my mind raced, searching for an escape route. Nate's eyes darted to mine, and in that instant, I saw the determination that had drawn me to him in the first place.

"We were just—" he began, but the nurse interrupted.

"Get back to the hospital. Now."

Her tone left no room for argument, and I could feel the ground shifting beneath us, the sanctuary we had carved out of rust and shadows slipping away. We were no longer the adventurous misfits; we were just two kids caught in the spotlight, and that spotlight was starting to feel painfully bright.

But before we could move, another sound echoed through the yard, a low rumble that vibrated the ground beneath us. The nurse turned sharply, her expression shifting from annoyance to alarm, as the train engine behind us began to shake violently.

"Nate! Ava! Get out of here!" she shouted, panic rising in her voice.

My heart raced, fear clawing at my chest. I grabbed Nate's hand, pulling him away from the looming danger. The ground trembled beneath us, and the reality of our fragile escape closed in, threatening to engulf us both.

And just like that, the night took a turn I could never have anticipated, the world around us twisting into chaos as the darkness descended, the train yard now a battleground of choices and fears.

Chapter 4: The Storm

Rain drummed against the window, a relentless reminder of the storm that raged outside. It echoed the turmoil swirling inside me, where each drop felt like a memory, each gust of wind a haunting whisper of my past. The sterile scent of antiseptic filled the air, mingling uneasily with the warmth of the thick woolen blanket that cocooned me, providing a false sense of comfort. I glanced at the clock on the wall, the ticking hands as loud as my racing heart. It was almost time for Nate's visit, and with each minute that ticked away, I felt the tension knot tighter in my chest.

Nate had become my lifeline over the past few weeks. He arrived like a breath of fresh air in the suffocating atmosphere of the hospital, his presence illuminating the bleakness of my days. The way he teased me, his laughter rolling like soft thunder, made me forget—if only for a moment—that I was trapped within these four walls, my body tethered to machines that beeped and hummed like an orchestra of despair. I had grown fond of his mischievous smile and the way his eyes sparkled with mischief, as if he were harboring secrets meant just for me. He brought me books to read, comic strips to chuckle over, and stories from the outside world that felt like a dream I could barely reach.

But today, a darker cloud loomed on the horizon. My father was coming, and with him, a tempest of emotions I had long since tried to bury. Mark's reappearance after months of silence felt like a crack of thunder in an already stormy sky, jolting me awake to the reality of my pain. I had spent years longing for his approval, for the gentle touch of a father who always seemed just out of reach. Now, his looming presence threatened to pull me away from the fragile peace I had found with Nate. I had rehearsed the conversation a hundred times in my mind, every possible scenario swirling like the storm outside.

When the door creaked open, my heart sank. My father stepped into the room, and for a moment, the world fell silent. He looked unchanged, his features hardened by the weight of indifference, the gray in his hair a stark contrast to the youthful image I had clung to in my mind. His eyes, however, betrayed a flicker of something—was it regret, or merely curiosity? The silence stretched between us like an unbridgeable chasm, filled with the unsaid words of years gone by.

"Ava," he said, his voice a gravelly echo of familiarity that felt foreign on my ears. It held no warmth, no reassurance. Just a hollow sound bouncing off the walls of the sterile room.

"Why are you here?" I asked, my voice trembling despite my efforts to sound strong. The question hung in the air, heavy with all the emotions I had packed away for far too long.

He took a step forward, the clinical whiteness of the room contrasting sharply with the shadows of our shared history. "I thought it was time we talked."

"Talked? After all this time? You vanished, Dad," I retorted, the words spilling out before I could stop them. "I needed you when everything fell apart, and you just... disappeared."

His gaze dropped to the floor, avoiding the storm brewing in my eyes. "I had my reasons, Ava."

"Reasons? What reasons could justify leaving your daughter to fend for herself?" My voice cracked, and I felt the walls close in around me. "Do you even know how hard this has been for me? For months, I've been fighting to feel alive, and you weren't even there to see me struggle."

He shifted, his discomfort palpable. "I wasn't ready to face your illness. It scared me."

"Scared you?" The incredulity in my tone made me want to laugh, though it felt more like a cry. "It scared me too, Dad. But I didn't have the choice to run away. I had to confront it every single day. I had to learn how to survive."

He opened his mouth as if to say something but closed it again, the words dying on his lips. I could see it now, the fear in his eyes—a reflection of my own. In that moment, I wanted to reach out, to connect, to forge a bond that had been severed by time and neglect. But the chasm between us felt insurmountable.

"I'm trying to be here now," he said finally, a hint of desperation creeping into his voice. "I want to understand what you're going through."

"Understand?" I let out a laugh that was more bitter than joyful. "You think you can just walk back into my life and everything will be fine? I need more than just words, Dad. I need you to see me, really see me."

The weight of my confession hung heavily between us, a reminder of all the years I had spent feeling invisible, a mere afterthought in his life. His expression shifted, a flicker of guilt passing across his features, but it was quickly masked by his usual stoicism.

"Maybe you should focus on getting better first," he replied, the words tinged with a dismissive edge that cut deeper than any physical pain.

My heart sank, an anchor pulling me into the depths of despair. "You don't get it," I whispered, fighting back the tears that threatened to spill. "I am better when I feel loved, and I feel loved when I'm with Nate."

His brow furrowed slightly at the mention of Nate, as if he had stepped into an unfamiliar territory. "Who is Nate?"

"Someone who cares," I said defiantly. "Someone who's been here for me when you weren't."

For a moment, the tension hung in the air, electric and charged. I could feel the weight of my father's judgment, the disapproval radiating off him like heat from a fire. But what could he possibly understand of my life now? He had abandoned me, and yet he stood there, expecting to pick up the pieces as if nothing had happened.

"Maybe it's time to let go of that illusion, Ava," he said, his tone icy. "People leave. That's just how life works."

I flinched at his words, a part of me wanting to lash out, to shout that he was wrong, that life could be different. But instead, I swallowed hard, my throat tight with emotions I didn't know how to express. The storm outside roared back to life, lightning flashing through the window, illuminating the stark reality of our situation.

"Maybe you're right," I finally murmured, my voice barely above a whisper. "Maybe I should learn to live without you."

And with that, the words hung in the air, unresolved, a fragile peace shattered by the harsh truth of our reality.

The storm outside raged on, a relentless percussion that matched the chaos within me. My father's presence lingered like a heavy fog in the room, obscuring my thoughts and clouding my heart. I could still feel the sting of his words hanging in the air, the icy dismissal cutting deeper than any physical pain I had endured. It was as if he had taken a scalpel and sliced through the delicate fabric of my emotions, leaving me raw and exposed.

As I sat on the edge of my hospital bed, my hands clenched in frustration, I could hear the soft murmur of voices in the hallway, a reminder that life continued beyond these sterile walls. Nurses flitted by, their laughter a ghostly echo of joy that felt worlds away from the storm brewing in my soul. I longed for Nate's presence, his laughter a balm against my jagged edges, but today, he was late. Perhaps he sensed the tempest within me and was trying to gather the right words to bridge the distance between us.

The door creaked open, and my heart leaped, but it was not Nate who walked in. Instead, it was a nurse, her name tag reading "Maya." Her warm smile instantly brightened the room, and I felt a flicker of relief, as if the sun had momentarily broken through the clouds.

"Hey there, Ava," she said, adjusting the IV drip beside me. "How are we holding up?"

"Surviving," I replied, attempting a smile that felt more like a grimace. "Though I think I might need a lifeboat."

Maya chuckled, her laughter a comforting sound in the otherwise somber atmosphere. "Well, we can't have you sinking. How about I bring you some of that awful hospital jello? It's practically a rite of passage at this point." She winked, and I couldn't help but laugh, the sound bubbling up despite the heaviness that lingered in my heart.

"Just what I need—gelatinous encouragement," I teased back, grateful for the distraction. "Maybe if I eat enough of it, my father will just... disappear again."

Maya's expression softened, the humor fading as she settled into the chair beside my bed. "I know it's hard, Ava. It can feel so isolating when you're going through this. But remember, it's okay to be angry. It's okay to feel hurt."

"Is it? Because it seems like everyone expects me to just roll with it, to forgive and forget." My voice wavered, the vulnerability spilling out with each word. "I thought my dad's absence was a choice, but now it feels like I'm just a reminder of something he can't bear to face."

"Sometimes people don't know how to cope, and their fears drive them away. It's not your fault," Maya said gently. "You're fighting a battle most people can't even begin to understand. You deserve to be seen and loved, not to be sidelined."

Her words lingered, a lifeline I desperately clutched onto. "I want to believe that," I admitted, my voice barely above a whisper. "But it's hard when the person you need most is the one who hurt you."

Before Maya could respond, the door swung open again, and this time Nate stepped in, his presence a beacon of warmth amidst the chill. His hair was damp from the rain, and he shook it out like a wet dog before gracing me with a smile that lit up the room. "Hey, sunshine," he said, his tone playful despite the weight of my earlier encounter. "I came as soon as I could. Traffic was hell, and I swear my car almost floated away."

"Did you bring a life raft?" I quipped, my spirits lifting just from his presence.

"Only my charming self, but I hear it's quite buoyant," he shot back, a grin breaking across his face. He leaned against the wall, arms crossed, eyes sparkling with mischief. "What's the update? Have you threatened your father yet?"

A soft snort escaped me, the tension in my chest easing slightly. "It didn't go quite that way. More like a mild verbal exchange punctuated by my father's emotional unavailability."

Nate's expression shifted from humor to concern, and he walked over, perching himself on the edge of my bed. "I hate that he's here. You deserve better than that."

"Better would be an understatement," I replied, picking at the fraying edges of the blanket. "It's just... how do you reconcile a lifetime of absence with a single visit? He acts like I'm just supposed to welcome him back with open arms."

"Because it's easier to think that way, right? It's simpler to pretend like you can just pick up where you left off." Nate's voice was low, his gaze steady on mine. "But you're allowed to set boundaries, Ava. You're allowed to demand what you need from him."

"What if I don't even know what I need?" I sighed, the frustration bubbling back to the surface. "I feel like I'm constantly in the eye of a storm, unsure of where it's going to hit next."

"Then let's weather the storm together." He reached for my hand, his warmth wrapping around me like a soft blanket. "Whatever happens, you don't have to go through this alone. I'm here, even when things get messy."

The sincerity in his eyes made something inside me shift, a fragile hope flickering to life. "You really mean that?" I asked, my voice barely above a whisper.

"Absolutely," he replied, his thumb brushing over my knuckles. "But I'm also going to need you to promise not to scare me away with tales of jello and your father. It's not a very enticing prospect."

"Deal," I said, a laugh escaping my lips. "Though I can't promise I won't bring up the jello again. It's practically a character in this hospital drama."

Nate chuckled, the tension easing further as we settled into a comfortable rhythm. The storm outside continued to rage, but within these four walls, we carved out our own little sanctuary. "So, tell me about this epic battle you fought with your dad," he urged, leaning closer, eyes sparkling with interest.

I took a deep breath, feeling the weight of the earlier confrontation lifting, even if just a little. "It was nothing short of a disaster. I told him he had a habit of vanishing at the worst times, and he said I should focus on getting better."

"Classic," Nate replied, rolling his eyes dramatically. "I mean, who wouldn't want to hear that during a hospital stay?"

"Right? And when I mentioned you, he gave me this look like I was smuggling in contraband. I swear, if he had a monocle, he would've adjusted it in that moment."

"Sounds like he's the one missing out," Nate said, a softness creeping into his tone. "You're amazing, Ava. You don't need someone like that in your life if they're just going to add to your struggles."

"You really think so?" I asked, my heart swelling with the weight of his words.

"Definitely. Anyone who doesn't see your light is blind, and you deserve people who see you clearly."

The sincerity in his voice washed over me, a soothing balm for the wounds I had carried for so long. In that moment, I felt a connection with Nate that went beyond words—a bond formed through shared struggles and laughter, an understanding that transcended the chaos of our surroundings.

With the storm raging outside, we sat together in the eye of our own tempest, two souls finding refuge in each other's presence, and for the first time in a long while, I felt the faint stirrings of hope take root within me.

The rain continued its relentless patter against the window, the sound almost hypnotic, as if it were trying to lull me into a sense of calm I couldn't quite grasp. The hospital room felt like a ship caught in a tempest, and I was navigating the rocky waters of my heart with little more than a flimsy sail. The air was thick with unsaid words, each moment stretching out like a long, winding road with no end in sight.

Nate leaned closer, his warm breath brushing against my cheek as he whispered a joke about hospital food that had me giggling. It felt like a small reprieve from the storm brewing not just outside, but inside me as well. "You know, if they serve any more of that jello, I might just start a protest," he said, a mock-serious expression on his face. "I'm pretty sure it's secretly plotting against us."

"Right? I think it's working for my dad. He's just here to remind me of how lonely the world can be." The playful banter was a lifeline, pulling me out of the depths of despair. "But if he's in league with the jello, then that's a power couple I can't compete with."

Nate chuckled, but there was a flicker of concern in his eyes. "Your dad doesn't get to dictate how you feel or what you need. Just remember that. You're stronger than he knows, and it's time you show him."

A wave of gratitude washed over me. I didn't have the words to express how much Nate's support meant, but I felt it deeply, as if he were stitching together the frayed edges of my heart. The door opened abruptly, and in walked my father again, his presence slicing through the air like a sharp knife. The moment he crossed the threshold, the energy in the room shifted, like the calm before a storm.

"I need to speak with you, Ava," he said, his tone rigid, as though the mere act of addressing me required immense effort.

"Fantastic," I replied, my voice dripping with sarcasm. "I just love unplanned family reunions in hospital rooms. What's next, a surprise party?"

"Please, let's not make this harder than it needs to be." His eyes narrowed, the frustration evident in his stance. "I want to understand why you're pushing me away. You're sick, and you need help."

"Help?" I echoed incredulously. "You're the last person I need help from. I've been fighting this battle on my own, and now you decide to swoop in and play the concerned father? It feels a bit too late for that."

"Do you really think it's easy for me?" he shot back, his voice rising slightly. "I've watched you suffer from a distance, and it's—"

"It's what?" I interrupted, my anger bubbling over. "It's painful? It's hard? Well, welcome to my reality! You made that choice. You've been absent, and I've had to deal with the consequences."

Nate stood by me, his presence a steady anchor in the whirlwind of emotions. I could feel the tension crackling in the air, like static electricity before a thunderstorm. "Ava, maybe you should take a moment," he suggested gently, his hand brushing mine, grounding me.

But I wasn't ready to take a moment. "No, I need him to understand. This isn't just about his feelings or my illness. It's about the years of silence and the weight of his absence."

Mark crossed his arms, his gaze hardening. "You're still my daughter, and I'm here now, trying to do the right thing."

"The right thing?" I laughed bitterly. "You think showing up now, after months of silence, is the right thing? I've been living in a nightmare, and you think you can just pop in and be my savior? That's not how this works."

"I never wanted to hurt you, Ava," he said, his voice quieter, but the edge remained. "I thought giving you space would be best, but clearly, I misjudged things."

"Space? Is that what you call it? Abandonment, perhaps?" I shot back, feeling the fire of anger fueling my words. "You think I haven't felt your absence every single day?"

Nate stepped closer, sensing the rising tension. "Maybe this isn't the best time for this conversation," he suggested, his voice calm but firm. "Ava, you need to take care of yourself. Let's just breathe for a second."

But I couldn't breathe. Not with the weight of my father's silence pressing down on me, suffocating any semblance of peace I had managed to find. "You don't get to dictate what I need, Dad. I need you to acknowledge my pain, to see me for who I am—not just some version of me that fits into your narrative."

Mark's expression shifted, a hint of something resembling regret flickering across his features. "I'm trying to see you," he said, his voice softening. "But it's hard when you won't let me in."

"It's hard because you've built walls around yourself, and now you want me to lower mine. It doesn't work that way. You have to meet me halfway." I felt the weight of my words crash against the walls we had both erected.

Nate watched us with a mix of concern and determination, clearly unsure how to navigate this delicate terrain. "Maybe we should take a break and—"

"No," I interrupted, my heart racing. "This isn't going away, Nate. I can't pretend everything is fine while I'm still wrestling with this. It's exhausting."

Mark ran a hand through his hair, frustration etching deeper lines on his forehead. "Ava, I don't want to hurt you, but I need you to know that I'm here now. I want to help."

"Help? You don't even know where to start," I shot back, my heart pounding in my chest. "You don't even know what I need."

"Then tell me!" he replied, the urgency in his voice cutting through the storm. "What do you need?"

In that moment, I felt the ground shift beneath me, the stakes suddenly high as I considered my answer. The room felt charged, every moment heavy with unspoken truths, with emotions simmering just below the surface. I could feel Nate's eyes on me, urging me to be brave, to confront the truth I had been hiding for so long.

"I need you to admit that you were wrong," I said finally, my voice steadier than I felt. "I need you to acknowledge that your absence was a choice, and that choice hurt me more than anything else. I need you to accept that I am not okay, and that I need help navigating this—not just from you, but from the people who've been here all along."

Silence enveloped the room as my words hung in the air, a declaration that shifted the very foundation of our relationship. The rain pounded against the window, mirroring the tumult in my heart.

Mark opened his mouth to respond, but before he could form the words, there was a sudden knock at the door. My heart raced again, an uneasy tension creeping in as I turned my gaze toward the entrance.

"Excuse me?" a nurse's voice called out, her tone urgent. "We need to discuss Ava's treatment plan, but I can come back if this is a bad time."

"Actually, we were just—" Nate started, but I cut him off with a wave of my hand. My heart raced, my thoughts spiraling as the weight of my father's unspoken apology hung in the air.

"No, it's fine," I said, my voice trembling. "We can talk later."

But as the nurse stepped into the room, the charged atmosphere shifted yet again. I glanced at Nate, then back at Mark, whose expression had transformed into something unreadable.

"Ms. Jennings," the nurse said, her voice clipped, "we have a situation."

And just like that, the storm outside felt like the calm before an even more violent tempest, as the room braced itself for the unexpected twist that was about to unravel everything I thought I understood.

Chapter 5: The News

I could hardly remember the last time I had stepped outside the sterile embrace of the hospital. The fluorescent lights hummed above me, casting an unflattering glow on everything they touched. I'd spent so many hours here that the smell of antiseptic had begun to seep into my very bones. Today, it felt particularly suffocating, a tangible reminder of the gravity of our situation. Nate lay there, the faint beeping of the monitor marking the rhythm of his weakened heartbeat. The lines on his face, once so vibrant and full of life, now seemed etched in shadows, and it took everything in me not to crumble under the weight of despair.

With every shift of the chair, I felt like a fish floundering in a net, desperate to grasp at something solid, something that would pull me back to the surface. I curled my fingers around Nate's, tracing the familiar grooves of his palm, every rise and dip telling the story of our time together. I focused on the warmth emanating from his skin, a flickering candle in a darkened room. The doctors had come in moments ago, their hushed voices like distant thunder, rumbling with the kind of news no one ever wants to hear. Their eyes avoided mine, as if the mere act of looking at me might shatter the fragile facade I was desperately trying to uphold.

"Hey, superstar," I whispered, my voice barely above a breath, afraid that even my words could tip the balance toward the dark side of reality. "It's me. I'm right here." I leaned closer, hoping to draw strength from him as much as I was trying to provide it. His eyelids fluttered, and a faint smile broke through the veil of pain etched across his face.

"I'm still here," he murmured, his voice raspy, as if each word were a precious gem he had to save for the right moment. "You're my sunshine, you know that?"

I could almost laugh at the irony, how he always seemed to find light even in the darkest corners. "And you're my moon," I replied, my heart twisting at the thought of his light dimming. "Always shining, even when things get tough."

But tough was an understatement. I could feel the doctor's words lingering in the air like unwelcome ghosts. "We're doing everything we can," they had said, their faces a mask of professionalism that only hinted at the seriousness of his condition. But there was no avoiding the truth—they had shifted from hope to a kind of resignation that felt like a noose tightening around my throat.

With every moment spent in this limbo, my heart sank deeper. I had once imagined our future filled with wild adventures and lazy Sunday mornings, but now those dreams felt as distant as the stars I used to gaze up at with him, the twinkling reminders of everything that could be. I could almost see them—our future self, laughing and sharing coffee at sunrise, planning trips that seemed too wild to dream. I clutched his hand tighter, anchoring myself to the present, hoping that my love could somehow tether him to life.

"Remember that time we got lost hiking?" Nate's voice broke through my reverie, low but imbued with a mischievous lilt. "You insisted we were taking the scenic route, but really, we were just going in circles."

I laughed, the sound feeling foreign and electric in the oppressive quiet. "You say 'going in circles,' I say 'embracing spontaneity.'" My eyes danced with the memory of his exasperation, his brow furrowed as we trudged through the underbrush, both too stubborn to admit defeat.

"We should've just followed the sound of my stomach growling," he chuckled, the sound of it was a melody I wished I could record and replay forever. "But you were so set on that view. I knew you were just trying to impress me."

"Or maybe I just wanted an excuse to get you alone in the woods." The banter flowed between us, a lifeline thrown amidst the encroaching darkness. I felt the tension in my chest ease, if only slightly. In this moment, we were not just patient and caretaker; we were two people who had danced through life together, weaving memories that would linger even when the music faded.

His laughter turned into a cough, a harsh reminder of the fragility of this moment. I stroked his hair, feeling the soft strands beneath my fingertips, and leaned in closer, searching his eyes for that spark that had first drawn me to him. "Nate, we've got so many more adventures ahead of us, you know that, right? Just imagine—maybe a beach in Mexico or hiking the Alps. We'll even get lost, but this time I'll pack snacks."

"Only if I get to carry the backpack." His grin was wry, a ghost of his former self, but it was still there, alive in the depths of his blue eyes. "That way I can complain about the weight the entire time."

"Deal," I said, fighting against the knot forming in my throat. "You know I wouldn't want it any other way."

In that quiet room, we carved out a sanctuary, a moment of levity against the heavy backdrop of reality. For a brief flicker, we returned to the world we had built together, each laugh an anchor against the tide of fear that threatened to wash us away. But even as we shared those lighthearted moments, the ever-looming shadow of impending loss weighed heavily on my shoulders. The doctors had spoken in hushed tones, their expressions grave, and I couldn't shake the feeling that time was slipping through our fingers like grains of sand.

The laughter subsided, leaving an echo of longing in its wake. I squeezed Nate's hand, wishing my strength could flow into him, a surge of love and defiance against the encroaching darkness. "You'll fight, right?" The question hung in the air, a fragile whisper, and for a moment, the world outside faded, leaving only the two of us suspended in this poignant bubble of hope and fear.

I didn't want to think about the possibility of losing Nate. It was an idea so absurd that it felt like trying to imagine life without sunshine or air. Yet, as the seconds ticked away, that absurdity morphed into a palpable fear, coiling around my chest like a tight band. The air in the hospital room had turned thick and stale, heavy with unspoken words. Each breath felt like a reminder of everything I stood to lose.

A nurse came in, her soft smile a stark contrast to the reality surrounding us. "Good morning, Nate! How are we feeling today?" she asked, her tone almost buoyant, but I could see the fleeting glance she cast in my direction—a mix of sympathy and concern. Her clipboard, a silent witness to Nate's condition, seemed to vibrate with unsaid truths.

"Better than yesterday," Nate replied, though his voice cracked slightly, revealing the lie nestled within his bravado. He turned to me, a glint of mischief sparking in his eyes. "Just don't let her know I tried to sneak out last night to grab a burger. Can't let them catch me being too adventurous, you know?"

I snorted, unable to contain my amusement. "Because sneaking out of a hospital is definitely the most rebellious thing you could do right now." I crossed my arms, feigning exasperation. "What kind of wild plan would you hatch next? Scaling the walls for a midnight run to the drive-thru?"

Nate's laughter was strained but genuine, and it made my heart swell with affection and dread all at once. "Well, if you think about it, we'd make a great team. You distract the guards, and I'll shimmy out the window like a rogue ninja." He feigned a dramatic escape pose, his arm extended as if to leap into action.

"Rogue ninja? Please, you can hardly lift a spoon right now without sounding like a wounded dinosaur." I couldn't help but smile at his determination, the way he clung to our lighthearted banter as if it were a lifebuoy. But deep down, I was terrified. Each laugh felt like a small rebellion against the fear that clawed at my insides.

As the nurse finished checking his vitals, she offered a few kind words before slipping out, leaving us in a fragile bubble of our own making. I leaned in closer, resting my forehead against his. "Promise me you'll keep fighting, Nate. I can't do this without you."

He took a breath, the kind that seemed to take a monumental effort, and nodded. "I promise. I'm not going anywhere, not while we have so many more adventures to plan." The sincerity in his voice brought warmth to my heart, but it was tainted with a shadow of uncertainty. How could he promise that when the reality felt so precarious?

Moments passed in a comfortable silence, filled only with the sounds of the hospital—distant beeping, murmurs of staff, and the occasional rattle of carts being wheeled down the hall. I wished I could freeze time, capture this moment where the world faded away, leaving just the two of us entwined in our hopes and fears. But reality was insistent, and I felt the weight of it pressing down harder as I caught sight of a figure lingering in the doorway.

Dr. Peters, the lead physician, stepped in with an air of gravity that turned the atmosphere electric. My stomach dropped, and I shot a glance at Nate, whose expression had shifted from playful to guarded in an instant. The doctor's eyes flitted between us, an unspoken communication passing in the stillness.

"I'm glad to see you both are keeping spirits high," he said, his tone neutral yet firm. "However, we need to discuss Nate's condition further." The way he said it felt like a stone dropping into water—ripples of dread spreading outward.

I straightened, a sense of urgency washing over me. "Is it bad?" My voice trembled slightly, betraying the calm I desperately wanted to maintain.

Dr. Peters hesitated, searching for the right words. "Nate's condition has indeed worsened. His body is not responding to treatment as we had hoped."

I felt as though the floor had dropped away beneath me, plunging into an abyss of uncertainty. I glanced at Nate, whose jaw tightened, eyes narrowing as if bracing for impact. "What does that mean?" he asked, his voice steady, but I could hear the tremor beneath it.

"It means we need to consider alternative treatments. We're looking into a more aggressive approach," Dr. Peters explained, each word hanging in the air like a weight. "However, I want to be clear. These options come with risks, and there are no guarantees."

I fought to swallow the lump rising in my throat. "Risks?" The word felt like a blade, sharp and cruel. "What kind of risks?"

"Side effects could be severe. We're talking about invasive procedures that may take a toll on his already weakened body," Dr. Peters replied, his voice unyielding but not without compassion.

I squeezed Nate's hand tighter, the warmth between us a fragile lifeline. "You don't have to decide right now, Nate. We can talk through everything, weigh the options," I said, glancing back at the doctor. "There has to be something we can do. We can't just... give up."

Nate turned his gaze toward me, his expression softening. "Ava, I refuse to go out without a fight. I want to know all the possibilities." He shifted slightly, determination etched in his features. "Let's figure this out together."

The doctor nodded, a glimmer of respect flickering in his eyes. "That's a strong mindset, Nate. I'll have the team put together the information you need. We can schedule a meeting later today to discuss your options in detail."

As the doctor stepped out, leaving a charged silence in his wake, I couldn't shake the feeling of dread that lingered in the air. Nate turned to me, a small smile playing on his lips despite the tension. "I'd say we're pretty much professionals at handling crises by now. Just add this to our list of adventures."

"You mean to say our next thrilling escapade will involve doctors and needles instead of beaches and bonfires?" I quipped, trying to inject levity into the dark cloud that loomed above us.

"Exactly," he replied, feigning seriousness. "I can picture it now: 'Ava and Nate's Medical Mayhem!'"

We both burst into laughter, the sound a fragile yet defiant challenge to the gravity of our circumstances. For a moment, it felt like we were simply two people sharing a joke, but the laughter only highlighted the underlying reality, a bittersweet reminder of what was at stake.

But even amidst the chaos, there was comfort in knowing we had each other. With every shared laugh and every moment of vulnerability, we were crafting our own story, one filled with love, fear, and the fierce determination to face whatever lay ahead together. In that hospital room, surrounded by the sterile trappings of modern medicine, we were still alive, still fighting for the dreams we had woven together. And that, I realized, was worth everything.

The moments that followed felt suspended in time, as if the world outside the hospital walls had turned into a distant memory, each tick of the clock amplifying the heavy silence in the room. Nate's expression had shifted from playful banter to a resolute determination, a stark contrast that left me reeling. I studied his face, looking for cracks in his facade, a glimmer of doubt, but all I found was an unwavering strength that both inspired and terrified me.

"Okay, so medical mayhem it is," Nate declared, attempting to sound cheerful as he pushed the sheets down slightly. "I'm ready for all the chaos you can throw at me." The bravado in his voice was admirable, but it only underscored the fear clenching my heart like a vice.

"Just remember," I replied, forcing a lightness into my tone, "I'm not sure how well I handle needles. My fainting spell last week should give you an idea."

"Perfect," he said, a smirk tugging at the corners of his lips. "We can make it a two-for-one deal: I get a treatment, and you get a couch in the corner for your dramatic fainting episodes. You know, I've always wanted to be the star of a hospital drama."

"More like the supporting character who swoons every time the lead shows up." I couldn't help but roll my eyes, though a smile broke through my worry. "But if you're the star, I guess I'll have to up my game. I can wear scrubs and call myself Nurse Ava, here to save the day."

"Just no fainting during critical moments, please," he said, eyes twinkling. "I can't afford any additional drama when I'm already the main act."

The banter flowed easily between us, a thread of humor weaving through the looming reality. But with each laugh came a lingering tension that crackled in the air, a reminder of the fragile balance we were trying to maintain. I could feel the weight of uncertainty in the pit of my stomach, a heaviness that threatened to suffocate me if I allowed it to take root.

As the afternoon wore on, the room grew dim, the sunlight outside softening into a warm glow. It was the kind of light that made everything feel deceptively serene, almost picturesque—a stark contrast to the turmoil brewing within. I glanced out the window, watching leaves sway gently in the breeze, and I yearned to be outside, away from the suffocating walls of the hospital. The world beyond felt alive, while we were trapped in this liminal space, teetering on the brink of hope and despair.

Suddenly, the door swung open, and my breath caught in my throat. It was Dr. Peters again, his demeanor more serious this time.

I felt the laughter in the air dissipate, replaced by a dense cloud of unease.

"Ava, Nate, I need to discuss something with you," he said, his voice firm yet gentle. I exchanged a glance with Nate, who was now sitting upright, his face mirroring my own apprehension.

"Is it about the treatment?" Nate asked, his voice steady, though I could hear the slight tremor beneath it.

Dr. Peters nodded, stepping further into the room. "We've reviewed Nate's case, and I want to be transparent about what we're dealing with. The treatments we discussed have potential, but there are complications we need to address. We can start with the aggressive options, but they could lead to a significant deterioration in his quality of life."

The words hit me like a punch, leaving a sickening emptiness in their wake. I felt my pulse quicken, a panic clawing at my throat. "What do you mean by quality of life?" I whispered, my heart racing. "Are you saying the treatments could make him worse?"

"There's a possibility," he said, his gaze steady but sympathetic. "I don't want to sugarcoat anything. It's crucial that you both understand the risks involved. The alternative is to focus on palliative care, which would prioritize comfort over aggressive treatment."

I could feel the walls closing in on me, the room spinning slightly as I processed his words. "No," I blurted out, the word escaping before I could stop it. "We can't just give up. There has to be a way to fight this."

Nate squeezed my hand, grounding me as I wrestled with my emotions. "Ava, let's just—"

"I know you want to fight, Nate. I want to fight too," I interrupted, my voice rising with desperation. "But what does that even mean if it comes at the cost of your comfort? If you're suffering, what's the point?"

He opened his mouth, ready to argue, but Dr. Peters interjected softly, "I think it's important to take some time to consider all your options. This decision is not just about fighting; it's about quality of life and what that means to both of you."

A heavy silence enveloped us, the air thick with unspoken fears. I could feel my heart racing, each beat echoing the weight of the moment. The thought of losing Nate sent tremors through me, but the idea of prolonging his suffering felt even more unbearable.

"We could discuss it with your family, maybe gather some opinions," Dr. Peters suggested, his tone gentle yet firm. "But ultimately, the choice is yours."

Nate's gaze flickered between us, and I could see the conflict brewing within him. "I want to do this my way," he finally said, his voice low but resolute. "If that means fighting, then that's what I'll do. I want to feel like I've done everything I could."

"Even if it means more pain?" I challenged, my heart aching.

"Pain is part of life, Ava," he replied, his expression unwavering. "But I won't go down without a fight, not when there's a chance, however small, that we could turn this around."

I searched his eyes, desperately wishing for a sign that he wasn't just trying to convince himself. "Okay, then," I said finally, my voice steadying. "But we do this together. We research everything, we weigh the options, and we don't rush into anything."

Nate nodded, a flicker of relief crossing his features. "Together," he echoed, and I felt a warmth bloom in my chest.

Before we could delve deeper into the conversation, the sound of frantic footsteps echoed outside the door, breaking the moment. My heart raced again, a wave of anxiety washing over me. "What's that?" I asked, a sense of dread creeping in.

Dr. Peters stepped toward the door, his brows furrowed. "Stay here, both of you. I'll check it out."

Nate and I exchanged glances, a shared worry amplifying in the silence. The commotion outside grew louder, a cacophony of voices punctuated by urgent calls for help. I gripped Nate's hand tighter, a silent promise that I would be there, no matter what.

Dr. Peters opened the door just as a flurry of activity burst into the room. I could barely make out the frantic expressions of nurses rushing by, but my heart dropped as I caught snippets of their conversation: "Code blue... Room 307... Need immediate assistance."

Panic clawed at my insides, a chill sweeping through me. I turned to Nate, who looked just as alarmed. "What's happening?" I whispered, dread pooling in my stomach.

And then, amidst the chaos, I noticed a figure stumbling into the doorway, a nurse desperately trying to regain control. She gasped, her face pale, eyes wide with fear. "We need to move now! Someone's collapsing—"

Before she could finish, the lights flickered ominously, and the hospital intercom crackled to life with an urgent announcement. My heart raced as I clutched Nate's hand, bracing for whatever came next, knowing that everything was about to change.

Chapter 6: The Reckoning

The air in the room felt thick with the weight of unsaid words, a palpable tension that hummed between us like an electric current. I had spent years building my life around this moment, rehearsing every line, each inflection like an actor preparing for the performance of a lifetime. Now, standing in front of my father, I could hardly muster a breath. The walls felt like they were closing in, painted a dull beige that mocked the vibrant turmoil raging inside me.

"Why, Dad?" I finally managed, the question emerging from my throat like a strangled cry. "Why did you choose to be absent during the hardest part of my life?"

Mark looked at me, his blue eyes—once a mirror of my own—now clouded with something I couldn't quite place. Shame? Regret? They darted away, refusing to meet mine, and I felt a wave of frustration surge through me. His presence had always been like a ghost; there, but never truly engaged, drifting in and out of my life as if he could simply will away the discomfort of fatherhood. The silence that stretched between us was deafening, a vast chasm filled with years of disappointment and unfulfilled expectations.

"I—" he started, the word hanging on the precipice of his lips, quivering like a leaf in a gust of wind. But the thought seemed to evaporate as quickly as it had formed. Instead, he clenched his jaw, his expression hardening as if my question had struck a nerve he didn't want to expose.

"Just tell me," I pressed, my voice softer now, though still edged with the sharpness of old wounds. "Was I not worth fighting for?"

With a deep sigh, he raked a hand through his thinning hair, a gesture so familiar it felt like I was watching a rerun of a show I'd long grown tired of. "You don't understand," he finally said, his voice a low rumble. "I thought I was protecting you by staying away.

I thought…" His voice trailed off, and I felt the heaviness of his words settle between us like a thick fog.

"Protecting me from what? Your shame? Your fear?" I spat, each word dripping with the venom of a hurt I had carried for too long. "Because all I've felt is your absence. It's a gaping hole that I can't fill with anything else."

He flinched at my words, as if I had struck him. "You think I wanted to be this way?" His eyes finally met mine, and in that moment, the walls he had built around himself seemed to crack, revealing a glimpse of the man he might have been. "I couldn't cope, Ava. I couldn't bear to watch you fight, to see you suffer. It tore me apart."

The honesty in his admission surprised me. For years, I had painted him as the villain in my life's story, the absent father who had chosen his own discomfort over my pain. Yet here he was, raw and unguarded, standing in the ruins of our relationship. My heart softened, even as my anger simmered just below the surface.

"But I needed you," I said, my voice trembling. "I still need you. I don't want to fight this battle alone."

A flicker of emotion crossed his face, a spark of something that resembled vulnerability. "And I needed to be strong for you," he confessed, his voice barely above a whisper. "But every time I thought about coming back, I felt like I would crumble. I thought I was helping you by staying away, letting you focus on your fight without having to worry about mine."

My breath hitched as I processed his words. This wasn't just about me; this was about him too. His fear had woven itself into the very fabric of our relationship, binding us both in a silence that had become deafening. "You're not the only one fighting here, Dad. You have to know that I would have understood if you had just been honest. If you had just tried to be there."

The corners of his mouth twitched, an echo of the man I remembered before the illness had shrouded my life in darkness. "I didn't know how," he admitted, his voice breaking, the defenses he had built collapsing around him like a house of cards in a storm. "I thought if I stayed away, it would hurt less. But it just made everything worse."

"Then let's stop this," I urged, my voice a mixture of desperation and hope. "Let's figure it out together. You don't have to go through this alone either."

He looked at me then, truly looked, and for the first time, I felt a connection between us, a thread weaving its way through our shared pain. "I don't deserve your forgiveness," he murmured, a hint of sorrow lacing his tone.

"Maybe not," I replied, surprised by my own candor. "But it's not about what you deserve. It's about what we both need. We're still here, aren't we? Isn't that something?"

The silence that followed was charged, the kind of silence that promises change. As the truth of my words hung between us, I realized that we were both clinging to the remnants of a life marked by silence and fear. It was a starting point, however fragile. In the midst of our pain, perhaps there lay a flicker of hope—small and fragile, yet undeniably present.

"I don't want to lose you again," he said finally, his voice thick with emotion, as if he were admitting something monumental, something that could alter the very course of our lives.

"You won't," I promised, the words tumbling out before I could second-guess them. "Let's make it work this time. Together."

In that moment, something shifted between us. The foundations of our estranged relationship began to tremble, the roots of understanding intertwining amidst the rubble of years past. We stood on the precipice of something new, something raw and unfiltered, ready to confront the wreckage together.

The warmth of understanding lingered in the air, the silence between us charged with possibilities that had been dormant for far too long. I could almost taste the faint sweetness of hope—a flavor I had long abandoned. My father, still standing before me, looked both vulnerable and fragile, like a piece of porcelain on the edge of a shelf. In that moment, I realized we were both mere players in a game we had never agreed to, forced to navigate the wreckage of our pasts.

"Okay, so where do we go from here?" I asked, my voice steady yet cautious, as if any sudden movement might shatter the delicate truce we had forged. Mark shifted his weight, running a hand through his hair again, and I recognized the familiar sign of his discomfort. It was as if he were trying to gather his thoughts but found himself grappling with a tangled mess instead.

"I suppose we start with the truth," he said, a faint tremor betraying his bravado. "But truth has a way of splintering everything it touches."

I raised an eyebrow, a small smile breaking through my earlier resolve. "Well, when has anything ever been easy between us? We might as well embrace the chaos."

His lips twitched in a response that might have been amusement, though it quickly faded as he glanced away. "The last thing I wanted was to hurt you. I thought if I stayed away, you'd find the strength to fight on your own. I never wanted to be a burden."

"A burden?" I echoed, disbelief coloring my tone. "You were a ghost, Dad. You could've been a presence, a source of strength. Instead, you chose to be nothing."

He flinched, and I felt a pang of guilt, but the truth was too heavy to disguise. "I know," he admitted, his voice almost a whisper. "And I'm sorry. I thought I was doing the right thing, but I see now how wrong I was."

The words hung in the air, fragile yet transformative. I didn't want to get lost in his apologies; I needed action, a plan. "What's your idea of the right thing now?" I asked, curiosity edging my tone.

"I want to help," he said, meeting my gaze with newfound determination. "I want to be there for you, for every treatment, every appointment. No more avoidance. If you'll have me, I'll show up. I swear."

It was an offer laden with promise and risk, a delicate balance that made my heart race. The memory of every empty chair at my side during those hospital visits loomed large, but could I really allow myself to trust him again? "Okay," I said slowly, weighing the word. "But it can't be half-hearted. I need you to be all in, or not at all."

"I can do that," he replied, earnestness flooding his features. "But I also need you to understand that I'm scared too. I've never been good at facing these kinds of things."

The vulnerability in his voice was disarming, yet a flicker of irritation ignited within me. "Scared? You think I'm not? I've been fighting this battle every day, and it's terrifying. But I can't afford to have you back in my life just to disappear again when it gets tough."

His shoulders slumped as if I had taken a physical toll on him. "I promise, Ava. I won't run. I've been running from my fears for too long. It's time I stopped."

"Then let's do this together," I said, the weight of my words heavy with possibility. "Let's figure out what that means."

We stood there, two people on the brink of something new, yet tinged with the uncertainty of old scars. I could feel the warmth of potential blooming between us, the fresh air of a shared resolve sweeping away some of the dust of our past.

"Are you ready for the next round?" I asked, attempting to lighten the mood, a playful glimmer dancing in my eyes.

"Next round?" he questioned, feigning confusion. "I'm not sure I signed up for a boxing match."

"Sure you did!" I grinned, the tension easing. "This is like a championship fight, Dad. You either step into the ring or get knocked out. We can't afford to be spectators anymore."

"Alright, champ," he chuckled, a sound that felt almost foreign yet achingly familiar. "But I must warn you, I might be a bit rusty."

"Just like riding a bike," I shot back, my heart lightening. "Except instead of a bike, it's my emotional baggage, and instead of a helmet, you're going to need a full suit of armor."

His laughter filled the room, a sound that danced in the air like sunlight breaking through clouds. "I'll have to find something suitable for that. Maybe a knight's suit?"

"Perfect! The dad who fought dragons," I teased, warmth spreading through me as the image took root in my mind. "Can you just imagine the battle scenes?"

The laughter continued, a balm for the wounds we had both carried. As we exchanged banter, I caught glimpses of the man my father had once been—full of life, humor, and warmth. It made the ache of his absence a little less sharp, the possibility of a renewed relationship a little more tangible.

Yet, as the laughter faded, I couldn't shake the unease that lingered at the edges of our newfound camaraderie. Each moment felt precarious, like standing on a tightrope strung high above the ground, unsure of what awaited us on the other side. "But Dad," I said, my tone shifting as reality intruded once more, "this isn't just a fun ride. There are real stakes here. This is my life."

He nodded, the gravity of my words sinking in. "I know, and I don't want to take that lightly. But we have to be honest with each other from here on out. No more secrets."

"Agreed," I said, feeling a knot in my stomach tighten at the thought of what lay ahead. "This is going to be messy, but I'm willing to fight through it. Are you?"

"Absolutely," he replied, a determined glint returning to his eyes. "I'll be there, every step of the way."

"Then let's suit up for battle," I said, an unexpected smile breaking through my apprehension. "And may the odds be ever in our favor."

As I looked into his eyes, I saw a flicker of understanding, of shared resolve. We were no longer just father and daughter; we were comrades facing an uncertain future, united by the promise of healing and the hope that lay within the shadows of our past.

The air had shifted between us, transforming the tension into a palpable energy that felt almost electric. I could see the determination in my father's eyes, a light that flickered like a candle fighting against the wind. It was a fragile hope, but it was hope nonetheless, and I couldn't help but feel the stirrings of my own resolve. Yet, beneath that warmth lay an undercurrent of uncertainty, a reminder that this delicate truce could unravel at any moment.

"So, what's the game plan?" I asked, trying to inject some levity back into the atmosphere. "Will you be my sidekick, or do you need a superhero costume?"

Mark chuckled, the sound a little more confident this time. "How about I settle for being your humble servant? I can fetch coffee and hold your hand during treatments. I might even wear an apron if that helps."

"An apron?" I smirked, leaning into the banter. "What, are we baking cookies now? Because that sounds dangerously close to becoming my new coping mechanism."

"Well, we can try that too," he replied, the twinkle in his eyes sparking joy in my chest. "I'm all for cookie therapy. Chocolate chip or oatmeal raisin?"

"Chocolate chip, obviously," I shot back with mock seriousness. "Oatmeal raisin is a trap dressed as a cookie. The kind of betrayal that shatters trust."

His laughter rang out again, a beautiful sound that filled the room, but it faded too quickly. The laughter was just a momentary balm, and the gravity of our situation crept back in, reminding me of the stakes involved. I knew that beneath the playful repartee lay the serious business of fighting my illness, an enemy that showed no mercy.

"Alright, but what if we run into a situation where a cookie can't save the day?" I asked, my tone turning somber. "What happens when the treatments get tough, or the news isn't what we hope?"

Mark's smile faltered, replaced by the shadows of worry that had clouded his face before. "Then we face it together. That's what this is all about, right? I won't shy away, even when it gets dark."

"That's a big commitment," I said, my voice barely a whisper. "Are you sure you're ready for that? Because I can't be the only one in this fight."

He paused, clearly weighing my words. "I can't promise that I won't stumble. I'm still figuring out how to deal with all of this, but I can promise to be there, to at least try."

A moment of silence hung between us, heavy yet tender, a shared understanding forging an unbreakable bond. I wanted to believe him. I needed to. "Okay then," I said, pushing past the doubt, "let's start small. You come with me to the next appointment. We can tackle the unknown together."

"Consider it done," he replied, nodding, his resolve appearing firmer now.

As we settled into a more comfortable rhythm, I caught a glimpse of what our relationship could be—a partnership forged in the fires of adversity, tempered by laughter and shared vulnerabilities. The thought was exhilarating and terrifying all at once.

"So, after the appointment, we'll celebrate with those cookies?" I suggested, my heart racing at the prospect of reclaiming some semblance of normalcy.

"Absolutely! We'll have a full cookie celebration. I'll even let you pick the music," he replied with a playful smirk. "Just no ballads about heartbreak. I'm not ready for that."

"Deal," I laughed, "but you can't complain if I bust out some '90s hits."

"Now we're talking!"

The moment felt surreal. We were exchanging glances filled with unguarded laughter, where the past seemed like a shadow slowly fading from view. I leaned back, allowing a smile to bloom on my face, feeling like a little girl who had just been handed the keys to a kingdom. For the first time in a long while, I felt like we were on the brink of something real, something that could redefine our relationship.

But then, as if the universe had sensed my elation, a sudden ding from my phone shattered the fragile peace. The sound cut through the air like a knife, and I felt my heart skip a beat as I glanced at the screen. The words "New Test Results Available" flashed before me in bold letters, the very embodiment of anxiety that I had tried so hard to suppress.

My breath caught, the lightness of the moment dissipating in an instant. "I— I need to check this," I stammered, the phone shaking slightly in my hand.

"Do you want me to come with you?" Mark asked, his concern palpable.

I hesitated, torn between wanting his presence and the suffocating weight of dread. "No, it's fine," I said, forcing a smile that felt brittle. "I can handle it. Just... give me a second."

I turned away, staring at the phone as if it were a ticking time bomb. The room felt like it was closing in on me, and I took a deep breath, trying to steady myself. My thumb hovered over the screen, each second stretching into an eternity.

Finally, I pressed the button, and the screen populated with the results. My heart raced as the words blurred together, the reality of my situation crashing over me in a wave of icy fear. I could barely read the first line before the world tilted beneath my feet. "Elevated markers indicate potential complications..."

"No," I whispered, dread washing over me like a cold tide.

Just then, a sharp gasp broke through the air, and I looked up to see Mark watching me with wide eyes, the laughter that had filled the room moments before vanishing entirely. "Ava, what is it?" His voice trembled with concern, and I could see the fear reflecting in his gaze, mirroring my own.

"I—I don't know," I stammered, my mind racing. "It's just... it doesn't look good."

"What do you mean?"

"I don't think it's what we hoped for," I said, my voice shaky as I took a step back, as if the words were physical objects pushing me away.

The air felt electric, thick with unspoken fears as my father approached, his eyes scanning the screen for answers that I still struggled to comprehend. "Let me see," he urged gently, but I held the phone tight, a lifeline I wasn't ready to share.

"What if I can't do this?" I blurted out, the question bursting from me like a dam breaking. "What if I can't fight this?"

"You can," Mark said firmly, his voice steadying mine. "You've already proven that. You're stronger than you know."

But as the weight of his words sank in, the reality of the results settled like a heavy stone in my gut. A chilling sense of despair started to creep in.

Just then, the phone buzzed again, a notification that felt like a cruel twist of fate. "Another message?" I mumbled, more to myself than to him, fumbling to unlock the screen. The words on the new message caught my breath—"Doctor wants to discuss treatment options."

My heart dropped, and I exchanged a glance with my father. The unspoken understanding passed between us, heavy and thick. This wasn't just another appointment; it was a crossroads. A choice we both needed to make, and the gravity of it loomed large.

The laughter, the hope, the renewed bond we had just forged—it all felt fragile, like a house of cards caught in a breeze. I felt the walls closing in again, the light dimming, and the shadows creeping back.

"Dad, what if—"

Before I could finish, the phone slipped from my fingers, tumbling to the floor with a sickening crack. A deep silence enveloped us, the reality of my situation crashing down like waves against a rocky shore. My heart raced as I looked into my father's eyes, searching for the strength I needed but feeling only a growing uncertainty.

"Maybe we're not ready for this after all," I whispered, a chill crawling down my spine.

As the reality of my future loomed before us, I felt the ground shift beneath my feet, teetering on the edge of the unknown, waiting for the next wave to hit.

Chapter 7: A Fragile Hope

The hospital garden breathed a quiet serenity, an oasis carved from the relentless clamor of beeping machines and sterile linoleum corridors. It was a fragile sanctuary, dotted with wildflowers that somehow managed to flourish in spite of the heavy shadows cast by looming sycamore trees. As evening dipped into twilight, the air turned cool, carrying the faint scent of damp earth and blooming jasmine. I found solace here, lying on the soft grass beside Nate, our fingers intertwined like the branches above us, whispering secrets only the stars could overhear.

"I never thought I'd find myself here," Nate mused, his voice a low murmur that harmonized with the rustling leaves. He stared up at the sky, his deep brown eyes reflecting the first twinklings of stars. "It's kind of poetic, don't you think? A garden in a hospital. It's like they're trying to remind us that life persists, even in the most unexpected places."

His words hung in the air, a delicate reminder that beauty could thrive amidst chaos. I felt a warmth unfurl in my chest, an ember ignited by his unyielding optimism. "Maybe it's a metaphor for us," I replied, turning my head to meet his gaze. "Struggling to bloom in a place that feels more like a cage than a sanctuary."

Nate chuckled softly, a sound that danced around the silence of the night. "Cage or sanctuary, I'd choose to be here with you over anywhere else." There was a sincerity in his voice that tugged at my heartstrings, making me wonder if I had inadvertently stumbled into a fairy tale where the heroes were just two broken souls searching for a glimmer of hope.

As the stars twinkled overhead, I felt a spark of creativity ignite within me, one I hadn't realized had lain dormant, stifled by the weight of my own struggles. Inspired by Nate's resilience, I whispered, "Do you remember the night we spent at the lake, skipping stones?" My mind replayed the moment like an old film reel—Nate's laughter blending with the sound of water splashing, our dreams weaving together like the ripples spreading across the surface.

He nodded, his eyes sparkling with the memory. "Of course. You almost took out that duck with your throw. I still can't believe you tried to skip a rock that was practically a boulder."

"Hey, ducks have to watch out for flying debris too!" I countered playfully, the weight of the hospital's fluorescent lights fading from my mind. "Besides, I was aiming for the perfect skip!"

Nate grinned, and in that moment, it felt as though the weight of our circumstances slipped away, leaving only the essence of us—two flawed beings carving joy from shared memories. "You know," he began, shifting slightly to face me, "I've always wanted to capture that moment. Not just in words, but in art."

Art. The thought settled over me like a soft blanket, warm and inviting. "What do you mean?" I asked, genuinely curious.

"I mean," he replied, his voice dipping into a conspiratorial whisper, "sketching it out. I've always carried this little sketchbook, hoping to turn our memories into something tangible." His fingers brushed against his pocket, where the worn leather of his sketchbook nestled against him. "Would you want to try it? To create together?"

A rush of excitement surged through me, intoxicating and intoxicatingly unexpected. I had always thought of writing as a solitary endeavor, a personal refuge where I could lose myself in the maze of my thoughts. But here, with Nate, the idea of blending our worlds into something new felt as thrilling as standing on the edge of a cliff, ready to leap into the unknown.

"Let's do it," I said, my voice bubbling with eagerness. "Let's bring our memories to life."

The next few moments unfolded like a dance, both of us moving with a newfound rhythm as Nate retrieved his sketchbook. He opened it to a blank page, the crispness of the paper almost gleaming under the soft glow of the moonlight. With a pencil poised between his fingers, he looked at me, a spark of inspiration igniting in his eyes. "Okay, what do you see?"

"Um," I started, searching for the right words to paint my thoughts. "I see... the lake, obviously. But also, the laughter—like the way the sunlight danced on the water and made everything shimmer."

"Got it," he replied, the pencil gliding across the paper with practiced ease. I watched as the strokes formed a beautiful scene, each line imbued with the spirit of our memory. It was intoxicating to witness, as if the past was resurrecting itself before my eyes.

"And you?" I nudged him, intrigued to see how he perceived our memories. "What do you see when you think of that day?"

He paused, his brow furrowing slightly. "I see you," he admitted, his voice softer now. "You laughing, hair a mess, hands splashing water everywhere. That's the image that sticks with me."

My heart fluttered at his honesty, the depth of his observation rendering me momentarily speechless. There was something profound in the way he expressed himself, an innate ability to capture the essence of a moment with just a few words. "You really see me," I said, a sense of warmth enveloping me. "Not just the surface, but everything beneath."

Nate's gaze held mine, and for a heartbeat, the world around us faded into obscurity. The hospital, the pain, the looming shadows—all dissipated under the intensity of that connection. "How could I not?" he murmured, his voice a soothing balm against the backdrop of our struggles.

In that shared silence, I felt a fragile hope take root within me, an awareness that even amidst the chaos, we could forge something beautiful together. As we continued to create, our laughter mingling with the sounds of the night, I realized that our art was not merely an escape; it was a testament to our resilience, a declaration that we would not be defined by our circumstances, but by the moments we chose to embrace. And perhaps, just perhaps, there was a future waiting for us—a canvas yet to be painted with the colors of our dreams.

The moon hung low in the sky, draping everything in its silvery glow, casting long shadows that danced around us like specters of our worries. I watched Nate sketch with an intensity that felt both magical and oddly comforting. Each stroke of his pencil seemed to breathe life into the paper, transforming our shared memories into a vibrant tapestry of dreams. It was as if the garden itself held its breath, watching him create, while I quietly marveled at the way he poured his soul into every line.

"Do you think we'll ever really get out of here?" I asked, unable to suppress the worry that twisted in my gut. My voice was barely a whisper, but the words hung between us, heavy and real. The stars twinkled above, indifferent to the weight of our fears.

Nate paused, his hand hovering over the page. He looked at me, his expression thoughtful, and then he said, "Maybe it's not about where we are, but what we make of it. Even in a hospital, we're creating something beautiful, aren't we?"

His optimism wrapped around me like a warm blanket, but the reality of our situation still felt sharp and jagged. "Sure, but wouldn't it be nice to create something outside these walls? To breathe fresh air without the smell of antiseptic lingering in our nostrils?"

He chuckled, his eyes crinkling at the corners. "I mean, who wouldn't want a break from the aroma of cleaning supplies? But maybe we're just getting our feet wet for something bigger. This could be our launchpad, our underground art movement!"

I laughed, the sound bubbling out of me like champagne. "An underground art movement? In a hospital garden? You might be onto something. I can see the headlines now: 'Two Hospitalized Artists Create Revolutionary Works Amongst the Wildflowers!'"

"Right?" he grinned, and for a moment, the weight of our struggles lifted, leaving only the buoyancy of shared laughter. "And we could have our own gallery opening. Just imagine—'The Flowerbed Collection: Hope from Sickness.'"

"Maybe we could even serve hospital food at the opening," I quipped, rolling my eyes. "Nothing says fine dining like a mashed potato sculpture."

"Art is subjective!" he shot back, pretending to hold a monocle up to his eye. "I can see the critics now, raving about the 'visceral texture' of your mashed potato masterpiece."

The banter danced around us, an ephemeral bubble that momentarily shielded us from the reality outside our laughter. But even in the warmth of our playful exchange, the undercurrents of uncertainty still lingered, like the distant rumble of thunder that promised rain.

"I've never written poetry before," I confessed, feeling a sudden urge to share. "It's like standing on the edge of a cliff and looking down. Scary, but exhilarating."

"Why not give it a shot? You've already got the perfect inspiration right here," he said, motioning to the sketchbook and the pages filled with our memories. "You could write about us, about this moment. It doesn't have to be perfect; it just has to be real."

His encouragement washed over me, filling me with a rush of energy I hadn't felt in what seemed like ages. I closed my eyes for a moment, letting my thoughts swirl like autumn leaves caught in a gentle breeze. The garden was alive with nocturnal sounds, the chirping of crickets harmonizing with the faint rustle of leaves. A poem began to form in my mind, a fragile hope wrapped in words.

"Alright, here goes nothing," I said, propping myself up on my elbows, the grass cool beneath me. "Just don't judge me too harshly, okay?"

"I promise, I'll only judge you moderately harshly," he replied with a teasing wink.

I rolled my eyes but couldn't suppress my smile. With a deep breath, I began to recite the lines that had taken shape in my mind, letting my heart pour out with each syllable. "In a garden of whispers, beneath a moonlit shroud, where laughter dances softly, and the stars hum aloud..." My voice wove the imagery into existence, a tapestry of vulnerability and strength.

Nate listened intently, his gaze fixed on me, an open book of admiration. "That's beautiful," he murmured when I finished, his voice thick with sincerity. "You've got a gift, Ava. I knew you did."

I felt heat rise to my cheeks, a mix of embarrassment and pride. "Thank you. It felt... freeing, in a way. Like I was unearthing something buried deep inside."

"Maybe we're both unearthing things," he replied, his eyes glimmering with something deeper. "Art, poetry... it's all about exploring the layers we hide beneath the surface."

Just then, the distant sound of footsteps interrupted our moment, breaking the bubble of intimacy that had enveloped us. A group of nurses walked past, laughter spilling from them like sunlight piercing through clouds. I watched as they moved with an ease that felt almost foreign, their bright scrubs a stark contrast to the muted tones of our world.

"Do you think they ever stop to dream?" I mused, glancing back at Nate. "Or is it all just... duty and routines?"

"I think they do," he replied, his voice thoughtful. "Every now and then, I catch glimpses of their smiles, like they're sharing a secret we can't quite hear. Everyone has their own battles, even those who seem to have it all together."

His words resonated, reminding me that hope could be a universal thread, weaving through every soul, binding us together despite our different struggles. As the laughter faded into the distance, I felt a flicker of determination ignite within me. "We should do this more often," I declared. "Create art, write, dream. Even if it's just here in this garden, let's make it a habit."

"Absolutely," Nate said, his enthusiasm infectious. "And next time, I'll bring my watercolors. We'll paint the sky and the flowers and maybe even the cafeteria's infamous jello—though I can't promise it'll be a masterpiece."

I laughed, imagining the chaos of splattering colors and clashing designs. "As long as we keep it chaotic, I think we'll be fine. Who needs rules, anyway?"

"Exactly! Life is much more fun when you toss the rules out the window." He leaned closer, his eyes alight with mischief. "We could even have a rebel art show—'Breaking Boundaries with Brush Strokes!'"

"Now you're speaking my language." The promise of our shared creativity filled me with a sense of purpose, turning the hospital garden into a sanctuary of possibilities.

And as the stars twinkled above, I felt the weight of my fears begin to dissipate, leaving only the shimmering threads of hope weaving through the fabric of our shared experience. In that moment, lying on the grass beneath a canopy of stars, I knew we were just beginning to write our story—one filled with art, laughter, and the courage to dream beyond the confines of our reality.

The sun dipped below the horizon, casting long shadows across the hospital garden, while the lingering warmth of the day clung to the air. As we sprawled on the grass, the world around us morphed into a canvas of color, the twilight blues and purples mingling with hints of pink. I turned to Nate, who was busy adding delicate details to his latest sketch, his brow furrowed in concentration. It was mesmerizing to watch him transform simple memories into art, each stroke revealing not just the image but the emotions we'd shared.

"Do you think you could sketch a future?" I asked suddenly, surprising myself with the question. "Like, if we really could imagine what's next?"

He paused, pencil hovering just above the paper. "What would it look like?" His curiosity lit up his features, drawing me in.

"Maybe a little house by the sea," I said, my mind racing with the possibilities. "Where we could paint sunsets and listen to the waves crash. Maybe a garden full of wildflowers. And an endless supply of jello cups."

Nate laughed, the sound rich and warm against the encroaching night. "Definitely jello cups. But let's not forget the cats. I'm picturing at least three. They'd probably stage a coup if we didn't have enough."

"Right, and one of them will definitely be a diva," I added, grinning. "You know, demanding the best sunspot and knocking things off the counter just to assert dominance."

"Ah yes, Queen Mittens, ruler of the household." His voice dropped to an exaggerated, regal tone. "Bow before her fluffiness or face her wrath!"

The laughter bubbled between us, filling the air with a sweetness that felt as nourishing as a homemade meal. But beneath the levity, a subtle tension brewed, an awareness that we were both clutching at the future like it was made of fragile glass. As Nate resumed sketching, the atmosphere shifted, the stars above bearing witness to our fleeting moments, and I couldn't shake the weight of what lay ahead.

"Sometimes, it feels like I'm in this endless loop," I admitted, my voice dropping. "Like I can't see past today, let alone tomorrow."

Nate glanced at me, his expression softening. "I get that. But maybe that's where our creativity can save us. We can break the cycle through art, through writing, whatever we need."

"Do you really believe that?" I asked, genuinely curious.

"Absolutely. Creativity has this magical way of turning chaos into something beautiful," he replied, his confidence grounding me. "And it gives us control, even when everything else feels out of our hands. I mean, look at us—here we are, creating in a garden of uncertainty."

His words resonated, the spark of inspiration igniting once more within me. "Alright then, let's make a pact," I proposed, fueled by a sudden surge of determination. "We'll create something every day, no matter how small, until we leave this place. A painting, a poem, even a sketch of the cafeteria's unidentifiable casserole."

Nate's grin widened, and he nodded vigorously. "Cafeteria casserole it is! I can already hear the critics clamoring for a taste."

"Right? 'A true reflection of hospital cuisine: artfully bland with hints of despair!'" I laughed, picturing the ridiculous reviews we could craft for our imaginary exhibition.

But as our laughter faded into the crisp evening air, I felt a shift, a whisper of unease sliding into my thoughts. The garden felt less like a sanctuary and more like a fragile shell, precariously holding the weight of our dreams. The soft rustle of leaves became a reminder of how transient everything was—our moments together, our hopes, the very air we breathed.

As we continued to create, a shadow flitted at the edge of my vision. I turned instinctively, my heart racing, but found only the wind stirring the branches. "Did you see that?" I asked, trying to shake off the creeping chill that enveloped me.

"See what?" Nate replied, his brow furrowing.

"I thought I saw someone... never mind. It was probably just my imagination." I laughed nervously, though a knot formed in my stomach.

"Your imagination can be quite vivid, especially with that poetry brewing inside you," he teased, though there was an edge of concern in his tone. "Just focus on the art, okay? I'll keep watch for any rogue squirrels."

The moment of levity was fleeting. I watched as he returned to his sketching, but the unease lingered. I couldn't shake the feeling that the darkness around us was more than just the night closing in; it felt almost like a premonition, a harbinger of something yet to come.

We continued our creative escapades under the stars, the moonlight a gentle guide illuminating our journey. I sketched words across the page, letting my thoughts tumble out like the petals of a daisy scattered by the wind. As the minutes stretched into hours, I could feel the heaviness of fatigue settling in, but something compelled me to keep going, to push past the weariness.

Suddenly, the sound of footsteps crunched on the gravel path behind us. My heart skipped, and I turned, bracing myself for whatever shadow had emerged. There stood a figure—tall, silhouetted against the fading light, the outline familiar yet shrouded in uncertainty.

"Hey, you two lovebirds!" called a voice that sent a jolt through me. It was Ethan, Nate's older brother, his grin wide, but it didn't reach his eyes. "The doctors said you might be out here. What are you doing, plotting your escape?"

Nate shot me a glance, his expression tightening for a fleeting moment. "Just... making some art. Want to join?"

Ethan stepped closer, the air around us thickening with unspoken tension. "Art, huh? Looks more like you're hiding from the world." His tone was light, but the undertone felt heavy, like the weight of an unseen storm.

"Maybe we are," I replied, trying to match his lightness. "But we're also creating something real. It's a form of rebellion, you know."

Ethan's gaze flicked between us, the playful demeanor faltering for a moment. "Well, I hope you're both ready for some real talk because I just got off the phone with Mom, and she's worried sick about you, Nate."

A heaviness settled in my chest, the lightness of our previous conversations slipping away. "What did she say?" Nate's voice was steady, but I could sense the tension creeping in.

"She wants to come visit. Soon. She thinks it'll help," Ethan replied, crossing his arms as if bracing for impact.

"Great," Nate muttered, his frustration palpable. "Just what I need—more pressure."

Before I could respond, a sudden commotion erupted from the main building, a flurry of activity breaking through the stillness of the night. Voices raised, urgent and sharp, sending a shiver down my spine. I glanced at Nate, whose eyes widened in alarm.

"What's happening?" I asked, a feeling of dread twisting my stomach.

Ethan turned sharply, his earlier levity vanished. "Stay here," he commanded, already moving toward the chaos.

I watched him disappear, the darkness swallowing him whole. Nate remained frozen beside me, a storm brewing behind his dark eyes. "This isn't good," he murmured, his voice laced with fear.

The tension in the air thickened, an electric current that surged between us. My heart raced, echoing the mounting anxiety that pulsed through the garden. Just as I opened my mouth to speak, a loud crash reverberated from the hospital, followed by frantic footsteps.

"What if it's..." I started, my voice trembling.

"Don't say it," Nate interrupted, his tone urgent. "We can't think like that."

But as the sound of chaos echoed again, reality pressed against us, the fragile hope we'd woven feeling more like a thin thread unraveling before our eyes.

And in that moment, I realized that whatever lay ahead would demand more than art or poetry; it would test the very essence of our resilience, thrusting us into a reality we couldn't escape.

Chapter 8: The Intervention

The fluorescent lights buzzed softly overhead, casting a sterile glow across the hospital room that felt as unwelcoming as a foggy dawn. My heart raced with each echoing beep from the monitor, a mechanical reminder that I was still tethered to this life, though I sometimes wished I could float away into oblivion. Every breath felt like an uphill climb, a stubborn reminder of the illness clawing at my insides, refusing to let go. Just yesterday, I had convinced myself that today would be different—brighter, lighter, a slice of normalcy amid this harrowing chaos. But despair had a way of creeping in like the chill of winter, uninvited yet relentless.

The door creaked open, revealing Nate, my steadfast anchor in this tempest. He stepped in with that charming smile, the one that could light up the darkest of corners, but today it flickered like a candle fighting the wind. His brown hair was tousled, as if he had run a hand through it one too many times, and the worry lines etched into his forehead deepened with every passing moment. "Hey," he said, a single word that was both a greeting and a plea, a soft bridge connecting us in this unforgiving space.

"Hey," I replied, my voice barely above a whisper, hoarse and rasping like sandpaper. I wanted to reach out, to pull him close and absorb some of his warmth, but the weight of the blankets felt like an anchor, pinning me to the bed. I watched as he crossed the room, his footsteps soft against the linoleum floor, a stark contrast to the cacophony of beeping machines.

"What's on the agenda today?" he asked, attempting a light tone that fell flat in the heaviness of the air. The question was a familiar ritual, a gentle probing for hope amidst the despair that shadowed us. "More of this?" He gestured to the hospital room, the sterile white walls echoing our unspoken fears.

I shrugged, the movement making my shoulders ache. "Same old, same old."

Nate sat at the edge of the bed, the warmth of his presence a soothing balm against my fraying nerves. "I brought you something." He fished in his pocket, pulling out a small, squished paper bag. "Your favorite."

My heart warmed slightly as I reached for the bag, recognizing the familiar aroma of cinnamon and sugar wafting up to meet me. The hospital diet had been a relentless parade of bland meals that left me feeling more like a test subject than a patient. "You shouldn't have," I managed, a ghost of a smile playing at the corners of my mouth.

"Too late now," he quipped, unwrapping a churro with exaggerated care. "It's already been smuggled past the food police."

I took a bite, the sweetness exploding on my tongue, igniting a long-buried craving. The taste was a fleeting moment of joy in this sea of gray, and I closed my eyes, savoring it as if it were a forbidden treasure.

Nate watched me, his gaze a mixture of affection and concern, the two emotions swirling together like the autumn leaves outside my window. "Ava," he began, hesitating as though the words might sprout wings and fly away. "I was thinking... maybe it's time for an intervention."

The word hung in the air, heavy with implications. An intervention? The very notion made my chest tighten. It felt like the universe had shifted beneath my feet, leaving me teetering on the brink of something I couldn't yet comprehend. "You mean...?" I started, my mind racing to catch up.

"Yeah," he said, his voice softer now. "Bringing everyone together. Your family, my family. I think it's time they faced each other. We've been avoiding it for too long."

I swallowed hard, a mix of dread and curiosity swirling within me. The thought of my parents and Nate's parents sitting in a room together felt surreal, like trying to fit a square peg into a round hole. "They won't want to," I whispered, the weight of my reality pressing down on me like a thick fog.

"Maybe they need to," Nate countered, his eyes earnest and resolute. "You've always been the glue, Ava. It's time they start holding each other up."

The thought of my family—my mom, with her tightly wound worries, and my dad, who masked his fear with silence—sitting across from Nate's equally well-meaning but emotionally reticent family sent shivers down my spine. They had always lived in separate worlds, each blissfully unaware of the other's turmoil. But now, here I was, the bridge between them, frail and fragile, hoping they could find common ground in their shared love for me.

"Will it help?" I asked, the question barely escaping my lips.

"I don't know," he admitted, running a hand through his hair, a gesture I had come to recognize as a sign of his internal struggle. "But I think it's worth a shot. We can't keep pretending everything's okay."

As I lay there, the churro now a sweet aftertaste in my mouth, I contemplated his words. The walls that had built up around my family felt insurmountable, yet here was Nate, my beacon of unwavering support, suggesting a way to break them down. It was terrifying and beautiful, this idea of bringing together the shards of our lives.

"I'll think about it," I said finally, my voice a mere tremor of its usual strength. I could feel the swell of emotions just beneath the surface—fear, hope, resentment—tugging at the corners of my heart. It felt like standing on the edge of a precipice, teetering between the familiar safety of solitude and the raw vulnerability of connection.

Nate nodded, relief flooding his features, and in that moment, I realized that no matter how murky the waters of my mind became, he would always be there, ready to plunge into the depths with me. The idea of the intervention loomed like a storm cloud on the horizon, but perhaps it could also be the cleansing rain that washed away the debris of our past. With Nate by my side, I felt an inkling of strength seep into my bones, a flicker of hope that maybe, just maybe, I could face whatever lay ahead.

The next few days passed like an elaborate game of chess, each move calculated yet riddled with uncertainty. The sterile walls of my hospital room felt less like a haven and more like a cage, the air thick with anticipation. I was aware of every passing hour, each tick of the clock reverberating in my mind like the tolling of a distant bell, echoing reminders of the impending intervention Nate had proposed. As the date approached, a swirling maelstrom of emotions took root within me—anxiety, hope, fear—each pulling me in different directions, like leaves caught in an autumn gust.

Nate's presence was a comfort, a steady lighthouse guiding me through the murky waters. He spent his afternoons curled up in the awkward hospital chair, flipping through old magazines, though I suspected he was simply buying time until he could bring his plan to fruition. "You know," he said one afternoon, glancing up from an article about pet fashion—an absurdity that had me chuckling despite myself—"if my parents try to bring any casserole dishes, I'm hiding them in your closet."

"Wouldn't want to spoil the ambiance with their culinary masterpieces, huh?" I quipped, imagining the gelatinous mass of something they'd insist was 'comfort food.'

"Exactly! A hospital is no place for mystery casseroles," he shot back, laughter bubbling up between us, momentarily dispelling the heaviness looming over our lives. Yet beneath the light banter lay an unspoken understanding; we were both aware of the emotional battlefield that awaited us.

As the intervention day dawned, the sun streamed through the hospital windows, bathing the room in a warm glow that felt like a cruel jest. I lay in bed, the crisp sheets a stark reminder of my vulnerability. My family and Nate's would soon converge, and I could feel the tension in the air—like the calm before a storm. Each heartbeat echoed in my ears, a steady rhythm that reminded me I was still here, still fighting.

The clock ticked relentlessly, and soon the moment arrived. The first knock on the door startled me, making my heart leap into my throat. I looked at Nate, who gave me a reassuring nod. "You got this," he whispered, though the tremor in his voice betrayed his own nerves.

As the door opened, my parents stepped inside, their expressions a careful blend of concern and steely resolve. My mother, her usually vibrant eyes dulled by worry, took in the scene before her. "Ava," she said softly, her voice barely a whisper.

"Hi, Mom." The word felt heavy on my tongue, loaded with everything unsaid between us.

My dad shuffled in behind her, his broad shoulders tense, hands shoved deep in his pockets. He offered a nod, the unspoken words swirling in the air like a dense fog. Neither of them was quite ready to breach the chasm that had grown between us, but here we were, thrown into the arena together, and I felt like the reluctant gladiator.

"Are we really doing this?" I muttered, half to myself.

Nate's parents followed shortly after, Mr. Jensen's booming voice cutting through the tension. "Ah, there's my girl! How are you holding up?" His jovial tone clashed with the somber mood, and I couldn't help but roll my eyes.

"Like a wounded deer in a room full of hunters," I replied, forcing a smile despite the tightening in my chest.

With everyone seated, an awkward silence enveloped us, each family member stealing furtive glances at one another, unsure of how to initiate this monumental task. I could almost hear the wheels turning in their heads, their minds racing to fill the gaps left by years of avoidance.

Nate took a deep breath, and the silence shattered like glass. "Okay, everyone," he began, his voice steady, "I think we all know why we're here. Ava needs us, and it's time we address the elephant in the room."

At that moment, I felt like a deer caught in headlights, the spotlight glaring down on me. The warmth of Nate's hand over mine was grounding, reminding me that I wasn't alone in this.

"Let's just be honest," he continued, locking eyes with each of our parents in turn. "We've let Ava bear the weight of this illness alone for too long. We've been living in separate bubbles, ignoring the fact that we're all struggling."

My mother inhaled sharply, and I could see her processing his words. "It's not that simple, Nate," she said, her voice wavering slightly. "We all care about Ava. We're just... scared. We don't know how to help."

"Scared?" Nate echoed, a flicker of frustration flashing across his face. "Scared is sitting in the waiting room, wondering if she's going to pull through! Ava needs us to be brave now, not cower in our corners."

"Bravery looks different for everyone," my father interjected, his tone defensive. "We've been trying to respect everyone's feelings—"

"Feelings?" Nate cut in. "What about Ava's feelings? She's been fighting this battle with you all watching from the sidelines! If you're afraid to show up for her, what does that say?"

The words hung in the air, electrifying the atmosphere, and I couldn't help but feel the sharpness of the truth slicing through the defenses we'd all built. This intervention was becoming a raw, messy amalgamation of emotions, and I felt myself spiraling into a whirlwind of thoughts.

"Okay, can we all just take a breath?" I said, interrupting the rising tension. "I appreciate the passion, really, but we need to focus on what's going to help us, not hurt us."

My voice felt fragile, but it cut through the escalating conversation. "I'm scared too. I'm scared of what this illness means for me, for us. But I don't want my health to become a battleground for you all. We need to talk—really talk—about how we can support each other."

The room fell silent again, this time heavier than before, as each person grappled with their emotions. I could see the flicker of realization in my mother's eyes as she absorbed my words, a flicker that suggested she was beginning to understand the chasm we had all contributed to.

"I've felt so helpless," she finally admitted, her voice thick with unshed tears. "And I thought being strong meant staying quiet."

"Strength can mean vulnerability," I replied, my heart racing as I watched the walls slowly begin to crumble, the cracks widening as honesty seeped in. "We can't heal unless we're willing to let each other in."

As we sat in that hospital room, surrounded by the ghosts of our past conversations, I could feel a fragile sense of unity emerging. It was still delicate, like a spider's web glistening with dew, but for the first time in ages, I felt a glimmer of hope. Perhaps this wasn't just an intervention for me, but a chance for all of us to step into the light together, to confront our fears, and to finally find a way to support each other in this unpredictable journey ahead.

In the wake of that pivotal moment, something shifted within the cramped confines of my hospital room. The walls, once a source of suffocating pressure, felt less imposing, allowing flickers of warmth and light to seep through. My family had bared their souls, and for the first time, it seemed as if we might stitch together the tattered fabric of our relationships. The air crackled with unspoken promises, as if we were all silently agreeing to walk this path together, no longer isolated in our fears.

"Maybe we can make this a regular thing?" Nate suggested, glancing around the room with a hopeful expression. "You know, family meetings. No casserole required."

A snort escaped my lips, breaking the tension as I shot him a teasing smile. "Let's banish all casserole dishes for good, shall we?"

Laughter bubbled up around us, the kind that chases away shadows, and for a moment, the looming specter of my illness retreated. But as the laughter faded, I could feel the weight of reality creeping back in. The truth was still there, lurking just beyond the walls of this fragile unity, and I feared that our shared honesty might soon splinter under the strain.

"What if we start small?" my father proposed, the timbre of his voice both soothing and firm. "We can schedule a weekly video call, just to check in. Maybe we can even try some family activities online."

I raised an eyebrow, half-amused, half-dismayed. "Family activities online? Is that your way of suggesting we all take up knitting?"

"Hey, don't knock the art of knitting," Nate chimed in, his eyes twinkling. "I could see you leading a virtual knitting circle. You'd be the hipster queen of hospital crafts."

"Imagine the Instagram following," I quipped back, feeling the weight in my chest lift a little more. The thought of absurdly styled knitting needles becoming my unlikely claim to fame was ridiculous enough to give me hope that we could navigate the choppy waters of our new reality.

Amid the banter, a palpable shift took place, an unspoken agreement that we were all in this together. But just as the mood began to lift, a nurse entered, her crisp scrubs and purposeful stride grounding us back in reality. "Sorry to interrupt, but we need to take some tests," she said, a clipboard in hand and a smile that was both apologetic and professional.

I nodded, suppressing a sigh as I prepared to roll up my sleeve for yet another blood draw. The easy camaraderie dissolved, the laughter fading like a wisp of smoke in the wind. I turned to Nate, who squeezed my hand, a silent promise of support.

"Don't be too long," he said softly, a hint of worry creasing his brow.

"Just enough time to have a little fun with my favorite nurse," I replied, feigning bravado.

As they wheeled me out, the fluorescent lights overhead hummed, casting shadows that danced along the walls. I could hear my parents and Nate exchanging quiet words behind me, their voices blending into a low murmur, but the feeling of unity remained, wrapping around me like a comforting blanket.

The testing room was stark, with machines that hummed ominously. I sat on the edge of the bed, the coolness of the metal surface sending a shiver down my spine. The nurse was quick and efficient, her movements practiced as she prepared for the draw.

"You've been a trooper, Ava," she said, her smile genuine. "How are you holding up?"

"I've been better," I admitted, trying to sound lighter than I felt. "But I'm fighting. It's all I can do."

Her gaze softened, and I saw a flicker of understanding in her eyes. "That's all we can do sometimes. Just keep pushing through."

I nodded, the words resonating within me. As the needle pierced my skin, I felt the familiar pinch, followed by the warmth of blood pooling into the vial. I breathed through the discomfort, trying to focus on the nurse's kind smile.

"Just a few more vials, and then you can get back to your family," she reassured me. "They'll be waiting for you."

Moments later, I was wheeled back to my room, the familiar sight of Nate and my parents filling me with a sense of belonging. But as I settled back onto the bed, an uneasy energy crackled in the air, prickling the skin on my arms.

"Hey, you missed a riveting discussion about online board games," Nate said, his tone light but his eyes flickering with something more profound.

"Board games? Sounds thrilling," I replied, feigning interest as I scanned the room for clues of what had transpired in my absence. My parents exchanged glances, their expressions unreadable, and a sense of foreboding unfurled in my stomach.

"Actually, it's more serious than that," my mother finally said, her voice steady yet tinged with apprehension. "We need to talk about your treatment plan."

The gravity in her tone immediately stilled the air, the laughter evaporating like a summer storm cloud. My heart began to race, each thump a drum echoing in the silence. "What do you mean?"

Nate's grip on my hand tightened, his thumb brushing reassuringly over my knuckles, but I could see the worry flickering in his eyes. "Ava, what's going on?"

My mother glanced at my father, and he sighed heavily, the sound resonating with all the unspoken fears we had been tiptoeing around. "There are some new options available, but they come with significant risks," he explained, his voice steady but thick with concern. "We want you to be aware before you make any decisions."

"New options? Risks?" My mind raced, grappling with the implications. "What are you talking about?"

My father took a deep breath, his face a portrait of the emotions he had spent so long trying to mask. "The doctors are suggesting a more aggressive treatment plan. It could mean more hospital time, more invasive procedures."

I felt the ground shift beneath me, the world tilting slightly off its axis. "More invasive? What does that even mean?" I could feel the walls of the room closing in, the weight of their words pressing down on me.

Nate squeezed my hand tighter. "Ava, we'll face this together. You don't have to decide right now."

My mother's eyes shimmered with unshed tears. "We just want you to be aware, to have all the information before you choose. We can't let fear guide our decisions anymore."

"Fear? Is that what this is about?" My voice cracked, frustration boiling up. "You think I haven't been scared enough? You think I haven't been fighting every single day?"

"We know," my father said, his voice low and steady. "But we also know that sometimes you have to confront fear to truly live. It's a risk, but it might be your best chance."

The tension in the room was palpable, a heavy weight settling over us. My mind raced, torn between the allure of hope and the dread of what those "risks" might entail. As my heart pounded in my chest, I suddenly felt light-headed, my vision swimming at the edges.

"Just give me a moment," I managed, needing to process the whirlwind of information crashing around me.

But before I could catch my breath, an alarming beep erupted from the monitor beside my bed, the sound escalating into a frantic rhythm that sent panic racing through the room. The nurse rushed in, her face paling as she assessed the situation.

"Her vitals are dropping!" she called out, the urgency in her tone slicing through the tense atmosphere like a knife.

"Wait! What's happening?" I gasped, feeling the world spin as the room swirled into chaos. Nate's grip slipped from my hand as he stepped back, his expression a mix of fear and confusion.

As the nurse began barking orders, a sense of impending dread settled over me, closing in like a vice. I could feel consciousness slipping, my heart racing as my vision blurred, the edges of reality darkening.

And then, amidst the cacophony of voices and hurried footsteps, everything went black.

Chapter 9: The Farewell

The hospital room was an odd blend of sterile white and the warmth of memories we had woven together. The beeping of machines kept a rhythm that felt far too calm for the chaos of emotions swirling inside me. Sunlight filtered through the half-drawn blinds, casting stripes across the floor that reminded me of the way light danced on the lake during our summer picnics. Those moments felt like a lifetime ago, and yet here I was, still clinging to the threads of our shared laughter, as fragile as the stitches holding my heart together.

Nate lay there, propped up against a pile of pillows, the corner of his mouth twitching into a smile that didn't quite reach his eyes. Even in this moment of inevitable farewell, he managed to find humor in our situation. "You know," he said, his voice a raspy whisper, "if I have to go, I'm taking the best pillow with me. This thing has become my confidant." He motioned dramatically toward the oversized, floral-patterned pillow that had become his steadfast companion, stained with the remnants of our late-night conversations, the laughter, and the tears.

I chuckled, the sound breaking through the heaviness in the air. "Just be sure to leave it behind if you're heading for a better place. No need to subject anyone else to your pillow talk."

He laughed lightly, and I felt a pang of sorrow at the sound—a reminder that laughter, even in the face of loss, was still part of our language. It was how we had built our world, piece by piece. With each shared joke, we transformed mundane moments into extraordinary memories. Now, every word felt like a coin tossed into a wishing well, each wish echoing the hope that somehow, some way, this wasn't really the end.

"Remember the time we nearly sank the canoe?" Nate asked, his eyes sparkling with the remnants of that adventurous summer day.

"You insisted on racing that family with the double kayak, and we ended up doing the doggy paddle for half a mile."

"How could I forget?" I leaned forward, the weight of my memories creating a bittersweet ache in my chest. "You were supposed to be my expert canoe captain, and instead, you panicked like a chicken being chased by a toddler."

He feigned offense, clutching his heart in mock dismay. "I'll have you know that was a strategic retreat. Survival instincts kicked in!"

The laughter bubbled between us, but even as we reminisced, the truth loomed larger than life. I had taken the liberty of charting out our "goodbye tour," a rather pretentious name for a series of trips to our favorite spots, but I needed to fill our days with the laughter and warmth we had always known. I wanted to remember Nate not for his declining health but for the vibrancy of the moments we shared—the wind in our hair, the sun on our faces, the taste of ice cream melting on our tongues during sweltering afternoons.

"Let's go to the lake today," I suggested, even as a knot twisted tighter in my stomach. "Just for a little while."

Nate's gaze softened. "You really think they'll let me out of here?"

"Only one way to find out." I shot him a determined smile, my heart thumping like a drum in my chest. We could do this. We could capture one more piece of the world outside these sterile walls.

After a few rigmaroles with the nurses, whose sympathetic smiles both comforted and frustrated me, we were granted permission for a brief outing. The ride was filled with a mix of excitement and apprehension, the hum of the engine somehow resonating with the unspoken fear hanging in the air. I glanced over at Nate, who seemed lost in thought, his fingers absently tracing patterns on the worn fabric of his jeans.

The sun blazed brightly when we finally arrived, casting ripples of light across the water. The smell of pine trees mixed with the earthy aroma of damp earth, creating an intoxicating perfume that stirred memories of lazy afternoons spent splashing in the lake. Nate and I walked slowly, hand in hand, letting the crunch of gravel underfoot ground us in the moment.

"Do you remember the first time we came here?" Nate asked, and I could see the nostalgia painting his face. "You dared me to jump off that ridiculous rock, and I almost didn't make it back."

"Almost," I teased. "You flopped like a fish. I thought you'd given up on swimming for good."

He laughed, a rich sound that echoed against the backdrop of the lake. But beneath the laughter was a vulnerability that tugged at my heart. "You know, I always felt like a part of me was meant to sink. But with you..." His voice trailed off, the weight of his words hanging in the air like the clouds gathering above.

With a surge of affection, I squeezed his hand tighter, feeling the warmth of his skin against mine. "You've always floated, Nate. You might not see it, but you do."

"Maybe I'm just afraid of drowning." His eyes searched mine, and in that moment, I realized that while I had been trying to fill our remaining days with laughter, he was grappling with the reality of our impending separation.

I wanted to be strong for him, to shoulder the weight of our love like a shield against the storm brewing on the horizon. Yet, as I looked at him, vulnerability stripping away the bravado, I felt the tears welling up. "Promise me something," I said, my voice a mere whisper.

"Anything."

"Promise me you'll carry my spirit with you, wherever you go."

A moment of silence hung between us, heavy and poignant. "And you'll carry mine?"

I nodded, tears spilling over as I pulled him close, feeling the warmth of his breath against my skin, the fragility of this moment tattooing itself into my heart. Our love had been a fleeting flame, but the light it cast would linger long after the fire had burned out. Even in the face of the inevitable, we chose to savor each heartbeat, to embrace the bittersweet tapestry of our memories, knowing that love was never truly lost, only transformed.

The lake shimmered beneath the sun, each ripple capturing fragments of light like scattered diamonds, a stark contrast to the heaviness in my heart. As we sat on the rocky shore, the cool breeze tousled Nate's hair, and I couldn't help but marvel at how he remained a source of warmth and laughter even as the world around us felt like it was dimming. I watched him, his profile framed against the vast expanse of water, a mixture of joy and sorrow flickering in his gaze as he breathed in the familiar scents of pine and wet earth. This was our sanctuary, the place where laughter once danced unburdened, and now it felt like a final act in a play we weren't quite ready to leave.

"What do you think the fish are doing right now?" he mused, breaking the silence, his voice teasingly serious.

"I don't know, Nate. Probably discussing the best techniques for avoiding our fishing lines," I replied with a smirk. "I mean, we were hardly expert anglers."

He chuckled, and I noted how his laughter was becoming increasingly rare, like a beloved song I hadn't heard in ages. "I think they'd be giving each other pep talks. 'Stay low, fellas! Don't take the bait! She's a menace with that rod!'"

"Me? A menace?" I feigned offense, placing my hand over my heart. "I prefer the term 'enthusiastic novice.'"

His smile widened, a flash of the vibrant man I had fallen in love with. "Enthusiastic? Sure. Novice? Debatable." The teasing glint in his eyes was a reminder of the easy banter we shared, a lifeline in this storm. I wished desperately that we could keep trading quips like this, stacking our moments like building blocks, but the crumbling foundation beneath us loomed too large to ignore.

As the sun dipped lower in the sky, casting a warm golden glow over everything, Nate turned serious. "Ava, do you ever think about what comes next? I mean, after this?"

I hesitated, the air thickening with the weight of his question. I had been trying to keep my thoughts on the present, focusing on our shared moments rather than the uncertain future. "I try not to," I admitted finally, my voice barely above a whisper. "But sometimes I wonder if I'll be able to breathe without you."

His gaze softened, and he reached out, brushing my fingers with his. "You will, you know. You're stronger than you think."

"Maybe. But what if I don't want to be strong?" The vulnerability hung between us, a fragile thread that could snap at any moment. "What if I just want to be weak for a while? To wallow and cry and pretend everything is okay?"

"Then I'll be here, wallowing right alongside you." His words wrapped around me like a warm blanket, a soothing balm in a world that felt increasingly chaotic. "I'll bring the popcorn for our pity party."

"And I'll make sure it's that fancy, organic kind," I replied, smiling through the tears that threatened to spill over. The playful banter felt like a lifeline, yet the reality of our situation loomed larger than life. It was a bittersweet reminder of how little time we had left.

After a while, I broke the silence, glancing sideways at him. "You know, I always imagined my life would follow a different script. You know, the whole 'meet the love of my life, settle down, have kids' kind of deal."

"Ah, yes, the classic romantic comedy arc," he replied, a hint of mischief dancing in his eyes. "But what if you're the lead in a tragicomedy? You know, lots of laughs followed by a deeply emotional twist at the end?"

"Let's hope for more laughs than tears," I said, my heart aching. "What I wouldn't give for one last ridiculous adventure. Maybe we could do that road trip we talked about? Just you and me, singing off-key to our favorite songs, with the windows down?"

"Now that sounds like a plan." He paused, and for a fleeting moment, the glimmer of hope sparkled in his eyes. "Let's do it. Just give me a few more days to get a little stronger."

I nodded, feeling the weight of the world pressing against my chest, every breath becoming a reminder of what we were losing. But the idea of one last adventure sparked something deep within me—a flicker of determination that threatened to push through the despair.

"Alright, then. Let's make a list," I said, pulling out my phone. "Top ten must-see places, and let's pick the craziest activities we can think of. Like, I don't know, swimming with sharks or bungee jumping!"

"Or we could just find the nearest ice cream parlor and engage in an epic sundae showdown," he suggested with a playful grin.

"Now that's more like it," I laughed, the lightness of the moment pushing away the shadows that loomed. The thought of devouring scoops of ice cream until we couldn't move felt liberating.

As we sketched out our plans, Nate's laughter rang like music, filling the empty spaces in my heart with warmth. We were creating memories—one after another—like a patchwork quilt, each square a testament to our love, the colors vibrant and rich, reminding me that even as we faced the impending darkness, we could still savor the light.

Yet, in the back of my mind, a question loomed. What if our time ran out before we could check off our list? What if this road trip remained nothing but a daydream, forever out of reach? I shoved the thought aside, unwilling to let it taint the precious moments we had left.

As the sun began to set, painting the sky in hues of pink and orange, I took a deep breath, savoring the warmth of Nate's presence beside me. We may have been on the edge of goodbye, but today, we were alive, weaving our memories into a tapestry of love that would linger long after the laughter faded.

The air was thick with the sweet scent of blooming wildflowers as we strolled along the familiar paths of the park, a place that had witnessed the birth of countless memories between us. The vibrant colors of spring enveloped us, creating a stark contrast to the somber reality we were navigating. I caught Nate glancing at the cherry blossom trees, their delicate petals fluttering down like confetti celebrating our existence in this moment, and I wondered if he felt the bittersweet nostalgia tugging at his heart as fiercely as I did.

"Look at them," he said, a hint of melancholy in his voice. "They're beautiful, but they never last. Just like us."

His words hung in the air, and I felt a sharp pang in my chest. "Maybe their fleeting nature makes them more precious. Just like us."

"Ah, the philosopher speaks!" he said, raising an eyebrow playfully. "So, what's your philosophy on ice cream? I'm convinced it's the cure for everything."

"Easy. It's an emotional support food, and I require a pint of mint chocolate chip to deal with your existential musings," I replied, nudging him gently.

Nate laughed, the sound ringing like bells through the soft hum of the park. "Then we must get to the nearest ice cream shop immediately. My survival depends on it!"

"Your survival? I'm the one with the emotional turmoil here!" I protested, though the smile creeping onto my face betrayed my feigned indignation. "You're the one getting all philosophical."

"True, but that just means I need ice cream more than you do. It's a sacrifice I'm willing to make."

With each step toward the ice cream shop, the laughter we shared felt like a protective shield, warding off the encroaching shadows. The sight of the little shop, adorned with whimsical colors and the enticing aroma of freshly made waffle cones, brought an unexpected rush of joy. I could feel the tension easing, if only for a moment, as we approached the counter lined with vibrant flavors.

"What's your poison?" Nate asked, eyes gleaming as he surveyed the options.

"I'm feeling adventurous. How about lavender honey?" I suggested, raising my eyebrows playfully.

He made a face. "Lavender? Seriously? I came here to indulge, not to question my life choices."

"Fine, Mr. Chocolate Connoisseur. You stick to your usual, and I'll take the plunge into floral flavor," I said with mock seriousness.

As we stood there, our ice cream cones in hand—his a towering mound of fudge brownie and mine a delicate swirl of lavender honey—I couldn't help but think about how these simple, sweet moments were what I wanted to remember. I wanted to etch the taste of his laughter, the crunch of the cone, and the warmth of the sun on my skin into my heart.

"Cheers to lavender!" I declared, raising my cone high.

Nate clinked his cone against mine. "And to whatever bizarre combination of flavors we can think of next."

As we licked our cones, savoring the sweetness, Nate's gaze wandered to the nearby playground where children laughed and played. "It's funny, isn't it? When you're young, you think life is endless. Every day is a new adventure waiting to be had. And then it hits you—life doesn't last forever."

"Are you sure you're not a poet on the side?" I teased, trying to lighten the heavy air again.

"I might be. A very obscure poet, writing about ice cream and existential dread," he joked, but his eyes were serious, reflecting the weight of our conversations.

We stood in silence for a moment, our thoughts swirling around us like the petals dancing in the breeze. I could feel the inevitability creeping in, a reminder that our time was limited. The laughter of children mixed with the distant sounds of nature felt like a soundtrack to our farewell, a sweet symphony that I desperately wanted to drown in.

"I want to take you somewhere," Nate said suddenly, his tone shifting.

"Where?" I asked, curiosity piqued.

"Just trust me. You'll love it."

I raised an eyebrow, skeptical but intrigued. "That's how horror movies start."

"Only if you don't follow my lead," he quipped, grinning. "Come on. I promise it's not an abandoned cabin in the woods."

As we walked, the path narrowed, leading us away from the bustling park and into a quieter stretch of trees. Sunlight filtered through the leaves, casting dappled shadows on the ground. The air felt charged, almost electric, and I found myself leaning into Nate, letting his presence guide me through the unfamiliar terrain.

Finally, we emerged into a small clearing, and my breath caught in my throat. Before us lay a hidden meadow, a lush tapestry of wildflowers swaying gently in the breeze, a secret garden I had never known existed. The colors exploded in a riot of vibrancy, each petal an affirmation of life's beauty, starkly juxtaposed against the shadow of our reality.

"It's perfect," I whispered, taking a step forward. The beauty of the place enveloped me, and I felt the weight of our situation lift, if only for a moment.

"I thought you'd like it," Nate said, a hint of pride in his voice. "I've been coming here for a while, just to think. It feels...alive."

"Like us," I said softly, turning to face him. "Even in the face of everything."

He stepped closer, the air thick with unspoken words, his expression softening. "I wanted to share this with you, Ava. To give you a piece of my world."

"And it's beautiful," I replied, feeling a swell of emotion rise within me.

Just then, the sound of rustling came from behind a cluster of bushes, and a pair of bright eyes peered out at us. A deer, delicate and graceful, stepped cautiously into the clearing. It regarded us for a moment, as if sensing the weight of our hearts, before bounding away into the trees.

"See? Even the wildlife appreciates our moment," Nate said, his eyes twinkling.

I smiled, but as quickly as the joy filled the space, a wave of uncertainty crashed over me. I reached out, grasping Nate's hand, feeling the warmth seep into my skin, grounding me. "Nate, can we promise to keep this moment close? Even when...even when it's hard?"

He nodded, a flicker of something deeper passing through his gaze. "Always. This will be our secret."

The world around us felt suspended in time, a fragile bubble protecting us from the chaos beyond. But even as I felt the love between us solidify in that enchanting meadow, a sharp pain shot through my chest, a cruel reminder of the reality waiting beyond our secret haven.

"Let's take a picture," I suggested, pulling out my phone. "I want something to remind me of this."

As I posed, he knelt down, framing the shot perfectly. Just before the shutter clicked, I noticed a flicker of distress cross his face, a momentary shadow that eclipsed the joy of the scene. I lowered my phone, concern replacing the laughter in my heart.

"Nate?"

But before I could ask what was wrong, he stumbled back, clutching his chest, a look of panic seeping into his features. My heart raced, the beauty of the meadow fading as a sense of dread washed over me. "Nate!"

He gasped, the color draining from his face. "Ava, I—"

The world around us blurred, the flowers losing their luster, and in that instant, the truth crashed down like a tidal wave. My heart thundered in my chest, dread coiling tight within me as I rushed to his side, the vibrant life around us morphing into a haunting echo of the inevitable loss that loomed just beyond the horizon.

Chapter 10: Shifting Sands

The antiseptic scent of the hospital clung to me like an unwanted second skin, a stark contrast to the vibrant chaos of life just beyond these walls. I spent my days in a cocoon of beige and blue, where time seemed to stretch like taffy—sweet yet painfully slow. Sunlight filtered through the blinds, casting stripes on the floor that felt like rays of hope. Every morning was a silent promise that maybe today would bring some semblance of normalcy. I tried to hold onto that thought as I sat up in my bed, my fingers dancing nervously over the blank pages of my journal.

Nate was my anchor, his presence as grounding as the earth beneath my feet, yet I could feel him shifting like sand beneath me. Our laughter had once been a soundtrack to my life, a melody so sweet that it drowned out even the most ominous of thoughts. But lately, the laughter had dulled, replaced by an uneasy silence that hung in the air like fog—thick and suffocating. I often caught him staring out the window, his brows knit in concentration, as if he were trying to solve a puzzle that was never meant to be pieced together.

My letters became an outlet for the unspeakable. Each one was a delicate thread weaving through the fabric of my fears and dreams. I would scribble furiously, pouring my heart onto the page. "Dear Nate," I wrote one afternoon, the ink pooling under the weight of my emotions. "Some days, I think the sun is just pretending to shine, like a child hiding behind a curtain, hoping no one notices their absence. I can't shake this feeling that the darkness is creeping closer, ready to wrap around me like a winter coat that's two sizes too big. I wish I could tell you that everything will be okay, but sometimes I wonder if that's just a lie I'm telling myself to avoid the truth." I folded the letter, sealing it with the remnants of my courage.

Yet even as I penned my worries, a part of me knew that Nate was fighting his own battles. When he entered my room, his smile often felt like a mask—bright yet fragile, as if a mere breath could shatter it. I'd see the way his hands trembled ever so slightly as he poured coffee from the small thermos I'd convinced him to bring. "You know, Ava," he said one morning, stirring the coffee with an absentminded flick of his wrist, "if I didn't know any better, I'd think you were trying to steal all the sunshine for yourself."

I raised an eyebrow, a playful smirk tugging at my lips. "Oh please, I'm just trying to ensure you have enough caffeine to make it through the day. And, let's be real, I could use a little extra sunshine, too."

His laughter was a brief respite, but the underlying tension lingered in the air. I could see the way he rubbed his temples as if trying to chase away a headache that was more than physical. It was the kind of ache that dug deep into the marrow of his being, a worry that had taken root in his heart. There was something unspoken between us, a chasm that widened with every passing moment.

As I settled into the rhythm of my days, the hospital room transformed into a strange kind of sanctuary. I decorated the sterile walls with a collage of memories—photos of sun-soaked afternoons spent at the beach, my hair a tangled mess from the ocean breeze, Nate's laughter echoing through the waves. I would gaze at those images, feeling a bittersweet pang in my chest, knowing that the world outside continued to spin while I felt trapped in this surreal limbo.

"Are you still writing those letters?" Nate asked one day, his tone casual yet tinged with curiosity.

I nodded, a shy smile creeping onto my lips. "Every single one. They're my way of keeping you close when everything else feels so far away."

He leaned back in his chair, his gaze drifting toward the window. "You know, sometimes I wish I could just write everything down instead of talking. It feels easier that way. Less pressure."

I tilted my head, intrigued. "You? The king of witty comebacks and spontaneous rants? Writing instead of talking sounds like a personal apocalypse."

"Touché," he replied, a half-smile breaking through his earlier façade. But as quickly as it appeared, the smile vanished, leaving behind that familiar tension.

The days blended together like colors in a watercolor painting, blurring the lines of reality. I found myself waiting for the moment when Nate would share what weighed heavily on his heart. Yet, with each passing day, that moment felt increasingly out of reach. His eyes, once bright and full of mischief, were now shadowed with something darker, a storm brewing beneath the surface.

Then came a day that began like any other, with sunlight filtering through the curtains, painting the walls in hues of gold. I sat up, adjusting the pillows behind me, ready to dive into another round of letters. But the air felt different, charged with an electricity that tingled against my skin. Nate entered, his expression unreadable.

"Ava," he began, his voice steady yet laced with an urgency that made my heart race. "We need to talk."

My pulse quickened, an instinctive knot tightening in my stomach. I could sense the gravity of the moment, the shift in the air that promised a revelation, perhaps one I wasn't ready for. As he settled into the chair beside my bed, I took a deep breath, preparing for whatever storm he was about to unleash.

Nate's gaze held mine, steady yet uncertain, as if he were balancing on the edge of a cliff and could tip either way at any moment. "Ava," he repeated, his voice steady, yet there was an underlying tremor that danced through the syllables. "We need to talk."

The urgency in his tone snatched the air from my lungs, leaving me to wonder if I should brace for impact. I shifted slightly, my fingers clutching the edges of my blanket as if it could anchor me to this moment. "Is it good news or bad news?" I managed, my voice playful despite the tightness in my chest.

Nate's lips quirked into a ghost of a smile, but the humor didn't reach his eyes. "Well, if I had to rank it, I'd say it's a solid middle ground—like oatmeal, neither here nor there, but with a sprinkle of cinnamon."

"Oatmeal? Really? Now I'm starving." I couldn't help but laugh, even if the sound was laced with anxiety. Humor had always been our go-to defense, a shield against the reality we were grappling with.

He took a deep breath, letting the silence hang between us like the delicate pause before a storm. "It's about your recovery," he began, his voice growing serious. "The doctors think you might need more intensive treatment than what's been planned."

My heart sank like a stone dropped into a lake. The words hung heavy in the air, rippling outward with an unsettling clarity. "More intensive? You mean... longer? Or different?" The tremor in my voice betrayed the calm I attempted to project.

Nate nodded slowly, his expression softening. "They want to try a new therapy, something they think could speed up the process. But it requires a commitment. You'd be staying here longer than we expected."

I processed his words, my mind racing through possibilities. Longer days, longer nights, more time confined to these four sterile walls. "And what about you? Will you still be able to be here?"

"Of course," he said, leaning forward, a fierce determination flickering in his eyes. "I wouldn't leave you. Not now."

The sincerity of his words wrapped around me like a warm embrace, but beneath it lingered a shiver of uncertainty. "But what if it's not enough?" The question slipped from my lips before I could stop it, a raw, jagged piece of fear that cut through the moment.

"It will be enough," Nate replied, but even as he spoke, I could see the doubts lingering behind his bravado. His smile faltered, and

I felt the tremors of unease that rippled beneath the surface of his steadfastness.

The quiet stretched between us, and I took a moment to collect my thoughts. The weight of it all threatened to smother me, but then a flicker of resolve ignited deep within. "Alright," I said, my voice firmer now. "If they think it's the best option, then I'll do it. I just want to get better."

A look of relief washed over Nate's face, his shoulders visibly relaxing. "You're stronger than you think, Ava. And I'm here to remind you of that every single day."

Our eyes locked, and for a brief moment, the world outside faded into the background. It was just us, two souls tethered together amidst the uncertainty, like a pair of ships battling the storm.

"I'll hold you to that," I said, a playful challenge dancing in my tone. "But only if you promise to keep bringing me coffee and those awful hospital pastries."

"Deal," he laughed, the sound brightening the room, pushing back the shadows that threatened to engulf us.

As the conversation shifted, the weight of the morning felt a bit lighter. We delved into plans—how we'd tackle this new phase together, the uncharted territory ahead of us. Each suggestion felt like a small victory, a reminder that while the path was uncertain, I wouldn't be walking it alone.

Later that afternoon, as the sunlight dipped lower in the sky, casting a golden glow through the window, I decided it was time to put pen to paper again. The letters had become my solace, a space where I could untangle the web of emotions that knotted inside me.

I began with a simple salutation, my heart spilling out onto the page as I wrote to Nate. "Dear Nate, sometimes I feel like I'm playing a game of chess, and the rules keep changing. Every day is a new move, and I can't quite figure out the strategy. But with you by my side, I think I might just have a shot at winning."

Lost in the rhythm of my thoughts, I became enveloped in my words, unaware of the world around me. The sound of the door creaking open broke my concentration. I looked up to find a nurse entering, her cheerful demeanor an unexpected burst of energy.

"Hey there, Ava! Just doing my rounds. How's our star patient?" she asked, her bright scrubs a stark contrast to the muted tones of the room.

"Star patient? I think you've got the wrong room," I shot back, my smile wide and teasing. "This place could use some serious renovation."

She chuckled, adjusting the clipboard tucked under her arm. "Well, I'm not an interior designer, but I can assure you that your personality adds a certain charm to this sterile environment."

I could feel my cheeks warm with embarrassment, but I leaned into the banter. "Oh, you mean the 'I-may-or-may-not-have-a-slight-addiction-to-hospital-blankets' vibe? It's all the rage, you know."

"Absolutely," she laughed, her eyes sparkling. "Have you thought about starting a trend? I'd be your first follower!"

Just then, Nate reentered, a small stack of papers in his hands. "I have news!" he declared, the excitement in his voice palpable. "I found a list of activities we can do together while you're stuck here!"

"Activities?" I raised an eyebrow, intrigued. "Are we talking about arts and crafts, or are we going full circus with juggling?"

He feigned seriousness, squinting at the papers. "Well, let's see... Ah yes! It says here we can paint, do puzzles, or even set up a movie marathon. Although, juggling does sound like a fantastic idea."

"Oh, please. I'd pay to see you try to juggle popcorn without making a mess," I replied, laughter spilling over as I imagined the scene.

"Challenge accepted," Nate said, puffing out his chest dramatically. "I will master the art of popcorn juggling if it means entertaining you."

The nurse smiled, shaking her head. "You two are a riot. Just promise me you'll stay out of trouble."

"Trouble?" I gasped in mock disbelief. "Us? Never! We're like two peas in a very un-troublesome pod."

With a wink, she departed, leaving us to our antics, a bubble of laughter and warmth enveloping the room. The darkness that had loomed earlier began to recede, replaced by the flickering light of camaraderie and hope. In that moment, I felt a little less like a patient and a little more like Ava—the girl who still had a spark to fight, a light to share, and a future to reclaim, even amidst the shifting sands of uncertainty.

Nate and I spent the next few days enveloped in our little bubble of defiance against the hospital's sterile reality. Our time was filled with laughter that echoed through the room, a sweet counterpoint to the beeping machines and whispered conversations from the corridors. I took to heart his promise to entertain me, and before long, we were knee-deep in the eclectic world of hospital activities, which, surprisingly, was more entertaining than it had any right to be.

On one particular afternoon, Nate suggested we attempt the most ridiculous arts and crafts project we could find in the activity book—making friendship bracelets. "You know, the kind you used to make at summer camp," he said, his eyes twinkling with mischief. "Except this time, we'll make them extra special with a touch of hospital charm."

I couldn't help but chuckle at the idea. "What's that? A bead shaped like a syringe?"

"Exactly!" he replied, feigning seriousness. "We'll call it 'Ava's Apothecary of Friendship.' I can see the name in lights now."

With a small table set up beside my bed, we spread out an assortment of colorful strings and beads—everything from neon pink to the delightfully absurd shades of hospital green. As we worked, our fingers tangled in the threads and our laughter mingled with the soft sounds of the hospital. "This might just be the worst idea we've had yet," I said, squinting at the confusing jumble of knots in front of me.

Nate picked up a bead shaped like a tiny pill. "You're not the only one who struggles with commitment, Ava. This bracelet is a symbol of our unbreakable bond... and my inability to choose colors."

"More like a representation of my questionable life choices," I replied, struggling to untangle my creation.

"Don't knock it until you've seen the final product!" he teased, his voice melodramatic. "This could be the next big trend—hospital chic."

As we worked, a sense of normalcy washed over me, pulling me momentarily away from the weight of my situation. With every laugh and playful jab, the walls of my room transformed into a sanctuary filled with warmth and camaraderie, a safe haven from the outside world. We adorned our wrists with our handmade creations, laughing as they turned out more like unfortunate art projects than any semblance of fashion.

"Look at us, the epitome of style," Nate said, holding up his wrist like a runway model, the mismatched strings dangling awkwardly. "We're basically trendsetters."

"I think we just set the trend for hospital humor," I replied, unable to contain my laughter. "We're going to revolutionize the way patients perceive their stay!"

Just then, the door swung open, and in walked a doctor, clipboard in hand, his brow furrowed in concentration. "Ah, what do we have here? Looks like a craft disaster in progress."

Nate straightened up, puffing out his chest. "We're redefining hospital decor, doctor. Care to join us?"

The doctor chuckled, shaking his head. "I'm afraid I'm not equipped to handle such cutting-edge art. I'll stick to healing patients."

As he continued his examination, I couldn't shake the feeling that something was shifting beneath the surface. The doctor was unusually serious today, his demeanor edged with concern. "Ava, I need to talk to you about your treatment plan," he said, glancing between Nate and me.

The warmth from earlier evaporated, replaced by a chill that ran down my spine. "Is everything alright?" I asked, my heart racing as uncertainty bloomed like a wildflower in my chest.

"We've seen some complications in your lab results, and we need to adjust the treatment moving forward," he replied, his tone professional yet tinged with an undertone of urgency.

Nate's expression fell, his bravado slipping away like sand through fingers. "What kind of complications?" he asked, his voice laced with an edge of worry.

The doctor hesitated for a moment, as if weighing his words. "It's nothing to panic about, but we need to be proactive. The current therapy isn't yielding the expected results, and we want to ensure that we're doing everything we can."

My heart thudded in my chest, every beat echoing in my ears. "Proactive? You mean more treatments? Different ones?"

"Yes," he confirmed, scribbling notes on his clipboard. "But it's essential that we discuss this in detail. I'd like you to meet with the specialist tomorrow."

"Specialist?" I repeated, the word tasting foreign on my tongue. It felt like a step into a realm I wasn't ready to explore. "What kind of specialist?"

"An oncologist," he replied gently, his eyes searching mine for understanding.

I swallowed hard, the weight of the word hanging heavy between us. The reality of my situation began to settle in, cold and unyielding. "But... I'm not—" I stammered, the denial racing through my mind.

Nate's hand found mine, his grip firm and reassuring. "Ava, we'll get through this together. Just like everything else."

The doctor nodded. "This is about being thorough, making sure we're covering all bases. I promise, we're on your side."

I wanted to believe him. I wanted to cling to the fragments of hope that sparkled like stars in the darkness. "What if... what if I don't want to meet with this specialist?" I asked, my voice shaking.

"Then we'll figure it out," Nate said, his voice steady. "But you're not alone in this. We're a team."

As the doctor continued to explain the next steps, I felt a swell of panic rising in my chest, threatening to overflow. I glanced at the bracelet adorning my wrist, a ridiculous symbol of our time together, and for a fleeting moment, I questioned everything. I had fought so hard to keep my spirit intact, yet now the looming presence of uncertainty felt like a shadow creeping closer.

Once the doctor left, silence enveloped us, thick and suffocating. Nate shifted in his chair, his eyes filled with an earnest concern that twisted my heart. "Ava, we can face this. Just promise me you won't shut me out."

I looked at him, my mind a whirlwind of thoughts and emotions. "I promise, but..." My voice faltered. "What if this is too much?"

His gaze softened, a mixture of empathy and determination etched on his features. "Then we'll find a way to make it manageable. Together."

The sun dipped low outside, casting long shadows that danced across the room, and as I watched the light fade, a sense of foreboding crept in. "What if I can't?" I whispered, the question hanging heavy in the air.

Nate leaned closer, his voice barely above a whisper. "You can, Ava. I know you can."

But even as he spoke, I could feel the tide shifting beneath us, the ground unsteady, and I couldn't shake the feeling that something darker was on the horizon, waiting just out of sight. My heart raced as a shiver ran down my spine, an instinctive awareness that the real battle was just beginning.

And then, just as I was about to speak, the overhead lights flickered ominously, plunging us momentarily into darkness. The sudden loss of illumination sent a surge of panic through me. Just as quickly, the lights returned, but the chill that had settled into my bones remained, gnawing at me.

"What was that?" I asked, my voice a thread of uncertainty.

Nate glanced at the door, the concern etched across his face mirroring my own. "I don't know, but..."

Before he could finish, the intercom crackled to life, its static punctuating the air with an urgency that felt almost palpable. "Attention, please. We're experiencing a system malfunction. All staff to emergency stations."

A deep sense of dread enveloped the room. The quiet hum of the hospital had transformed into an eerie silence, and I felt my heart drop into my stomach. The world around me felt suddenly perilous, the walls closing in as a realization began to dawn. This wasn't just a routine hiccup. Something was off—something more than just the flickering lights, something that threatened to unravel the fragile peace we had fought so hard to maintain.

I turned to Nate, fear mirrored in his eyes, and in that moment, I knew—everything was about to change.

Chapter 11: Fragile Conversations

The scent of antiseptic hung in the air, mingling with the faint floral notes from the small bouquet of wilted daisies perched on the window sill. I watched the sunlight filter through the glass, casting a warm glow across the sterile room. It was a stark contrast to the chill that seeped into my bones whenever I thought about why we were both here. The muted hum of machines and the distant chatter of nurses created a backdrop to our unexpected sanctuary, a place where the outside world faded away, leaving only Nate and me.

"Did I ever tell you about the time my brother tried to fix our car and ended up making it worse?" Nate leaned back in his chair, a playful glint in his eyes. His dark hair fell slightly over his forehead, and for a moment, I was lost in the way he animatedly recounted the tale. "We were stranded in the middle of nowhere, surrounded by cornfields. I swear, the only thing missing was a banjo playing in the background. The car was sputtering like it had a mind of its own, and he had the audacity to insist it was perfectly fine. The next thing we knew, the entire thing was making sounds I'd never heard before. We ended up waiting for hours for a tow truck that never came, just sitting there, staring at the sky."

I chuckled, picturing the two of them, a snapshot of brotherly misadventure. "I can just see it. Did he at least have a good excuse for being so utterly useless?"

Nate grinned, and I could see a flicker of nostalgia in his eyes, a glimpse into a happier time that felt far away from the hospital's whitewashed walls. "Oh, he claimed he was 'experimenting with a new method of automotive repair.' I think he just wanted an excuse to spend more time outside."

His laughter was like a breath of fresh air, cutting through the heaviness that often lingered in our conversations. But as the humor ebbed, I sensed a shift. The laughter faded, and a shadow crossed his features when I casually asked about his mother. It was a simple question, yet it struck like a thunderclap. The silence that followed hung between us like an unspoken agreement, a fragile conversation caught in the web of our shared realities.

"She's... she's doing her best," Nate finally said, his voice low, almost hesitant. "I think she's more scared than she lets on." He stared at the floor, as if it held the answers he was searching for, the weight of his words settling heavily on my chest.

My heart ached at his admission. The bravado that often surrounded him cracked, revealing a vulnerability that I hadn't seen before. "It's tough, isn't it?" I asked softly, trying to bridge the distance that had suddenly opened up between us. "When the people we love are hurting, and we feel so helpless?"

Nate nodded, his gaze lifting to meet mine, and in that moment, the room around us felt smaller, the air thicker with unspoken emotions. I could see the battle waging within him, a struggle between wanting to protect me from his pain and the need to share the burden. It was a delicate balance, like a high-wire act where one misstep could send everything tumbling.

"I guess I just always thought my mom was invincible," he confessed, running a hand through his hair, a gesture that seemed to echo the frustration brewing inside him. "You know, like superheroes don't get sick. But here we are."

The honesty in his words stirred something deep within me. I could relate all too well. My own family was navigating the stormy seas of illness, and the once-solid foundation I'd taken for granted felt like quicksand beneath my feet. "I thought the same about my dad," I admitted, the memories swirling to the surface. "He always seemed so strong. But when he got sick, it felt like the world tilted on its axis. I wasn't ready for it."

Nate's expression softened, and the moment stretched, the quiet intimacy enveloping us like a warm blanket. It was a shared understanding, forged in the fires of our fears and insecurities. "Do you think they know how much we worry?" he asked, his voice barely above a whisper.

I pondered the question, the weight of it heavy in the air. "Maybe they do, but it's hard for them to show it. I mean, what if our worry makes them feel worse? I think they try to protect us from the pain, just like we want to protect them."

He nodded slowly, absorbing my words as if they were a balm for his soul. "It's a funny thing, love," he mused, a wry smile creeping onto his lips. "We want to shield them from everything, yet here we are, both struggling with our own battles."

Laughter bubbled up between us again, lighter this time, but it danced precariously along the edges of sorrow. I felt a connection deepen, a bond forged not just in our shared experiences but in the understanding that came with them. It was as if we were both holding a fragile glass ornament, our hearts, and fears intertwined within its translucent beauty.

As the afternoon sunlight shifted, casting long shadows across the floor, I caught a glimpse of something profound in Nate's eyes—a flicker of resilience mingled with hope. The moment was a delicate dance, one I never wanted to end. Together, we were navigating the storm, tethered by the knowledge that we were not alone in our struggles.

And in that hospital room, amid the beeping machines and the sterile walls, we found a small, sacred space where laughter and vulnerability intertwined, creating a fragile yet beautiful tapestry of connection.

The silence that followed hung in the air like a thick fog, wrapping around us and making the space feel even smaller. I could sense Nate grappling with thoughts that roamed just beyond the reach of his words, each one fighting to be heard but tangled in the web of his emotions. The tension in his shoulders relaxed a fraction as I let the moment linger, a fragile balance where vulnerability danced on the edge of revelation.

"Do you ever feel like we're just characters in some tragic soap opera?" Nate finally asked, a hint of laughter threading through his voice, trying to lighten the mood. "Like any moment now, the dramatic music will swell, and we'll find ourselves swept up in a plot twist that nobody saw coming."

"Tragic, indeed. Perhaps with a sprinkling of dark humor," I replied, raising an eyebrow playfully. "I can see it now: 'Tune in next week as our heroes navigate the treacherous waters of hospital coffee and existential dread.'"

He chuckled, the sound warm and rich, almost like a comforting blanket against the chill that permeated the room. The laughter we shared was like a lifeline, pulling us from the depths of our worries, even if just for a moment. I had always believed that humor was the most powerful antidote to pain, a truth Nate seemed to grasp instinctively.

"Maybe we should start a podcast," he mused, leaning forward with that infectious enthusiasm. "We could share our charming tales of waiting rooms and the strange conversations that occur while sitting on uncomfortable chairs. I bet we could attract a loyal audience of other hospital dwellers."

"Right, and we could sell merch too," I added, my imagination taking flight. "'I Survived the Waiting Room' t-shirts, complete with inspirational quotes about coffee and life's unpredictability."

Nate threw his head back, laughter spilling forth in a way that made my heart do a little flip. "Now that's a million-dollar idea! Just think of the tagline: 'Life's a hospital, and we're all waiting for something!'"

As the laughter faded, the comfortable rhythm of our conversation shifted. I sensed the undercurrents of seriousness reemerging, pulling us back toward the reality we both tried so hard to navigate. It was a delicate dance, one we were still learning, but I felt the weight of Nate's unspoken fears drawing us closer together.

"I really do worry about her," he said quietly, his gaze drifting back to the floor, the playful spark dimming. "It's like I can see the light fading sometimes. I just want to do something, anything, to make it better. But I feel so... helpless."

"Helplessness is one of the hardest emotions to swallow," I replied softly, letting the words hang in the air. "You want to be the hero, but sometimes all you can do is stand by, watching."

Nate nodded, his expression one of quiet understanding, and I marveled at how we had both stepped into this role—witnesses to our families' struggles, caught in the throes of a fight that felt far too large for us. "It's so unfair," he murmured, a hint of anger creeping into his voice. "Why do we have to go through this? Why can't life just play fair for once?"

"Maybe life thinks it's funny," I suggested, attempting to weave humor back into the conversation. "Like some cosmic prankster watching us squirm."

He smirked, but there was an edge to it, a reflection of the frustration simmering just beneath the surface. "If that's the case, I'd like to have a word with that cosmic joker. I have some grievances I'd love to air."

We fell into a comfortable silence, the kind that felt like a shared breath, where everything unsaid flowed between us like an invisible thread. I couldn't shake the feeling that this moment—this delicate exchange of fears and laughter—was somehow transformative, an exploration of our shared humanity in the face of adversity.

Then, the door creaked open, and a nurse stepped in, her presence a welcome interruption. "Hey there, you two. How are we doing?" she asked with a warm smile, her cheerful demeanor lighting up the room.

"We're just plotting world domination through hospital-themed merchandise," Nate replied, a quick smile flashing across his face, the weight of his earlier concerns momentarily lifted.

"Ah, I see! I'll put in a good word for you with my contacts in the t-shirt business," she quipped, and for a moment, it felt as if the air had shifted back to lighter, brighter territory.

"Thanks! Just make sure the colors are flattering; we want our audience to feel good about their choices," I added, a playful twinkle in my eye.

The nurse chuckled, shaking her head as she moved to check the machines, her movements efficient yet graceful. "You two are something else. If only all my patients had your sense of humor."

Once the nurse left, the moment stretched again, the light banter giving way to deeper reflections. Nate turned toward me, his expression earnest. "I know I've been more of a downer lately, but thank you for sticking around. It's nice to have someone to talk to who understands."

I felt a warmth spread through my chest at his words, a feeling of being seen in a world that often felt isolating. "I get it. It's hard to find someone who truly understands. And honestly? You've been my lifeline too. It's comforting to share the weight, even if just a little."

A smile crept onto his face, and in that moment, I realized how crucial our connection had become. We were both navigating uncharted waters, and with every shared laugh and heartfelt conversation, we were crafting a lifeboat, something to cling to amidst the waves of uncertainty.

Just as we settled back into our easy rhythm, a loud commotion echoed from down the hall. Shouts and laughter mingled with the sterile sounds of the hospital, pulling our attention like a magnet. Curious, we exchanged glances, eyebrows raised in unison, a silent agreement to investigate the source of the disturbance.

"Care to join me on a little adventure?" Nate asked, a mischievous glint in his eye.

"Absolutely! Who knows? Maybe we'll discover a secret underground lair or an unexpected gathering of disgruntled penguins," I replied, my heart racing at the prospect of breaking free from the confines of our conversation.

As we rose from our chairs, the heavy atmosphere of the room shifted, replaced by an exhilarating sense of possibility. The world outside awaited us, filled with unpredictable moments that could spark laughter or illuminate our struggles. Together, we stepped into the unknown, ready to face whatever awaited us, hearts a little lighter and spirits a bit brighter.

The commotion that echoed through the hall was like a siren call, pulling us away from the heaviness that had settled around our shoulders. Nate and I exchanged a look that was part confusion, part excitement, both of us ready for a reprieve from our earlier conversation. With a shared nod, we ventured into the corridor, the world outside our small bubble of conversation expanding into an unpredictable adventure.

As we stepped into the hallway, the vibrant energy felt electric, almost palpable. The fluorescent lights hummed above us, and the sound of laughter bounced off the walls, mingling with the scents of antiseptic and something strangely sweet, like cotton candy. "I'm starting to think we've stumbled into a carnival," I quipped, feeling the weight of my worries lift just a little.

"Let's hope they have popcorn," Nate replied, scanning the area with an exaggerated seriousness that made me laugh. "I hear popcorn is the key to all great hospital escapes."

We followed the sounds to a small gathering near the nurses' station. A few staff members were crowded around a cart filled with brightly colored balloons and a sign that read "Welcome Back, Lucy!" in cheerful, crooked letters. It appeared one of the nurses was returning from maternity leave, and the atmosphere was brimming with joy and celebration.

"Look at that!" Nate said, his eyes lighting up as he nudged my shoulder. "It's a party! I bet they have cake."

Just as he finished his sentence, a small girl, no older than five, bounded past us, her tiny arms outstretched as she sprinted toward the balloons like they were enchanted. She stopped short, her eyes wide with wonder, before jumping up to reach the lowest one. "Balloons!" she squealed, her voice high and joyous.

Nate and I chuckled, caught up in the innocent exuberance of her excitement. The warmth radiating from the group was contagious, a spark of life that momentarily brightened the dim corners of our minds. I felt a flicker of something I hadn't felt in a while—hope.

"Okay, so now I'm convinced we should crash this little gathering," I said, a playful glint in my eye. "If they have cake, we'll be the unofficial ambassadors of joy."

"Ambassadors of joy? That's quite a title," Nate teased, arching an eyebrow. "Do we get badges? Maybe capes?"

"Only if we save the day!" I declared, and with that, we moved toward the group.

As we approached, I could hear snippets of conversation—stories about sleepless nights, the challenges of motherhood, and a flurry of congratulations. The nurse, Lucy, beamed, her eyes sparkling as she recounted the misadventures of her first few weeks as a mother. It was heartwarming, a reminder that even in this stark environment, life continued to flourish outside of hospital rooms and illness.

"Do you think we can at least score some snacks?" Nate whispered as we hovered at the edge of the gathering. "I mean, isn't that the least they can do for two bedraggled hospital dwellers like us?"

"Why don't you ask?" I nudged him, feigning confidence. "You're much better at charming people than I am."

"Fine. But if this backfires, I'm blaming you," he replied, his voice laced with mock seriousness.

As he approached the group, I hung back, trying to read the mood. Nate turned on his trademark smile, effortlessly engaging with the staff as if he were a regular at the party. I watched as they laughed at his quips, each smile serving as a reminder of the warmth that lingered in spaces filled with hardship.

"Excuse me, ladies," Nate said, his voice rising above the laughter. "We couldn't help but notice your lively celebration. Any chance you'd share some of that famous hospital cake with two of your most loyal patrons?"

The nurses exchanged amused glances, and after a moment of playful deliberation, one of them responded, "You'd be surprised how much cake we have. You'll have to show us your best party dance to earn a slice, though!"

"Challenge accepted!" Nate declared, throwing me a wink. My stomach fluttered as he launched into an impromptu dance, his movements a blend of awkward charm and sheer enthusiasm. Laughter erupted around him, and for a moment, the weight of our earlier conversation seemed to dissolve.

I joined in, unable to resist the infectious atmosphere. The little girl from earlier watched, her wide eyes sparkling as she attempted to mimic our goofy moves, arms flailing in sheer delight. It felt so liberating to let go, if only for a few moments, to feel the joy washing over us like a gentle tide.

"See? I knew we'd find a way to escape the doom and gloom," Nate said, breathless from his antics as he returned to my side, a satisfied grin plastered on his face. "What do you think? Should we go professional?"

"Only if we can incorporate balloons into our act," I joked, glancing at the colorful decorations that bobbed above us. The atmosphere had shifted, the laughter weaving a tapestry of connection that momentarily drowned out the hospital's clinical reality.

But just as I felt the joy taking root, a sharp cry pierced the air, cutting through the laughter like a knife. The room fell silent as heads turned toward the source. The little girl, who had been reveling in the balloon display, had stumbled, her face crumpling in an instant of shock and pain.

"Oh no," I breathed, instinctively moving toward her.

Nate followed closely, and together we knelt beside her as the nurses rushed forward. The girl's mother appeared, panic etched across her face, and I felt a pang of recognition in the mother's frantic movements. The scene shifted again, the playful atmosphere transforming into one of concern, the laughter evaporating as if it had never existed.

"Lucy! Honey, what happened?" her mother knelt beside her, worry palpable in her voice.

"I want my balloon!" the girl sobbed, tears streaming down her cheeks. Her small body shook with the force of her distress, and it felt like the whole world had ground to a halt.

Nate looked at me, his expression mirroring the concern etched across my face. "What do we do?" he whispered, the lightheartedness of moments ago slipping away.

"I think we should help," I replied, my heart racing as I glanced around at the nurses who were now tending to the girl. I felt a surge of determination as I knelt beside them, ready to offer comfort in whatever way I could.

As the commotion unfolded, I realized that amid our laughter and joy, we were still part of this world—a world filled with both laughter and pain, joy and heartbreak. Our fragile lives were interwoven in ways we couldn't fully understand. Just as I prepared to comfort the little girl, a strange sensation gripped my chest—a cold, creeping dread that something else was looming just beyond the veil of our laughter.

Before I could articulate the feeling, a familiar voice rose above the chaos, slicing through the air with an intensity that sent a chill down my spine. "Ava?"

My heart dropped as I turned, meeting the gaze of a figure standing at the entrance of the ward, their expression unreadable. It was a face I hadn't expected to see—a face from my past that I had hoped to leave behind.

"Ava!" The voice again, sharper now, as if it were a knife carving through the fragile barrier I had built around my heart.

The laughter faded into a heavy silence, and I felt the world around me tilt, the balance of the moment shifting dramatically. Everything I had felt in those last moments—the laughter, the hope—hung precariously, teetering on the edge of something that could change everything.

Chapter 12: The Unexpected Visit

The antiseptic smell of the hospital was a constant reminder that life, in all its fragility, could be painfully mundane. I sat in the small room, staring out the window where the sun blazed overhead, oblivious to the turmoil brewing within. The fluorescent lights buzzed softly, mingling with the rhythmic beeping of the machines that surrounded my mother's bed. She lay there, a still figure wrapped in white sheets, her breath shallow and intermittent. The sight of her fragile state knotted my stomach, twisting and tightening like a stubborn vine, and all I could do was wish for a moment of peace amid the chaos.

It was one of those days when my mind refused to quiet down, each thought looping back to the memories of my father, Mark, who had long ago drifted out of my life like a wisp of smoke. I could almost hear his laughter echoing through my childhood home, a sound that now felt like a distant melody I could no longer recall clearly. Anger and sadness mingled in my chest like oil and water, creating a tempest of emotions I struggled to navigate. The absent figure of my father was a puzzle with too many missing pieces, a constant reminder of everything I had lost, and I had buried those feelings beneath layers of indifference and resentment.

Then came the knock at the door, sharp and unexpected, slicing through the haze of my thoughts. My heart stumbled, an errant drumbeat, as the door creaked open. There stood Mark, my estranged father, his tall frame awkwardly outlined against the sterile backdrop of the hospital room. His face was a mixture of concern and something akin to fear, his brow furrowed as if he were bracing for impact. It was like seeing a ghost—one that had lingered too long in the shadows of my memory, and suddenly, he was here, standing in the flesh, alive and too real.

"Ava," he said, his voice a rasp, like gravel grinding against itself. The name hung in the air, heavy with the weight of years unspoken. I narrowed my eyes, searching his expression for the familiar comfort I had once known, but instead, I found only the unfamiliar shape of regret.

"What are you doing here?" I managed to croak out, each word laced with the sharp edge of resentment. The tension coiled between us like a tightly wound spring, ready to snap. I was acutely aware of my mother's stillness in the background, her quiet breath a contrast to the storm brewing in this small room.

"I heard about your mom," he replied, stepping closer, though the distance between us felt insurmountable. "I wanted to see if you were okay."

"Okay?" I echoed, incredulous. "You disappeared for years, and now you think you can just stroll in and play the concerned father? How is that supposed to make any of this better?" Each word dripped with the bitterness of abandonment, a flavor I had grown accustomed to but was still not ready to swallow again.

He ran a hand through his hair, a gesture that felt all too familiar yet foreign. "I know I've messed up, Ava. I know I haven't been there. I—" he paused, searching for the right words, his voice cracking under the weight of the moment. "I'm sorry."

I couldn't let the words wash over me like some soothing balm. Apologies felt cheap when they arrived too late, like flowers sent to a grave. "Sorry doesn't change anything. You can't just show up and expect everything to be okay."

"Maybe I'm not expecting that," he said, his voice barely above a whisper, and for a fleeting moment, I saw the flicker of vulnerability in his eyes, a hint of the man I used to know. But it was drowned out by the flood of memories: the empty chair at family dinners, the birthdays celebrated without him, the hollow ache that never quite went away.

"I don't need you here, Mark," I snapped, each word laced with all the hurt and anger I had pent up over the years. "You left when I needed you the most. Why should I believe you now?"

His expression shifted, a storm brewing behind his eyes. "Because I'm trying to make it right. I can't change the past, but I want to try and be here for you now."

The truth in his words tugged at something deep within me, a long-buried hope that perhaps, just perhaps, this man standing before me wasn't just the ghost I had imagined but a real person with real regrets. Still, doubt clawed at my insides, relentless and unforgiving. Trust was a fragile thing, and I had spent years building walls strong enough to keep out the pain. "How do I know this isn't just another empty promise?" I shot back, my voice trembling with the weight of the question.

"I don't expect you to trust me right away," he replied, his voice steady despite the quaking atmosphere. "But I'm here. I'm not going anywhere this time."

Those words hung in the air, and I felt the prick of tears welling in my eyes. I hated that he could still affect me this way, that after all this time, I could still feel the pull of his presence, like gravity drawing me toward him. Yet I also felt the familiar walls rising, reinforced by years of hurt. How could I let myself be vulnerable again?

The silence stretched, heavy and oppressive, filled only by the soft sounds of the hospital—the distant laughter of nurses, the chirping of machines, and my mother's rhythmic breaths. I turned my gaze to her, a fragile figure trapped in the throes of illness. A part of me wanted to shield her from the man who had abandoned us both, while another part, one that had long been dormant, ached for connection, for understanding.

"Look, Ava," he said gently, as if sensing the storm brewing inside me. "I know I can't erase the past, but I want to try and help you through this. We can face it together. I want to be part of your life again."

The sincerity in his voice reached for the parts of me I had buried deep, where hope flickered like a dying flame. Would I dare to let it breathe? Would I be willing to risk another fracture in my already shattered heart? As I grappled with these questions, I realized that the answers wouldn't come easily; perhaps, they never would.

His presence loomed like an ominous cloud, one that threatened rain at any moment, and I felt the rush of emotions surge through me, waves crashing against the fortress I had meticulously built around my heart. My mind raced with the potential fallout of his unexpected visit, each scenario more dramatic than the last. I could picture myself hurling the closest hospital chair at him, or perhaps I'd break down in tears, the walls of my carefully constructed indifference crumbling into dust. Instead, I opted for a middle ground: sarcasm.

"Is this the part where you tell me you've joined a support group for deadbeat dads?" I quipped, crossing my arms in defiance. The words hung between us like a challenge, a gauntlet thrown at his feet. His expression faltered for a moment, the flicker of surprise in his eyes giving way to something softer, perhaps even a hint of admiration.

"No, but I probably should. Clearly, I need to work on my re-entry strategy," he replied, attempting to match my wry tone, though his voice trembled slightly. There was a vulnerability in his admission that made me want to scoff and cry all at once. This was a man who had allowed the weight of life to crush him under the burden of his own mistakes, yet here he was, willing to bare himself before me, as raw as my emotions felt.

"Re-entry? Is that what we're calling it now?" I retorted, the bitterness seeping into my voice. "Because it feels more like you've parachuted into a war zone without any warning. You can't just come back and pretend everything's fine. You can't be an absent parent for years and suddenly decide to show up, ready to play the hero."

He ran a hand through his hair, a gesture I remembered from childhood—his way of signaling he was on the brink of saying something important. "I'm not pretending, Ava. I've messed up, and I own that. I didn't know how to be there for you, so I convinced myself it was easier to be somewhere else. I see that now, and it kills me."

I wanted to scream, to shake him until he understood the chaos he had left in his wake. The loneliness of family dinners where I had become the invisible guest, the birthdays where my wishes had felt like echoes in a vast empty room. "You think it's just about you feeling bad? It's not! I had to navigate my life without you, and I'm tired of your guilt overshadowing my pain. You have no idea what I've been through."

His face fell, and for a moment, I could almost see the inner conflict reflected in his eyes—the man who had left and the father who desperately wanted to make amends. "You're right. I don't. But I want to learn. I want to be here for you now, even if it means facing the consequences of my absence."

The honesty in his words sliced through the thick atmosphere, and I felt my resolve start to waver. Did I want to believe him? Could I risk reopening the wound that had taken so long to scab over? My heart ached with indecision, caught in the tension of past hurt and the flicker of potential healing.

Before I could respond, the door swung open, and a nurse poked her head in, her bright blue scrubs contrasting sharply with the drab walls. "Excuse me, but visiting hours are almost over. I just wanted to remind you to take care of yourself, Ava. You need to eat something." Her tone was soothing, yet her presence felt intrusive, a reminder that the world outside was still spinning while we fought our own battle.

"Right, because I'm really in the mood for a five-star meal right now," I muttered, my sarcasm returning like a loyal friend. The nurse smiled kindly, unfazed by my sarcasm, before slipping back into the hall.

"Look, let's not end this conversation here," Mark urged, his voice low, almost pleading. "I know I can't fix everything, but I want to try. Can we at least start somewhere? I'll take what I can get. Just a few minutes of your time."

I leaned back against the wall, my heart thundering in my chest as I weighed my options. The urge to slam the door on him, to close the chapter before it could start anew, battled fiercely against the small part of me that yearned for a connection. I had always been a sucker for redemption arcs, even if I found them annoying when they happened to other people.

"I can give you five minutes," I finally replied, my voice steady but laced with defiance. "But if you screw this up, you won't get another chance."

"Fair enough," he said, a flicker of hope igniting in his expression. I could almost see the wheels turning in his head as he prepared to lay bare the thoughts that had simmered beneath the surface for too long.

"Okay, let's get one thing straight," I began, leaning forward, my voice lowering to a conspiratorial whisper as if the walls themselves might listen. "I'm not your therapist. I'm not here to comfort you about your feelings. If you want to talk, you better be ready to hear what I have to say without trying to fix it. Can you do that?"

He nodded, the corners of his mouth twitching in what might have been a smirk or a grimace. "I can try. I promise I won't interrupt your ranting session."

"Good," I said, folding my arms defiantly. "Now, let's see if you really want to hear what I have to say."

His expression shifted, the seriousness returning as he leaned closer, inviting the vulnerability of the moment. "I'm listening."

I took a deep breath, the weight of years resting on my shoulders like a heavy cloak. "You left me when I needed you the most, and every time I thought about you, it felt like a punch to the gut. I had to figure out who I was without you. That's not something you can just sweep under the rug with a few apologies and puppy-dog eyes."

The silence that followed felt monumental, like the stillness before a storm. Mark's gaze bore into mine, his expression a mix of sorrow and understanding. "I can't change what happened. But I can promise to be present now, to let you lead this conversation wherever you need it to go. I just want to be a part of your life again, Ava."

His sincerity made me hesitate, my defenses quaking under the weight of honesty. But as I gazed into his eyes, searching for the truth behind his words, I felt something shift—an unfamiliar, tentative flicker of hope that perhaps, against all odds, we might find a way back to each other, even if the path was riddled with potholes.

The tension between us crackled like static electricity, each word we exchanged holding the potential to either bridge the chasm of years or ignite a fire that would scorch us both. My heart raced as I fought the urge to retreat into the comforting numbness I had perfected. This wasn't just a conversation; it was a negotiation of our very existence, a tentative dance around the unsteady ground of our fractured relationship.

"I want to know who you are now, Ava," Mark said, his voice earnest, grounding me in a way I hadn't anticipated. "Tell me about your life. What makes you happy? What makes you angry? I want to know the real you, the person I missed out on for so long."

His eyes, deep and searching, felt like a gentle push against the barricades I had erected. It was easy to stay angry, to cling to the hurt like a shield. But the flicker of sincerity in his gaze stirred something within me, an urge to break the silence that had defined us for years.

"Fine," I said, the sharpness in my tone a reflex. "You want the real me? Here it is. I work at a coffee shop, grinding through the daily grind of overly complicated lattes and customers who think they're more important than they are. I have a roommate who plays the ukulele at two in the morning, and I'm still trying to figure out what I want to be when I grow up, which, spoiler alert, hasn't happened yet."

Mark nodded, absorbing every word, as if I were handing him pieces of a puzzle he desperately wanted to complete. "That sounds... relatable. The coffee shop life sounds tough, though. Do you enjoy it?"

"Enjoy is a strong word," I replied, raising an eyebrow. "It pays the bills and keeps my brain somewhat engaged. Plus, I get free coffee, which is a huge perk. But if I had a nickel for every time someone tried to impress me with their knowledge of artisan coffee beans, I'd probably be able to open my own coffee shop."

A chuckle escaped him, surprising me with its warmth. "I didn't realize I was talking to a coffee connoisseur. Maybe I should start taking notes."

I smirked, the walls around my heart softening slightly. "Good luck with that. My coffee expertise doesn't extend much beyond ordering a double shot of espresso and hoping it doesn't taste like burnt rubber."

"Noted," he said, mirroring my grin. "And what about hobbies? Do you have any that don't involve caffeine?"

I hesitated, the familiarity of my interests feeling too personal to share. "Well, I dabble in writing," I admitted, the words spilling out before I could stop them. "I've been working on a novel for the past year, but it's more like a collection of abandoned ideas at this point."

"Writing? That's incredible! What's it about?" His enthusiasm caught me off guard, and I felt a flicker of pride mingling with the anxiety of revealing something so deeply personal.

"It's a love story," I said, unable to suppress a sheepish smile. "Or at least, it was supposed to be. But it seems to have turned into this convoluted mess of characters making terrible decisions and everyone ultimately being unhappy. Kind of like my life, I guess."

"Ah, the classic tale of love lost and found again," Mark mused, his expression thoughtful. "Maybe it just needs a twist. Like, the protagonist suddenly gets a long-lost parent dropping back into their life and complicating everything."

My eyes widened, and I laughed, unable to help myself. "So, you're saying I should write you into the story? You'd be the charming but flawed father figure who pops in at the worst possible time. Sounds riveting."

"I'd be a terrible character, trust me," he shot back with a playful glint in his eyes. "I'm the one who caused the plot twist in your life, remember?"

"True," I said, feeling the heat of our banter bring a warmth to the cold room. "But at least the story might have a chance to redeem itself."

"Redemption is a tricky business," he replied, his tone shifting, grounding the lightheartedness we'd just shared. "But I'm willing to fight for it."

The words hung between us, heavy with implications. I could see the flicker of hope in his eyes, but it felt precarious, like a candle teetering on the edge of a table. Would I be able to balance the light he brought into my life against the darkness of his past?

Just as I opened my mouth to respond, the door swung wide, and a doctor strode in, clipboard in hand, wearing the all-too-familiar expression of someone about to deliver news that could change everything. "Ava," he said, glancing between us, his voice devoid of the lightness that had filled the room moments before. "I need to speak with you."

Panic surged through me. "Is it my mom?" I asked, dread pooling in my stomach, my earlier levity evaporating into thin air. I shot a glance at Mark, who wore a mask of concern that mirrored my own turmoil.

The doctor hesitated, his expression softening, which only deepened the pit in my stomach. "Yes, it's about your mother's condition. There have been some complications."

I felt the walls of the room close in, the sterile air thickening with unspoken fears. "What kind of complications?" I pressed, my voice trembling despite my efforts to sound steady.

"Her health has deteriorated more rapidly than we anticipated," he began, the words slicing through the air like a knife. "We need to discuss her options and what this means moving forward."

My breath caught, the world around me fading into a dull roar. I looked at Mark, his eyes wide with the weight of unasked questions and fears of his own. "What does that mean?" I whispered, my voice barely audible above the rush of my heartbeat.

The doctor's gaze remained steady but sympathetic. "It means we need to consider the possibility of palliative care. We want to ensure she's as comfortable as possible during this time."

I felt my heart plummet, crashing into a void of despair. The fragile connection I'd been building with Mark felt like a thin thread in the face of the reality that loomed before us. "No," I whispered, shaking my head, desperation clawing at my throat. "No, we can't—she can't—"

"Let's take this one step at a time," the doctor interjected gently, but I barely registered his words. I felt the room spin, the air thick with the weight of my mother's fragility and the sudden resurgence of every unresolved feeling I'd been wrestling with.

Mark reached out, his hand brushing against mine, grounding me in a moment that felt utterly chaotic. "Ava, I'm here," he said softly, his presence a lifeline in the storm. "We'll face this together."

But as I looked into his eyes, a flicker of uncertainty crept in. Could I truly let him in when everything felt so precarious? The uncharted territory of our relationship hung in the balance, poised on a knife's edge.

Just as the doctor began to explain the next steps, a loud crash echoed from the hallway, followed by a flurry of voices. The sound jolted my heart back into overdrive, and I glanced toward the door, dread pooling in my stomach once more. Whatever was about to unfold would change everything—again.

Chapter 13: Healing Through Art

The sun hung low on the horizon, spilling liquid gold across the train yard, transforming the rusting cars into canvases of color. Each creaking metal frame whispered stories of long-forgotten journeys, echoing the hidden narratives buried deep within my heart. I clutched my notebook, pages worn and dog-eared, my pen poised above the paper, trembling with anticipation. This spot had become my sanctuary, a place where the weight of the world lifted just enough for me to breathe, to think, to feel.

Nate arrived moments later, his silhouette framed against the dying light. He wore his usual slightly crooked grin, a hint of mischief dancing in his blue eyes, as if he had secrets to share—little treasures waiting to be uncovered. The way his presence illuminated the dimming yard filled me with warmth, igniting sparks of inspiration I hadn't realized were dimming within me. He sauntered over, hands shoved deep into the pockets of his faded jeans, hair tousled as if he had just rolled out of bed, and I couldn't help but smile.

"Did you bring the goods?" he asked, raising an eyebrow, his tone playful. I couldn't tell if he was referring to my poems or the iced coffee I had hastily packed. Maybe both.

"Only the finest poetry this side of the tracks," I replied, trying to sound grandiose, but failing miserably as a giggle escaped my lips. "And maybe a little caffeine."

"Perfect combination for a night of artistic genius," he declared, plopping down next to me on the splintered wooden planks. I could almost hear the train whistles in the distance, harmonizing with the murmur of our laughter, a melody that chased away the shadows lurking in my mind.

I flipped through my notebook, skimming the lines that had poured out of me in moments of solitude and despair, each verse steeped in a bittersweet authenticity. As I began to read, the familiar lines wove around us, each word a thread binding our unspoken understanding. I felt Nate's gaze pierce through the veil of my insecurities, his focus unwavering as he absorbed my thoughts, my feelings, my soul laid bare.

"'In the chaos of the storm, I found a flicker of light,'" I recited, feeling the weight of the words resonate. "That's how I felt when we found this place, like chaos could breathe beauty into the wreckage."

His expression shifted, deepening with recognition. "And sometimes, the wreckage is where the real art is, isn't it?" he mused, his voice low and thoughtful. "It's in those moments we discover who we are."

I looked at him, searching for the secrets behind his eyes, and saw the light reflecting my own struggles—his laughter and vulnerability intertwined in a delicate dance. He leaned closer, and for a fleeting moment, the world faded away, leaving just the two of us and the harmony of our shared experiences.

"Read me another," he urged, a hint of eagerness in his tone, his fingers brushing against the pages. I hesitated, the words suddenly feeling too personal, too raw. But I could see the encouragement in his eyes, a gentle nudge towards authenticity, and I felt the fear ebb away.

"Alright, here goes." I cleared my throat and dove into a piece I had penned just days ago, the ink still fresh and tinged with the fragility of my emotions. "'Love isn't always found in perfect moments; sometimes, it lingers in the unguarded seconds between laughter and tears.'"

"Damn," Nate breathed, a smile breaking across his face. "That's beautiful. You capture what it means to be human so perfectly." His praise washed over me like a warm embrace, stirring a whirlwind of butterflies in my stomach.

"Coming from you, that means a lot," I admitted, the corners of my mouth tugging upward. "You have this way of seeing the world that makes everything seem... well, a little more magical."

Nate chuckled, his eyes twinkling like the stars that were beginning to punctuate the twilight sky. "Magical, huh? Maybe it's the coffee talking, but I'll take it. You know, we should do something with your poetry—something more than just reading it in a train yard."

I raised an eyebrow, intrigued. "What did you have in mind?"

He paused, the gears in his head visibly turning. "Illustrations. Your words are vivid enough to paint a picture already, but what if we created something together? You write, and I draw. We could blend our talents."

The idea took root in my mind, sprouting tendrils of excitement and fear. "That sounds... incredible. But what if it turns out terrible?"

Nate shook his head vehemently. "Art isn't about perfection; it's about expression. And I'd much rather work on something that captures our messy, complicated lives than anything pristine."

A thrill coursed through me at the prospect, igniting a spark of inspiration. "Okay, let's do it. I'm in."

"Awesome," he said, his enthusiasm infectious. "Tonight, we brainstorm. Tomorrow, we start creating."

As we plotted our artistic endeavor, the air thick with possibility, I couldn't help but marvel at how this unlikely collaboration had become a refuge for both of us. In sharing my poetry with Nate, I was finding pieces of myself I had long hidden away, while he, with his playful charm and unwavering belief in me, was drawing out my voice from the shadows, one word at a time.

Under the canopy of stars, laughter erupted between us, the sounds intertwining with the gentle rustle of the wildflowers swaying in the breeze. I felt a rush of gratitude, not just for this moment but for the journey that had led me here—one filled with heartbreak, healing, and unexpected beauty. As we dove into the depths of our creativity, I knew this was only the beginning, a new chapter woven from the threads of our shared experiences, waiting to be explored and immortalized in vibrant hues.

As the days melted into a warm, inviting haze, our impromptu project began to take shape, much like the colorful murals sprawling across the walls of our town. Each evening, we found ourselves back at the train yard, a haven where creativity flowed as freely as the nearby river. With Nate's sketchbook sprawled across the uneven wooden planks, we crafted a world where my poetry danced off the page, intertwining with his illustrations in a vibrant display of expression.

Nate had a knack for drawing the most mundane objects in ways that turned them into something enchanting. A simple rusted bolt transformed into a whimsical creature, its limbs outstretched as if caught mid-dance, while a cluster of wildflowers sprouted from the pages, blooming with colors that rivaled a sunset. The sketchbook quickly became a treasure trove of our shared dreams and hopes, a sanctuary where nothing was off-limits.

"Okay, so what about this?" I suggested one afternoon, my pen poised above my notebook as we lounged against the worn wooden beams of the train yard. "For the piece about finding light in the chaos, we could have a lighthouse surrounded by stormy waves, the beam cutting through the darkness."

Nate's brow furrowed in concentration, his pencil gliding across the paper. "Love it, but what if we added a twist? The lighthouse could be made of shattered glass—representing how beauty can emerge from brokenness. And maybe there are tiny ships navigating through the tempest, lit by the lighthouse's glow."

I leaned closer, mesmerized. "You really have a gift for turning my words into something more. It's like you can see into my soul or something."

"Maybe I'm just a good guesser," he replied, winking playfully. "Or perhaps I'm just really good at eavesdropping."

As we laughed, the air around us shimmered with possibility. Our playful banter quickly transformed into a deeper exploration of the themes within my poetry, weaving layers of our experiences into every stroke of his pencil. The collaborative nature of our work created an intimacy I hadn't anticipated, allowing us to navigate our vulnerabilities together, layer by layer.

Each new poem birthed fresh ideas, spiraling us into debates about the imagery we wanted to portray. On a particularly warm evening, the golden hour cloaking us in soft light, I shared a piece that had been haunting me—one about love that danced on the edge of destruction, a raw reflection of my own fears.

"I think it's important to show that love isn't always perfect," I said, my voice trembling slightly as I read. "Sometimes, it feels like a delicate balance between holding on and letting go."

Nate nodded, his fingers pausing above the paper. "Maybe for this one, we illustrate a couple standing on a tightrope, with storm clouds swirling around them. They could be reaching for each other but also teetering on the brink."

"Brilliant," I replied, feeling a rush of exhilaration at how effortlessly our minds intertwined. "And we could add little echoes of their past selves below, watching them from the shadows. It shows how past experiences linger, even when we try to move forward."

"Or maybe they're throwing rocks at them," he joked, his laughter mingling with the soft rustle of the grass around us. "You know, just to keep it light and breezy."

"Right, because that's what every couple needs—an audience heckling them from below!" I shot back, giggling at the absurdity of it all.

As the weeks drifted by, our artwork became a living testament to our shared journeys. The train yard transformed into our studio, where the air was thick with the scent of fresh ink and laughter. We painted vibrant canvases that hung precariously from the rusty train cars, transforming our little corner of the world into an explosion of color and life.

One evening, as dusk settled in, I noticed Nate staring intently at his latest drawing—a girl standing at the edge of a cliff, wind whipping through her hair as she gazed into the abyss. There was something hauntingly beautiful about it, a raw emotion captured in the delicate lines.

"What's going on in your head?" I asked, curiosity piquing as I settled beside him.

He sighed, the weight of his thoughts palpable. "Just thinking about how sometimes we find ourselves at that edge, right? It's terrifying, but also exhilarating. The fear of what lies below can be paralyzing, but maybe it's also what pushes us to leap."

I pondered his words, feeling a flicker of recognition in my chest. "That's exactly it. It's that very moment—the choice between retreating to safety or embracing the unknown—that shapes who we are."

"Maybe we should illustrate that," he suggested, his eyes lighting up. "A series of cliffs, each one representing a different leap we've taken. We could draw our characters in various stages of their journey—some ready to jump, others hesitating, and a few already soaring."

A sense of urgency ignited within me, sparking a new wave of creativity. "Let's do it! Let's create something that embodies every leap we've made, every fear we've conquered."

Nate's enthusiasm was infectious, and as we sketched into the night, the moonlight casting silver shadows on our pages, I realized how much this project had become a mirror of our lives. It was more than just art; it was an exploration of our souls, our fears, and our dreams, all wrapped up in the bond we had forged amidst the chaos.

As we moved through the work, I couldn't help but feel the threads of our connection tightening, each shared laugh and whispered fear knitting us closer together. There was an unspoken understanding that transcended words—a kind of magic only created through vulnerability and trust. And as our project evolved, so too did we, each new piece a chapter in our unfolding story, rich with color and depth.

The sun dipped below the horizon, casting the train yard in hues of purple and gold as we dived deeper into our artistic endeavor. Days of laughter, creative frustration, and quiet moments had woven a rich tapestry of memories. Our project had morphed into something both exhilarating and terrifying, each brushstroke carrying the weight of our unspoken truths.

On this particular evening, I stood before a canvas splattered with vibrant colors, my heart racing with the prospect of what lay ahead. Nate had sketched a figure standing at the edge of a cliff, the wind swirling around her, hair a wild halo. It mirrored my own journey—one that had been filled with leaps into the unknown and moments of hesitation. We were reaching a pivotal point in our collaboration, and the air crackled with anticipation.

"Okay, what's the next leap?" Nate asked, leaning against the easel, arms crossed, his blue eyes sparkling with mischief. "What's the big revelation you're keeping from me?"

I feigned surprise. "Revelation? Me? Never! I'm just an open book." But my pulse quickened as I thought of the piece I had yet to share, the one that felt too raw, too personal.

"Right, like a book that's missing the last chapter," he shot back, raising an eyebrow. "Seriously, Ava. Spill it."

I took a deep breath, the weight of his gaze urging me to reveal more. "It's about fear. How it can be paralyzing but also a catalyst for growth. There's a line about stepping into the fire, about how sometimes you need to get burned to learn how to rise."

Nate's expression shifted, the playful banter giving way to something more profound. "Sounds like you're speaking from experience."

"Touché," I replied, meeting his gaze with equal intensity. "It's scary how much we hold back, isn't it? How the fear of getting burned stops us from taking risks."

"Exactly. But what if we painted that fire?" he suggested, a spark igniting in his eyes. "What if we illustrate the burning and the rising? We could show flames around the figure, but instead of being consumed, she's lifting off the ground, as if she's transforming through the heat."

I loved the way his mind worked, always twisting ideas into something new and vibrant. "And maybe there could be shadows lurking in the flames, representing the fears that try to hold her back."

"Now you're talking," he grinned, clearly enjoying the exchange. "Let's make those shadows look like little monsters; everyone loves a good monster in their story."

Laughter bubbled between us as we worked, the sound echoing off the metal walls, our energy building with each stroke. The sunlight faded, replaced by the gentle glow of string lights we had hung in our makeshift studio, casting a warm ambiance around us. I felt at home in this world we had created together, where each layer of paint and poetry brought us closer, revealing depths of understanding I hadn't known existed.

As the flames took shape on the canvas, I couldn't shake a lingering anxiety. It was as if my fears were trying to claw their way back into my thoughts. "Nate," I said suddenly, hesitating. "What if this project makes everything real? What if it exposes things we're not ready to confront?"

"Then we confront them together," he said, his voice steady, a grounding force in the whirlwind of my emotions. "We've come this far; we're in it together, remember?"

His reassurance washed over me, yet a part of me still quaked with uncertainty.

A few moments passed in silence, the sounds of paintbrushes gliding across canvas filling the air. Then, without warning, the distant echo of laughter morphed into something more jarring—raised voices, sharp and harsh. The tranquility of our art was suddenly pierced by an argument nearby, spilling out from behind the shadows of the train cars.

I looked at Nate, his expression shifting from playful concentration to concern. "What the hell is that?" he whispered, glancing toward the source of the noise.

"Should we check it out?" I suggested, curiosity battling against a flutter of apprehension in my stomach.

Nate shrugged, his brow furrowing slightly. "Probably not a great idea to get involved, but... I'm kind of curious."

We crept closer to the edge of our sanctuary, peering around a rusty boxcar. The scene before us sent a chill racing down my spine. A small group of teenagers, their faces twisted in anger, surrounded another boy who was backed against the metal wall, fear etched into his features.

"What do you want?" he pleaded, his voice barely a whisper.

One of the older boys shoved him, sending him stumbling backward. "You think you can just waltz in here? This is our turf!"

My heart raced as I pulled back instinctively. "Nate, we can't just stand here. We have to do something."

Nate shook his head, eyes narrowed. "And what? We're going to take on five of them? It's not our fight."

"But what if he gets hurt?" I insisted, a surge of anger mixing with fear. "We can't just turn our backs on this."

Before Nate could respond, the situation escalated. The boy stumbled again, his hands raised in a defensive gesture. A sense of urgency prickled at the back of my mind. "Nate, please!"

With no more time for debate, I made my decision and stepped forward, the adrenaline propelling me into the light. "Hey! Leave him alone!"

The group turned, their surprise morphing quickly into scornful laughter. "Look who it is, the poetry girl," one of them sneered, recognition flashing in his eyes. "What's she going to do? Write a sonnet about us?"

"Just walk away," I demanded, my voice steady, though my heart raced. "You don't want to make this worse."

The boy I had defended glanced at me, his eyes wide with disbelief. I could see the panic reflected in his gaze, and it fueled my resolve.

"Are you serious?" the leader laughed. "And what makes you think you can take us on? This is none of your business."

I took a step closer, my heart pounding in my chest. "It is my business when I see someone being bullied. So why don't you let him go and save yourselves the trouble?"

Nate moved behind me, a protective presence, though I could feel his tension radiating through the air.

"Look, we're not looking for trouble," he said, his tone cool and collected, trying to defuse the situation. "Just let him walk away."

The leader's laughter faded, replaced by a cold, calculating expression. "Or what? You think you can intimidate us with your little art project?"

And that's when I saw it—a glimmer of something sharp in his hand, catching the faint light. My breath caught in my throat, and the air grew thick with tension.

"Get back!" Nate shouted, stepping in front of me, his body shielding mine.

In that moment, time seemed to stand still, the threat hanging in the air like the first crack of thunder before a storm. Everything I had learned about stepping into the fire felt painfully irrelevant. I realized I wasn't just stepping into a creative leap; I was teetering on the edge of something far more dangerous, and the flames that had once inspired me now flickered ominously in the shadows.

Chapter 14: Daring Dreams

The gravel crunched beneath the tires of Nate's old truck, the rhythmic sound matching the erratic beating of my heart. As we sped away from the sterile confines of the hospital, the world outside unfurled like a story waiting to be told. The dusky sky melted into shades of pink and orange, a watercolor canvas illuminated by the setting sun, and I could feel the warmth of the evening wrapping around me, as inviting as a favorite sweater. It felt almost surreal to be here, freedom coursing through my veins, dispelling the shadows of the sterile white walls I had known for too long.

"Are you sure you're up for this?" Nate shot me a sideways glance, his eyes dancing with mischief, the corners of his mouth lifting in that lopsided grin I had grown fond of. There was something undeniably charming about him, a blend of boyish exuberance and quiet confidence that made it easy to forget our surroundings. The truck's worn leather seats cradled us like a familiar embrace, every bump in the road punctuating the thrill of the moment.

"Please," I scoffed, trying to sound tougher than I felt. "I've faced down needles and IV drips. A little moonlit adventure isn't going to scare me."

He chuckled, the sound rich and full, and I felt a flutter in my stomach that had nothing to do with the remnants of my treatment. This was different—alive, electric. We raced through the winding roads, and the scent of pine and fresh earth seeped in through the cracked window, invigorating my senses. Each mile that put distance between us and the hospital felt like shedding a layer of my reality, like peeling away the constraints of my illness, if only for a little while.

As we neared the lake, the air shifted, infused with the scent of damp earth and water. The sun sank lower, spilling its last rays across the water's surface, transforming the lake into a shimmering mirror of twilight. I could hardly contain my excitement as we pulled up to the small clearing that opened up to the dock. The crickets began their evening serenade, a chorus of chirps harmonizing with the soft lapping of water against the shore.

Nate parked, and without a second thought, we hopped out, the cool grass tickling my bare feet. "This place is perfect," I said, gazing at the tranquil water, a feeling of calm washing over me.

He grinned and gestured toward the dock. "Come on, let's get closer."

The wooden planks creaked beneath our weight as we stepped onto the dock, the cool breeze ruffling our hair and carrying with it the whispers of the evening. I sat down, letting my legs dangle over the edge, toes skimming the water's surface, sending little ripples dancing away. Nate settled beside me, our shoulders brushing, a simple touch that felt monumental in its familiarity.

We sat in comfortable silence for a moment, the kind that only comes when two people feel safe in each other's presence. The lake stretched out before us, an expanse of shimmering darkness punctuated by the fading light. As the stars began to emerge, I could almost believe that anything was possible.

"What do you dream about?" Nate asked, breaking the silence, his voice soft yet curious.

I looked out at the horizon, searching for the right words, the dreams I had been too scared to voice. "I dream about a life where I can wake up every day and not think about my illness. A life where I can travel, see new places, and meet new people without feeling like I'm dragging an anchor with me."

His gaze was steady on me, encouraging. "Where would you go first?"

"Anywhere but here," I said with a playful smile. "But if I had to choose, I think I'd like to go to Italy. I want to sip wine in a café in Florence, eat pasta that's not from a hospital tray, and wander through streets that look like they belong in a painting."

Nate chuckled, a rich, deep sound that vibrated through me. "I can see you there, twirling pasta like you were born to do it."

I laughed, the sound echoing into the night, the heaviness of the hospital slowly dissipating. "And you? What do you dream about?"

He hesitated, a flicker of something shadowy crossing his features before he spoke. "I dream about building something... more. Not just a career or a house, but a life that feels like home. Somewhere that I can bring people together. Maybe a little café by the beach where everyone knows your name."

"That sounds perfect," I said, imagining him as the charming owner, whipping up coffee and pastries while greeting customers like old friends. "And what's stopping you?"

"Maybe fear," he said quietly, staring at the water as if it held the answers. "Fear that I'll fail or that it won't be enough. But talking about it with you makes it feel... doable."

A comfortable silence wrapped around us again, but the air shifted as if holding its breath. Just then, a soft plop echoed in the stillness, drawing our attention to the water below. A frog leaped from the edge, creating concentric ripples that danced outward.

"See?" I nudged him playfully. "If a little frog can jump into the unknown, so can we."

Nate turned to me, a spark of something unnameable in his eyes. "What if we're not just frogs, Ava? What if we're the ones building bridges?"

My heart skipped at the thought, fluttering wildly in the cage of my ribcage. There was an intensity in his gaze, a connection that felt almost palpable. But just as quickly as the moment bloomed, shadows from the past lurked at the edges, reminding me of the fragility that defined our lives.

I forced a smile, but the weight of reality settled over me like a heavy blanket. "We just have to keep jumping, right?"

Nate's expression shifted, the hope mingling with concern. "Yeah, but I don't want you to jump alone."

I looked away, swallowing the lump forming in my throat. The truth was, I didn't want to jump alone either, but the thought of tethering someone else to my unpredictable fate felt like a betrayal. The balance of dreams and fears danced between us, and I could sense the shift, the delicate tension that always loomed in the spaces we dared to fill with hope.

The night deepened around us, a cocoon of shadows, and I could feel the pull of vulnerability threatening to unravel everything we had built in this fleeting moment. Yet, in that breathless quiet, I realized that maybe, just maybe, I could allow myself to dream a little bigger, to leap a little farther.

The stars began to blink awake, dotting the indigo canvas overhead like scattered diamonds, as Nate and I sat there, suspended in a moment that felt infinitely more precious than the life I had left behind at the hospital. The air was thick with the scent of pine and damp earth, and the gentle lapping of the water against the dock created a soothing rhythm that almost made me forget the incessant thrum of worry lodged in my mind. I tucked a strand of hair behind my ear, glancing sideways at Nate, who was still staring out at the water as if he could divine the secrets of the universe from its depths.

"Did you ever think we'd end up here?" I asked, my voice barely above a whisper, as if speaking too loudly might shatter the tranquility that surrounded us.

"Honestly? I thought you'd be stuck in that hospital room, living off bland jello and wondering why your doctor didn't give you a Netflix password." His grin widened, but there was a softness in his eyes that belied the humor in his words.

I laughed, the sound bubbling up freely. "Well, if that was the case, I'd definitely have a very different outlook on life. Maybe I should thank my doctor for the forced vacation."

"Or thank me for the audacious plan that got us here," he countered, nudging me playfully with his shoulder. "You know, I'm not just a pretty face and a questionable fashion sense."

"Questionable is a generous term," I shot back, glancing at his mismatched socks peeking out from his sneakers. "But seriously, you did this. You took me away from all that. I needed this."

He paused, the weight of my words hanging between us. "Sometimes, we all need a little escape. Especially you." His voice turned serious, and the lightness faded, replaced by something raw and honest. "I don't want you to feel like you're stuck, Ava. You deserve to see the world, to feel free."

The way he said my name sent a shiver down my spine, a reminder that I wasn't just a patient or a label. I was Ava. A girl with dreams and desires, a girl who craved adventure and spontaneity. But the reality of my situation loomed like a storm cloud, threatening to darken the horizon of this perfect evening.

"You make it sound so easy," I replied, the weight of my heart heavy in my chest. "What if my reality is... different?"

His expression softened. "I get that it's hard, but what if we just allow ourselves to dream a little? You know, what if we decide that tonight is just for us? No hospitals, no charts, no worries?"

I studied him, the earnestness in his eyes igniting a flicker of courage within me. "Okay," I breathed out, allowing myself to lean into the hope he was offering. "Tonight is for dreaming."

With that unspoken pact hanging in the air, we began tossing around our wildest dreams as if they were pebbles skipping across the lake. Each idea rippled outward, creating waves of laughter that danced through the night. I painted vivid pictures of adventures we could take—café-hopping in Paris, hiking through the Rockies, or getting lost in the vibrant streets of Tokyo. Each destination blossomed in my mind, bright and colorful, pulling me away from the sterile world I was used to.

Nate matched my enthusiasm with dreams of his own, each one more whimsical than the last. "I want to build that café, but I'd also love to learn how to surf. Imagine me, a total novice, wiping out spectacularly while the locals cheer. It'll be a viral sensation," he joked, his eyes twinkling.

I snorted at the thought. "I'd pay good money to see that. But first, you'd better find a shirt that matches those socks."

"Hey! They're statement pieces!" he protested, feigning offense, and I couldn't help but chuckle at his seriousness. The lightness of our banter created a protective bubble around us, a fortress against the realities that awaited when dawn broke.

As the evening wore on, the stars became our witnesses, twinkling approvingly as we poured our hopes and dreams into the night air. With every story shared, we built a bridge—a connection forged not just through our shared experiences, but through the boldness of dreaming together.

But just as I felt myself floating in the warmth of this newfound connection, a faint, haunting sound pierced through the tranquility. A soft beep, a distant reminder of the hospital's sterile buzz, crept into my mind, pulling me back to reality. The transition was jarring, like a splash of cold water on warm skin. I instinctively clenched my fists, nails digging into my palms as I fought to hold on to the dreamlike state we had woven together.

Nate must have sensed the shift because he turned to me, concern etched on his face. "Hey, what's going on in that brilliant mind of yours?"

I bit my lip, weighing my words carefully. "It's just... I feel like I'm walking on a tightrope. One wrong move, and I could fall back into that world, the one I'm trying so hard to escape."

His expression softened further, and he reached for my hand, his grip warm and reassuring. "Then don't look down. Just keep your eyes on what's ahead. You can't let fear dictate your dreams."

The sincerity of his words struck me like a thunderclap. For a fleeting moment, I could almost believe it—could almost envision a life where fear was a mere whisper, a shadow that faded with the dawn. But I was still tethered to reality, the frayed edges of my hope gnawing at me.

"Easier said than done," I muttered, the frustration evident in my voice. "What if I wake up tomorrow, and the dreams we've shared tonight shatter into a million pieces? What then?"

"Then we pick them up, piece by piece. We don't stop dreaming, Ava. Not ever," he insisted, his gaze steady on mine, as if he could see the flickering flame of my hope and wanted to stoke it to life.

In that moment, I felt something shift—a weight lifted, even if only slightly. I knew the road ahead would be riddled with uncertainty, but Nate's unwavering support grounded me. It was as if he had handed me a lifeline, a thread to pull me back to the surface every time the waves threatened to swallow me whole.

And as we sat there, hands clasped together, surrounded by the whispering trees and the shimmering lake, I realized that perhaps I could dare to dream a little bigger. I could allow myself to envision a future where I didn't just survive, but thrived. A future where the boundaries of my reality were defined by my willingness to leap, not my fears.

"Okay, I'll try," I finally replied, a small smile breaking through the uncertainty that had clouded my heart. "I'll keep dreaming."

Nate beamed at me, and in that smile, I saw a glimpse of a future I could chase, a future where every leap didn't have to be a plunge into the unknown, but an exhilarating ride through the exhilarating chaos of life.

As the stars twinkled overhead, weaving a blanket of light across the night sky, I felt a sense of exhilaration mingled with trepidation. My heart thrummed with the rhythm of Nate's words, still resonating within me. "I'll keep dreaming." The promise had tasted sweet on my tongue, a momentary release from the clutches of uncertainty. Yet the shadows of reality were not far behind, lurking just beyond the edges of our laughter.

Nate was leaning back, propping himself on his elbows, his tousled hair catching the breeze. "So, what's the first thing you're going to do when you get out of here? You know, when you've officially escaped the clutches of the hospital?" He spoke lightly, but I could sense the underlying weight of concern behind his playful tone.

I hesitated, staring at the dark waters of the lake, its surface reflecting the stars like a million tiny mirrors. The question sent a jolt of excitement through me, but it was quickly tempered by a familiar dread. "I suppose... I want to feel alive again. Really alive," I finally admitted, my voice barely above a whisper. "I want to go hiking in the mountains, feel the wind in my hair and the sun on my face. No hospital gowns, no IVs—just me and the world."

He nodded thoughtfully, and for a moment, his expression was almost solemn. "That sounds incredible. We can make that happen. Just think of the places we could explore." The sincerity in his eyes made my heart swell, and I dared to believe that perhaps there was a path leading away from the confines of my illness.

As the night wore on, we drifted into deeper conversations, each one revealing layers of dreams and fears. Nate shared his own ambitions, the details of his café evolving into a vivid vision filled with laughter, delicious aromas, and a sense of belonging. "I want it to be a place where everyone feels at home," he said, his gaze unwavering. "Where people come together over good coffee and better conversations."

"And your questionable socks will be the main attraction?" I quipped, unable to resist the teasing spark that ignited between us.

"Hey! They're a part of my charm," he replied with mock indignation, shooting me a playful glare. "But really, it's about creating a space where people can escape their lives for a moment. Just like we are right now."

The way he articulated his dreams made my own seem more attainable. It was a push and pull of ambition, each of us feeding off the other's hope. But with each laugh and shared dream, I felt the specter of my illness lurking ever closer. It was a constant reminder of the ticking clock I was always aware of, the one that dictated my every move.

"Do you ever think about the 'what ifs'?" I asked, my voice catching in my throat. "Like what if I don't get better? What if this is all I ever have?"

He turned to me, his expression unflinching, and for a moment, I wondered if I had stepped too far into vulnerability. "What if you do get better?" he countered, leaning in closer, his earnestness palpable. "What if you travel, meet amazing people, and live a life you can be proud of? That's a better 'what if,' don't you think?"

I opened my mouth to respond, but the words caught like butterflies in my throat. What if I didn't have the strength to do all that? What if my dreams were nothing more than whispers in the dark, destined to fade with the first light of dawn?

But Nate was undeterred. "You know, you're not alone in this, Ava. You've got me, and I'm not going anywhere."

"Even if I turn into a full-blown drama queen?" I smirked, attempting to lighten the air.

"Especially then," he shot back, his grin infectious. "Just think of it as a character-building exercise."

The banter flowed easily, a balm for the deeper uncertainties swirling within me. Yet just as the laughter filled the air, a sharp sound broke the peaceful ambiance—a rustle in the bushes, followed by an unmistakable voice calling out.

"Ava! Nate! Are you out there?"

I froze, the joyous bubble we had created instantly bursting. The voice was familiar, urgent, and it sent a chill racing up my spine. My heart plummeted. It was my brother, Kyle.

"Damn it," I muttered, my excitement from moments earlier evaporating like mist in the morning sun. I looked at Nate, panic dancing in his eyes.

"Maybe we should—" he started, but the sound of footsteps crunching on the gravel cut him off.

The next moment, Kyle emerged from the shadows, his face a mix of concern and relief. "There you are! I've been looking all over for you!"

I opened my mouth to explain, but the words caught in my throat. The thrill of the evening felt fragile in the wake of reality. Kyle didn't understand; he'd never grasp the allure of escaping the hospital even for a moment.

"Why did you sneak out?" he continued, his voice laced with exasperation. "You're supposed to be resting! What if something happened?"

Nate stood, shifting uncomfortably as if he was caught in the crossfire of a family debate. "Hey, we were just... getting some fresh air," he interjected, trying to lighten the tension.

Kyle shot him a look that would have turned a lesser man to stone. "Fresh air? You know she shouldn't be out here, especially at night! What if—"

"What if she needs to live a little?" Nate countered, his voice rising to meet Kyle's intensity. "She's not just a patient; she's a person with dreams."

"Enough!" I finally burst out, surprising even myself with the force of my words. "I didn't come here to argue about my life choices. I needed this, Kyle! For one night, I needed to feel normal."

The words hung heavy in the air, a taut thread that threatened to snap. Kyle's expression softened, a mixture of concern and frustration written all over his face. "I get that, but you're not normal right now. You need to be careful."

As the weight of his words settled around me, a different kind of tension crackled in the atmosphere, electric and unpredictable. I could feel the heat of Nate's gaze on me, urging me to hold my ground.

But the world around us suddenly felt charged, as if the night was holding its breath, waiting for the inevitable clash between dreams and reality to unfold. My brother's protective instincts battled against Nate's determination to remind me of the life I yearned for.

"Look, Kyle," I said, trying to keep my voice steady, "I know you care. But I need to take risks. I want to feel alive, even if it's just for a moment."

"I just want to protect you," he replied, his tone softening, but the conflict in his eyes remained.

Nate stepped closer to me, and the connection between us was palpable, a silent agreement that we were in this together. "We're just trying to enjoy the night. It's not like we're doing anything reckless."

Kyle's frustration simmered, and the tension escalated, a storm brewing in the heart of our conversation. The moment hung suspended, fragile as the delicate balance between fear and freedom.

Just then, as if fate had decided to intervene, the unmistakable sound of sirens echoed in the distance, piercing through the night and sending a wave of panic coursing through me.

"Do you hear that?" Kyle said, eyes wide. "We need to get you back. Now."

My heart raced. "What's going on? Are they looking for us?"

"Don't know, but we need to go."

Nate took a step back, his brow furrowing. "Wait, what if it's not about us? What if it's something else?"

The sirens grew louder, closing in, drowning out everything else, and in that moment, a shiver of unease curled around my spine.

"What if tonight was only the beginning?" I wondered aloud, dread creeping in as the implications of that sound sunk in.

As Kyle reached for my arm, I caught Nate's gaze one last time, and in that fleeting look, a hundred unspoken words passed between us—hopes, fears, and dreams all crashing together, teetering on the brink of uncertainty.

And then, before I could grasp what was truly happening, the night erupted into chaos.

Chapter 15: The Edge of the Abyss

The hospital room felt like a cave, both cold and oddly comforting, a refuge from the chaos of the outside world. Fluorescent lights hummed softly, casting a sterile glow over the walls painted in muted pastels. I stared at the peeling floral wallpaper, tracing the faded petals with my fingers, as if willing them to bloom back to life. Every second ticked by with the weight of eternity, echoing my heartbeat, quickening whenever I caught sight of Nate's shadow by the door. He looked so alive, all strong lines and stubborn curls, but the energy in his body was shifting. I could see it in the way he stood, hands shoved deep into his pockets, shoulders hunched slightly as if he were bracing himself against a wind that didn't exist.

"Did you bring me anything fun?" I asked, forcing a grin that felt more like a grimace. The joke had lost its humor, but I clung to it, as if laughter could stitch together the fraying edges of my reality.

Nate's smile was tentative, a fragile thing that could shatter if nudged wrong. "I thought maybe some gummy bears," he said, pulling a crinkled bag from his jacket. "I figured they'd at least match your hospital gown."

I chuckled softly, picturing the neon colors against the drab fabric I'd been forced to wear, the joke landing somewhere between light-hearted and bleak. The truth was, my body felt like a stranger's—one that was slipping away from me, bit by bit. The weight of it all sat in my chest, a tangible pressure that made it hard to breathe, harder still to accept.

As the evening slipped into night, a silver slice of moonlight cut through the blinds, illuminating the space with an ethereal glow. It danced across Nate's face, highlighting the deep shadows under his eyes and the tight set of his jaw. I wondered how long he could keep up this charade, this game of pretending that everything was okay when the air between us crackled with unsaid words.

"Hey," I said softly, breaking the silence that had grown thick and heavy. "You know you can talk to me, right? I'm not just your patient. I'm... I'm still here."

He turned, those dark eyes of his searching mine. There was a flicker of something behind them—fear, maybe, or something deeper, a tether that stretched between us, fraying at the edges but still holding on. "It's just... it's hard," he admitted, his voice cracking like a dry branch underfoot. "I don't want to burden you with my worries when you're already carrying so much."

"Since when do you care about burdening me?" I shot back, feigning indignation but unable to mask the tremor in my voice. "I mean, you've been dragging my ass around for years, and now that I'm down, you want to be noble?"

He laughed, a sharp bark that surprised even him. "Fair point." But the mirth didn't linger; it faded like a summer rain. "It's just that every time I see you in this bed, I'm reminded of how fragile everything is. The thought of losing you..." He paused, swallowing hard, his expression shifting into something raw and vulnerable. "It keeps me awake at night, Ava."

The air hung heavy with unspoken fears, wrapping around us like an old, familiar blanket that was both comforting and suffocating. I wanted to reach out and smooth the lines of worry from his brow, but I hesitated. "I'm not going anywhere," I said finally, forcing conviction into my tone. "You're stuck with me, for better or worse. Besides, who else would put up with your constant need for snacks?"

His lips quirked in a half-smile, but the weight of his anxiety remained, unshakable. "What if the worst happens?"

"Then we deal with it," I replied, my voice steady, though inside, my heart lurched at the thought. "One step at a time. I refuse to let fear dictate our lives."

"Easier said than done," he murmured, his gaze dropping to the floor, as if the tiles held answers.

"Yeah, well, since when have I backed down from a challenge?" I challenged, trying to pull him back into the light. "You and I? We're a team. We're unstoppable."

The silence that followed was thick, laden with the weight of truth. Nate finally looked up, and I could see the shadows in his eyes flickering, wrestling with the flickering light of hope. "I don't know what I'd do without you," he admitted, the words spilling from his lips like a confession, honest and haunting.

"Good thing you'll never have to find out," I shot back, unable to hold back the quirk of my lips. But as soon as the words left my mouth, I felt a cold shiver snake up my spine, a whisper of doubt threading through my bravado.

We settled into a comfortable silence, the kind that felt like an embrace, both warm and heavy. In that moment, I resolved to fight—not just for myself, but for Nate, too. I wanted him to know that even in the face of uncertainty, love could thrive, could illuminate even the darkest corners.

But as the moonlight faded, giving way to the shadows of night, I couldn't shake the feeling that we were teetering on the edge of something far more profound than either of us could bear. A quiet terror lurked in the depths, whispering that love might not be enough to conquer the abyss that lay ahead.

The following days drifted by like slow-moving clouds, heavy with the promise of rain yet somehow never quite breaking. I found myself falling into a rhythm of routine that felt both stifling and oddly comforting. Doctor's visits became part of my daily dialogue, the sterile scent of antiseptic mingling with the artificial sweetness of the candy Nate brought on his visits. He'd transform the bland room into a pocket of normalcy, even as my body betrayed me more with each passing day.

One afternoon, when the sun blazed relentlessly outside, Nate pushed the door open, his entrance punctuated by the sudden rush of cool air from the hallway. He was all smiles and warmth, a human sunbeam with tousled hair and a grin that could spark joy in the dreariest of places. "You would not believe the epic battle I just had with the vending machine. It tried to eat my dollar." He held up the crumpled bill as if it were a war trophy, and I couldn't help but laugh, the sound lifting some of the lead that had settled in my chest.

"Oh, the horror! Do you need backup next time? I could send in a rescue team," I teased, fighting to keep my spirits high, even as I could feel the pulse of unease thrumming just beneath the surface.

"Only if they come equipped with snacks." He dropped the dollar bill onto my bedside table, the sharp thud of paper on plastic a reminder of the absurdity of it all. "What's the battle plan today? More magazine articles about celebrity cat outfits? Or should we dive into the world of obscure crossword puzzles?"

"Please, I can't handle that level of commitment." I waved a hand dramatically. "I still haven't recovered from last week's 'easy' sudoku."

Nate rolled his eyes, a good-natured exasperation that I cherished. "You, my friend, are not cut out for intellectual pursuits."

"Oh, you're one to talk! Didn't you get stuck on a puzzle that involved a chicken, a fox, and a bag of grain?"

He chuckled, a rich sound that filled the room. "Okay, that was one time, and it was late! You know I operate best after 8 PM."

Just then, the door creaked open, and the nurse stepped in, her demeanor all business, as she deftly adjusted the IV line with a practiced hand. "How are we feeling today, Ava?" she asked, her voice bright but professional, a stark contrast to the laughter Nate and I had just shared.

"Like I just lost a battle to a vending machine," I quipped, shooting a sidelong glance at Nate, who grinned sheepishly. The nurse chuckled, jotting something down on her clipboard, but the laughter felt fragile against the backdrop of my reality.

"I'll take that as a good sign," she said, adjusting her glasses as she turned to check the monitor. "Your vitals look stable, but I'll be sure to keep an eye on things."

With the nurse gone, Nate's laughter faded into a thoughtful silence. The weight of our earlier banter hung like a mist in the air, a protective veil that couldn't shield us from the truth. I felt the walls of the room close in, and I turned to Nate, the vulnerability creeping back in. "Do you think about it?" I asked, my voice softer, almost hesitant.

"Think about what?" He looked up, the light in his eyes dimming, replaced by something heavier.

"About... the worst-case scenarios."

He was quiet for a moment, the only sound in the room the steady beeping of the heart monitor. "Yeah, I think about it a lot," he admitted, his voice low. "But I don't want to burden you with my fears. You have enough on your plate."

"Burden? Nate, we're in this together, remember? If you're worried, I want to hear it. Let me shoulder it with you." The words came out more urgent than I intended, but they felt necessary.

He shifted in his chair, rubbing the back of his neck as if the gesture could ease the tension tightening around us. "Okay, but it's not pretty. I can't shake the thought of what life would look like without you. The idea of you—of losing you—it's... it's terrifying."

There it was, the unvarnished truth laid bare between us. His honesty hit me like a punch to the gut, a reminder of how close we were to the edge of the abyss.

"What do you see?" I pressed, needing to know, to understand what haunted him in the quiet hours of the night.

"I don't know, Ava. It's like... like waking up and realizing the world is muted. Everything loses its color. I see a life where I have to move forward without you, and I can't imagine it."

"God, Nate," I whispered, the gravity of his words pulling me under. "But you have to believe that I'm fighting. I'm not going anywhere without a fight."

He nodded, but I could see the uncertainty lingering in his eyes. "What if it's not enough?"

I leaned forward, closing the distance, the air between us thick with shared dread. "Then we'll figure it out. Together. I refuse to let this define us."

He searched my gaze, a flicker of hope igniting before it was snuffed out again by fear. "It's easy to say that, but reality doesn't always cooperate."

"Reality can be a jerk," I replied, a smirk tugging at my lips, my attempt at levity sinking into a pit of seriousness. "But we can be the outlaws. Rewrite the rules. Challenge everything."

He laughed softly, but I could see the fight within him reigniting, a reluctant spark. "You're exhausting, you know that?"

"I've been told I have that effect," I shot back, teasing despite the heaviness weighing us down. "But you love it. You love me."

"Damn right I do." His voice softened, the corners of his mouth turning up, but I could feel the tension still coiling in the air.

For a moment, we held each other's gaze, two souls tethered to a fragile hope. I thought of all the battles still ahead, the uncertainty lingering like a storm on the horizon. But in that small room, with Nate by my side, I felt the power of our connection—the unshakeable belief that love could withstand even the darkest of nights.

The days continued to blur into one another, each filled with a strange mix of laughter and despair. I became a master of distraction, wrapping myself in the threads of conversation with Nate, knitting together our shared moments to stave off the creeping shadows. The hospital room transformed into a cocoon of sorts, where we spun our own stories amidst the sterile smell of antiseptic and the persistent hum of machinery, creating a bubble that sometimes felt invincible.

As the sun dipped low in the sky, painting the room in shades of amber and gold, I watched Nate pace by the window, his silhouette framed against the twilight. The way he moved spoke volumes, an unending loop of worry and protectiveness that he wore like a second skin. He stopped suddenly, turning to face me with an expression I couldn't quite read, a curious blend of determination and apprehension.

"Ava," he said, his voice low, almost conspiratorial. "I was thinking we should make a list."

"A list? Like grocery items or top ten movies to watch?" I asked, cocking an eyebrow playfully, though I felt a twinge of dread.

"Not quite," he said, biting his lip. "More like... things we want to do, places we want to go. You know, when you're feeling better."

His optimism washed over me like a gentle tide, but there was an underlying current that pulled at my heartstrings. "A bucket list?"

"Exactly! But without the death part, please," he added, his eyes sparkling with mischief, even as they held the weight of his unspoken fears. "We need to make some big plans. And what's life without a little chaos?"

"Chaos, you say? You do realize I'm currently residing in the epicenter of chaos, right? I'm pretty sure my life has a permanent reservation here." I gestured dramatically around the room, but beneath the humor, my heart raced with both hope and uncertainty.

"Then let's shake things up!" He plopped down on the edge of my bed, his enthusiasm infectious. "We can start small. How about a weekend at the beach? Just you and me, sand between our toes, ice cream melting faster than we can eat it?"

"Sounds dreamy," I replied, imagining the sun warming my skin, the salty breeze whipping through my hair. "But I'm not sure if the hospital will approve of sand in the IV line."

"Details, details!" he laughed, brushing off my concerns. "We'll figure it out. What else? Skydiving? You've always said you wanted to experience freefall."

"Skydiving? I think you've misinterpreted my zest for life. I said I wanted to feel alive, not plummet to my imminent doom."

Nate rolled his eyes, a playful smirk dancing on his lips. "You're such a chicken. What if we aim for something a bit less 'life-threatening' then, like a road trip? Just the two of us, blasting our favorite music, and getting lost in each other's company."

The idea sent a thrill through me, a heady mixture of excitement and longing. "Okay, I could get behind that. I mean, what's the worst that could happen? I could get sick in a car? We could argue over the radio station? Or—"

"Let me stop you right there," he interrupted, his eyes narrowing teasingly. "No arguing allowed. Just happy, blissful road trip memories."

"Fine! But you do realize that no matter how many playlists we create, I'm still going to end up humming the wrong lyrics, right?"

Nate laughed, the sound brightening the room and pushing back the shadows that loomed. "Oh, I look forward to your interpretations of the classics. 'I'm on the highway to hell' sung as a show tune will always be my favorite."

Our laughter filled the space, a temporary shield against the harsh reality outside. But as the moment stretched, I felt the weight of it return, thick and uncomfortable.

"What if... what if we can't do any of it?" I blurted out, the words tumbling from my lips before I could catch them.

Nate's smile faltered, the light dimming in his eyes. "What do you mean?"

"I mean, what if this—" I gestured vaguely around the room, the sterile walls closing in on me, "—is it? What if we're just running out of time?"

He shook his head, his expression resolute, but I could see the flicker of fear lurking beneath. "We can't think like that. We're going to make it through this. I refuse to let the what-ifs consume us."

"But the reality is there, Nate. You know that, don't you?" My voice cracked as I spoke, the dam of emotions threatening to spill over.

Before he could respond, the door swung open again, and the doctor stepped in, a clipboard clutched tightly in her hand. The sterile aura she carried felt heavy, suffocating in its finality.

"Good evening, Ava," she said, her tone professional but lacking warmth. "I wanted to discuss your recent test results."

The air thickened, and Nate's grip on my hand tightened, his expression morphing from playful to serious in an instant. "What's wrong?" he demanded, his voice barely above a whisper.

The doctor hesitated, her eyes darting between us. "I'd prefer to discuss this in a more private setting. It's important."

"Just tell us," I insisted, my heart racing, panic bubbling beneath the surface.

The doctor cleared her throat, a heavy pause hanging in the air like a guillotine. "Ava, we've seen some concerning changes in your condition. We need to take immediate action, and I'd like to discuss your options."

A cold knot formed in my stomach, the laughter of moments ago slipping away like sand through my fingers. The words hung heavily in the air, and I felt the walls close in, the brightness fading. I searched Nate's face, his expression a mirror of my own dread.

"What options?" I managed to ask, the question escaping my lips like a plea.

But before the doctor could answer, the monitor beside me began to beep erratically, the sound sharp and jarring against the fragile atmosphere. Nate's eyes widened, the worry etched deeply across his features.

"Hold on, Ava," he murmured, panic slipping into his voice as the alarms grew louder, blaring a warning that echoed in the stillness of the room.

And just like that, the laughter faded into silence, replaced by the urgency of a world spiraling out of control.

Chapter 16: Unraveling Threads

The soft glow of late afternoon light filtered through the sheer curtains, casting delicate patterns on the floor like the remnants of a dream just on the edge of consciousness. I was sprawled on the couch, surrounded by a collection of throw pillows that offered a haphazard kind of comfort. The scent of fresh coffee danced through the air, mingling with the faint fragrance of old pages, nostalgia swirling around me like a warm blanket. It was a familiar chaos—my sanctuary, where I sought refuge from the outside world. Just as I settled deeper into my makeshift nest, the doorbell rang, shattering the calm and sending a flicker of anticipation racing through me.

Mark was standing on the other side, his smile wide and infectious, radiating an energy that could easily light up the dimmest of rooms. He had this way of turning the mundane into something magical, even if it was just a simple visit. I opened the door, my heart fluttering a little more than I cared to admit. He stepped inside, the cool autumn air trailing behind him like a reluctant guest. "I brought something," he said, his eyes sparkling with mischief.

"What is it this time?" I asked, feigning annoyance as I crossed my arms, trying to suppress the eager grin threatening to break free.

With a flourish that would make any magician proud, he revealed a scrapbook, its worn edges suggesting it had been lovingly handled over the years. "You'll love it. I promise," he declared, his enthusiasm contagious. I couldn't help but feel a swell of curiosity as I took the scrapbook from him.

As we settled onto the couch, the world outside faded, leaving only the sanctuary of my living room and the flicker of excitement that hung in the air between us. I opened the cover, the spine creaking gently, releasing a sweet scent of aged paper and memories. Page after page revealed snippets of my childhood—photos of me, a small girl with wild curls and a mischievous grin, adorned in oversized dresses that swirled around my knees. I could hear the laughter of my younger self echoing in my mind as I flipped through the memories, each image pulling me deeper into the past.

"Remember this?" Mark pointed at a photograph of my fifth birthday party, where I was in the center of a cluster of brightly colored balloons, cake smeared across my cheeks like some culinary war paint. I couldn't help but chuckle, the sound bubbling up unbidden.

"I thought I looked so sophisticated," I said, mock seriousness dripping from my tone. "Like I was ready for my first gala instead of just a backyard barbecue."

Mark laughed, a rich sound that filled the room. "You definitely looked like you were ready to take on the world."

There was a comforting intimacy in our shared laughter, but beneath it lay an undercurrent of tension I could never quite shake. Each photo unearthed a mix of joy and pain, laughter tinged with the bittersweet taste of longing for what had been lost. My father, the ghost in the corners of my mind, loomed over every joyful memory like a shadow refusing to fade.

"Your dad had such a knack for capturing the moments," Mark said, flipping to a picture of a family picnic, my dad grinning, arms wide as if he could embrace the entire world. "Look at how happy he is here."

My heart clenched at the sight, the warmth of the memory conflicting with the cold reality of our relationship. "Yeah, he was something," I replied, the words tumbling out heavier than I intended.

Mark glanced at me, his expression shifting from playful to concerned. "Do you want to talk about it?"

The invitation hung in the air, both inviting and intimidating. Part of me wanted to bury the unease beneath layers of nostalgia, to linger in the happiness of the moment. But another part, a more honest part, recognized that I had to confront the lingering wounds. "I want to, but I'm not sure where to start," I admitted, my voice barely above a whisper.

"Maybe just start with the good," he suggested gently, nudging the scrapbook closer, as if to remind me that there were still threads of joy woven into the fabric of our family history. "We can unravel the bad later."

I nodded, allowing the vulnerability to creep in as I recalled our family gatherings—the smell of my mother's famous pot roast, the warmth of a summer sun that seemed to linger forever. We would laugh until our stomachs hurt, stories spilling out like confetti, each one more ridiculous than the last. But just beneath those memories lay a thread of loss, a gnawing absence that had turned laughter into a bittersweet reminder of what should have been.

Flipping the pages, we came across a photo of me with my father on a fishing trip, his arm slung around my shoulders, the world behind us a blur of blue sky and shimmering water. "That was one of the few times we had together," I murmured, tracing the outline of my young face in the photograph. "He was so present that day."

"Was that before everything changed?" Mark asked, his voice gentle, inviting me to peel back the layers I had kept tightly sealed.

"Yeah," I replied, a lump forming in my throat. "It was before he decided to walk away from everything." The words stung like cold air on a winter morning, and I could feel the weight of history pressing down on us.

Mark remained quiet, his gaze steady and encouraging, giving me the space to unravel the tangled emotions swirling within. I took a breath, gathering courage as I spoke. "I want to forgive him, I really do. But it's hard when all I can think about is the pain he caused." The vulnerability of the moment hung between us, thick with unspoken truths and shared understanding.

He reached out, placing a hand on my knee, a simple gesture that sparked warmth in my chest. "Forgiveness isn't easy, Ava. It's messy, just like life."

Our eyes met, and in that shared gaze, I found a flicker of hope—a reminder that perhaps I wasn't alone in this tangled web of emotions. As we continued to flip through the pages, Mark's presence was a steady anchor amidst the storm of memories. With each photo, I felt the past lifting slightly, allowing for the possibility of healing, a path toward forgiveness illuminated by the connections we forged in the present.

The pages of the scrapbook flickered with vivid memories, each photograph a portal to a moment I once cherished but now viewed through a lens of ambivalence. I could feel the warmth of my childhood memories mingling with the coolness of reality, a bittersweet concoction that left me feeling lightheaded. Mark's presence was both grounding and exhilarating, a paradox I couldn't quite decipher. He shifted slightly, his knee brushing against mine, igniting a spark that sent ripples through my already turbulent emotions.

"You know, I've always found it fascinating how memory works," he mused, his voice low and thoughtful. "It's like our brains are little filing cabinets, but sometimes, they forget to file things away properly."

I chuckled, grateful for his attempt to lighten the mood. "So, what you're saying is that I need to get my brain an organizer? Maybe one of those fancy ones with color-coded tabs?"

"Absolutely. Perhaps a little label maker too?" His grin was infectious, making me forget for a moment the weight of our earlier conversation. But then I remembered the way my father had abandoned me, and the joy dimmed ever so slightly.

As we continued to sift through the scrapbook, I found myself captivated by a picture of my mother. She was radiant, her laughter captured mid-chortle, a kaleidoscope of happiness. "She always knew how to bring everyone together," I said, my voice softening. "Even when things were falling apart, she had this way of making everything feel... whole."

Mark's eyes darkened slightly, a flicker of understanding passing between us. "You took after her in that regard, you know. You have this amazing ability to draw people in, to make them feel seen."

The compliment washed over me like a gentle wave, warming the corners of my heart. "You're just saying that because I fed you that cinnamon roll last week," I teased, attempting to deflect the sudden swell of emotion that threatened to choke me.

"Hey, that was a life-changing cinnamon roll," he replied, mock-seriousness etched on his features. "I might need a support group now, thanks to your baking prowess."

We laughed, the sound echoing against the walls, temporarily pushing away the lingering shadows of our conversation. But laughter only lasts so long before reality nudges its way back in. As we turned to the next page, a more somber photograph caught my eye—my father sitting alone on the porch, a faint shadow of melancholy clouding his usually bright demeanor.

"Do you ever think about why he chose to leave?" Mark asked, his voice gentle, probing yet respectful.

I swallowed hard, the question hanging in the air like an uninvited guest. "All the time. It's like trying to piece together a puzzle without all the pieces," I confessed, each word feeling heavier than the last. "Sometimes I wonder if he even thought about how his absence would affect us."

Mark's expression softened, an empathy radiating from him that felt both comforting and unsettling. "You have every right to feel that way. It's okay to be angry, Ava. Anger is just another form of love, after all. It shows you cared."

"Is it wrong that I still want him to be proud of me?" I asked, my voice barely a whisper. "Even after everything?"

"No, it's perfectly human." He reached for my hand, a gesture so simple yet profound that it momentarily stole my breath away. "Wanting approval from a parent, no matter how flawed they may be, is one of the most universal desires we have. It's okay to hold onto that hope."

His words wrapped around me like a protective blanket, shielding me from the biting chill of self-doubt. I took a moment, letting the warmth of his hand seep into my skin, feeling a connection bloom between us that seemed almost otherworldly. "What about you? Did you ever have that kind of relationship with your parents?" I asked, trying to redirect the intensity of my own emotions.

Mark hesitated, his eyes flickering away momentarily. "Well, my dad was more into fishing than family bonding," he admitted, a playful lilt returning to his tone. "But my mom? She had this way of making every moment feel like a lesson, even if it was just about the right way to fold a towel."

"That sounds... organized," I laughed, picturing his mother meticulously lining up the dish towels in a perfect row.

"Oh, it was downright militaristic," he replied, feigning a grimace. "But it taught me a thing or two about attention to detail. I'm pretty sure that's why I'm now so obsessed with properly arranging my books by color."

"You've got me beat there. My books are a chaotic mess." I chuckled again, my heart feeling lighter, even as the conversation still lingered on heavier subjects.

We continued flipping through the scrapbook, the photographs gradually blending into a visual tapestry of my life, interspersed with snippets of laughter and echoes of old pain. My gaze landed on a picture of a family vacation, a bright summer day captured in full splendor. My dad, in his quintessential Hawaiian shirt, was lifting me above his head, my laughter frozen in time, a reminder of a fleeting happiness I had almost forgotten.

"Look at that," I said, the weight of nostalgia settling back in. "That was one of our best trips. I felt so loved back then."

"It's incredible how a moment can feel like eternity, isn't it?" Mark mused, his gaze thoughtful. "Yet, sometimes those moments are built on foundations that crumble later."

I let the truth of his words sink in, the layers of my childhood peeling away like the pages of the scrapbook. "I wish I could bottle those feelings, you know? Save them for the days when I feel lost."

"Maybe that's the trick—bottling up the good while working through the bad." He leaned closer, his expression earnest. "You can hold on to the happiness without letting the pain define you."

The weight of his words hung in the air, and for the first time, I felt the stirrings of hope unfurling within me. "You make it sound so simple, like I just need to add a dash of positivity and a sprinkle of resilience."

"Hey, don't underestimate the power of a good recipe," he teased, a spark of mischief dancing in his eyes. "If only life had a set of instructions. Maybe we could figure it all out with the right ingredients."

"Or at least a better label maker," I quipped, laughter bubbling back to the surface, lighter and more buoyant than before.

But beneath our laughter, a tension lingered, a delicate thread weaving through our banter. I couldn't shake the feeling that each visit, each shared moment, was nudging me toward a precipice. A line drawn between the past I longed to mend and the future I craved to embrace. The warmth of Mark's hand on mine grounded me, but I knew I had to confront the shadows lurking in the corners of my heart. It was a journey I couldn't take alone, and for the first time, I felt ready to take the plunge.

The soft afternoon light bathed the room in a warm glow as I leaned back on the couch, still buzzing from our conversation. Mark's presence lingered like a comforting echo, his laughter weaving a spell around me that dulled the sharp edges of memory. The scrapbook lay open between us, its pages a vivid tapestry of my past. Yet, as I absorbed the colors and smiles, a flicker of apprehension danced just out of reach.

"I never would have guessed you were such a sentimental hoarder," Mark teased, nudging the scrapbook with his elbow. "What's next? Are you going to drag out the old trophies you earned in kindergarten for the ultimate nostalgia tour?"

"Hey, those trophies were hard-won!" I protested playfully. "I still remember the pride swelling in my tiny chest when I received the 'Best at Napping' award. Truly a crowning achievement."

Mark roared with laughter, the sound warm and genuine, but as the joy washed over me, I felt a shiver of anxiety slither down my spine. "You know, I think your mother had a point when she said you were destined for greatness," he replied, his tone shifting slightly. "Even if greatness was measured in nap time."

"Clearly, I peaked too early," I shot back, but there was a tremor in my voice that betrayed the laughter. Mark's eyes narrowed slightly, the shift in atmosphere palpable.

"Do you want to talk more about him?" he asked, his expression earnest. "About your dad, I mean."

The question hung in the air like a heavy curtain, thick with expectation. I felt my heart race, the old hurt pulsing to the surface as I forced a smile that didn't quite reach my eyes. "I think I've shared enough childhood trauma for one day. Let's save my therapy session for next week."

Mark chuckled, but I could see the concern etched on his features. "Just remember, you don't have to hide behind humor all the time," he said softly. "It's okay to feel vulnerable around me."

"Trust me, I have enough vulnerability stored up for a lifetime," I countered, shifting the focus back to the scrapbook, but the shift felt feeble against the weight of our conversation. I hesitated, torn between the urge to keep my defenses up and the allure of honesty. "He was never really there for me. I keep thinking maybe I could just... forgive him. But how do you forgive someone who turned their back on you?"

Mark regarded me, his brow furrowing with thought. "You start by understanding that forgiveness isn't for him. It's for you. It's about letting go of the weight he's left behind."

I nodded slowly, processing his words like a slow dance of understanding. "It just feels like a betrayal to forget," I whispered, more to myself than to him.

"Then don't forget," he replied, leaning closer, his voice steady. "Keep the memories that matter, and leave behind the pain. You're allowed to carve out your own path."

Just then, the shrill sound of my phone breaking the atmosphere shattered our moment, the sharp ring slicing through the thick air. I fished it out of my pocket, glancing at the screen. My heart dropped as I saw my father's name flashing across it. An electric jolt shot through me, freezing me in place. I didn't want to answer. Not now, not after everything I had just shared with Mark.

"Are you going to get that?" Mark asked, a hint of curiosity in his voice.

"Maybe I should just ignore it," I said, a tremor of uncertainty creeping in.

"Or maybe you should find out what he wants," he suggested, his tone gentle but firm. "You've been doing so well peeling back the layers. It might be the next step."

"Next step or next disaster?" I quipped, the sarcasm barely masking my rising panic. "I don't think I'm ready to have a heart-to-heart with a ghost."

"Maybe he's ready for a wake-up call," Mark countered, his eyes steady, urging me to make the leap.

With a sigh, I reluctantly swiped to answer. "Hello?" I said, my voice betraying the swell of emotions raging within me.

"Ava, it's me," my father's voice came through the line, deep and slightly strained, as if he had rehearsed this moment a hundred times yet still couldn't find the right words.

"What do you want?" I replied, my tone sharper than I intended.

"I—" he paused, and I could hear the hesitation in his voice, the weight of years hanging heavy in the air. "I just wanted to talk. Can we meet?"

"Meet?" The word felt foreign on my tongue, like an echo of a past I was trying to escape. "Why now? After all this time?"

"I know I haven't been there for you, and I can't change the past. But I want to try to make things right," he said, a thread of desperation woven into his words.

My heart raced, conflicting emotions surging to the forefront. "Try? You think that's enough?" I shot back, each word laced with a cocktail of hurt and anger.

"Ava, please," he pleaded, his voice softer now, vulnerable. "I know I've hurt you, but I've changed. I want to show you that."

"Show me? How? By dragging up old ghosts?" I snapped, feeling the walls I had carefully built around my heart begin to crack.

"I'm in town. I can come over—" he started, but I interrupted him.

"No. No more half-hearted attempts. You can't just waltz back into my life as if nothing happened. That's not how this works," I retorted, my voice a mixture of defiance and uncertainty.

"Just hear me out, Ava," he urged, his tone laced with desperation. "I need you to know that I regret everything. I want to make amends."

"Regret isn't enough," I shot back, frustration bubbling over. "You can't just erase years of silence with a few well-placed words."

"I know. But I'm asking for a chance to explain," he insisted.

I paused, the weight of his request pressing down on me like an anchor. "And why should I trust you?"

"Because I'm still your father," he said, the honesty in his voice catching me off guard. "And I'm not asking for forgiveness, just a chance to talk."

My pulse quickened, the anxiety coiling tightly in my chest. "Where do you want to meet?" I finally asked, my voice trembling slightly.

"Can we do it at your favorite coffee shop? You know, the one with the terrible Wi-Fi?" he replied, a faint chuckle attempting to lighten the gravity of the moment.

"Fine," I said, more to give myself time to think than anything else. "But this doesn't mean I'm welcoming you back with open arms."

"I understand," he said, a note of relief in his voice. "I'll see you soon."

As I hung up, the silence in the room felt oppressive, the air thick with unspoken words and unresolved tension. I turned to Mark, whose expression mirrored my own turmoil. "So, that just happened," I said, my heart racing.

"Are you okay?" he asked, concern etched on his face.

"I don't know," I admitted, the reality of my father's impending visit crashing over me like a wave. "I thought I was ready to forgive, but now I just feel... lost."

Mark leaned forward, his eyes intense. "You don't have to have all the answers right now. Just take it one step at a time."

But even as he spoke, a cold sense of dread settled over me, wrapping around my chest like a vice. I had opened a door I wasn't sure I could close again. The path to forgiveness felt steep and rocky, and now it lay before me, fraught with uncertainty and old wounds waiting to be reopened.

As Mark's hand lingered on mine, grounding me, I couldn't shake the feeling that this was just the beginning. The quiet chaos in my heart echoed a warning, one that hinted at more than just a meeting with my father. It whispered of buried secrets and painful truths that would soon claw their way to the surface, and as I met Mark's steady gaze, I realized that the real unraveling was just beginning.

Chapter 17: The Breaking Point

The sterile scent of antiseptic clung to the air, sharp and clinical, mingling with the faint hum of fluorescent lights overhead. I blinked up at the ceiling tiles, those tiny squares that had become far too familiar over the past few days. Each small crack and stain seemed to whisper secrets of the many patients who had come before me, but today, it felt different—heavier. A rhythmic beeping punctuated the silence, a metronome marking time in a place that was supposed to offer healing. But all I could feel was the encroaching dread that clutched at my throat like an invisible noose.

"Ms. Sinclair," the doctor said, her tone a curious mix of clinical detachment and empathy, as if she were reciting a script written by someone who had long ago lost the ability to truly connect. "We've reviewed your test results, and I need to discuss the implications." The words rolled off her tongue like a bitter pill, each syllable sinking deeper into the pit of my stomach.

Implications. The word hung in the air like a storm cloud, heavy with unspoken fears. I tried to focus on her face, but all I could see were her lips moving, my mind racing ahead to the possible scenarios she would lay out like a tarot card reader revealing fates I was not ready to accept.

She continued, her gaze steady yet somehow distant. "The treatment options we discussed previously have not yielded the desired results. We will need to consider more aggressive measures." Each phrase sent ripples of anxiety coursing through me. My heart, which had somehow managed to keep its rhythm through the uncertainty, now raced like a frantic horse bolting from the starting gate.

I opened my mouth, desperate to speak, to claw my way back to some semblance of control, but no sound emerged. Instead, I felt a hot wave of tears stinging my eyes. How had I arrived at this precipice, teetering on the edge of something I could not comprehend?

As the doctor continued, I found my thoughts drifting to Nate. His presence had become my anchor amid this turbulent sea of fear. When he was around, I could forget—if only for a moment—about the incessant beeping of machines and the ominous weight of my diagnosis. He could make me laugh with just a quirk of his eyebrow, as if humor was a spell he cast to ward off the darkness.

A few moments later, as if summoned by my thoughts, Nate burst through the door. His brown hair was tousled, and his shirt was slightly wrinkled, suggesting that he had rushed from somewhere—likely his favorite coffee shop, where he always insisted on grabbing me a caramel macchiato, even though I had told him a thousand times how I preferred it without the caramel. He carried an air of warmth that somehow filled the cold, sterile room, and my heart fluttered, grateful for his presence.

"What did I miss?" he asked, concern etching lines on his forehead as he scanned the room, his gaze settling on the doctor, who had become too engrossed in her clipboard to notice the shift in energy.

I wished I could tell him it was just the usual updates, just another round of uninvited news. Instead, the lump in my throat thickened.

The doctor shifted her focus, her professional demeanor softening just a touch. "We need to discuss Ava's treatment plan moving forward."

I braced myself for the inevitable disappointment. I could see it in Nate's eyes—the flicker of fear behind the façade of bravery he always wore for me. He stepped closer, and I could almost feel his warmth wrapping around me like a protective cocoon, his hand slipping into mine with an ease that grounded me.

"Hey," he said softly, squeezing my fingers. "You okay?"

"Not really," I admitted, the truth slipping out before I could reign it back in. "I don't think I'm ready for whatever she's about to say."

He nodded, his thumb brushing over my knuckles in a soothing motion. "We'll get through this together, okay? You're not alone in this fight."

The doctor cleared her throat, and I steeled myself for the onslaught of words that felt like stones tumbling down a mountainside, one after the other. "Ava, I know this isn't easy to hear, but we need to be proactive. The current treatment isn't working, and we have to consider our options."

My breath caught, a tightness settling in my chest as she listed alternatives. Each option sounded more intimidating than the last, laden with complications and risks I had never wanted to think about. I could feel Nate's fingers tightening around mine as I fought to maintain composure, to stay afloat amidst the rising tide of uncertainty.

"We'll take it one step at a time," Nate whispered, and I could hear the determination in his voice, even as my own wavered.

"Can you give us a moment?" he asked the doctor, his tone shifting from concerned boyfriend to something more protective, a bear ready to fight for his territory.

The doctor hesitated but nodded, leaving us alone. The door clicked shut behind her, and suddenly the air felt thick with a tension I could hardly bear.

"What do we do now?" I asked, my voice barely above a whisper.

Nate met my gaze, those brown eyes so full of compassion and resolve. "We breathe. We don't make any decisions until we're ready. We've got time."

I wanted to believe him, wanted to cling to the hope he offered, but doubt crept in, whispering that time was a luxury I might not have. In that moment of shared vulnerability, I caught a glimpse of the strength I had buried beneath layers of fear and despair. Nate was right; I wasn't alone, and perhaps that was enough to keep the darkness at bay, at least for now.

The afternoon sun filtered through the thin hospital curtains, casting a soft, dappled light that danced across the sterile floor, but it felt like a cruel joke. In the midst of such beauty, I felt trapped in a place devoid of color or warmth. Nate sat beside my bed, his brow furrowed in thought as he absently twirled a pen in his fingers, the clicking sound mingling with the rhythmic beeping of the machines that monitored my every breath. I could almost feel my heart synchronize with their mechanical pulses, a constant reminder of my fragility.

"Are you sure you want to order hospital food?" he asked, raising an eyebrow as he scrolled through the menu on his phone, a playful smirk attempting to ease the heaviness that had settled between us. "I mean, I don't know about you, but the last thing I want is a side of mystery meat with a dollop of regret."

I laughed, a sound that surprised me in its brightness. "What if the mystery meat is actually a gourmet delicacy? Maybe it's the next big culinary trend—hospital chic."

He chuckled, but I could see the worry lurking in his eyes. "If it's a trend, I want to be a trendsetter in something else, like... well, definitely not this hospital food situation." He paused, a glint of mischief lighting up his features. "Let's take a gamble, then. How about we just order a whole pizza? We'll call it a party and add balloons to the mix."

I could imagine it: a gaudy, balloon-filled fiesta right here in the confines of this sterile room. The thought made me smile wider, and for a fleeting moment, I felt the weight of my fears lighten. "As long as it's pepperoni and not Hawaiian. I refuse to have fruit on my pizza, even in a hospital."

"Pepperoni it is," he declared, mockingly raising an imaginary glass in a toast. "To fighting hospital food one slice at a time!"

Our laughter filled the small space, the warmth of our banter wrapping around us like a comforting blanket. But beneath the surface, the cold reality still loomed. I could feel it creeping back, the fear threading its way through the jokes. The uncertainty of my diagnosis loomed like a storm cloud, threatening to eclipse the brightness Nate brought into my life.

As I leaned back against the pillows, I caught sight of the window, a stark reminder of the world outside. The trees swayed gently in the breeze, their leaves a vibrant green, a sharp contrast to the pale blues and whites of my hospital room. Each rustle of the leaves seemed to whisper promises of freedom, adventures that felt tantalizingly out of reach.

"Hey," Nate said, breaking through my reverie. "What are you thinking about?"

I hesitated, grappling with how to voice the tumult in my chest. "I was just thinking about how nice it would be to be out there. To feel the sun on my face instead of this sterile blanket."

His gaze softened, and for a moment, I saw the fierce protectiveness flicker in his eyes. "I promise we'll get you out of here soon. Once you're up and about, I'll take you on a road trip. Just you, me, and a car full of snacks. We'll blast our favorite songs and pretend like we're on the run from our responsibilities."

"Or from reality," I quipped, rolling my eyes. "Sounds like a solid plan."

"Right? I can see the headlines now: 'Two Misfits Escape to Find Freedom on the Open Road—Caution: May Contain Excessive Laughing and Ice Cream.'"

I snorted, picturing us driving through small towns, stopping at roadside diners, the wind whipping through our hair. "Maybe we could even get matching tattoos to commemorate the occasion. Something like, 'Surviving One Slice at a Time.'"

Nate feigned horror. "Tattoos? Aren't those permanent? I'm not sure I'm ready for that level of commitment."

"Ah, but what if we got something small and cute? Like a little slice of pizza or something equally ridiculous?"

"Now we're talking! A pizza slice tattooed on your ankle so you can always remember your culinary preference."

Our laughter rippled through the room once more, lifting the veil of gloom just a little further. But as Nate's expression shifted to something more serious, I felt my heart drop.

"Ava," he began, his voice low, "I know we're making jokes, but I want you to know that whatever happens, I'm here. I'm not going anywhere."

The sincerity in his voice wrapped around my heart, squeezing it tight. "I know," I said, my voice catching in my throat. "And I can't tell you how much that means to me."

For a moment, silence enveloped us, a gentle pause where the world outside faded, and all that remained was the palpable bond between us.

"Do you ever think about the future?" Nate asked suddenly, his tone shifting to one more serious, though still soft. "Like what we'd do after this?"

I bit my lip, feeling the gravity of his question. The future felt like a distant, nebulous concept, so far removed from my present reality. "I used to think about it all the time," I admitted. "What I wanted to do, where I wanted to go. But now? It's like every time I try to envision it, I hit a wall."

Nate nodded, his brow furrowing as he considered my words. "It's okay to feel that way. We're in a unique situation—who wouldn't feel uncertain?"

"Unique is one way to put it," I replied, my voice laced with irony. "I never imagined I'd be living the hospital life at twenty-eight. Not exactly the dream I had."

"Yeah, me neither," he said with a wry smile. "But you know what? Even if our plans are a little different now, it doesn't mean we can't still have fun. We can find joy in the weirdest places."

"Like this hospital room?" I gestured around us, the starkness of the environment suddenly a little less suffocating in the light of his words.

"Exactly! Who knows? Maybe we'll start a trend. Hospital-themed parties might be the next big thing."

"Complete with a DJ who only plays beeping sounds!" I added, laughter bubbling up again.

"Now that's a party I'd love to crash," he said, grinning widely.

Our banter flowed effortlessly, and for a while, we existed in our own little bubble, shielded from the outside world. The weight of my diagnosis lingered, but it felt lighter somehow, tempered by Nate's unwavering presence. Each laugh we shared seemed to dim the shadows, inching me closer to a realization I hadn't been ready to face before: I didn't have to fight this battle alone. In our shared moments of laughter and vulnerability, I found a flicker of hope—a reminder that even in the darkest times, connection could light the way.

As the hours melted into one another, the rhythm of laughter became our lifeline, pulling me away from the looming darkness that danced just out of reach. Nate's charm, woven with wit and a warmth that felt like a balm, transformed the hospital room into something akin to a sanctuary. I couldn't help but marvel at how he managed to turn my fears into fodder for playful banter. Each quip was like a tiny rebellion against the constraints of my reality.

"Okay, new game," Nate declared, leaning in closer, eyes sparkling with mischief. "Let's invent outrageous scenarios that could make this hospital stay a bit more entertaining."

I raised an eyebrow, intrigued. "Like what? 'Survivor: Hospital Edition'?"

"Exactly! Only the strongest patients make it through to the next round." He mimicked a dramatic voiceover. "In a world where the food is inedible and the waiting room chairs are uncomfortable, one woman must fight against her greatest enemies: boredom and unflattering hospital gowns."

I couldn't suppress the laughter bubbling up, picturing a battle of epic proportions. "I can see it now: our fearless heroine, armed with nothing but a remote control and a jello cup, takes on the dreaded nurse who insists on drawing blood every hour!"

Nate put on a solemn expression, nodding gravely. "That nurse is relentless. But don't worry; our hero always finds a way to distract her. Maybe with an impromptu dance party?"

"Right! And the jello becomes a prop in a high-stakes dance-off, complete with dramatic slow-motion shots."

"Perfect! But we'll need a twist. Just when it seems like victory is in her grasp, she discovers her best friend has traded all the food in the fridge for... wait for it... kale smoothies!"

I groaned dramatically. "The betrayal runs deep. Now she must not only conquer the hospital but also rescue her friend from the clutches of healthy eating!"

We spiraled into fits of laughter, and for a moment, I could almost forget the sterile walls that surrounded me. I found solace in the absurdity of our game, a distraction from the very real fears gnawing at my insides. It was moments like these that reminded me of the beauty of connection, even amidst chaos.

But just as our laughter faded into a comfortable silence, a sharp knock interrupted us. The doctor entered, her clipboard in hand and a grave expression on her face. The air shifted, turning heavy once again as the reality we had evaded seeped back in.

"Ava," she said, her tone serious, "I need to talk to you about your test results."

Nate's hand tightened around mine, a silent promise of support. The lightness evaporated, replaced by a thick blanket of apprehension.

"Have you decided on the next steps?" I asked, trying to inject a semblance of normalcy into the conversation, though my heart raced like a marathon runner.

The doctor hesitated, glancing at Nate before focusing on me. "We need to consider an experimental treatment that just became available. It carries risks, but it could be your best chance at a positive outcome."

My breath caught in my throat. Experimental treatment? It sounded like something out of a science fiction movie, a gamble that could either yield miraculous results or send me spiraling into a deeper abyss.

"What kind of risks are we talking about?" Nate interjected, his voice firm, protective.

"Side effects can vary greatly. Some patients report significant improvement, while others experience complications that require hospitalization," the doctor replied, her voice devoid of emotion, as if reciting statistics rather than discussing my life.

I swallowed hard, the weight of her words crashing down on me like a tidal wave. "And if I don't do it?"

"Without treatment, your current trajectory is concerning. I can't guarantee how much time we have left if we choose to wait."

The silence that followed felt suffocating, the unspoken truths hanging in the air like a dense fog. I could feel Nate's presence beside me, a solid anchor, but even he couldn't drown out the cacophony of thoughts swirling in my mind. The doctor's words played over and over, each syllable igniting a different fear.

"Can I have some time to think about it?" I managed to say, my voice trembling slightly.

"Of course," the doctor replied, her gaze lingering for a moment longer before she stepped back into the hallway, leaving us alone in the unnerving stillness.

Nate turned to me, his expression a mix of concern and determination. "Ava, whatever you choose, I'm with you. You don't have to face this alone."

"I know," I said, the warmth of his words wrapping around me. "But it's such a huge decision. What if I take the risk and it doesn't work? Or what if the side effects are unbearable?"

"Then we figure it out together," he said, his voice steady. "I believe in you, in your strength to handle whatever comes next."

I looked into his eyes, seeking solace in his unwavering support. But beneath his reassuring words, a flicker of doubt burned in my chest. "What if my strength isn't enough? What if this is all too much?"

His brow furrowed, and he squeezed my hand tighter. "You are more than enough, Ava. You've fought so hard already. This is just one more battle, and we're going to tackle it together."

I nodded, feeling the swell of gratitude and fear collide within me. He was right; I had faced challenges before, and somehow, I had come out the other side. But this was different. This was life and death, and the stakes felt impossibly high.

"Okay," I said finally, my voice barely above a whisper. "I'll consider the treatment. But I need to talk to you about it more, weigh the pros and cons. I can't make this decision lightly."

"Absolutely," Nate agreed, his gaze steady. "We'll draw up a list, maybe even chart it out like we're back in high school."

I couldn't help but smile at the image of us sitting cross-legged on my hospital floor, frantically scribbling pros and cons while clutching colored markers. But just as I started to feel a semblance of hope, a sudden commotion erupted outside the room, shattering the fragile bubble we had created.

"What is that?" I asked, glancing towards the door.

Before Nate could respond, the door swung open, and a nurse rushed in, her expression frantic. "I need you both to stay calm," she said, her voice taut with urgency. "There's been an emergency on the floor. We need to evacuate this wing immediately."

My heart dropped. "Evacuate? What do you mean?"

"Please, just follow my lead. We'll take care of everything," she insisted, her eyes darting between Nate and me.

Panic surged through me as I exchanged a glance with Nate, his face mirroring my concern. "What's happening?" I pressed, my voice shaking.

"Just trust me. We need to move."

In that moment, the world outside my hospital room collapsed, leaving only uncertainty in its wake. As we followed the nurse into the chaotic hallway, the weight of the decision ahead pressed down on my chest. Would I be forced to confront my fears in the midst of an emergency? What if this moment changed everything?

The sound of sirens echoed in the distance, and my heart raced, teetering on the edge of the unknown, ready to plunge into whatever lay ahead.

Chapter 18: The Secret Garden

The world outside was a cacophony of sirens, bustling nurses, and the relentless beeping of machines, a stark reminder that I was trapped in a clinical nightmare, but the moment Nate slipped his hand into mine and led me toward the unassuming door, a flicker of hope ignited within me. "Trust me," he murmured, his voice low and conspiratorial, laced with an enthusiasm that felt almost infectious. I wanted to roll my eyes, to toss his optimism back at him like an unwanted gift, but something in his gaze—the way his blue eyes sparkled with mischief—compelled me to follow.

Behind that door, the corridor morphed into a shadowy passageway, the antiseptic smell of the hospital fading into a distant memory. The air thickened with anticipation, and I could feel the weight of the unknown pressing against my chest. Each step felt like a secret I was about to uncover, the tension curling in my stomach like a vine in search of something solid to cling to. "Where are we going?" I finally asked, my curiosity blooming amidst my anxiety.

He grinned, his confidence washing over me like sunlight breaking through clouds. "A place where the outside world can't reach us."

As we navigated through the dimly lit corridor, I noticed the soft, muted colors of the walls transitioning into something warmer, something alive. With each footfall, a vibrant pulse thrummed beneath my skin, urging me onward. I let out a breath I didn't know I was holding when Nate halted in front of an inconspicuous door, its surface worn and unassuming. He turned to me, his expression a mix of playful secrecy and profound sincerity. "Ready?"

I nodded, though I wasn't entirely sure what I was preparing for. He swung the door open, and I stepped inside.

What lay before me was a breathtaking contrast to the sterile confines of the hospital: a hidden garden that spilled forth with color, life, and the sweet perfume of blooming flowers. Sunlight cascaded through a glass ceiling, illuminating the delicate petals of peonies, daisies, and violets, their hues vibrant enough to make even a rainbow envious. I was immediately enveloped in warmth, the kind that seeps into your bones, as if the garden itself were embracing me.

"This... is incredible," I breathed, taking a cautious step forward. The ground was soft beneath my feet, a gentle carpet of moss interspersed with colorful stones, and I felt as if I'd stumbled into a painting, each stroke vivid and alive.

Nate chuckled, clearly pleased with my reaction. "I found this place last week. Thought it could be our little secret." His voice was filled with delight, and I couldn't help but smile back at him, the tension in my body easing like the release of a tightly wound spring.

I wandered deeper into the garden, my fingers trailing along the edges of lush foliage. A butterfly, delicate and shimmering, flitted past me, and I watched, mesmerized, as it danced from flower to flower. Each bloom seemed to stretch upward, eager to showcase its beauty to the world, even when the world outside remained grim. It was then that I felt a rush of exhilaration coursing through me, the kind that comes from discovering a piece of magic hidden in plain sight.

"Can you believe this is behind a hospital?" I said, turning to Nate, who was busy inspecting a particularly stunning marigold. "It's like something out of a storybook."

He looked up, his expression thoughtful. "Maybe that's exactly what we need—a storybook moment. Just for us."

I laughed softly, the sound escaping my lips like a rare melody. "So, what do we do here? Make wishes on dandelions? Whisper our secrets to the flowers?"

"Why not?" He smirked, crossing his arms with an air of mock seriousness. "I mean, if you want to spill your deepest, darkest secrets to a daisy, I'm not going to stop you."

"Oh, please," I replied, rolling my eyes dramatically. "I'm saving those for a rain-soaked evening, not for a sunlit garden."

"Then what about our dreams? We can share those."

There was a glimmer in his eyes that made my heart flutter—a combination of earnestness and playfulness that felt like a beacon guiding me through the dark. "Alright, but only if you promise to share yours first."

Nate leaned back against a stone bench, feigning deep contemplation. "Okay, let's see. I dream of traveling the world, of finding hidden spots like this garden everywhere I go. I want to see the Eiffel Tower, dive into the Great Barrier Reef, and maybe even dance in the rain on some exotic beach." He looked up, his expression filled with fervor. "What about you?"

My heart raced at the question. I'd spent so much time thinking about the past, the hospital, the chaos, that I had nearly forgotten what it meant to dream. "I want to write," I said slowly, the words unfurling like petals in the sunlight. "I've always wanted to write stories that make people feel. I want to create worlds where they can escape, even if just for a little while."

"That's amazing," he replied, his admiration palpable. "You have the perfect voice for it. You should start a blog or something."

"Sure, right after I become a world-renowned author," I quipped, my tone light but the weight of reality looming just behind the laughter. "I'll just need a few extra hours in the day."

"Who says you can't create those hours?" He shot back, a teasing grin dancing on his lips.

I shook my head, feeling the warmth of our playful banter weaving an invisible thread between us, pulling me closer to him. "I think you're confusing dreams with delusions."

"Maybe. But I'd like to think delusions can lead to something wonderful."

The garden, with its secret beauty, its wildflowers bending in the gentle breeze, felt like a sanctuary—a place where the weight of the outside world slipped away, even if just for a moment. With Nate by my side, I felt the fragile spark of hope flickering to life, igniting a warmth that spread through my chest. As we continued to share our dreams amidst the vibrant blooms, I realized that perhaps resilience wasn't just about enduring the chaos but also about embracing the beauty that managed to thrive in its shadow.

The days melted into one another, a sweet routine blossoming in our hidden sanctuary. With each visit to the garden, the world outside faded further into a muted backdrop, a distant hum of chaos that couldn't quite reach us. Nate and I began to claim the space as our own, our laughter blending with the rustling leaves, the soft buzzing of bees weaving an enchanting melody around us.

One afternoon, as I sprawled on the mossy ground, I found myself lost in the swirl of colorful petals, imagining them as vibrant characters in a story only I could tell. "What if flowers had their own lives?" I mused aloud, propping myself on my elbows to look at Nate. "What if daisies were secretly in love with the sun and waited all day just for a glimpse of its golden rays?"

Nate's laughter echoed like a chorus of bells, bright and contagious. "You think daisies have such lofty aspirations? I'm pretty sure they're just happy to be alive and occasionally pecked at by passing bees." He leaned back against the cool stone bench, his arms folded behind his head, and stared at the sky, where wisps of clouds floated lazily, casting playful shadows over the garden.

"I bet they dream big," I replied, a grin tugging at the corners of my mouth. "If I were a flower, I'd want to be a peony—full of color, never afraid to bloom big and bold."

"Peonies are overrated," he countered with mock seriousness. "I think I'd be a cactus. Tough, resilient, and a little prickly around the edges." He raised an eyebrow, as if daring me to disagree.

"Cacti? Really?" I rolled my eyes, stifling a laugh. "You would choose the most unapproachable plant possible. How very on-brand for you."

He feigned hurt, clutching his chest dramatically. "I'm wounded. You wound me deeply with your words."

The playful banter continued, a dance of words as we spun our imaginative tales. Each session felt like a world-building workshop, crafting characters that felt almost real—at least as real as the blooms around us. I could see Nate as a swashbuckling hero, leaping through deserts to save a delicate flower from the grips of winter. Meanwhile, I would play the spirited flower, bursting into a thousand colors at his triumphant arrival.

It was a whimsical escapade, and for the first time in what felt like ages, I could almost forget the hospital's sterile walls and the ever-looming specter of illness.

But as the sun dipped lower in the sky, painting everything in shades of gold and lavender, a shadow crept in, casting a pall over our sanctuary. "What do you think it's like?" I asked, the lightheartedness of our conversation giving way to something more profound. "You know, to be truly free. To not have any of this weighing you down."

Nate turned his gaze from the horizon to me, the playful spark in his eyes momentarily replaced by something deeper, a flicker of vulnerability. "I think it's like standing on the edge of a cliff, the wind whipping through your hair, knowing you can jump without fear."

I nodded, feeling the weight of his words settle in the space between us. "And what if you fall?"

"Then you fly," he replied, his smile a beacon of reassurance, though it didn't quite reach his eyes.

A silence fell, stretching out as the sun's last rays bathed the garden in a warm glow. I felt the heaviness of unsaid thoughts swirling around us. There was a reality that clung to Nate, a flicker of something I could sense but didn't quite understand. "What about you?" he asked, breaking the silence. "What does freedom mean to you?"

It felt like an invitation to bare my soul, but I hesitated, considering the weight of my own thoughts. "Honestly?" I took a deep breath, the words tumbling out before I could second-guess myself. "Freedom feels like the ability to breathe without a thousand thoughts competing for space in my head. Like feeling safe enough to explore every corner of who I am without the fear of judgment or rejection."

"Then you should start with this garden," Nate said softly, leaning forward, his intensity pulling me in. "This is your safe space. You can explore whatever parts of yourself you want here."

I looked around, at the flowers standing proudly against the creeping shadows, and nodded slowly. "You're right. Maybe I can find pieces of myself hidden in the petals."

As I spoke, I felt something shift in the air—a rustling, an energy that made the hairs on my arms stand on end. It was as if the garden itself was listening, its colors deepening in the twilight, a magical tapestry woven from our unspoken hopes and fears.

But before I could dwell on the sensation, a sudden rustling from the bushes caught my attention. Nate and I exchanged curious glances, our playful mood momentarily eclipsed by the unexpected sound. I half-expected a raccoon or a wayward squirrel to make an appearance, but instead, a woman stepped into the clearing, her presence electric and enigmatic.

She looked out of place, dressed in vibrant bohemian attire that seemed to mirror the garden itself. Long, flowing skirts and an array of bracelets adorned her arms, each piece jangled as she moved. Her hair cascaded in wild waves, capturing the evening light like spun gold. "Well, well," she said, a knowing smile curling at her lips. "What do we have here? A couple of dreamers?"

Nate straightened, his demeanor shifting slightly. "We were just—"

"Playing with words?" she interjected, her voice lilting like the wind through the flowers. "I can feel the magic in the air. You're weaving a tale, aren't you?"

I blinked, a mixture of surprise and curiosity bubbling within me. "Uh, yes? Kind of. Just enjoying the garden."

"Enjoying?" she mused, stepping closer, her eyes twinkling with mischief. "This isn't merely a garden; it's a sanctuary of secrets. The blooms here hold stories, and so do you."

Her gaze shifted to Nate, a knowing look passing between them. I couldn't help but feel a twinge of jealousy, like a child standing in the shadow of someone taller. "Secrets?" I echoed, trying to regain control of the conversation. "What secrets?"

"Ah, my dear," she said with a dramatic flair, "every flower, every petal here whispers a truth. What do you seek in this sanctuary?"

Nate opened his mouth to speak, but I interjected, my curiosity outweighing my reticence. "What do you mean by 'truth'? Is it about finding ourselves?"

The woman chuckled, a melodious sound that seemed to dance among the flowers. "Oh, honey, finding yourself is only the beginning. It's about unearthing what lies beneath the surface, the layers of yourself that even you might not know exist."

Her words resonated like a low hum, stirring something deep within me. "And how do we do that?" I pressed, feeling the walls I had built around myself begin to crumble, brick by brick.

"By embracing the chaos, my dear. By daring to dive into the unknown." She waved her arms dramatically, gesturing toward the vast expanse of the garden. "Every bloom has a story, just waiting for someone to uncover it."

The air thickened with an intoxicating mix of possibility and apprehension. I exchanged a glance with Nate, whose eyes sparkled with a blend of intrigue and skepticism. "What do you think?" he whispered, a playful challenge dancing on his lips.

"I think we're in for an adventure," I replied, a smile spreading across my face, the garden now pulsing with the promise of untold stories, inviting us to explore the depths of our own. The woman nodded approvingly, as if she knew that the spark of curiosity had ignited something between us, urging us to uncover the mysteries that lay ahead.

The air in the garden crackled with an energy I hadn't anticipated, a strange mix of excitement and trepidation that danced between the three of us. The woman—mysterious, almost ethereal—stood there with an air of knowing, her bright eyes flickering like candle flames, and I felt as if I were about to step onto the precipice of something monumental. "So, tell me," she said, tilting her head slightly as if she were gauging our souls. "What secrets have you tucked away? What dreams do you dare to unearth?"

I shared a quick glance with Nate, who seemed just as taken aback by this unexpected intrusion as I was. He cleared his throat, breaking the momentary spell. "Um, we were just, you know, dreaming about flowers and, uh, things."

The woman's laughter rang out, rich and warm, echoing through the garden. "Dreaming about flowers! Delightful. But you see, flowers are just the beginning. You both are on the brink of discovering something far more profound."

A shiver ran down my spine. "And what's that?" I asked, my curiosity piqued despite the warning bells chiming in my mind.

"Ah, the big question!" she exclaimed, her arms sweeping wide like a conductor leading an orchestra. "It's about transformation, about peeling back the layers to reveal your true selves. Each of you has the potential to bloom in ways you can't yet imagine."

Her words resonated, a siren song pulling at the edges of my consciousness. Transformation. It was a word I had heard many times, especially during my recent battles with my own identity and fears. "What do you mean, 'reveal your true selves'?"

"Let's just say that every flower here has a story, but not every story has been told," she replied cryptically, her smile deepening, hinting at secrets untold.

Nate raised an eyebrow, his skepticism evident. "And how exactly do we go about this transformation? Is it some sort of magic trick, or do we need to wave a wand?"

"Much better than a wand!" She grinned, her eyes sparkling. "You need to be willing to dive deep. The garden will guide you, but only if you're ready to face the truth. You both have walls that need to come down."

"Walls?" I echoed, feeling the heat rise to my cheeks. "What walls?"

"Walls built by fear, doubt, and the pain of your pasts," she said, her voice softening, almost tender. "You've been through so much, haven't you?"

I wanted to deny it, to brush aside the weight of her words, but something about her presence made it difficult to hold onto the familiar masks I wore. Instead, I nodded, my defenses crumbling slightly. "Yeah, I guess you could say that."

"Then let's do something about it." With that, she stepped further into the garden, beckoning us to follow. "Come. Let me show you."

Nate hesitated, a flicker of uncertainty crossing his features. "Wait, are we really going to follow a stranger into the depths of a garden? I mean, she could be a plant witch for all we know."

"A plant witch?" I stifled a laugh, glancing at the woman, who appeared more amused than offended. "I think she seems harmless."

"Harmless? That's what they all say before it's too late," Nate whispered, leaning in closer as if to shield himself from her perceived danger.

"I promise, I won't turn you into toads," the woman quipped, her tone playful. "Trust me, my magic is much more profound than that."

Finally, curiosity won over caution. Nate sighed dramatically, rolling his eyes as he took a step forward. "Fine, lead the way, oh wise one."

With a flourish, she turned and walked deeper into the garden. "You'll see," she said over her shoulder. "It's time to explore the uncharted territory of your hearts."

We followed her into a thicket of foliage, where the vibrant colors morphed into a lush tapestry of greens and blossoms, the air fragrant with the scent of earth and wildflowers. The path twisted and turned, revealing more of the garden's beauty as we moved further away from the familiar clearing.

"What are we supposed to do?" I asked, glancing at Nate, who looked equally bewildered yet intrigued.

"Feel," the woman said simply. "Feel what lies beneath the surface, what you've buried under layers of expectation and fear. The garden will help you unearth it."

I was about to protest, to ask for a more concrete plan, when suddenly the woman halted in front of an archway draped in ivy and blossoms. "Here is where the magic begins," she announced dramatically. "Step through, and you'll each find what you need most."

"What if I don't know what I need?" Nate asked, crossing his arms, skepticism still evident in his posture.

"Exactly!" she exclaimed, her eyes sparkling with mischief. "That's precisely the point. You'll discover it on the other side."

"Great, so we're just supposed to waltz through and hope for the best?" he muttered, casting a wary glance at me.

"Waltzing might be too much to ask, but yes, that's the idea," she replied, almost teasingly. "But trust me, it will be worth it."

I could feel the pulse of the garden, the way it vibrated with life and energy, almost begging us to take that leap of faith. My heart raced, anticipation bubbling within me. "What's the worst that could happen? A few weeds and a bit of dirt?"

"Right," Nate said, rolling his eyes again. "Because that's what every wise person says before entering a portal to another realm."

"Just trust me," I urged, taking a step forward. "We've come this far."

With a shared glance of determination, we took a collective breath and stepped through the archway, the world around us shifting as the light dimmed momentarily. As we crossed the threshold, an intoxicating fragrance enveloped us, one that spoke of secrets and untold stories.

On the other side, the garden opened up into an expansive space that felt almost surreal. The colors were more vibrant, the air charged with an electric anticipation. Flowers of every hue and shape stretched out in all directions, a riot of beauty that was overwhelming yet enchanting. I felt the ground shift beneath me, as if I were standing on the cusp of a dream.

"What is this place?" Nate whispered, awe mingling with disbelief.

"Welcome to the heart of the garden," the woman said, her voice a soft melody that seemed to blend with the rustling leaves. "This is where your true selves begin to emerge."

Before I could ask more questions, I noticed something fluttering in the distance—a flicker of movement that caught my eye. As I turned my head, I felt a strange sensation creeping up my spine, like an alarm bell ringing deep within me.

"What is that?" I breathed, pointing toward a shadow darting between the flowers.

The woman's expression shifted, her previous playfulness giving way to a look of concern. "Ah, it seems the garden has its own surprises," she murmured, her voice suddenly low and serious. "You must be careful."

"Careful of what?" Nate asked, his bravado slipping away as the tension thickened around us.

Before she could respond, a figure emerged from behind a massive sunflower, cloaked in darkness, its face obscured by shadows. A chilling sense of foreboding washed over me, and I could feel my heart pounding in my chest, each beat resonating like a warning drum.

"Who dares enter the sanctuary?" the figure rasped, its voice a low growl that sent shivers racing down my spine.

The garden that had felt like a haven just moments before now transformed into a maze of uncertainty. I glanced at Nate, whose earlier confidence had evaporated, leaving him wide-eyed and tense. The woman stepped forward, her demeanor shifting from welcoming to commanding.

"You have no power here," she declared, her voice steady and unwavering. "They seek knowledge, not conflict."

But the figure remained unmoved, an ominous presence that loomed larger with each passing second. I could feel the air thickening with tension, a storm brewing just beneath the surface, and I couldn't shake the feeling that the garden held more secrets than we were prepared to uncover.

As the figure took a step closer, I felt my breath catch in my throat, anticipation crackling like static electricity. "What do you want from us?" I managed to ask, my voice barely a whisper against the backdrop of the shifting garden.

"Only the truth," it hissed, the shadows around it swirling like a tempest, and in that moment, I realized that our journey through the garden was only just beginning.

Chapter 19: The Fragile Thread

The golden hour wrapped around us like a tender embrace, the sunlight filtering through the branches of the ancient oak in the park where we often found refuge. It felt like time itself had slowed down, allowing us to savor every second. I nestled against Nate, my head resting on his shoulder, inhaling the comforting scent of his cologne mixed with the earthy aroma of fallen leaves. His warmth enveloped me, and I could almost forget the world outside our little bubble, the one brimming with uncertainties and the specter of loss that loomed over our heads like an ominous storm cloud.

"Do you think the sky knows something we don't?" I mused, watching as the sun dipped lower, painting the horizon in shades of amber and rose. The beauty of it all made my heart swell and ache simultaneously, a paradox that had become all too familiar.

Nate chuckled softly, his deep voice resonating like a melody. "Maybe it does, but I'm pretty sure it's just showing off." He tilted his head, glancing at me with those sea-glass green eyes that seemed to see right through my bravado. "What's on your mind, Ava?"

I hesitated, the words tangling in my throat like vines. I had wanted to share my fears, the gnawing anxiety that had taken root within me since the day our hearts had intertwined. It was a beautiful connection, yet the fragility of it weighed heavily, as if it were balanced on a tightrope stretched high above a canyon. What if one wrong step sent us tumbling into the abyss? I opened my mouth, ready to unleash the turmoil, but I couldn't. Instead, I allowed a half-smile to slip onto my lips, attempting to mask the tremors beneath.

"Just wondering if the squirrels in that tree have any secrets," I replied, gesturing to a particularly plump one chattering away as it scurried along the branch. It was a flimsy diversion, but I could feel Nate's gaze intensify, searching for the truth behind my words.

"Secrets, huh?" He raised an eyebrow, feigning seriousness. "Let's see... perhaps they're planning a coup against the birds? Or maybe they're just really passionate about acorns." He paused, a grin spreading across his face. "Or they're trying to figure out how to build a rocket ship."

I laughed, a sound that felt like sunlight piercing through my anxiety. But as the laughter faded, so did my smile. "Sometimes I think I'm the only one trying to build a rocket ship, and I'm not even sure where I want it to go."

Nate's expression shifted, concern etching deeper lines around his mouth. "You don't have to do it alone, you know. I'm right here." He took my hand, intertwining our fingers, a small gesture that felt monumental. "Whatever you're facing, we'll face it together. You don't have to carry it all."

His sincerity was like a balm to my aching heart, but the weight of my fears threatened to suffocate me. I wanted to believe him, to lean into that promise of shared burdens, but the past had taught me that love was often accompanied by heartache. What if I lost him? What if life, in all its unpredictable glory, decided to play its cruel games?

"I'm just afraid, Nate," I finally admitted, my voice barely a whisper. "Afraid of losing you. It's like standing at the edge of a cliff, and every day I get a little closer to that edge." I could feel tears prickling at the corners of my eyes, and I fought them back, unwilling to unravel in front of him.

Nate's grip tightened around my hand, his thumb tracing gentle patterns across my skin, a soothing gesture that reminded me of the way the ocean lapped at the shore—steady, persistent. "You're not going to lose me," he said, each word deliberate, as if he were building a fortress against my fears. "I'm not going anywhere. We're in this together, remember?"

I wanted to scream, to shake him and make him understand that love was inherently risky, that the closer we got, the more vulnerable I felt. But instead, I breathed deeply, grounding myself in the warmth radiating from him. "You make it sound so easy," I said, my tone teasing but laced with sincerity. "Like you've cracked the code to eternal happiness."

"Maybe I have," he replied, his voice dripping with mock seriousness. "It's all about sharing snacks and not letting squirrels take over your thoughts. They can be very distracting, you know."

I rolled my eyes, the heaviness in my chest lightening for a fleeting moment. "You think squirrels are distracting? Try having your heart in the hands of someone who could walk away at any moment."

His expression softened, and he leaned closer, his breath mingling with the crisp autumn air. "That's the thing, though. It's not just in my hands, Ava; it's in both of ours. We've built something beautiful, something worth fighting for. And I promise you, I'm not walking away. Not now, not ever."

The conviction in his words wrapped around me like a security blanket, yet a lingering doubt gnawed at the edges of my mind. The world outside our cozy enclave remained chaotic, unpredictable, and it took every ounce of my strength to suppress the worries threatening to spill over. I wanted to believe in our love as fiercely as he did, but the fragile thread binding us felt precarious, a delicate whisper that could unravel at any moment.

As the sun sank beneath the horizon, casting a soft twilight glow, I nestled deeper into Nate's side. He was my anchor, my lifeline in a turbulent sea, yet I couldn't shake the haunting feeling that storms were brewing just out of sight, ready to crash into our carefully crafted haven. I closed my eyes, hoping that in the warm cocoon of his presence, I could find the courage to face whatever lay ahead.

The following days flowed like a slow river, each moment stretching out before us, both precious and suffocating. As autumn deepened, the world around us exploded in a riot of color, vibrant reds and oranges clinging to the trees, while the air turned crisp and sweet with the scent of falling leaves. Yet despite the stunning beauty enveloping us, a weight settled heavily in my chest, like a stone dropped into still water, sending ripples of unease throughout my being.

We spent our evenings in that tiny coffee shop down the street, a cozy little nook with mismatched chairs and the faintest hint of cinnamon wafting through the air. Nate was in his element, his laughter echoing off the walls, a melody that pulled me in like a siren's song. I watched him as he animatedly recounted a story about a disastrous attempt at baking cookies—one that had resulted in a flour explosion that would have made a perfect scene for a slapstick comedy. The way his hands moved, gesturing wildly, sent warmth spiraling through me, but in the back of my mind, an insistent whisper reminded me that the clock was ticking.

"What's wrong?" he asked, the light in his eyes dimming slightly as he caught the change in my expression. "You look like you just found a hair in your latte."

I offered a shaky laugh, a poor imitation of the joy I felt moments before. "I think it might be the sugar rush from your cookie disaster story. It's a little overwhelming." I took a sip of my steaming chai, hoping the spice would warm the icy tendrils of fear creeping up my spine.

"Right, the sugar rush," he teased, but his voice held an edge of concern. "You know, if it helps, I can make us a fresh batch of cookies, or we could just stick to takeout pizza and board games. That always cheers you up."

The very mention of our chaotic game nights filled me with a surge of nostalgia. Our living room transformed into a battlefield of laughter, pizza crumbs, and fierce competition. But the thought of losing those moments, of losing him, gnawed at my insides. I could almost hear the clock ticking louder in the silence between us, as if it were counting down to something inevitable.

"I don't think it's the cookies or the games, Nate," I said softly, struggling to maintain a façade of levity. "It's just... I feel like everything is so fragile right now. Like we're walking on a tightrope, and I'm terrified of falling."

He leaned forward, his expression shifting from playful to serious, a deep furrow forming on his brow. "You keep saying fragile. What do you mean? Is it us? Because if it is, I'm not going anywhere. You know that, right?" His voice was steady, but I could hear the underlying tremor, a reflection of my own fears.

"It's not just us," I admitted, my heart pounding like a drum in my chest. "It's everything. Life has a way of throwing curveballs, and I don't know if I'm ready to catch them. What if we don't make it through? What if something happens and..." I trailed off, unable to voice the dark thoughts swirling in my mind.

Nate reached across the table, his fingers brushing against mine, grounding me. "Ava, we're not a fairy tale, and I can't promise that everything will always be perfect. But I can promise that I'm here. No matter what."

His sincerity melted the ice encasing my heart, if only a little. I squeezed his hand, allowing myself to lean into the warmth of his words, though the shadows of doubt continued to swirl around us. "You say that now, but what happens when life gets messy? When it's not just about cookies and board games?"

"Then we get messy together," he replied, a hint of mischief in his eyes. "Look, if things go sideways, we'll handle it. You know how many times I've spilled coffee on my shirt before a big date? It's practically a ritual at this point. And hey, if the worst happens, we'll just make it a funny story to tell later. Think about it—'Remember that time I spilled coffee all over myself and Ava almost cried because she thought I'd lost my charm?'"

The image of Nate, coffee-stained and laughing, broke through the thick veil of worry that enveloped me. I couldn't help but chuckle at the thought, the absurdity of it lightening my heart. "You do have a knack for turning disasters into comedy."

"Exactly! And we'll figure it out, one awkward moment at a time," he said, his eyes sparkling. "We can be the best disaster duo this town has ever seen."

The corners of my mouth twitched upward, the weight of my anxiety lessening, even if just for a moment. "So you're saying we'd be like a rom-com that's less 'happily ever after' and more 'unexpectedly hilarious misadventures'?"

"Precisely!" He leaned back, crossing his arms triumphantly. "With an excellent soundtrack. Think of all the wild memories we'll create. Besides, isn't that what makes it all worthwhile?"

It was hard to resist his optimism. I wanted so badly to believe him, to let go of the worries that tied me down like anchors. "Okay, but what if we're not just awkward? What if something truly terrible happens?" My heart raced, and I could feel the shadows creeping back in. "What if—"

"Ava." His tone shifted to one of unwavering certainty, a softness that cut through the chaos. "We've faced challenges before. You don't get to this point without some bumps along the way. You think I didn't panic when I first met your family? Or when I introduced you to mine? I had visions of my mother trying to marry you off to the neighbor's dog."

"Not the dog!" I exclaimed, laughter bubbling up despite my fears. "What kind of a first impression would that be?"

He grinned, the warmth of his laughter infectious. "Exactly! But we survived, didn't we? We navigated those awkward moments together. That's the beauty of it all. Life is unpredictable, yes, but it's the unpredictability that makes it exciting."

I let his words wash over me, their warmth pushing back the chill of uncertainty. Maybe there was truth in what he said. Perhaps the chaos was a testament to our resilience, a reminder that love could thrive even in messiness. I sighed, feeling the tension ease in my shoulders. "Okay, Mr. Disaster Duo. I'm in. Let's embrace the chaos together."

"Now that's the spirit!" Nate beamed, his enthusiasm radiating like the sun breaking through the clouds. "Together, we can face anything. Squirrels, spilled coffee, questionable cooking skills—bring it on!"

As we shared another laugh, I allowed myself to believe that perhaps, just perhaps, we could weave our fragile threads into something beautifully resilient. The world might be unpredictable, but within the safety of his presence, I felt a flicker of hope igniting deep within me.

Our late-night conversations stretched on like the shadows cast by the flickering candlelight, each word a delicate thread weaving us closer together. The coffee shop had long since closed, and we found ourselves sprawled on the couch in my living room, the remnants of our dinner littering the coffee table—crumpled napkins and empty pizza boxes, an ode to our shared delight in culinary chaos. Outside, the wind howled, rattling the windowpanes, as if nature itself wanted to join in our late-night musings.

"I still think you owe me a rematch at Monopoly," Nate declared, tossing a discarded pizza crust into the air and watching it land aimlessly. "You can't just claim victory because I was distracted by my opponent's charming smile."

I rolled my eyes, playfully swatting him with a throw pillow. "Please, you were the one who decided to mortgage everything for a chance at Boardwalk. It's a classic rookie mistake, Nate. A little charm isn't going to save you from bad decisions."

He feigned hurt, placing a hand dramatically over his heart. "It's always my charm that gets me in trouble. I should've known better than to let you distract me with your dazzling wit and pizza toppings."

"Right, because I'm the villain in your Monopoly saga." I laughed, feeling the warmth of his presence seep deeper into my bones. Yet, beneath our lighthearted banter, a heaviness lingered, tugging at the edges of my mind. How long could we keep the facade of carefree moments alive before the shadows caught up to us?

Nate shifted, his expression softening as he leaned closer, searching my eyes. "You're still worried, aren't you?" The lightheartedness in his voice faded, replaced by an earnestness that made my heart ache. "I can see it, Ava. Just tell me what's bothering you. I promise I won't spill my guts this time—figuratively, at least."

"Sometimes it feels like we're on borrowed time," I admitted, my voice barely above a whisper. "Every laugh, every touch—like they're just fleeting moments waiting to be stolen away."

"I get that," he said, his thumb brushing over my knuckles, sending a rush of warmth through me. "But don't let those thoughts poison what we have right now. We can't control the future, but we can make this moment count."

"Moments don't feel like enough," I replied, frustration bubbling to the surface. "What if tomorrow is the day everything falls apart? What if I wake up and you're gone, and I'm left wondering what happened to the 'us' we built?"

Nate's gaze hardened, his jaw clenching slightly. "We can't think like that, Ava. I refuse to let fear dictate our love story. Every relationship comes with its risks, but we're strong enough to face them."

A breath caught in my throat as I searched for the right words, the ones that would convey just how deeply I felt. "I don't want to lose you, Nate. I need you to promise me that no matter what happens, you'll always choose us." The urgency in my voice hung in the air, palpable and raw.

He nodded, a fierce determination glimmering in his eyes. "I promise. No matter what the world throws at us, I'll always choose you." His fingers tightened around mine, and I felt the weight of his promise settle between us—a tether against the chaos of our fears.

As we sat there, the warmth of his hand enveloping mine, I felt a flicker of hope begin to bloom. Maybe this wasn't just about the uncertainties we faced. Maybe, in choosing to embrace each moment, we could create a future worth fighting for. "Okay," I said, softening. "Let's make this moment count. No more morbid thoughts for tonight."

Nate grinned, relief washing over his features like the first light of dawn. "Now you're speaking my language. What's next on our agenda? A rousing game of charades? I've been practicing my terrible impressions."

"Impressions? Oh no, this I have to see," I teased, shifting my body closer, ready to indulge in the kind of silliness that reminded me of the beauty in everyday life.

But just as he was about to launch into an exaggerated impersonation of a famous actor, the atmosphere shifted. The wind outside howled again, stronger this time, rattling the windows with an urgency that felt almost foreboding. The lights flickered overhead, and for a brief moment, shadows danced along the walls, shifting in a way that sent a shiver down my spine.

"Did you feel that?" I asked, glancing at the window, anxiety bubbling back to the surface. "It's like the world is warning us."

Nate's expression changed as he turned to the window, his smile fading. "Maybe it's just a storm," he said, trying to sound casual, though I could sense the tension rising in him too. "But it's more than just a storm outside, isn't it?"

"Yeah," I murmured, feeling the electric charge in the air as if the very atmosphere held its breath, waiting for something to happen. "It feels... different. Almost like something is shifting."

Before he could respond, the power abruptly cut out, plunging the room into darkness. My heart raced as I fumbled for my phone, its light flickering to life, casting an eerie glow around us. The sudden silence was deafening, and a cold breeze slipped through the cracks of the window, chilling the air.

"Okay, this is creepy," Nate said, his voice steady, though I could hear the underlying tension. "Let's just sit tight until the power comes back. We're not going to let a little darkness ruin our night, right?"

"Right," I said, though doubt crept into my mind like the shadows closing in. "But what if it's not just a power outage?"

A moment later, the faint sound of footsteps echoed from outside, muffled by the wind but undeniably present. My heart raced, and I exchanged a worried glance with Nate. "Did you hear that?" I whispered, my voice trembling slightly.

"Yeah," he replied, his brow furrowing. "It's probably just some kids messing around. This neighborhood isn't exactly known for its raucous nightlife."

But the footsteps grew louder, closer, and a chill raced down my spine. The doorbell chimed, breaking the tension, a dissonant sound echoing through the stillness of the house. My heart lurched. "Who would be here at this hour?"

Nate's eyes narrowed as he stood up, moving toward the door cautiously. "Stay here," he said, a firm edge to his tone that both comforted and terrified me. "I'll check it out."

"No!" I exclaimed, panic bubbling up. "I'm coming with you."

He hesitated, then nodded. "Fine. But we stick together. No heroics."

As we moved toward the door, the footsteps stopped, and an unsettling silence enveloped us once more. My pulse pounded in my ears as Nate slowly turned the doorknob, his body tense with anticipation. I could feel the world holding its breath, a moment suspended in time, teetering on the edge of something we couldn't predict.

The door creaked open, and the cold air rushed in, swirling around us like a ghostly hand. Outside, the porch light flickered erratically, illuminating a figure standing just beyond the threshold—a silhouette shrouded in darkness, features obscured.

"Who are you?" Nate demanded, his voice steady but edged with caution.

I stepped closer to him, a sense of dread pooling in my stomach. The figure didn't respond, merely taking a slow, deliberate step forward, and in that heartbeat, I felt the fragile thread of our evening fray, unraveling at the seams as the unknown loomed before us.

Chapter 20: A Flicker of Light

The garden welcomed us like an old friend, its vibrant colors spilling over the edges of our lives, transforming our mundane routines into a symphony of possibility. The air was thick with the sweet scent of blooming flowers, a heady mix that hung between us like a secret. With each visit, we wove our love deeper into the soil, nurturing not just the plants but also the fragile threads connecting our hearts. I had never known how a place could feel so alive, pulsating with energy that lifted my spirits and melted away the day's worries.

As we approached the garden one particularly radiant afternoon, the sunlight filtered through the leaves, creating a mosaic of light and shadow on the ground. The earth beneath our feet felt warm, almost alive, as if it had been waiting for us to return. Nate's laughter broke through the serene stillness, a sound so infectious that it made my heart leap. He was leaning over a patch of wildflowers, examining them as though he were uncovering hidden treasures. I loved how he could find joy in the smallest things—like the way a single daisy leaned bravely against a gust of wind, or how the bees buzzed about, completely unbothered by the chaos of the world around them.

"Look at this little guy," he said, holding up a tiny blue flower as if it were the rarest gem. "Think it's trying to impress us?"

I grinned, imagining it strutting about in its tiny blue petals, begging for our attention. "Absolutely. It knows it's got competition with those sunflowers over there, trying to steal the show."

We both turned our gaze to the sunflowers, their golden faces turned proudly towards the sky. They stood like sentinels in the garden, bold and unapologetic in their brightness. There was something about them—maybe it was their unyielding determination to seek out the sun—that resonated deeply with me. I could see the flicker of inspiration in Nate's eyes, a familiar spark that hinted at another idea brewing in that mind of his.

"What if we plant our own?" he suggested, brushing the dirt from his hands with a casual confidence. "We could make a little sunflower corner right here."

A thrill rushed through me at the thought. The idea of nurturing something together felt monumental, as if it symbolized a promise—one not just to the garden but to each other. "Yes! Let's do it! But we should find the biggest seeds we can." The excitement danced in my chest as I imagined the sunny patch we would create, our little sanctuary of hope amidst the shadows we often faced.

As we set to work, the sun dipped lower in the sky, casting a golden hue that felt almost magical. Nate and I dug into the earth, the soil giving way beneath our eager hands. The air buzzed with our laughter, mingling with the soft rustle of leaves and the distant hum of cicadas. Every shovelful of dirt we turned over felt like a small act of rebellion against the heaviness life sometimes pressed upon us.

"Did you know that sunflowers are actually heliotropic?" Nate said, his voice bright with enthusiasm as he helped me measure out the spacing for the seeds. "They follow the sun as it moves across the sky. It's like they're always searching for the light."

I paused, letting the weight of his words settle around us like the late afternoon sun. "That's beautiful," I replied, brushing my hair back and feeling a gentle breeze tug at the ends. "We could all use a little bit of that wisdom, don't you think? Always reaching for the light, no matter how dark it gets."

He met my gaze, a knowing smile playing at the corners of his lips. "Especially us. We've had our share of shadows lately, haven't we?"

The acknowledgment hung between us, a soft tension that hinted at the unspoken battles we fought outside this serene oasis. Yet, in this moment, with the warm earth beneath our hands and the promise of new life sprouting around us, I felt fortified against the uncertainties of the world. Together, we could create something beautiful, a testament to our resilience.

Once we finished planting the seeds, we stepped back to admire our work. The tiny, nestled seeds promised future sunflowers, bold and bright, eager to burst forth from the soil and claim their space under the sun. It was a small act, yet it felt monumental, a declaration that we were willing to invest in hope, even when the odds felt stacked against us.

As the shadows lengthened and the sky turned a deep, dusky blue, I turned to Nate, catching the glimmer of warmth in his eyes. "You know, I really needed this," I admitted, the words spilling out before I could stop them. "Just being here with you, planting seeds... it feels like we're building something, even if it's just a garden."

He nodded, his expression serious for a moment. "It's more than just a garden, Ava. It's a reminder that even in the chaos, we can grow something beautiful. And that beauty is worth fighting for."

His words wrapped around me, a soft blanket of understanding. In that twilight moment, I realized that we weren't just planting seeds in the soil; we were planting hope in our hearts. The sunflowers would soon stretch skyward, reaching for the light, and so would we.

The next few weeks unfolded like a well-loved book, each page turned revealing a new layer of color and texture in our lives. Every visit to the garden felt like stepping into a dream—sunlight dappled through the leaves, casting playful shadows that danced on the ground. It was a place where time seemed to pause, allowing us to savor the small joys that often slipped away in the chaos of the everyday. The world beyond the garden's walls was still fraught with challenges—uncertain job prospects, family pressures, and the lingering shadows of our pasts—but here, we were free to breathe.

One afternoon, the air was tinged with the sweet scent of honeysuckle, and I felt a spark of mischief flare within me as I turned to Nate, who was deep in thought, kneeling by a row of wildflowers.

"You know," I said, trying to mask my grin, "we could totally start a garden gnome collection. Think of the potential for ridiculousness!"

He looked up, a brow arched in that charmingly skeptical way of his, as if he were weighing the pros and cons of becoming a gnome collector. "Gnomes? Really? What's next? Flamingos? A yard full of lawn ornaments?"

I laughed, shaking my head. "Only if they're the quirky ones. You know, like wearing sunglasses and drinking a tiny cocktail." I leaned in closer, lowering my voice conspiratorially. "They'd totally fit the vibe of our secret garden."

Nate rolled his eyes, a mock-serious expression creeping onto his face. "Just what we need—an invasion of sunbathing gnomes. I can see it now: 'Welcome to Ava and Nate's Garden of Gnomey Delights.'"

"Hey, don't knock it till you try it," I replied, fighting back laughter. "A little whimsy could do us some good."

In that moment, I realized how much I cherished our lighthearted banter. It was an essential part of what we had built together—something that added a rich layer to the depths of our connection. With every jest and quip, I felt more and more rooted in this burgeoning relationship, the kind of bond that felt both fragile and unshakeable.

As the days turned into weeks, the sunflower seeds we had planted began to sprout, tiny green shoots pushing their way through the soil, eagerly reaching for the sun. It was a miracle to witness—an embodiment of hope thriving despite the odds. I often found myself lost in thought, reflecting on how much our lives mirrored the growth of those sunflowers. We were slowly emerging from the shadows, inch by inch, turning our faces toward the light.

On a particularly sunny afternoon, Nate suggested we have a picnic in the garden. The idea sent a thrill through me, and I quickly rallied to gather snacks, not wanting to miss an opportunity to make memories with him. I packed a woven basket with a haphazard assortment of goodies: sandwiches smeared with too much mustard, a bag of fresh strawberries, and two bottles of lemonade, their condensation trickling down the sides, promising refreshment.

When I arrived, Nate had already laid out a plaid blanket under the sunniest spot in the garden. The blanket was a glorious clash of colors, reminiscent of a summer carnival. "Welcome to our outdoor dining establishment," he announced with a flourish, gesturing at our spread. "Table for two, complete with a complimentary side of nature."

I set the basket down, chuckling. "I'm impressed. You must have some serious culinary skills to create a masterpiece like this."

He picked up a strawberry and pretended to inspect it like a sommelier assessing fine wine. "Ah yes, this one has a fine bouquet with notes of sunshine and just a hint of joy."

I rolled my eyes but couldn't hide my grin as I plucked a strawberry from the basket and took a bite. "Deliciously absurd, just like our lives."

We settled into our picnic, and laughter echoed through the garden, mingling with the gentle rustling of leaves. Between bites, we shared stories, weaving our dreams into the fabric of that afternoon. Nate spoke of his childhood—how he once tried to build a treehouse that ended up collapsing spectacularly, resulting in a summer spent mending bruised egos and broken boards. "In hindsight," he mused, "maybe I was just a little too ambitious. And my hammer skills? Well, let's just say they could use some work."

"I can't picture you as a tiny carpenter, but I love it," I said, my heart swelling with affection. "The world better watch out for you and your gnome collection. Next, you'll be tackling IKEA furniture assembly."

He feigned a gasp, placing a hand dramatically on his chest. "You dare to suggest I might fail at building a bookshelf? I'll have you know I'm very capable of following directions."

"Right, but do you know how to find the directions?" I teased, leaning closer. "Or will I have to come to the rescue with my superior IKEA assembly skills?"

Before he could respond, the air shifted, thickening with an unexpected tension. A figure appeared at the edge of the garden—someone I recognized but hoped to avoid. My heart sank as I caught sight of Mara, my sister, standing just beyond the blooms, her arms crossed defensively over her chest. Her face was a mixture of concern and annoyance, the lines of worry etched deeply into her brow.

"What are you doing here?" I called out, my voice tight. I hadn't expected her to find us, especially not in this haven we had created.

"I came to see if you were okay," she replied, her tone clipped. "Mom's worried. You just vanished, Ava."

Nate exchanged a glance with me, his expression shifting from playful to serious in an instant. I felt my heart race, the warmth of the picnic suddenly overshadowed by the chill of family obligations. This wasn't the moment I wanted to navigate, not in our sanctuary.

Mara's presence felt like a sudden storm cloud blocking out the sun. I could almost hear the vibrant colors of the garden dimming, the leaves rustling with an anxious energy. "You vanished? That's one way to put it," I replied, my tone edged with sarcasm, a weak attempt to mask the tumult brewing inside me. "I've just been busy... planting seeds, literally and metaphorically."

Nate shifted beside me, his expression a mix of concern and confusion. He knew my family dynamics were tangled, yet he didn't quite grasp how deeply entwined those roots ran. "Mara, it's okay," he said gently, trying to bridge the gap between my sister's intentions and my growing frustration. "We were just enjoying the garden."

But Mara was having none of it. Her gaze flickered between Nate and me, and I could almost hear her thoughts racing like a train on a track. "This isn't just about enjoying a garden. Mom's worried about you, Ava. You've been distant. You can't just pretend everything is fine."

The words struck hard, igniting a flurry of emotions I thought I had tucked away neatly. I wanted to retort, to fling back the pain of my family's expectations, but instead, I felt my defenses rise like a fortress. "I'm not pretending. I'm just... choosing to live my life how I want to."

"By hiding out here?" Her voice rose, laced with frustration. "You think running away will solve anything?"

Nate's eyes darted between us, caught in the crossfire. "Maybe we should take a step back," he suggested, his voice steady yet laced with an undercurrent of discomfort. "This is a private space for Ava and me. It's our escape."

Mara let out a sharp laugh, full of disbelief. "An escape? You think you can just bury your head in the ground and everything will magically resolve itself? That's not how life works, Ava."

I felt the heat rise to my cheeks, a mixture of embarrassment and anger. "I'm not burying my head. I'm trying to figure things out. Isn't that what growing up is about?"

"Figuring things out while also taking care of your family?" she shot back. "You can't just ignore us because you want to play house with your—"

"Play house?" Nate's voice was suddenly louder, sharper. "That's a bit dismissive, don't you think? What we're doing here is real. We're creating something meaningful."

I felt the tension in the air shift as Mara's expression turned wary. She opened her mouth, ready to unleash another round of skepticism, but then hesitated, her resolve faltering. "I didn't come here to fight. I just wanted to check on you. Mom's worried you might be... spiraling."

"Spiraling?" I echoed, incredulous. "What exactly do you think I'm spiraling into? A gnome-centric utopia?"

Nate chuckled, easing the intensity of the moment. "We should definitely consider it. It has potential." His lightheartedness was a balm against the tension, and for a fleeting moment, I felt a surge of gratitude. Yet, I also knew the conversation had shifted into dangerous territory, one where I had to tread carefully.

Mara sighed, her shoulders slumping slightly as she stepped closer, her tone softening. "Ava, please. Just talk to me. You've been so distant lately. You're not the only one who feels the weight of family expectations, you know."

I felt a pang of guilt; my sister always wore her heart on her sleeve, unguarded and earnest. "I didn't mean to shut you out. It's just... hard sometimes. I'm trying to carve out my own path, and it feels like everyone is watching, waiting for me to fail."

Her expression shifted, a mix of sympathy and understanding. "You won't fail, but you can't do it alone. That's not how this works."

Nate shifted again, seemingly caught between wanting to defend my choice of solitude and recognizing the validity of Mara's concerns. "Maybe we should all sit down and talk about this properly," he suggested, his tone diplomatic yet firm. "Ava's been going through a lot, and she's not alone in this."

Mara shot him a glance filled with appreciation, and I felt a rush of warmth towards him, grateful for his support. But as soon as I started to let down my guard, the ground beneath us shifted. I could see the sunlight waning, shadows stretching longer as the atmosphere grew thicker, charged with unresolved tension.

"Look," I said, attempting to reclaim control over the spiraling conversation. "I'm grateful for both of you, really, but I need some

---

space to breathe. Can we just enjoy the garden without the weight of family drama?"

Mara hesitated, her features softening into an expression I recognized—one of regret, but also determination. "I'll give you space, but you have to promise me you won't disappear. Don't make me track you down again."

"I promise," I replied, even as my heart sank at the thought of yet another confrontation looming in the distance.

She nodded, her shoulders relaxing slightly as she turned to leave. "Just remember, Ava, I'm here if you need me." With that, she walked away, leaving the three of us enveloped in the fading light.

The moment she vanished beyond the foliage, Nate turned to me, his expression serious. "Are you okay?"

I exhaled slowly, shaking off the remnants of the confrontation. "Yeah, I just—sometimes it feels like I'm being pulled in two different directions. It's exhausting."

Nate moved closer, brushing his hand against mine, the warmth of his touch grounding me. "I get it. But you don't have to face it all alone, Ava. You have me."

I smiled, grateful yet acutely aware of the storm brewing beneath the surface. Just as I opened my mouth to respond, a rustling sound broke through the tranquility of the garden, causing both of us to freeze.

"What was that?" I whispered, the hairs on my arms standing on end as I glanced around, searching for the source of the disturbance.

Nate's brows furrowed as he scanned the trees surrounding us. "I don't know, but it sounded like it came from over there." He pointed toward a thicket of bushes that looked thicker than they had before, shadows flitting beneath the leaves.

Without thinking, I stood up, an urge to investigate pulling me forward. "Should we check it out?"

Nate hesitated, his instincts clearly cautioning against it. "Maybe we should just—"

But I was already moving, the adrenaline coursing through me, compelling me to find out what lurked just out of sight. "Come on, it could be something interesting!"

As I approached the thicket, a sharp rustle echoed, followed by a low growl that sent a jolt of fear racing through me. My heart hammered in my chest as I turned back to Nate, who looked ready to bolt.

"Okay, maybe this wasn't such a great idea," he muttered, backing away slowly.

Just as I opened my mouth to agree, a figure broke through the underbrush—a flash of fur and eyes gleaming like embers in the fading light. I gasped as a wild animal emerged, not just any creature but a large, unmistakable shape—a coyote, its presence both striking and alarming.

And then, as if drawn by an invisible force, the coyote locked its gaze on me, the intensity of its stare cutting through the air like a blade, leaving me frozen in place.

Chapter 21: The Turning Tide

The hospital room was a kaleidoscope of white and gray, a muted canvas splashed with the occasional pop of color from the flowers cluttering the windowsill. I lay there, tangled in a web of sheets, my body both a stranger and a burden. The incessant beeping of machines and the shuffle of nurses were supposed to be comforting, but they only underscored my isolation. Each day felt like an eternity, the clock ticking with a malicious glee that mocked my inability to escape this clinical prison. I tried to focus on the good days—those fleeting moments when laughter danced in the air, when a gentle smile could chase away the encroaching shadows. But as the days wore on, those memories slipped further away, like grains of sand through my fingers.

It was one of those evenings when I was particularly aware of my fragility, the kind of night that wrapped around me like a heavy blanket, dulling my senses. The antiseptic smell, which once felt like a clean slate, now clung to me with a suffocating intimacy. I felt like a character in a play I never auditioned for, trapped in a role that demanded more courage than I believed I had. Just then, the door creaked open, and in walked Dr. Reynolds, her white coat swirling around her like a ghostly apparition. Her presence commanded the room, and though she was supposed to be a beacon of hope, I could see the weight of her own burdens etched on her brow.

"Ava," she said, her voice steady yet laced with an undertone of caution. "How are you feeling today?"

"Like I just swam the English Channel without a life jacket," I replied, forcing a smile that felt more like a grimace.

She chuckled softly, the kind of laughter that felt like a lifebuoy thrown to a drowning woman. "I wish I could say it gets easier. But you're a fighter, and we're not giving up."

I wanted to believe her, wanted to cling to the notion that I was a warrior battling some mythical beast. But that night, as I lay in bed waiting for sleep to come and steal away my worries, I overheard a conversation that shattered my fragile façade.

The door to my room was slightly ajar, and through the crack, I could see the nurse speaking with Dr. Reynolds in hushed tones. They were discussing me—my condition—an intricate tapestry of medical jargon and ominous undertones woven together in a way that made my heart race with a primal fear. "The clinical trials are our best option, but the odds are..." The nurse's voice trailed off, her expression grave.

I strained to hear more, my breath caught in my throat. The words "experimental treatments" and "slimmer chances" hung in the air like dark clouds ready to unleash a storm. My mind spun with the implications, the weight of their conversation pressing down on me like the oppressive hospital blankets. A chill raced down my spine, and I felt the walls of my room closing in, suffocating me with despair.

The moment stretched into infinity, time slipping through my fingers like a forgotten dream. I closed my eyes tightly, hoping to block out the reality that loomed beyond the door. I could feel fear creeping up my throat, a bitter taste of uncertainty that clung to my tongue. But amidst the rising tide of despair, a spark ignited within me—a familiar ember of defiance.

I reached for my journal, the pages worn and dog-eared from countless entries filled with my innermost thoughts, fears, and dreams. It was a lifeline, a way to reclaim my voice when the world threatened to drown it out. With trembling hands, I opened it to a blank page and began to write, the pen gliding across the paper as if it were a lifeboat navigating turbulent waters.

"Today, I heard whispers that cut deeper than any needle ever could," I scrawled, my handwriting a frantic dance of raw emotion.

"The odds may be against me, but I refuse to bow to fear. I am not just a patient; I am a story still unfolding."

With each word, I felt the weight of hopelessness lifting, replaced by a fierce resolve. I was determined to find joy in the smallest moments, to infuse life into this sterile existence. I remembered the times I had laughed with my friends, the way the sun felt warm against my skin on those rare outings when I could escape the confines of my illness. I wanted to live fiercely, even in the face of uncertainty.

Just then, the door swung open, and my friend Lily burst in, her vibrant energy infusing the room like a breath of fresh air. "Ava! You wouldn't believe what I just found in the gift shop!" She held up a ridiculous-looking stuffed giraffe with a neck that seemed to defy the laws of physics. "It's a guardian of good vibes, obviously."

I couldn't help but laugh, the sound bubbling up like soda fizzing over. "You're right. I'm definitely going to need that."

She placed the giraffe on my bedside table, its goofy smile a stark contrast to the sterile environment. "How's my favorite patient?" she asked, settling into the chair beside me.

I shrugged, unable to fully articulate the whirlwind of emotions swirling within. "Just fighting the good fight, I guess."

She reached for my hand, her grip warm and steady. "You're stronger than you think. We're all rooting for you, Ava. And I won't let you give up. We'll face this together."

In that moment, I realized that I didn't have to carry this burden alone. Hope flickered back to life, igniting a warmth in my chest that had been extinguished. With Lily by my side, I felt the storm begin to recede, just enough for me to breathe. Together, we would navigate this uncharted territory, forging a path toward healing with laughter and love.

The stuffed giraffe became an unintentional mascot of my resilience, sitting atop my bedside table with a goofy grin that somehow managed to lighten the atmosphere. Lily visited every day, turning my sterile room into a sanctuary of laughter and unfiltered conversation. She regaled me with tales of her latest culinary experiments, which invariably ended in culinary disasters that could rival any reality cooking show. "Today, I tried making soufflé," she announced one afternoon, rolling her eyes dramatically. "Let's just say it's no longer the fluffy cloud of deliciousness I envisioned. More like a dense, sad pancake that just lost its will to rise."

I burst out laughing, the sound ringing in the air, a welcome respite from the quiet tension that usually enveloped the room. "Did you at least have the forethought to save the ingredients before you gave up?"

Lily nodded, a mischievous twinkle in her eye. "Oh, I salvaged the chocolate. You can't mess up chocolate, right? I'm calling it 'chocolate pancake surprise.'"

"Honestly, I think you're onto something. They might sell it at hipster cafes."

We spent hours like that, weaving together a tapestry of stories filled with inside jokes and shared memories, while I clung to the comfort of our friendship like a lifeline. Each laugh felt like an antidote to the whispers of despair that crept in whenever I was alone with my thoughts. But even amidst the laughter, there was an undercurrent of tension that I couldn't shake. I often found myself staring out of the window at the bustling city below, the world moving at a dizzying pace, while I was confined within these four walls.

One evening, as twilight draped its soft embrace over the city, Lily pulled out a small bag from her purse. "Okay, I've got something special," she said, her voice conspiratorial.

I leaned forward, intrigued. "What is it? A snack? A magic trick?"

"Better!" She produced a tiny potted plant, its vibrant green leaves reaching eagerly toward the ceiling. "It's a bonsai tree! I thought you could use a little life in here."

"Isn't that kind of like bringing sand to the beach? I'm already drowning in life, even if it's mostly fluorescent lights and a sad excuse for a view."

She rolled her eyes, a smile tugging at her lips. "Exactly! It's a reminder that even the smallest things can thrive in less-than-ideal conditions. Just like you."

I took the bonsai into my hands, feeling its delicate trunk between my fingers. "You might be onto something," I said, my voice softening as I examined the tiny leaves. "This little guy is kind of like us. It's tiny, it's weirdly beautiful, and it's probably been through some serious storms."

"That's the spirit! Plus, if it survives my cooking experiments, it can survive anything."

As the days blurred into one another, the hospital began to feel less like a prison and more like a peculiar sanctuary. I started to find joy in the simplest moments—Lily's laughter echoing in the sterile hallways, the quiet dignity of the nurses who treated me with a grace that felt like a warm hug, and the soft rustle of the bonsai leaves as I gently tended to it. Each day, I watered it, and it seemed to flourish, almost as if it was rooting for me from its little pot.

But there were still moments of darkness that crept in, uninvited and insidious. Late at night, when the world was silent and my thoughts roamed free, the weight of uncertainty pressed down like a thick fog. I would clutch my journal, pouring my fears onto the pages in jagged handwriting, the ink pooling with anxiety and hope in equal measure. It became a ritual—my midnight confessions to the universe, a plea for strength amid the chaos.

One night, as I scribbled furiously, the door swung open, and in walked Dr. Reynolds, her expression unusually somber. I felt my heart skip a beat; her presence had always brought reassurance, but tonight, it felt like the air had shifted. "Ava, can we talk?" she said, the warmth in her voice replaced with an edge of seriousness.

I set down my pen, anxiety coiling in my stomach. "Sure, what's up?"

"We have some updates on your treatment plan. I want to make sure you're fully informed about the next steps."

"Next steps?" I echoed, feeling a tightening in my chest.

She pulled a chair closer, her gaze steady. "We're ready to start the clinical trials we discussed. There's a lot of promising research, and while the risks are significant, the potential benefits could be life-changing."

"Life-changing sounds great. But risks?" I asked, a tremor in my voice. "What kind of risks are we talking about here?"

Dr. Reynolds took a deep breath, her eyes searching mine. "Some patients have experienced severe side effects. I need you to consider this carefully. It's not a decision to be taken lightly."

The weight of her words sank into my bones. "So it's either embrace the trial or risk what? A fate worse than this?" I gestured vaguely to the sterile room around me.

"It's not about choosing between two evils, Ava. It's about seizing an opportunity to fight back. But you have to be honest with yourself about how far you're willing to go."

Silence enveloped us, thick and suffocating. I could feel the walls closing in, my mind racing with possibilities. "What if I don't want to fight anymore?" I whispered, my voice barely audible.

Dr. Reynolds reached across the table, her hand warm against mine. "Then we'll find another way. But I believe you have the strength to keep going. And I'm here to support you, no matter what."

As she spoke, the honesty in her gaze ignited something within me—a flicker of defiance mixed with a cautious hope. I didn't have all the answers, and I was terrified of the unknown that lay ahead, but there was also a fire within me that refused to be extinguished. With a deep breath, I straightened in my chair, determination mingling with my uncertainty. "Let's do it," I said, the words pouring out before I could second-guess myself. "Let's fight."

The resolve in my voice felt like a lifeline, a beacon cutting through the fog of despair. As I stared into Dr. Reynolds' eyes, I knew I was ready to embrace whatever came next, even if it meant navigating the treacherous waters ahead. With the support of my friends and the promise of new beginnings, I felt a sense of power returning, as if I had finally taken the first step toward reclaiming my story.

The decision to join the clinical trials hung in the air like the scent of antiseptic, thick and undeniable. After Dr. Reynolds left, I sank back into my pillow, the weight of choice pressing down on me as I stared at the ceiling. A ceiling that had become far too familiar, adorned with a haze of fluorescent lights flickering like the uncertainty within me. My mind raced with what-ifs and maybes, each thought echoing in the hollow space of my room.

Lily returned the next day, her energy as bright as ever, and I knew I had to share my news. She flopped down onto the chair, plucking the stuffed giraffe from its perch. "Guess what? I brought reinforcements!" she declared, producing a small, plush cactus this time. "This one is for you to poke at when things get prickly. We all need a little thorny encouragement, right?"

I chuckled, but there was a tension coiling in my gut. "I have something to tell you," I said, biting my lip, weighing how to drop this bombshell.

"Oh no. You're not pregnant, are you?" she gasped, eyes wide, fingers clutching the cactus as if it were a shield.

"No, no! I'm not even dating anyone!" I laughed, shaking my head. "It's about the clinical trials."

Lily put the cactus down, her expression shifting from playful to serious in an instant. "You're doing it, aren't you?"

"I am," I confirmed, my voice trembling slightly. "I told Dr. Reynolds I'm in."

Her gaze softened, and she reached for my hand. "Ava, that's huge. You're so brave."

"Or utterly insane," I replied, a wry smile curving my lips. "I'm not sure which yet."

"Either way, you're facing this head-on, and that's more than I'd ever do in your shoes. If I were in that room, I'd be curled up in the corner, begging for ice cream and Netflix."

I grinned at the visual. "It's not all heroic. I have my moments of doubt. Just last night, I wrote in my journal about how scared I am of what might happen."

"Writing is good," she said. "It's your way of processing. You're like one of those old-timey cowboys, journaling about your heroic adventures while simultaneously freaking out about the wild west of your own mind."

"Right? And the cactus is my trusty steed!"

As the laughter subsided, the weight of reality pressed back in. "What if I don't make it through the trial?" I murmured, the vulnerability slipping through the cracks in my bravado.

"Then we'll figure it out together. You have me, okay? And if that means I have to sit through another one of your weird hospital meals just to keep you company, so be it."

The laughter returned, and with it, a flicker of hope. We spent the rest of the afternoon plotting out the new reality of my treatment. We decorated the bonsai tree with tiny ribbons I'd saved from various holidays, turning it into a symbol of resilience and friendship. Each knot in the ribbon felt like a promise, tying us together even in the darkest moments.

The following morning, I was prepped for the trial. The nurses were cheerful yet efficient, bustling around as if they were on a mission to execute a flawless heist. I lay on the hospital bed, the crisp sheets cold against my skin. Just before the doctor arrived, I felt a surge of anxiety, the kind that grips your heart and squeezes. I couldn't help but glance at the door, wondering if escape was a possibility. But then I thought of Lily, of the cactus, of the bonfire of laughter we had lit in this place. I inhaled deeply, reminding myself of the courage buried beneath the layers of fear.

When Dr. Reynolds entered, she had the reassuring demeanor of a coach preparing her team for the championship game. "Today is a new beginning, Ava," she said, her voice calm and steady. "This is your chance to take control of your journey."

With that, they rolled me into the treatment room, a sterile space filled with shiny machines that hummed with life. I couldn't help but think of them as a sci-fi movie set, each device a character in a story that I was about to become a part of.

"Just relax, and we'll get started shortly," a nurse said, adjusting the IV line that snaked into my arm. "You're doing great."

I focused on the ceiling tiles, counting them as if they held the answers to life's greatest mysteries. One, two, three—each one a moment closer to the unknown I was bravely stepping into. Then came the first dose, a cocktail of hope and fear coursing through my veins, and I felt the familiar tickle of anxiety bubbling up again.

The nurse glanced at me, a kind smile on her face. "It's normal to feel a little uneasy. Just breathe."

As I focused on my breath, the atmosphere in the room shifted, growing heavier as if charged with a looming storm. Suddenly, I heard an alarm blaring, piercing through the steady beeping of the machines. My heart raced.

"Is that—?" I stammered, fear lacing my voice.

The nurse sprang into action, her demeanor shifting from calm to alert. "Stay calm, Ava. Just a precaution."

I wanted to believe her, but the tension in the room felt palpable. The door swung open, and Dr. Reynolds rushed in, her expression serious, cutting through the levity of the moment like a knife through butter.

"Dr. Reynolds, what's happening?" I asked, my voice shaking.

"Something's come up with the trial. We need to monitor your vitals closely."

Panic surged through me, and I gripped the edges of the bed, feeling the cool steel beneath my fingertips. "What do you mean? Is there a problem with the treatment?"

Dr. Reynolds exchanged a glance with the nurse, and I could see the wheels turning in her head. "It's too soon to say, but we have to be thorough. Let's focus on your vitals for now."

I watched as she and the nurse began adjusting the equipment, and my heart thudded loudly in my chest, a drumbeat of dread and uncertainty. In that moment, as I lay there, fear clenching my gut, I felt a wave of clarity wash over me.

Whatever lay ahead—whether it was triumph or tragedy—I had decided to fight. But the storm brewing outside, the uncertainty swirling around me, felt insurmountable. The machines beeped louder, a chaotic symphony, and I wondered if I was still the one holding the reins to my story, or if I was spiraling into a plot twist I had not anticipated.

Chapter 22: Love in the Shadows

The hospital's sterile scent hung thick in the air, mingling with the distant sounds of beeping machines and hushed conversations that drifted through the hallways like ghosts of unspoken fears. It was one of those nights when the world outside felt light-years away, a vibrant cosmos that seemed indifferent to the somber reality we inhabited. Nate and I huddled together in the common area, a small alcove dimly lit by flickering fluorescent bulbs that buzzed intermittently, casting jittery shadows on the pale walls. The blanket we wrapped around ourselves felt like a flimsy fortress against the harshness of our surroundings, a reminder that warmth could be found even in the coldest of places.

Nate's sketchbook rested on his lap, a canvas of emotions just waiting to spill over. He flipped through the pages, revealing intricate lines and playful sketches that danced with life. Each stroke of his pencil was like a breath of fresh air, momentarily pushing away the weight of the world pressing down on us. I could see the concentration in his furrowed brow, the way his fingers danced with familiarity over the pages, as if they were crafting not just art but the very essence of our shared dreams.

"Tell me about it," he urged, glancing up with those deep-set eyes that sparkled with a mix of mischief and sincerity. It was a look that could melt the ice surrounding my heart, even in the darkest of moments. "Where do you want to go?"

I took a deep breath, inhaling the sharp antiseptic tang of the air mixed with the faint aroma of coffee brewing somewhere in the depths of the hospital. "The coast," I replied, letting the word roll off my tongue like a wave lapping at the shore. "Somewhere where the sun kisses the sea, and the sand is warm beneath my feet. I want to feel that salty breeze against my skin, you know? It's like...freedom."

He nodded, his pencil poised in the air as he listened intently. "Describe it to me," he said, a playful challenge in his tone. "Paint me a picture."

I closed my eyes, conjuring the vibrant images I longed to share with him. "Picture this," I began, my voice a gentle whisper against the backdrop of the hospital's hum. "We're standing on a cliff, overlooking the vast ocean. The sky is painted in shades of orange and pink, the sun dipping below the horizon like it's slipping into a warm bath. The waves crash against the rocks, each splash a jubilant dance, and we can taste the salt in the air, sweet and bracing."

As I spoke, Nate's pencil moved rapidly, sketching the scene as if he were etching the very essence of my dreams onto the paper. "And what about the sand?" he prompted, grinning at my enthusiasm.

"The sand," I continued, my heart racing with the thrill of imagination, "is like golden sugar, warm and inviting. I want to run my toes through it, feel it slip between my fingers, and build sandcastles that reach for the sky." I paused, allowing myself to bask in the warmth of the moment, the flickering lights casting a cozy glow around us. "I want to feel alive."

He looked up from his sketchbook, his expression softening. "And you will," he said, a certainty in his voice that pulled at my heartstrings. "We'll go. I promise. Just you and me, a road trip with the windows down and our favorite songs blasting. We'll stop at every quirky diner along the way, collecting memories like souvenirs."

The idea of it set my soul alight, an ember of hope flickering in the darkness that had been closing in on us for too long. "We could even get matching tattoos," I suggested, teasingly nudging him with my shoulder. "A tiny wave for me, and maybe a...what would you choose?"

He pondered for a moment, a grin slowly spreading across his face. "A lighthouse, guiding me through the stormy seas of life. It's a symbol of hope, right?"

"Or just a reminder that you need to be careful not to crash into the rocks," I countered, laughter bubbling up between us, dispelling the heavy shadows. "You always were a bit of a klutz."

"Guilty as charged," he said, his eyes twinkling with mischief. "But I'd rather crash into rocks with you than sail smoothly alone."

In that instant, the walls of the hospital seemed to fade away, replaced by the endless horizon of our dreams. We shared stories that intertwined like threads in a tapestry, each word building the world we both craved. I could almost hear the waves crashing against the shore, the laughter of strangers mingling with the salty air as we wove our fantasies into reality.

Yet, just as quickly as the warmth enveloped us, a shadow flickered in the corner of my mind. I could feel the uncertainty creeping back in, that gnawing fear that threatened to unravel the fragile tapestry we had begun to weave. Our laughter dimmed slightly, the lightness of the moment marred by the knowledge that time was a cruel thief, silently stealing moments away.

"What if..." I hesitated, the weight of the question heavy on my tongue. "What if we don't have that chance? What if—"

"Hey," Nate interrupted, his voice steady, grounding me like an anchor amidst a tempest. "Don't go there. Not tonight. Let's keep building our world, one dream at a time. We can tackle the shadows when they come, but for now, let's create our light."

His words wrapped around me like a comforting embrace, and I nodded, the flickering hope igniting once more. The shadows would linger, but in this moment, beneath the blanket fort we'd constructed against the world, we were safe. Together, we were invincible, two souls adrift yet intertwined, navigating the stormy seas of uncertainty with the promise of brighter days ahead.

The next evening, the air in the hospital was heavier than before, thick with an almost tangible tension that wrapped around us like a suffocating fog. The fluorescent lights flickered more insistently, their buzzing a reminder of our isolation. Nate and I found ourselves once again nestled together in our little corner, the familiar blanket cocooning us in a warm embrace that defied the chill of the clinical environment. He had a newfound determination in his eyes, an energy that seemed to pulse between us like an electric current.

"Okay, Ava," he said, his voice low but firm, as he flipped to a fresh page in his sketchbook. "Tonight, we're going to do this differently. I want you to really dig deep and tell me what your ideal adventure looks like. No filters."

I raised an eyebrow, intrigued. "You want the unfiltered version? That could get messy. You sure you can handle it?"

"Bring it on," he replied, grinning as he settled back, pencil poised and ready to capture the chaos that was my imagination. "I've seen worse. Remember the time you tried to cook that spaghetti? I'm still recovering from the trauma."

"Hey! The smoke alarm is still my greatest achievement in cooking," I shot back, laughing as I remembered the kitchen disaster, smoke billowing and pots clattering. "But fine, if you want the raw, unfiltered version of my wildest dream, here goes."

I closed my eyes again, taking a deep breath to summon the wildest corners of my imagination. "Picture this: A sprawling forest, thick with trees that stretch up to the sky, their leaves whispering secrets as the wind flows through. We're hiking, backpacks slung over our shoulders, laughter echoing through the woods. Sunlight filters through the canopy, dappling the ground with patches of gold, and there's this feeling, you know? Like we're the only two people in the world."

Nate's pencil flew across the page, capturing the essence of my words with surprising speed. "And then what?" he prompted, his eyes gleaming with excitement.

"And then," I continued, my voice gaining momentum, "we stumble upon a hidden waterfall, cascading down smooth stones into a crystal-clear pool. The water is so inviting that we can't resist. We dive in, laughter ringing out as we splash each other, and for a moment, it's just us, the water, and the sound of nature all around." I paused, imagining the sensation of cool water enveloping us, washing away our worries.

Nate glanced up, a smirk playing on his lips. "I'm guessing you have your swimsuit packed for this adventure?"

"Of course! You can't be unprepared for spontaneous waterfall encounters," I replied, waggling my eyebrows in mock seriousness. "That's just basic survival skills. What about you? What's your version of a wild adventure?"

He scratched his chin thoughtfully, eyes narrowed in concentration. "I'd probably have to say something along the lines of a cross-country road trip," he mused, a hint of mischief in his voice. "Picture it: a van filled with all the snacks we can carry, your playlist blasting from the speakers, and a map full of quirky roadside attractions. Maybe we even pick up a stray dog along the way."

"A stray dog?" I chuckled, shaking my head. "Are you sure that's wise? They can be a lot of work."

"Yeah, but think of the stories! The dog could be our sidekick," he argued, leaning forward with excitement. "Imagine us getting into wild adventures, like fighting off a band of squirrels that try to steal our lunch. Or... getting chased by a goat at a petting zoo because you thought it looked 'friendly.'"

"You're terrible!" I exclaimed, laughter spilling from my lips. "But also, kind of brilliant. I can see it now—Ava and Nate: The Adventures of the Snack Bandit and the Goat Whisperer."

"Exactly! We could have our own reality show. I'd be the star, obviously," he quipped, puffing out his chest dramatically.

"Star? More like comic relief!" I shot back, eyes sparkling with mischief. "But I'd totally be your number one fan. Just as long as I'm not the one trying to negotiate with goats."

A comfortable silence fell between us, punctuated only by the rhythmic scratching of Nate's pencil on paper. The world outside continued its relentless pulse, a cacophony of life going on as usual, while we forged our own reality within the cocoon of our shared dreams.

But as the laughter faded, an unspoken heaviness crept back in, tugging at the corners of my mind. The promise of adventure felt bittersweet when paired with the uncertainty that loomed over us. I could see it in Nate's eyes, too—the flicker of fear that tried to make itself at home amidst our lighthearted banter.

"Do you ever think about what happens next?" I asked, the question hanging in the air between us, thick with the weight of possibility.

He paused, pencil hovering above the page as he searched my gaze. "You mean after the adventures?" he asked cautiously, as if testing the waters. "Like what if we actually got to do all those things we dream about?"

"Yeah. What if we do? But what if we don't?" I could feel my heart racing, the tightness in my chest growing. "What if we get stuck here? What if—"

"Ava," he interrupted, his voice steady and strong. "You can't think like that. We're going to do all of it. I don't care how long it takes; we'll find a way. I refuse to let this place define us or our dreams."

His conviction was a balm, soothing the anxiety that had begun to swell within me. "And besides," he added with a wry smile, "if we get stuck here, I'll just start a sketching revolution. You can be my muse, and I'll draw our adventures in vivid detail until we're too famous for this hospital."

"Famous for hospital doodles?" I laughed, feeling the tension lift slightly. "Now that's a niche market."

"Hey, don't knock it until you've tried it," he replied with mock seriousness, before his expression softened. "We'll find our way back to the world out there, I promise. Just keep dreaming, and I'll keep drawing."

And in that moment, as the shadows danced around us, I realized that love—our love—was more than just the spaces we filled with dreams. It was the way we dared to confront the unknown together, weaving a tapestry of laughter and light amidst the uncertainties. We were building our own reality, one sketch and one whispered dream at a time.

As the evening wore on, the faint hum of hospital activity began to lull into an eerie quiet, the only sound punctuating our bubble being the sporadic beeping of a nearby monitor. I glanced at Nate, whose concentration had shifted to the sketchbook resting in his lap. He was lost in thought, his brow furrowed, and I wondered if he, too, felt the creeping weight of uncertainty pressing against the edges of our whimsical adventure.

"Nate," I said softly, breaking the stillness, "what's the most ridiculous thing we could do if we really let our imaginations run wild? I mean, no rules. Just pure chaos."

His eyes lit up, and a grin spread across his face like the dawn breaking over a darkened sky. "Oh, I love where this is going. How about we steal a boat and sail off into the sunset? Just you, me, and an overabundance of snacks. We could be pirates, but instead of plundering, we'd be hoarding gummy bears."

"Pirates of the Sugar Sea?" I laughed, leaning into him, reveling in the absurdity of the moment. "I'm on board! But we'd have to have some sort of treasure map, right? A guide to the best candy stores along the coast!"

"Exactly!" He took my suggestion to heart, sketching furiously as he articulated our imaginary heist. "We could chart a course from one candy store to another, risking it all for gummy bears, chocolate bars, and, of course, those ridiculously sour lemon drops that make your cheeks pucker."

"Oh, the ones that make you cry a little?" I teased, my heart fluttering at the sight of his enthusiasm. "Now that's what adventure is all about! The danger of dental disasters and the thrill of sticky fingers!"

The warmth between us swelled as we bounced ideas off one another, each sillier than the last. We conjured wild scenarios involving gummy bear treasure chests, elaborate escapes from sugar-hating authorities, and an imaginary crew of stuffed animals standing at attention on the deck, ready to defend our stash at all costs. Laughter filled the air, a sweet antidote to the darkness that loomed outside our little sanctuary.

But then, just as quickly as the joy surged, a shadow flickered across Nate's expression. His laughter faded, and a seriousness settled in its place, transforming our playful banter into something more fragile. "You know," he said slowly, the humor in his voice replaced by an edge of uncertainty, "the truth is, we might have to be pirates in real life sooner than we think."

"What do you mean?" I asked, my heart stuttering as the weight of his words hung heavily between us.

He hesitated, searching for the right way to express what was swirling in his mind. "I mean...if things don't turn around, we might have to steal our happiness, Ava. Make a break for it. Take the adventures we talk about seriously. Escape while we still can."

I felt a coldness creep into my veins as the implications of his words settled in. "You're talking about leaving the hospital? What about—"

"What about what?" he interjected, his voice rising slightly. "The doctors? The treatments? They can't guarantee anything, and sitting here waiting for a miracle feels like a slow death. I don't want to spend what little time we have left trapped in these walls. I want to live, even if it's just for a little while."

The vulnerability in his tone struck a chord deep within me. "You're right," I said, my heart racing at the thought. "We've talked about all these things we want to do, but what if we don't have time? What if—"

"Ava," he interrupted, reaching for my hand, his grip firm and reassuring. "Let's not waste another moment. Let's plan something outrageous. Something we'll never forget. Let's steal that boat of dreams and sail until we can't anymore."

The idea ignited a fire within me, but a flicker of doubt remained. "And what if we get caught? What if we're not ready?"

"We won't get caught, and we'll figure it out as we go," he said, his voice laced with determination. "But we can't let fear keep us from living. It's time we write our own adventure, even if it's just for a night."

A thrill coursed through my veins as the possibilities danced before my eyes. I could almost feel the cool breeze of the ocean against my skin, the rush of freedom tingling in my fingertips. The world beyond the hospital's sterile walls was calling to me, whispering promises of laughter and joy, and I knew I couldn't ignore it any longer. "Okay, let's do it," I said, my voice steady. "Let's plan the most ridiculous escape the world has ever seen."

His face broke into a smile, and for a moment, the darkness receded, leaving us basking in the light of our shared resolve. We spent the next few hours feverishly crafting our escape plan, scribbling notes and making lists of everything we would need: a getaway car, snacks galore, a map of the coast, and maybe even a pirate flag to fly above our imaginary ship.

Suddenly, the door swung open, the harsh fluorescent lights spilling into our little haven. A nurse stepped in, her expression unreadable. "Ava," she said, her tone clipped and professional, "we need to talk."

My stomach dropped, the excitement of our plans slipping through my fingers like sand. Nate's grip on my hand tightened, and I could feel the tension radiating from him. "What's wrong?" he asked, his voice suddenly serious, the spark of joy dimmed by the gravity of the moment.

The nurse shifted uncomfortably, glancing between us as if she were weighing her words. "It's about your latest test results."

Panic rose in my chest, choking the breath from my lungs. "What do you mean?" I managed to stammer, feeling the world tilt beneath me.

"There are... some concerning developments. We need to discuss the next steps."

In an instant, the vivid colors of our dreams dimmed, replaced by the stark reality of the hospital room. The walls felt like they were closing in around us, and I could see the shadows creeping back into Nate's eyes, threatening to swallow the light we had created.

As the nurse continued speaking, her words faded into a blur, drowned out by the pounding of my heart. I exchanged a glance with Nate, his expression a mixture of fear and determination. It was a look that said we were far from finished, that our adventure was just beginning, and somehow, I knew this was only the beginning of something we could never have anticipated.

But as the nurse's voice broke through the haze, delivering news that would change everything, I realized that our escape plan was no longer a fantasy. It was our only chance to seize whatever time we had left and turn it into the adventure we desperately craved.

Chapter 23: The Reckoning

The sterile smell of antiseptic permeated the air, mingling with the faint hint of lavender from the tiny sachet I had hidden under my pillow. I lay in the hospital bed, a thin white sheet draped over me, barely concealing the myriad of bruises that danced across my skin like a chaotic watercolor painting. Outside my window, the world continued its relentless motion, oblivious to the war that had raged within these four walls. I turned my gaze toward the door, my heart racing with anticipation and a hint of dread. Today was the day I would finally confront him.

When my father stepped inside, the light seemed to shift, casting long shadows that danced against the walls like specters of the past. Mark Davidson, a man whose very presence had always been imbued with a mix of authority and a peculiar distance, looked at me with eyes that flickered with something I had seldom seen: uncertainty. His normally impeccable appearance was slightly disheveled; the collar of his crisp shirt was wrinkled, and his usually slicked-back hair had a few rebellious strands escaping the confines of his control. For a fleeting moment, I wanted to reach out and smooth them down, to remind him of the father I once knew before the emotional barricades went up.

"Ava," he said, his voice low and gravelly, as if each syllable was coated with the dust of unspoken words. He took a tentative step forward, his hands shoved deep into the pockets of his trousers, a stance that screamed both vulnerability and reluctance. "How are you feeling?"

I swallowed hard, the weight of everything unsaid hanging between us like a thick fog. "You know, just peachy. Living the dream," I replied, injecting a wry humor into my words, though the irony felt bitter on my tongue. "Can we skip the small talk? I'm not in the mood for pleasantries."

He blinked, the surprise evident on his face. Perhaps he had expected the usual façade—the dutiful daughter ready to forgive, to acquiesce to his emotional unavailability. But I was done playing that role. I was tired of the ghost he had become in my life, the father who had retreated behind walls of silence as if I were a fragile vase that could shatter at the slightest touch.

"Ava, I—" he began, but I cut him off, urgency flooding my voice.

"No, Dad. I need you to listen. Why have you been absent all these years? It's like you've chosen to be a ghost in my life, haunting me from a distance but never truly showing up." My heart pounded in my chest, a steady rhythm of courage. "Was it easier to pretend I didn't exist than to confront what happened? Because let me tell you, that hurt more than anything you might have faced."

The air grew heavy, the silence wrapping around us like an oppressive blanket. I watched as his defenses wavered, the practiced stoicism giving way to something more raw and real. He ran a hand through his hair, a sign of agitation I had come to recognize. "It wasn't about you," he said, his voice barely above a whisper. "It was about me—about how afraid I was of losing you. The thought of it... it paralyzed me."

His admission struck me like a blow, reverberating through the emotional landscape I had spent years navigating. "So you thought disappearing was the answer?" I challenged, my voice laced with disbelief. "You left me to deal with everything alone. Your absence became the backdrop to my entire childhood, and now you stand here, expecting me to understand?"

"I thought I was protecting you," he confessed, his gaze dropping to the floor as if the weight of his own words had become too much to bear. "If I wasn't there, maybe the pain would be less for both of us. I thought I could find a way to cope without seeing you suffer."

"By pretending I didn't exist?" I countered, my voice shaking with the force of my emotion. "I needed you, Dad. I needed you to show up, to acknowledge the pain we were both feeling instead of burying it beneath silence. You don't get to play the martyr now."

He finally met my gaze, his expression a mosaic of regret and longing, the fissures in his facade revealing glimpses of the man he once was. "I know. I know I failed you. And I don't expect forgiveness; I just wanted... I wanted to be strong for you. But I realize now that strength isn't about avoidance. It's about facing our fears, together."

The honesty in his words cut through the lingering tension, igniting a spark of something I hadn't felt in years—hope. It was a fragile thing, like a newborn bird daring to unfurl its wings for the first time, but it was there, nestled in the corners of my heart. "Then let's face it, together," I said, my voice steadier now, infused with a newfound determination. "Let's start with the truth."

For the first time, the walls began to crack, and the ghost I had resented for so long stepped forward, vulnerable and human. The sterile room transformed as we peeled back layers of pain and misunderstanding, the hospital's fluorescent lights illuminating our raw emotions. What began as a confrontation shifted into a tentative reconciliation, the air buzzing with the electric tension of two people who had been lost but were now finding their way back to each other.

It was terrifying and exhilarating all at once. I wanted to cling to that feeling, to weave it into the fabric of our lives, even as we acknowledged the long road ahead. In that moment, as we shared our truths, the weight of the past began to lift, making space for something new—something that felt like healing. And in the quiet that followed, I dared to believe that perhaps, just perhaps, we could learn to navigate this world together again.

The air in the room was thick with the remnants of our exchange, the electric tension weaving through the sterile environment, tangling with the rhythmic beeping of machines that monitored my every breath. I could feel the tentative threads of connection forming between us, but the weight of our shared history still hung heavily in the air, threatening to pull us back into the shadows.

As we sat in silence, I studied my father's face, a landscape of lines and creases that told stories of regrets and choices made in the dark. The way his brow furrowed, as if each thought was a stone that weighed him down, stirred something inside me—a strange mix of empathy and frustration. I wanted to shake him, to ask why he hadn't chosen differently. "Dad, you're here now. Why did it take me getting hurt for you to realize you needed to be present?" I asked, my tone sharp but tinged with the softness of vulnerability.

His eyes flickered, and for a moment, I thought I saw a hint of anger flash across his features, but it was gone as quickly as it appeared. "I don't know, Ava. I've spent so long trying to protect myself that I forgot what it meant to be there for you. I thought if I stayed away, it would hurt less. But every moment I was absent, it hurt more."

"So you chose to be a spectator in my life?" I shot back, crossing my arms defiantly over my chest. "That's a hell of a way to protect someone."

Mark sighed, a deep sound that resonated with defeat, and ran a hand through his hair again, as if trying to comb through the mess of our past. "I know it sounds terrible, but I thought if I could avoid facing you and your pain, I could somehow shield myself from my own. I was wrong, obviously." He paused, looking directly at me, his gaze steady and intense. "I don't expect you to forgive me, but I need you to understand that it wasn't about you. It was all about my fear."

"Fear? You think your fear excuses your absence?" My voice was growing louder, fueled by a mix of indignation and hurt. "Do you know what it felt like growing up without you? Watching other kids with their fathers while I sat alone in my room, wondering what I did wrong?" Each word came out sharper than the last, a jagged edge that cut through the air.

"I didn't want to put that burden on you," he replied, his voice trembling slightly. "I didn't want you to see how broken I was."

"Too late for that." I leaned back against the pillows, frustration bubbling within me like a soda can shaken too hard. "You're not the only one who feels broken, Dad. I've been piecing myself together for years, and your absence was the biggest crack in my foundation."

A beat passed, the gravity of my words hanging heavily between us. Mark looked at me, his expression shifting as if he were finally starting to understand the true impact of his choices. "Then let's work on this together. I don't want to be a ghost anymore. I want to be your father." His words were earnest, but there was a lingering question in his eyes, as if he wondered whether it was even possible to bridge the chasm that had grown between us.

"Prove it," I challenged, my voice steady, even as my heart raced. "I need to see that you mean it. Words are just words unless there's action behind them."

He nodded slowly, the weight of my challenge settling in. "What do you need from me?"

"Start by not treating me like a glass doll. I'm not fragile. I'm not your little girl anymore." I leaned forward, a spark igniting within me. "I'm a survivor, and I'm tired of being treated like I'm broken. If you want to be my father, then show me how to stand tall instead of hovering over me like a shadow."

A silence fell again, but this one felt different. It was charged, alive with the possibility of change. I could see the gears turning in his mind, the recognition dawning that we were both capable of more than we'd ever allowed ourselves to believe.

"Alright," he said finally, a hint of determination coloring his tone. "What's next, then?"

I grinned, a rush of adrenaline flooding my system. "First, let's ditch the hospital food. I need a burger. I need fries. I need anything that doesn't taste like cardboard."

He chuckled, the sound echoing through the room like a breath of fresh air, and for the first time in what felt like ages, I saw a glimmer of the man I had longed to connect with. "You're serious?"

"Absolutely. If we're going to make this work, I need comfort food. Plus, I think the nurses would appreciate the break from my hospital drama. No more deep emotional conversations until after lunch."

Mark laughed again, this time with a lightness that hadn't been present before. "Alright, one burger and fries, coming right up. But you're stuck with me until we finish this conversation, deal?"

"Deal," I replied, the word tumbling from my lips with a sense of liberation.

As he stepped out of the room, a rush of warmth filled the space where despair had lingered moments ago. I allowed myself a moment to breathe, letting hope unfurl within me like a blooming flower. There was still a long road ahead, a complex web of emotions and memories to untangle, but at least we were finally taking the first steps together.

When he returned with a tray laden with food, the aroma filled the room, competing with the sterile scent that had been my constant companion. He set it down on the small table beside my bed, and we both dove into the meal, the air between us no longer heavy with unspoken words but vibrant with laughter and shared stories.

"Remember that time I tried to make pancakes, and you ended up covered in flour?" he asked, a smile breaking across his face.

"How could I forget? You looked like a baking yeti," I replied, laughter spilling from my lips as I recalled the chaos of that morning.

"Hey, it's all about the effort," he shot back, his eyes sparkling with mischief.

We shared more than just food; we shared memories that served as lifelines to a past that had felt so distant. With each laugh, with each bite, the cracks in our relationship began to fill, and I realized that perhaps forgiveness was not a destination but a journey we could navigate together, one meal at a time.

With the warmth of shared laughter still lingering in the air, the tension that had once suffocated our conversations felt like a distant memory. Each bite of the greasy burger had reignited something deep within me, a flicker of hope that, while delicate, was beginning to burn brighter. My father had surprised me—he was more than just the sum of his past mistakes. He was here, present, ready to build something new out of the rubble of our shared history.

"So, I was thinking," he said, chewing thoughtfully, his eyes narrowing with concentration, "what if we made a list? You know, a list of all the things you want to do while you're recovering. Things you've wanted to do with me that I've... well, avoided."

"A list? Like a bucket list?" I raised an eyebrow, half-amused and half-skeptical. "You know I'm not dying, right?"

He held up a hand, a playful smile on his lips. "No, not a bucket list. More like a 'let's-get-our-act-together' list. You can even pick the first thing on it, like a royal decree."

"Okay, King Dad," I smirked, my heart swelling with unexpected affection. "In that case, I decree that we go skydiving."

He blinked at me, his mouth frozen in mid-chew as if I'd just suggested we wrestle a bear. "Skydiving? Isn't that a bit extreme for someone who's just come out of the hospital?"

I laughed, the sound bursting out of me like the soda I had once shaken too vigorously. "It's either that or we spend the afternoon watching old reruns of The Golden Girls. And honestly? I think I'd rather dive from a plane."

"Touché." He put down his burger, clearly wrestling with the image of his daughter hurling herself from a plane. "How about something a little less... death-defying? Maybe a hike? Or a trip to that weird museum with all the taxidermied animals?"

"Now we're talking!" I said, a grin spreading across my face. "I could definitely get behind a road trip. Taxidermied animals and questionable roadside diners—it's practically the definition of adventure."

Mark leaned back, his expression softening, revealing the fatherly instincts I had thought were long buried. "Alright then, we'll plan that. A father-daughter adventure, no more ghosts."

The moment felt profound, the weight of years of silence lifting ever so slightly. We finished our meal amidst an array of silly stories and shared laughter, creating a tapestry of connection that I hadn't realized we were missing until now. Each recollection wove us closer, drawing back the layers of our past.

But just as we began to settle into this newfound ease, my phone buzzed insistently on the bedside table, shattering the fragile bubble of our moment. I reached for it, glancing at the screen, and my heart dropped. It was a text from my best friend, Sophie.

I need you to call me. Now. It's about Alex.

The mention of Alex sent a chill racing through me. My pulse quickened as I looked up at Mark, who was still absorbed in the remnants of his meal. "Uh, I need to take this," I said, my voice unsteady as I slid out of bed, the IV stand rattling ominously beside me.

"Everything okay?" he asked, concern etching his features.

"I don't know," I admitted, the weight of uncertainty heavy on my chest. I stepped into the bathroom for a moment of privacy, shutting the door behind me and leaning against the cool tile wall, my heart pounding.

"Please tell me you're not dying or something," Sophie said as soon as I answered, her voice laced with urgency.

"What happened? Is Alex okay?" I asked, dread pooling in my stomach like cold lead.

"I don't know how to say this..." She paused, and I could practically hear her biting her lip through the phone. "He's been acting strange, Ava. He's been pulling away, and today... today he didn't show up for practice. When I went to check on him, I found him... with someone."

A wave of nausea washed over me, my thoughts spiraling into a whirlpool of confusion and pain. "With someone? Like a date?"

"No, not like that." Sophie's voice cracked, and I could feel the tension radiating through the line. "It was worse. He was with a girl I know from school—the one who... you know, the one you've always had a weird vibe with. They were together, and it didn't look friendly."

"Why didn't you just tell me?" My voice was low, a mix of anger and disbelief.

"Because I didn't want to hurt you. But I thought you should know, especially since you just got out of the hospital. I don't want you to be blindsided."

I squeezed my eyes shut, my chest tightening. "I need to talk to him," I said, my tone firm despite the uncertainty clawing at me.

"Are you sure that's a good idea? You just got out of there. I mean, I get that you want answers, but—"

"I need to know," I interrupted, fear and rage coiling tightly within me. "If he's pulling away now... what does that mean for us? I can't just pretend it doesn't hurt."

"Okay, okay, but please take care of yourself, alright? Call me back after you talk to him," Sophie urged, her voice softening.

"I will." I ended the call and leaned against the bathroom sink, the cool porcelain grounding me. The reality of Alex's betrayal crashed over me like a tidal wave, my heart thundering in my ears. Just when I had begun to feel a glimmer of hope with my dad, this bombshell threatened to drag me back down into despair.

When I stepped back into the hospital room, Mark looked up, concern etched on his face. "What was that about?"

"Just... friend stuff," I replied, forcing a smile that felt more like a mask than a genuine expression. I needed to keep him in the loop, but I didn't want to taint this fragile moment of reconnection. "Nothing I can't handle."

His eyes searched mine, a flicker of doubt in his gaze. "You know I'm here for you, right? Whatever it is, we can face it together."

"Right," I said, but even as I spoke the words, doubt clung to my heart. "Thanks, Dad. I really appreciate it."

With every step toward the door, I could feel my resolve hardening, like steel being forged in fire. I didn't have all the answers yet, but I knew I needed to face Alex—needed to confront whatever truth lay hidden in his silence.

As I reached for my jacket, the air shifted, thickening with a tension I couldn't quite pinpoint. My phone buzzed again, this time a call from Alex. My heart raced, the familiar mix of anxiety and anticipation flooding my senses. With a deep breath, I answered. "Alex?"

"Ava," his voice came through, low and uncertain, laced with something that sounded almost like regret. "Can we talk? There's something you need to know."

The room seemed to tilt, the walls closing in as I braced myself for whatever truth he was about to unleash. I glanced at Mark, who was watching me closely, an unreadable expression on his face. I nodded, as if to assure him I was ready, even though the reality of it felt like a lie.

"Yeah, we can talk. Just... meet me at the park?" I suggested, my voice steady despite the turmoil within.

"Sure. I'll be there."

I hung up, feeling a storm brewing in the pit of my stomach. There were questions I needed answered, truths I had to confront, and as I stepped into the chaos of the world beyond the hospital, I couldn't shake the feeling that the answers would shatter the delicate truce I had begun to build with my father.

Outside, the sun dipped low in the sky, casting long shadows that danced across the pavement, much like the tumult of emotions swirling inside me. Each step felt heavier than the last as I made my way to the park, the weight of uncertainty hanging over me.

What awaited me would change everything.

Chapter 24: The Storm Within

The night air felt electric, charged with an energy that both invigorated and terrified me. I stood on the rooftop garden, the city sprawled beneath me like a treasure trove of shimmering lights, each one flickering with stories I might never know. The gentle rustle of leaves provided a soft backdrop to my thoughts, contrasting sharply with the turmoil raging inside me. I pressed my palms against the cool metal railing, feeling the pulse of the city through my fingertips, but it couldn't drown out the anxiety that had taken up residence in my chest.

The doctors had spoken in hushed tones earlier that day, their words weaving a dark tapestry of worry and uncertainty. Aggressive treatment. It sounded like a battle cry, but it was also a reminder of the war I was losing. With every syllable, my heart sank a little further, each beat heavy with the realization that my body had become an untrustworthy vessel. I had always prided myself on my resilience, but now, I felt like a ship caught in a storm, tossed between the waves of hope and despair.

I took a deep breath, inhaling the scent of damp earth and blooming jasmine, desperately trying to find solace in the familiar. My mind spiraled back to Nate, his laughter like a lighthouse in the tempest of my thoughts. The very idea of losing him felt like a noose tightening around my neck. We had carved out a world together, one filled with late-night conversations, impromptu adventures, and a love that was both sweet and spicy, like the perfect blend of chocolate and chili. The thought of it slipping away was enough to make my stomach churn.

As the tears began to flow, I could feel the weight of them, each one a tiny release of the pain that had accumulated inside me like sediment at the bottom of a river. I let them fall freely, not caring if the world below witnessed my breakdown. This was my moment, raw and unfiltered, and I was determined to embrace it. My heart ached with the truth I was learning: vulnerability wasn't a sign of weakness; it was the strongest form of bravery I could muster.

"Hey, are you planning to flood the rooftop or are you just trying to water the flowers?" Nate's voice broke through the haze of my tears, playful yet laced with genuine concern. I turned to him, his silhouette framed by the city lights, and for a moment, I forgot the storm raging within. There was a lightness in his eyes that calmed me, a strength I wanted to cling to like a life raft.

"Just giving the flowers a drink," I replied, attempting to infuse a bit of humor into my heavy heart. "I figured they could use it more than I can."

He stepped closer, the warmth of his presence enveloping me like a soft blanket. "They'd definitely appreciate your tears more than this artificial stuff they keep getting from the hose." He gestured to the small watering can beside the vibrant blooms that adorned the rooftop, their colors blooming even brighter under the city's glow.

I chuckled softly, wiping my eyes with the back of my hand, trying to regain a semblance of composure. "You always know how to make me feel better."

"It's a gift," he grinned, leaning against the railing beside me. "What else are best friends for?" The casual declaration felt like an anchor in my sea of uncertainty, but it also stirred a deeper ache. We had danced around our feelings for far too long, but now, in the face of looming uncertainty, it felt almost cruel to keep pretending.

Nate turned serious, his gaze fixed on the horizon, where the last slivers of sunlight had surrendered to the night. "You're stronger than you think, Ava. This... whatever this is," he gestured between us, "it's not just going to fade away. You've got people who care about you. I care about you." His words lingered in the air, the weight of them settling over me like a warm embrace.

"I know," I said softly, my heart swelling at the sincerity in his voice. But beneath the warmth, a shadow of fear lurked, whispering that my time with him was running out. I turned my gaze to the city, my mind racing through a list of what-ifs and maybes that could haunt me. "What if... what if I can't fight this anymore?"

Nate's eyes narrowed slightly, a protective fire igniting within them. "You are not alone in this. We'll face whatever comes together. I refuse to let you go without a fight."

A chill swept through me, not from the cold, but from the weight of his words. I wanted to believe him, to latch onto that sense of hope like a lifeline. Yet, the gnawing doubt was a persistent companion, whispering that this was an uphill battle, one I might not be strong enough to win. "But what if—"

"Stop," he interrupted gently, taking my hand in his, his thumb rubbing soothing circles over my knuckles. "No more 'what ifs.' You've got to focus on the here and now. Let's make the most of it. You and me."

His grip was firm, anchoring me to the present. The rooftop garden, the distant hum of traffic, the shimmering stars above—it all felt so achingly beautiful. I could almost forget the clouds that loomed ominously in the distance.

"Let's start with a plan," Nate suggested, a spark of mischief returning to his eyes. "How about a movie marathon? Your pick. I'll supply the snacks."

"Only if you promise to bring popcorn. I need some comfort food to drown out the existential dread," I teased, letting a smile break through the haze of my fears.

"Popcorn, check. Extra butter, double check. And maybe some of those ridiculous candy bars you love?" He was already plotting, his enthusiasm infectious.

As he began rattling off the names of various movies, I felt a warmth unfurling within me, pushing against the cold grip of uncertainty. Nate had a way of grounding me, of reminding me that even amidst chaos, there were still moments worth savoring.

We stood together, hand in hand, looking out over the city. And for a fleeting moment, the storm inside me quieted, as if the promise of shared laughter and stolen moments was enough to chase away the shadows lurking in the corners of my mind.

The sky darkened around us, the city lights twinkling like a blanket of stars fallen to Earth, and for a moment, I let the weight of my worries drift away. Nate's presence felt like a soft glow, illuminating the parts of me that had been consumed by darkness. I was grateful for his humor, his relentless optimism that seemed to bounce off the walls of our shared anxieties, and as we settled into the familiar rhythm of our banter, I found solace in the absurdity of our situation.

"Okay, so how about this?" Nate leaned against the railing, his eyes dancing with mischief. "We can start with a classic—'The Princess Bride.' But let me warn you, I may quote it line for line. It's a real talent of mine."

"Quoting movies is your only talent?" I raised an eyebrow, feigning disbelief. "I thought you were secretly a ninja or something."

"Only on weekends," he shot back, grinning wide enough to make me forget the heaviness in my chest. "But if you want, I can throw in a few karate moves while we watch."

"Only if it's the part where you get knocked out," I teased, nudging him with my shoulder.

We stood in comfortable silence for a moment, watching the flickering lights below, as if we were the only two people in a vast universe. My heart felt lighter, the storm inside me subsiding just enough to let a sliver of peace shine through. "You know," I said, my voice barely above a whisper, "it's moments like this that I wish could last forever."

Nate turned to me, his expression shifting to something softer, more serious. "Then let's make them last, Ava. You deserve that." His words hung in the air between us, a promise cloaked in sincerity, and for a brief second, I allowed myself to dream of a future—one where laughter was the soundtrack of our days, and love shielded us from the darkness.

But as quickly as that thought took root, the inevitable shadow loomed again, darkening the edges of my vision. I couldn't afford to indulge in fantasies. Reality was a relentless tide, threatening to pull me under. "You say that, but..." I hesitated, searching for the right words. "What if I can't be that person for you? What if I'm just a temporary chapter in your story?"

"First of all, stop with the melodrama," he chuckled, but the concern in his eyes was evident. "And second, you're not just a chapter, Ava. You're the whole book, and I refuse to let you close it just yet."

I looked away, letting his words wash over me like a soothing balm. Part of me wanted to argue, to push him away with the very fears that threatened to engulf me, but I couldn't deny the flicker of warmth igniting within.

"Fine, but I'm not wearing a princess costume," I said, hoping to steer the conversation back to safer ground. "If I'm the book, let's at least make it a thriller. Maybe a little romance, some comedy, and definitely a plot twist or two."

Nate's eyes sparkled with mischief as he leaned closer, lowering his voice to a conspiratorial whisper. "How about we add a touch of magic? You know, something that'll keep the readers on their toes."

"Magic?" I laughed, picturing him with a wand, trying to conjure a spell. "What are you going to do, turn me into a frog?"

"I think you'd make a lovely frog, actually. Very enchanting," he said, waggling his eyebrows in a way that made me laugh even harder.

As the laughter echoed around us, I felt a momentary reprieve from my worries. The world below continued its unrelenting pace, but here, suspended in our little bubble, I could forget, if only for a while.

Eventually, Nate pulled out his phone, scrolling through his movie library. "Okay, so what's it going to be? An epic love story? A heart-pounding thriller? Or are we in the mood for a laugh?"

"Let's go with the laughter. I could use more of that," I replied, trying to mask the quaver in my voice. "Something to distract me from... you know."

"Done," he said decisively, tapping the screen. "Prepare for laughter and possibly a few ridiculous quotes."

As the opening credits rolled, I leaned against Nate, his warmth seeping into my skin, making me feel safe. The movie unfolded, and I let the humor wash over me like a wave, erasing some of the shadows in my mind. Laughter filled the air, a healing balm that momentarily dulled the edges of reality. We shared inside jokes, mock-serious commentary on the plot twists, and before long, I found myself laughing so hard I nearly spilled popcorn all over us.

Halfway through, the movie's soundtrack shifted to a romantic scene, the kind that made the air thick with unspoken tension. I could feel it hanging between us, a delicate thread that dared to bridge the space separating friendship and something more. My heart raced, and I suddenly became acutely aware of the way Nate's shoulder brushed against mine, the way his laughter made my stomach flutter.

I stole a glance at him, watching as his eyes flickered between the screen and me. There was an intensity in his gaze that made my breath hitch. My heart wanted to leap, to dive headfirst into the moment, but the logical side of me clung to caution, reminding me of the weight we carried.

"Hey," he said, interrupting my thoughts, his voice low. "What if this is our thing? Movie nights, popcorn, ridiculous banter... just us?"

A wave of warmth washed over me, coupled with a twinge of fear. "Are you sure you want that?"

"Why wouldn't I?" He leaned closer, his expression earnest. "You make everything better. And you know I'm a sucker for a good rom-com."

My heart did a little somersault, caught between hope and dread. "You do realize that every good rom-com has a climax, right? And I'm not sure I can promise a happy ending."

"Who says we can't rewrite the ending?" he challenged, and there was something in his tone that set my nerves alight. "Life doesn't always hand us happy endings, but we can create our own moments. I'll take what I can get, as long as it involves you."

I bit my lip, processing his words, a whirlwind of emotions tumbling within me. I wanted to believe him, to lean into the warmth of his sincerity, but the specter of uncertainty still loomed large. "What if I'm just a hurricane waiting to happen? I could wreck everything."

"Or," Nate countered, his gaze unwavering, "you could be the calm in the storm. You just have to let me in."

In that moment, everything shifted. The fear that had tethered me to the ground began to unravel, and I realized that maybe—just maybe—letting someone in didn't equate to losing myself. I could still fight my battles while holding onto the light he offered.

"Alright," I said finally, a soft smile breaking through my earlier resolve. "Let's rewrite the ending, one movie night at a time."

Nate's grin widened, his eyes sparkling with mischief and warmth. And just like that, amidst the flickering screen and the laughter echoing in the night, I felt a tiny seed of hope begin to blossom. In the midst of the storm, there was still a flicker of light, and I was ready to explore it, even if it meant embracing the unknown.

The air around us crackled with an unspoken tension, the flickering screen casting playful shadows on Nate's face. The film had transitioned into a sequence of outrageous antics, where two hapless characters found themselves in increasingly absurd situations, and I couldn't help but laugh. Each chuckle felt like a small victory, a reminder that life, even in its darkest chapters, still had the capacity for humor.

"Okay, but let's be real," Nate said, leaning in as if he were about to share a state secret. "If we were in this movie, I would definitely be the sidekick. You know, the one who gives all the terrible advice but still manages to look good while doing it."

"Sidekick, huh?" I quipped, elbowing him playfully. "More like the comic relief. Just here to make the audience laugh while I carry the weight of the emotional journey."

"Touché. But let's face it: no one wants to be the protagonist when you can be the sassy sidekick who steals the show."

We both burst into laughter, the kind that comes so easily between us, the kind that erases the heaviness that clung to my heart like a damp blanket. But as the movie continued, my mind drifted, caught in the undertow of my reality.

The laughter dimmed as I contemplated the absurdity of our situation. Here we were, lost in a world of make-believe while my own life was a precarious balancing act. I cast a sideways glance at Nate, who was now fully invested in the antics on screen. There was something so comforting about watching him, the way his expressions shifted with each ridiculous plot twist. But beneath that comfort lay the gnawing fear of what lay ahead.

"Are you okay?" he asked suddenly, his attention snapping back to me, piercing through my reverie.

"Yeah, just... thinking," I replied, forcing a smile that didn't quite reach my eyes.

"Thinking about how many popcorn kernels you can fit in your mouth at once?" he teased, his tone light, but the concern lingered in his gaze.

"No, more like wondering how many more movies I'll get to watch before I'm stuck in the hospital again." My voice wavered, and I quickly turned back to the screen, pretending to be captivated by the characters' shenanigans.

Nate shifted closer, his knee brushing against mine. "You know you can talk to me about this, right? I'm not just here for comic relief. I'm your friend. I'm here for the heavy lifting too."

I swallowed hard, the lump in my throat a bitter reminder of the precariousness of my situation. "It's just—what if this next treatment doesn't work? What if I'm just prolonging the inevitable?"

"Okay, let's not go down that road," Nate interrupted gently, his voice steady as he gripped my hand. "What if it does work? What if it opens doors to new adventures?"

His optimism felt like a balm, but it also sparked an internal battle. "I don't want you to suffer through my battles. You deserve better than a friend who's constantly fighting for her life."

"I'm not going anywhere," he said firmly, his gaze unwavering. "Besides, I've already invested too much time in the 'Ava Chronicles' to back out now. I want to be here for every plot twist, every hilarious moment, and every battle cry."

A smile flickered on my lips, the warmth of his words wrapping around me like a comforting embrace. "You're ridiculous, you know that?"

"Absolutely," he shot back, his smile infectious. "But that's why you love me."

"I'm starting to think you're right," I admitted, my heart swelling.

As the credits rolled, Nate turned off the screen and settled back against the railing, the cool metal pressing into my back. "So, what's next on the agenda? More movies? A snack run? Or do you want to take a stroll and make the most of this beautiful night?"

The city sparkled below us, an invitation to explore, to escape the reality waiting at my door. "Let's walk," I decided, needing the fresh air and the freedom of movement to clear my head. "I could use a little adventure."

"Adventure it is!" Nate declared, jumping to his feet and extending a hand to help me up. His enthusiasm was contagious, and I felt a flicker of excitement ignite within me.

We descended the rooftop stairs, the hum of the city growing louder as we stepped into the night. The streets were alive, a symphony of laughter, chatter, and the occasional honk of a taxi. Nate pulled me toward a small café that glowed like a beacon, its warmth spilling onto the sidewalk. "Best hot chocolate in the city, hands down," he proclaimed, leading the way.

The café was a cozy nook filled with mismatched furniture, eclectic artwork, and the mouthwatering scent of freshly baked pastries. The barista greeted us with a friendly smile, and before I knew it, we were seated at a tiny table nestled in a corner, our steaming mugs in front of us.

"Cheers," Nate said, raising his cup.

"Cheers," I echoed, clinking my mug against his, the sound like a small celebration. As I took a sip, the rich, velvety chocolate enveloped me in warmth, a delicious distraction from the chill creeping in around the edges of my thoughts.

"So," Nate began, a playful glint in his eyes, "if you could go anywhere right now, no limitations, where would you want to be?"

"Somewhere far away, where I can't think about doctors or treatments or goodbyes," I admitted, surprised by the honesty in my words.

"Sounds perfect," he replied. "How about we turn this into a game? For every question, we have to come up with the most ridiculous scenario possible."

"Okay," I laughed, feeling lighter with each sip. "But I'm warning you, my imagination runs wild."

"Bring it on," he challenged, grinning.

We spent the next half hour spinning wild tales of adventure, from conquering volcanoes in the tropics to escaping from a secret lair filled with villains who had a penchant for collecting rare items. Laughter filled the air, wrapping around us like a warm blanket, chasing away the shadows that lingered in my mind.

But as we finished our drinks, a sudden wave of unease washed over me. The world outside seemed to dim, a reminder of the reality that awaited me. I glanced at Nate, who was engrossed in recounting his latest escapade at work, the energy radiating from him almost palpable. Yet, there was a gravity beneath his laughter, a sense that he too understood the stakes of our current situation.

"Nate," I interrupted gently, my heart racing. "What if things don't go as planned with my treatment? What if this is it?"

The light in his eyes flickered for just a moment before he met my gaze, his expression turning serious. "Ava, stop. We don't have to think that way. We're focusing on the here and now. And right now, we're having hot chocolate and planning our next great adventure."

But his words hung heavy in the air, and I could feel the truth thrumming beneath them. The weight of my condition felt insurmountable, like a storm ready to break loose at any moment.

As we stepped outside, the cool breeze kissed my cheeks, refreshing yet invigorating. The night felt alive around us, pulsing with possibilities. I wanted to believe that hope existed beyond the shadows, that adventure still awaited us.

But just as we started walking, my phone buzzed violently in my pocket, an unwelcome intrusion into our moment. My heart dropped as I pulled it out, the screen illuminating a message that sent a jolt of panic coursing through my veins.

It was from my doctor.

The words blurred as I read, my breath hitching in my throat. "Ava, we need to discuss your treatment plan. It's urgent."

The world around me began to fade, the sounds of laughter and city life slipping away like sand through my fingers. I looked at Nate, his expression shifting from playful curiosity to concern, the shift so swift it felt like a punch to the gut.

"Are you okay?" he asked, sensing the change in the atmosphere.

I swallowed hard, struggling to keep my voice steady. "I—I need to go. It's about the treatment."

Nate's face paled, and in that moment, I could see every possible outcome flashing across his features—fear, worry, uncertainty. The air between us thickened, heavy with the weight of the impending conversation, the storm that had been brewing within me now threatening to erupt.

"Let's go together," he said, determination replacing his earlier levity.

But as I opened my mouth to respond, the streets began to swirl around me, the lights blurring and the laughter fading into a distant echo. I felt like I was being pulled into a vortex, uncertainty wrapping around me like a vice. I couldn't shake the feeling that whatever awaited me in that office was going to change everything.

"I can't..." I murmured, my voice barely above a whisper, the storm within me surging to the forefront.

Nate stepped closer, his eyes searching mine. "Ava—"

Before he could finish, a distant rumble echoed through the night, resonating deep within me, mirroring the tempest I had fought to contain. And as the first drops of rain began to fall, heavy and relentless, I realized that this was the moment where everything shifted.

The storm had arrived.

Chapter 25: Memories Like Sand

Sunlight filtered through the dusty window of the hospital room, illuminating the scattered remnants of what had once been my sanctuary—a space decorated with vibrant paintings from local artists and hopeful quotes scrawled on cheerful post-its. The walls, a muted green, seemed to shrink inward, heavy with the weight of unspoken fears and fragile hopes. I sat on the edge of the narrow bed, my legs swinging lightly above the stark white linoleum floor, the scent of antiseptic mingling with the distant, comforting aroma of freshly brewed coffee wafting from the nurses' station.

Nate burst into the room with a playful energy that momentarily lifted the heaviness that clung to the air. He had his signature lopsided grin plastered on his face, the one that always made my heart flip. "Guess what I found?" he announced, brandishing a stack of colorful scrapbook supplies like a magician revealing his latest trick.

I arched an eyebrow, feigning disinterest. "Let me guess—glitter? You know how I feel about glitter, Nate."

"Okay, fine. No glitter. But we do have stickers, paper, and the most important ingredient of all: memories!" He twirled around, his arms outstretched as if embracing the moment.

My laughter spilled out, light and unexpected, a sound I hadn't realized I'd been missing. "You're serious about this, aren't you?"

"Dead serious. We're creating a scrapbook," he said, plopping down next to me, the bed creaking under his weight. "It'll be our time capsule, a visual representation of our epic adventures."

I tilted my head, allowing myself to be swept into his enthusiasm. The thought of assembling our memories—a tangible collage of laughter, love, and the bittersweet essence of time—was irresistibly tempting. "Alright, but we have to promise to make it as ridiculous as possible."

He raised an eyebrow, mirroring my earlier expression. "Ridiculous is my middle name. Let's do this."

We spent hours sifting through photographs, each one a portal to a moment in time. There was the shot of us grinning like fools at the local carnival, our faces smeared with cotton candy and joy. I remembered the taste of sugary sweetness lingering on my tongue, the thrill of the ferris wheel swaying gently beneath us as we soared above the lights, the world below a kaleidoscope of color.

"That was a dangerous game of ring toss," Nate chuckled, his eyes sparkling with the memory. "I still can't believe I won that giant stuffed dinosaur."

"It was a hideous dinosaur!" I countered, laughing as I recalled the day he insisted on carrying it home. "It practically took over the backseat of your car. I think it had its own seatbelt."

He leaned back, a grin spreading across his face. "But it was worth it to see you light up like that. And you secretly loved it."

"Alright, guilty as charged," I admitted, my heart swelling with warmth. I could almost hear the echoes of our laughter ringing in the air, a sound so familiar it felt like home.

We continued flipping through the snapshots, pasting them onto the thick pages of our scrapbook with the careful precision of artists at work. Each photograph held a memory, a story begging to be told. A quiet afternoon spent sipping coffee in our favorite café, the sun streaming through the windows like liquid gold; our clandestine stargazing sessions on the hospital roof, where the city lights below sparkled like a sea of diamonds; even the tender, fleeting moments we'd stolen amidst the chaos of treatments and uncertainty.

With every sticker we placed, every line of poetry we jotted down, I felt the weight of our time together crystallizing into something beautiful, something that transcended the fear of what lay ahead. Nate would read snippets of poetry he had collected, words that captured our love, the fleeting nature of life, and the beauty in the ordinary.

"Listen to this one," he said, his voice soft as he read aloud: "And when the world feels heavy, and the night stretches endlessly, remember, my heart is a song for you, an echo of laughter across the skies."

I looked up, my heart fluttering at the weight of those words. "Where did you find that?"

"It's just something I jotted down a while ago," he said, a hint of vulnerability creeping into his voice. "I figured we could use it as a header for our sunset page."

I nodded, my throat tightening. The sunset page would capture those quiet moments we'd shared on the hospital roof, wrapped in blankets, gazing out at the fading light. It had been our sanctuary, a place where time stood still, where the world outside faded away and it was just us, caught in a moment of serenity amidst the chaos of our lives.

As we cut and pasted, laughter echoed through the room, mingling with the distant beeping of machines and the soft shuffle of nurses outside. We crafted a narrative of our journey, complete with ridiculous inside jokes that only made sense to us. I added a small doodle of a cat, drawn with my signature awkwardness, and Nate erupted into laughter. "Is that supposed to be Mr. Whiskers?"

"Of course! He's our unofficial mascot," I defended, stifling a giggle.

"He looks like he's plotting world domination," Nate shot back, his eyes twinkling.

I leaned into him, our shoulders brushing together as we forged ahead with our masterpiece, the scrapbook slowly transforming into a tapestry of our love—a love that was vibrant and messy and, above all, real. Each turn of the page brought a new memory, a new laugh, and an echo of the tender moments that had filled our time together.

In that hospital room, surrounded by the chaos of life, we found solace in our creation, a reprieve from the uncertainty that loomed over us. Every snip of scissors, every carefully placed photo, wove a connection that felt unbreakable, a reminder that even though time was slipping through our fingers like sand, the memories we created would linger long after the moments had passed.

We fell into a rhythm, Nate and I, scissors snipping, paper rustling, laughter bubbling up like champagne in a toast. Each page we crafted became a time capsule, a testament to a love that felt both light as air and heavy as a stone, teetering on the brink of an uncertain future. I found solace in our shared creation, a cocoon spun from snippets of poetry, bursts of color, and the warmth of our intertwined fingers.

As we moved deeper into our project, the initial spark of humor took on a more profound tone. The sun began to dip lower in the sky, casting long shadows that danced along the walls of our temporary sanctuary. The light turned golden, bathing the room in a hue that felt like an embrace. It was in this glow that Nate reached for another photo, one that captured a moment I had almost forgotten—the two of us lounging in a park, sprawled on a picnic blanket, surrounded by the sweet chaos of crumbs and laughter.

"Remember that day?" he asked, holding the photo up as if it were a relic of an ancient civilization. "We spent more time trying to catch the squirrels than actually eating."

"Oh, I remember. You were convinced you could befriend them," I teased, nudging him with my shoulder. "Meanwhile, I was dodging flying breadcrumbs like they were grenades."

Nate chuckled, his laughter rich and full. "I maintain that if you just give them a chance, they might surprise you."

I rolled my eyes but couldn't help but smile. "Right, because nothing says romance like being ambushed by rodents in the middle of a lovely afternoon."

"Hey, it was a good strategy. They could have been our unofficial wedding planners," he shot back with a mock-seriousness that made me laugh even harder. "Can you picture it? Tiny tuxedos, tiny flowers, and they'd serve as the ring bearers. Talk about memorable!"

"Perfect! Just imagine Aunt Gladys trying to wrangle those little furballs," I said, my eyes sparkling at the mental image of our family's bemusement.

We continued, lost in our laughter, and I could almost feel the weight of the world shifting. As I cut and pasted, I caught glimpses of my own reflection in the glossy photographs—bright-eyed and carefree, laughing as if I had no cares at all. Those were the moments that tethered me to the earth, each one a thread in the fabric of our shared story.

The scrapbook grew thicker, pages piled with our lives. I lovingly arranged the photo of us at the carnival, where I had worn a neon pink wig that should have been deemed a crime against fashion. Nate leaned in, a conspiratorial whisper in his voice. "You know, I still think that wig had its own gravitational pull."

"Gravity? Or sheer embarrassment?" I shot back, laughter bubbling over.

"I prefer to think of it as an enhanced sense of style," he replied, pretending to straighten an imaginary tie. "Truly, a fashion icon in the making."

As we lost ourselves in our banter, I suddenly felt a wave of something darker wash over me. I caught Nate's eye, and his grin faltered slightly, the unspoken weight of our situation flickering between us like a candle about to be snuffed out. In that instant, the laughter turned brittle, hanging in the air like a fragile ornament ready to shatter.

"I love this," I said, attempting to shift the mood, my voice softer. "It feels... timeless."

His expression shifted, thoughtful yet tinged with sadness. "It's like we're building something that's going to last, right? Something that says we were here, that we mattered."

"Exactly," I agreed, determined to keep the moment light. "This scrapbook is our way of flipping time the bird. It's proof that even when things are hard, we still had a hell of a time."

Nate smiled, but I could see the cracks in the facade, the way his eyes glossed over as if he were peering through a foggy window into a reality we both feared. "You're right. We've had our share of moments. Some a bit crazier than others," he said, a hint of mischief creeping back into his tone.

Just as I was about to respond, a soft knock on the door interrupted us. It creaked open, revealing one of the nurses with a gentle smile that never quite reached her eyes. "I'm sorry to interrupt, but it's time for Nate's medication."

Nate sighed, glancing at me as if to gauge my reaction. "Ah, the dreaded meds. The necessary evil of this glamorous life."

I squeezed his hand, willing him to feel the strength of my support. "I'll be right here when you're done. No squirrels will escape my wrath in your absence."

The nurse nodded, her demeanor professional yet warm as she stepped into the room, her presence momentarily filling the space with a sense of normalcy. I watched as Nate stood, stretching his limbs as if trying to shake off the weight of impending reality. "I'll make it quick. I'll be back faster than you can say 'world's most ridiculous wedding planners,'" he promised, the sparkle returning to his voice.

"Just don't get sidetracked by the snack cart!" I called after him, unable to resist teasing even in the face of uncertainty.

He flashed me a grin over his shoulder, and I was left alone with the scrapbook, its pages now a testament to our journey. The silence that enveloped the room felt heavy, like a thick fog rolling in, pressing against my chest. I stared at the photos and snippets of poetry we had created together, the laughter still echoing in my ears, and wondered how long I could hold onto these fleeting moments.

As I flipped through our memories, I thought of the sunsets we had watched from the roof, the way the colors had mingled together in a breathtaking display that seemed to pause time itself. Each memory was a piece of us, an anchor against the tides of uncertainty that threatened to pull us apart.

I closed my eyes for a moment, allowing the warmth of our laughter to wrap around me like a blanket. Nate's vibrant spirit, even in the face of everything we were up against, fueled my own resilience. I opened my eyes and smiled at the pages of our scrapbook, knowing that the real beauty of life was captured in the tiny moments, the small joys amidst the chaos.

The door clicked softly as Nate returned, the energy in the room immediately shifting with his presence. I looked up from our project, trying to read the expression on his face. Was it the usual lightness I'd come to rely on, or something more profound hiding just beneath the surface?

"Mission accomplished," he declared, hands triumphantly on his hips. "And no snack cart ambushes this time. I was vigilant."

"Good to know you're on top of your game," I teased, leaning into the warmth of our banter, though I couldn't shake the feeling that something had changed during his brief absence. He returned to my side, his eyes scanning the growing scrapbook filled with our moments, and I watched as a flicker of pride danced across his features.

"Look at this!" he exclaimed, flipping open to a page adorned with a haphazard collage of our adventures. "We are practically professionals at this now."

"Professional scrapbookers? Who knew?" I quipped, nudging him playfully. "Next stop, reality TV fame! 'Scrapbook Wars: The Epic Showdown.'"

"Only if I get to wear a sparkly apron," he shot back, a grin spreading across his face. "Nothing says culinary prowess like a bedazzled outfit."

We continued to add to our masterpiece, our conversations flowing seamlessly between lighthearted teasing and deeper musings. I found myself caught up in the rhythm of our laughter, the way it intertwined with the gluing and cutting as if it were its own art form. The page we were currently working on featured a series of pictures from a beach trip—sandcastles and sunburns—each one a slice of carefree joy.

"I still can't believe you tried to ride that inflatable flamingo into the ocean," Nate chuckled, his eyes sparkling with mirth. "You looked like a walrus trying to surf."

I narrowed my eyes playfully. "That walrus was a brave soul! And it was either that or be swept away by the waves. I was merely trying to keep my dignity intact."

"Dignity? With a flamingo?" He laughed, his voice a rich melody of joy that filled the room. "You were just lucky that lifeguard was around to save you. What was his name? Kyle? He was swooning over you like a lovesick puppy."

"More like a love-struck seagull, trying to steal my fries," I retorted, the memory still tickling me. "Not that it mattered. I was too busy being a walrus."

The humor in our words was comforting, a distraction from the looming uncertainty that hovered like a dark cloud on the horizon. But just as I started to feel fully immersed in our lighthearted banter, I caught a glimpse of the clock on the wall, its ticking sharp and insistent, a reminder of the time slipping away. I bit my lip, trying to push down the unease that twisted in my stomach.

"Hey, remember that time we tried to cook together?" I asked, desperate to anchor myself back in laughter. "You nearly set the kitchen on fire!"

"Don't blame me for your terrible knife skills!" he shot back, feigning outrage. "You wield a chef's knife like it's a sword in a Renaissance fair!"

I laughed, the image of our chaotic kitchen escapade vividly flooding back—the smoke alarm blaring, flour exploding like a cloud of confetti, and Nate, ever the charmer, trying to salvage our charred masterpiece while pretending to be a gourmet chef. "If I recall correctly, I was the one putting out fires while you panicked over an undercooked chicken."

"Okay, fine, you were the hero in that story," he conceded, eyes twinkling. "But just wait until our next culinary adventure. I'll wear my fireman's helmet to avoid any hazards."

As we exchanged more tales, our laughter mingling with the fading light, a heavy knock shattered our bubble. The door swung open once more, but this time, it was not a familiar face. A tall figure in a crisp white coat stood there, clipboard in hand, a serious expression etched across their face. My heart sank. The energy shifted abruptly, and the room felt charged, every breath stilled in anticipation.

"Nate," the doctor began, their voice low and steady, cutting through the remnants of our laughter like a knife. "We need to talk."

Nate's grin faded, replaced by a look of confusion that mirrored my own rising dread. "Is everything alright?"

The doctor's gaze darted between us, and in that moment, time seemed to stretch, each heartbeat echoing painfully in the silence that followed. "There have been some developments regarding your treatment plan. I need to explain the implications."

Panic clawed at my insides, and I felt my heart race. Nate's expression hardened, a mix of concern and determination washing over him. "What kind of developments?"

The doctor hesitated, glancing at the scrapbook sprawled across the bed—a testament to our fight against time, our shared moments captured in vibrant colors. "It's about your condition, Nate. There are options we need to discuss, but I think you should be prepared for some difficult news."

"Difficult news? What are you saying?" I interjected, my voice trembling as I fought to keep my composure. I could feel the walls of our cozy world closing in, the laughter fading into a distant memory, leaving only the stark reality hanging heavily between us.

Nate's hand found mine, squeezing tightly, grounding me in the moment. "Just tell us," he urged, his voice steady despite the tension tightening around us. "Whatever it is, we can handle it."

The doctor took a deep breath, the weight of the moment palpable. "We've noticed changes in your tests, Nate. We need to consider the next steps, which may involve a change in your current treatment strategy."

Every word felt like a blow, and I fought against the tears threatening to spill over. The light from the window dimmed as clouds rolled in, casting a shadow over our sanctuary.

"What does that mean?" Nate's voice was a whisper, as if afraid to say the words that hung heavy in the air.

"It means we need to have an honest discussion about your prognosis," the doctor said, the gravity of their tone a weight that pressed down on my chest.

The moment stretched, fragile and tense, as we waited for the news that could shatter everything we had built. I looked at Nate, whose expression was a mask of determination mixed with fear. In that instant, I realized how precarious our situation was, how fragile the fabric of our lives had become.

As the doctor continued, words swirling into a haze around me, the world began to slip away, the laughter and joy fading into the background. I knew, deep down, that this was a turning point, and as Nate's grip tightened around my hand, the tension crackled in the air. I could feel the ground shifting beneath us, and suddenly, the pages of our scrapbook, once a testament to our journey, felt like a countdown clock ticking down to an unknown end.

"What do you mean?" I managed to ask, my voice a bare whisper as I held onto Nate, not ready for the impending storm.

Just then, a loud crash echoed from the hallway outside, a sound that rattled me to the core. I turned, eyes wide, and when I looked back, the expression on the doctor's face had shifted, eyes darting toward the door as if sensing the upheaval.

"Nate..." I started, my heart racing, not knowing if I was prepared for the answers that lay ahead or the chaos that had just begun.

Chapter 26: The Final Countdown

The sterile scent of antiseptic wafted through the air, a constant reminder of where I was, though it had become almost comforting in its own way. My hospital room was a patchwork of soft blues and greens, designed to soothe, but as I lay in bed, I couldn't shake the feeling of being trapped inside a glass jar—everything I wanted just out of reach. The walls felt as if they were closing in, an invisible weight pressing against my chest, squeezing out all the fresh air I had hoped to breathe. Friends and family flitted in and out like butterflies caught in a whirlwind, their vibrant presence a stark contrast to the monotony of the room, but their chatter echoed in my mind like a dull hum, a reminder that no matter how bright their words, they couldn't illuminate the darkness creeping at the edges of my thoughts.

When Nate walked in, his silhouette framed by the bright overhead lights, it felt like the clouds had parted. He held a bouquet of sunflowers, their golden heads bobbing cheerfully as he stepped closer. "Thought these might brighten the place up," he said, grinning as he set the flowers down on my bedside table. The sight of those sunflowers brought an unexpected warmth flooding back, evoking lazy summer days and the sweet tang of lemonade. It was impossible not to smile at him; his unruly hair fell over his forehead in a way that made him look slightly tousled, as if he had just rolled out of bed and into my life.

"Did you just break into a florist's shop?" I teased, plucking a sunflower from the bunch and examining it like it held the secrets of the universe. "Because these are ridiculously beautiful. And I can't tell if you're trying to cheer me up or audition for the role of a rom-com lead."

Nate chuckled, his laugh a warm, melodic sound that cut through my anxiety like a hot knife through butter. "Well, if I were auditioning, I'd at least need a better wardrobe." He gestured to his faded band T-shirt and well-loved jeans, the fabric worn soft from countless washes. "But I'd like to think I have the charm down pat."

"Oh, absolutely," I said, rolling my eyes with exaggerated amusement. "Charm is clearly your forte. How else would you convince me to dance in a hospital room? That should be in your résumé."

His grin widened, and I could see the familiar glint of mischief in his eyes. "Let's give it a shot. I brought a playlist," he declared, pulling his phone from his pocket, as if it were a magician's hat from which he'd conjure the impossible. Within seconds, the soft strumming of our favorite song filled the room, and I felt the corners of my lips twitch into a smile that was far more genuine than anything I had mustered since being admitted.

"Really? You brought the entire band too?" I laughed, a sound that felt like the first notes of spring breaking through a long, harsh winter.

"Just me and the hospital-approved acoustics," he said, stepping closer, extending his hand. I hesitated, glancing around the sterile room, the IV stand standing sentinel in the corner, the monitors beeping like a metronome. But then I took his hand, my pulse racing not from fear but from an exhilarating mix of joy and something deeper—something that dared to unfurl in the light of those sunflowers.

We swayed gently, his arm wrapped securely around my waist, as if he could shield me from the world outside these four walls. The music enveloped us, transforming the stark reality of my illness into a fleeting moment of bliss. The weight of my diagnosis slipped away like a feather caught in the breeze, and I was no longer just a patient in a hospital gown but a girl lost in a moment, twirling under the soft glow of muted lights and memories.

"This is nice," I whispered, leaning my head against his shoulder, letting the rhythm guide us. "I forgot what it felt like to just... breathe."

"Me too," he replied, his voice barely above a whisper, yet it resonated deep within me. "I thought we could use a break from all the reality for a while. Dance like no one's watching, right?"

"More like dance like the entire staff is watching, and they're probably judging our two left feet," I laughed, glancing toward the door, half-expecting a nurse to burst in and hand us a warning about disturbing the peace. But in that moment, the fear that usually coiled tightly in my stomach relaxed just enough to let the music flow freely, weaving an invisible thread that connected us.

As the final notes hung in the air, reality began to creep back in, a bittersweet reminder of why we were here. The weight of it loomed over us like dark clouds, an impending storm that refused to be ignored. I met Nate's gaze, and we shared a silent acknowledgment of the fragility of this moment. I felt my heart sink, the joy of dancing dissipating into an inevitable heaviness.

"What happens next?" I asked, my voice shaky, betraying the calm I had fought so hard to maintain. It was the question that loomed larger than life, larger than the walls around me, larger than the sunflowers brightening the room.

Nate's smile faltered for a brief moment, his brow furrowing in thought. "Next, we focus on getting you through this treatment," he said, determination flickering in his eyes. "But also... we plan something for after. A real adventure. One where you can breathe in all the sunshine you want."

I let his words wash over me, a glimmer of hope fighting against the shadows of uncertainty. "Like a trip to the beach? Because I can already feel the sand between my toes."

"Exactly," he said, his grin returning. "And maybe we'll build the world's largest sandcastle. I'll even let you decorate it with seaweed if you promise to take all the credit."

A laugh escaped me, rich and genuine, the kind that felt like sunshine breaking through after a rainstorm. But even as we shared this moment, I could feel the delicate balance of joy and fear hanging in the air, reminding us that while we could dance, sing, and dream, the reality of the situation was still waiting just outside the door.

Nate's presence filled the room with a vibrancy that clashed deliciously with the clinical atmosphere. After our impromptu dance, I sank back against the pillows, trying to catch my breath, both from the music and the sudden rush of emotions that had surged through me. The sunflowers stood proud on the bedside table, their bright petals a stark contrast to the stark white sheets and the metallic sheen of the IV stand. I wanted to hold onto that feeling, the fleeting joy that Nate had brought into my otherwise drab existence.

"Okay, but seriously," I said, my voice teasing yet earnest, "what's the plan for our epic post-treatment adventure? I'm thinking we could do something ridiculously reckless—like jumping out of a plane or eating something that could give me a food coma before they put me under."

Nate chuckled, running a hand through his hair. "I like the reckless vibe, but how about we save the extreme sports for a later date? We could start with a road trip to the coast. Picture it: the wind in our hair, music blasting, and me, of course, acting like a rock star behind the wheel. It's practically a must-do."

The idea hung between us, shimmering with possibility. "What kind of rock star? The kind who plays air guitar to the '80s classics, or the one who wears leather pants and smashes guitars on stage?"

"Definitely the former. Though I could be convinced to wear leather pants if it means scoring us some good food at the nearest diner." His eyes sparkled with mischief, and I couldn't help but laugh, imagining the sight of him trying to pull off such a look.

"Let's not make promises we can't keep. I'd hate to ruin your reputation as a suave gentleman," I teased, winking. The moment felt like a breath of fresh air, and I clung to it, desperate to ignore the impending shadow of treatment that loomed in my mind.

But just then, the door swung open, and my mom popped her head in, her expression a mixture of hope and concern. "Oh, I see you're up to your usual antics," she said, her eyes flicking between Nate and me.

"We're plotting world domination, Mom," I replied, deadpan. "But first, we need to figure out how to get out of this hospital."

She stepped fully into the room, holding a small bag that seemed to crinkle with the promise of snacks. "Well, world dominators need fuel. I brought cookies," she said, setting the bag down and pulling out a container filled with freshly baked chocolate chip cookies, the kind that seemed to radiate warmth just by being present.

"See, Nate? My mom's already ahead of us in the food department. We need her on our team," I said, stealing a cookie before she could even set it on the table.

"Who knew cookies were the secret weapon against the tyranny of hospital food?" Nate remarked, taking one for himself, and we both chewed contentedly as my mom settled into a chair across from us.

"You two seem quite cozy," she said, a knowing smile creeping onto her face. "I hope you're not planning any escapades without me."

I shot Nate a glance, raising my eyebrows playfully. "Well, if you're in, we might just have to add a secret agent theme to our adventure."

"Count me in, but just so you know, my version of a secret agent involves a lot of snacks and very little actual danger," my mom said, her tone light but her eyes revealing the seriousness of our situation. The laughter faded, replaced by a somber undercurrent as I remembered the reason I was here, the treatment that was waiting just beyond the cheerful banter.

"Speaking of danger," I said, hesitantly shifting the mood, "I have to prep for the next round of treatment. How long do you think I can keep the 'I'm totally fine' act up before it falls apart?"

Nate leaned forward, his expression suddenly serious. "You're going to be amazing, Ava. You've fought through so much already. This is just one more hurdle. Just think of it as an annoying speed bump on our road trip."

"Right," I replied, though doubt tinged my voice. "But speed bumps can be pretty jarring."

"True," he admitted. "But they also slow you down just enough to appreciate the view. You have to allow yourself to feel everything, the good and the bad. It's all part of the ride."

My mom nodded, her gaze steady. "You're allowed to feel scared, Ava. It doesn't make you weak. It makes you human. And we're all here for you, no matter how many cookies it takes."

"Thanks, Mom," I said, feeling a swell of gratitude and love. The moment felt precious, the three of us huddled together in this small room, a makeshift fortress against the outside world.

As the conversation flowed, Nate began recounting stories of our mutual friends, each tale laced with humor and the kind of nostalgia that sparked warmth in my chest. We laughed at the absurdity of it all—like the time Charlie tried to impress everyone at a party by attempting to dance on the roof of his car, only to end up falling spectacularly onto the lawn.

"Honestly, he should have just embraced the embarrassment," Nate said, smirking. "He could have owned it like a pro."

"Right? 'Look at me! I'm the human cannonball of the party!'" I mimicked, waving my arms dramatically and causing both Nate and my mom to burst into laughter.

The laughter wrapped around us, cocooning us in a moment of levity that felt both fragile and fierce. I clung to it like a lifeline, wishing it could stretch on forever.

As the hour wore on, though, the inevitable shadows crept back in, dimming the bright laughter. I glanced at the clock, its hands ticking down with a relentless certainty. "So," I began, hesitating, "when do I have to go for the pre-treatment stuff?"

"Soon," my mom replied softly, her voice steady but filled with an underlying concern that made my stomach twist. "But you don't have to think about that now. Let's just focus on these cookies and what kind of trouble we can get into later."

"Trouble sounds perfect," I said, forcing a smile. But even as I spoke, my mind raced with the knowledge that my world was about to shift again. It was a stark reminder that while laughter and cookies filled the room, the reality of my illness remained an unwelcome guest, lurking just outside the door, waiting to make its presence known once more.

Nate caught my gaze, sensing the shift in the air. "Hey, what if we made a list of all the places we want to visit on our road trip?" he suggested, an attempt to draw me back into the light. "It could be our secret mission, something to keep our spirits up."

I nodded, grateful for his effort, knowing that those little moments of normalcy could be my sanctuary amidst the chaos. "Let's do it. A top-secret mission to seek out the best cookies across the country," I declared, already feeling the warmth of hope push against the shadows as we dove into our plans, sketching dreams that shimmered brightly against the gray of uncertainty.

As we mapped out our imaginary road trip, each destination floated into the air, buoyed by laughter and anticipation. The thrill of planning felt almost illicit, like stealing moments of freedom from the clutches of hospital routines. I took a bite of my mom's cookie, still warm and gooey with chocolate, and the rich, buttery flavor melted on my tongue. For a moment, I could almost convince myself that life was simply about cookies and the laughter of friends, but as the sugar high faded, reality crashed in like a sudden wave, cold and unyielding.

"Okay, first stop: the ocean," Nate suggested, leaning back in his chair with that trademark grin of his. "We could build a sandcastle, or better yet, an entire sand kingdom."

"Sand kingdom? I love it. I can be queen; you can be my loyal subject," I said, pretending to regal a nonexistent court. "But only if I get a tiara made of seaweed."

Nate chuckled, shaking his head. "I'm not sure the seaweed look is your best. How about seashells instead?"

"Seashells are overrated. It's all about embracing the weirdness," I countered, twirling a piece of hair around my finger, feeling the familiar flutter of joy that came with our playful banter.

The door swung open again, this time with a nurse entering, clipboard in hand, her expression professional yet friendly. "Sorry to interrupt, but we need to get you prepped for your treatment, Ava," she said, the tone of her voice a reminder of the reality that lay beneath our levity.

"Perfect timing, as always," I muttered under my breath, frustration bubbling just below the surface. I shot Nate a glance that was half-warning, half-pout. "Looks like my royal reign is coming to an end."

He stood up, his playful demeanor shifting into something more serious. "I'll be right here when you get back," he promised, his gaze steady.

As I slipped out of bed, I felt the familiar pang of dread clenching my stomach. "You better, or I'll come back and haunt you,"

I shot back, trying to keep the mood light even as I felt the walls closing in again.

"Ghosts can't do much about my cookie stash," he retorted, and we shared a fleeting smile before I turned to follow the nurse out of the room.

The fluorescent lights hummed overhead as I walked down the corridor, the sterile smell of antiseptic permeating the air, mixing with the scent of my fear. Each step felt heavier, my heart racing in time with the steady beeping of monitors. I passed other patients, their expressions varying from weary acceptance to quiet despair, each one a reminder that I wasn't alone in this fight, yet loneliness hung in the air like a thick fog.

The nurse led me into a small prep room, its walls painted a calming shade of green, though it did little to calm my rising anxiety. "You can sit here for a moment, Ava. The doctor will be with you shortly," she said, gesturing to a chair that looked more like a throne of apprehension than a place of comfort.

I nodded, forcing myself to sit, the chair cool against my skin. I took a deep breath, trying to steady the rush of emotions surging within me. It felt surreal, sitting there, surrounded by the sterile environment, yet dreaming of sandcastles and cookies. The juxtaposition was maddening.

As I sat waiting, my phone buzzed in my pocket. It was a text from Nate, a simple "You got this" accompanied by a ridiculous gif of a dancing cartoon cat. I couldn't help but laugh, the absurdity of it cutting through my anxiety like a hot knife through butter. I replied with a thumbs-up emoji, feeling a surge of gratitude for his unwavering support.

Moments later, the doctor entered, clipboard in hand, a serious expression settling on his face. "Ava, how are you feeling today?" he asked, the standard question imbued with an air of genuine concern.

"I'm ready to fight. Just like a superhero with a cookie stash," I quipped, attempting to lighten the mood despite the sinking feeling in my stomach.

He chuckled, but his eyes remained steady, assessing. "That's the spirit. We'll go through the routine tests before the treatment begins, but I want to make sure you're mentally prepared for what's to come. This round might be tougher than the last."

I nodded, my throat tightening. "Tougher how?"

"There could be more side effects. Nausea, fatigue...you know the drill," he said, his voice measured but firm. "But I want you to focus on what's next for you—what you'll do after this is all over."

"Like jumping out of a plane?" I asked, half-joking, half-hoping he'd laugh.

"More like finding ways to enjoy life again," he replied, his expression softening slightly. "And don't hesitate to reach out if you need support. We're here for you."

"Thanks," I managed, though the weight of his words settled heavily on my chest.

As the doctor began his examination, I felt a sense of calm wash over me. It was easy to get lost in my thoughts, to envision sandy beaches and sun-drenched days. But as I pictured our future adventures, a flicker of doubt gnawed at the edges of my mind. What if this was the last moment of levity I could afford before the shadows crept back in?

Once the examination was over, I was escorted back to my room, the familiar surroundings offering a strange sense of comfort. Nate was still there, leaning casually against the wall, looking as though he belonged in this little bubble of my world.

"Survived the examination?" he asked, feigning a look of mock horror.

"Barely," I said, sinking back into bed. "They want me to jump straight into the next round of treatment. Apparently, I'm a superhero now."

"Superheroes need their sidekicks," he said, winking at me. "I'll be your trusty companion on this quest."

The nurse came in, ready to start the IV drip, and I took a deep breath, preparing myself for the familiar sting of the needle. Nate's presence was a reassuring balm against my rising anxiety, a tether to reality that grounded me.

As the nurse prepared the medication, I glanced at Nate, a question hanging in the air. "What if things don't go as planned?" I asked, the weight of my vulnerability spilling out.

"Then we adapt, just like we always do," he replied, his voice steady, a calmness radiating from him. "No matter what, we'll tackle it together."

Just then, the nurse turned back to me, her expression shifting. "Ava, I need to talk to you about something."

My stomach dropped, and I shared a quick glance with Nate, sensing the shift in the atmosphere.

The nurse hesitated, a flicker of something unreadable in her eyes. "It's about your test results... they came back with some unexpected findings."

The world tilted on its axis, the air growing thick as silence enveloped us, leaving only the faint beeping of the monitor echoing ominously in my ears.

Chapter 27: The Breakthrough

I often found solace in the rhythm of the hospital machines, the soft beeping a peculiar lullaby that played in the background of my life. Yet today, their insistence seemed more like a cacophony, drowning out my thoughts as I settled into the worn, vinyl chair for yet another treatment session. The sterile scent of antiseptic hung heavy in the air, mingling with the faint trace of something floral—probably a nurse's too-enthusiastic perfume. I wished I could bottle that scent and keep it for days when hope felt like a far-off dream, a treasure buried deep under layers of uncertainty.

Nate, with his untamed hair and the crooked grin that somehow made my heart race, shifted uncomfortably in his chair beside me. His fingers drummed against his thigh, a rhythm that matched the machines' pulse. "You know, they should really invest in more comfortable furniture for people enduring this kind of torture," he joked, his voice low, a conspiratorial whisper meant to break the tension that hung between us like a thick fog.

I snorted, the sound escaping before I could catch it. "And while they're at it, how about a few complimentary lattes? I could use a shot of caffeine to combat the existential dread."

He laughed, a sound that cut through the oppressive atmosphere, making me forget for a moment why I was here. "Just don't let them serve you decaf. I hear that can lead to a total meltdown."

"Trust me, I've had my share of meltdowns. I'd like to think I'm due for a quiet, uneventful day." I leaned back, trying to focus on the dull drone of the overhead lights rather than the anxiety that had been my constant companion for months.

The nurse entered, her smile bright and practiced. She was a woman who radiated warmth, the kind of person who made the sterile environment feel just a tad more bearable. "Ready for your session, Ava?"

I nodded, my throat suddenly tight. As she prepared the equipment, I glanced at Nate, whose expression had shifted from playful to serious. I could see the concern etched on his face, the way his brow furrowed as if he were silently calculating the odds of this treatment working, or perhaps, how much longer I would be trapped in this relentless cycle of appointments and treatments.

The first few minutes were a blur, the sharp prick of the needle jolting me back to reality. I closed my eyes, counting the beeps of the machines, the ticking of the clock on the wall—a steady reminder that time continued to move forward, even as I felt stuck in place.

It was during this hazy time that my phone buzzed, a loud interruption to the monotony of the session. I fumbled for it, managing to awkwardly pull it from my pocket without disturbing the IV drip. My heart raced when I saw the caller ID. The hospital's research department.

"Answer it!" Nate urged, his voice a mix of excitement and apprehension.

Taking a deep breath, I swiped the screen. "Hello?"

"Ava, this is Dr. Reynolds. We have some exciting news regarding a new clinical trial for a therapy that may be a fit for you." His voice was smooth, but the words carried a weight that sent shivers down my spine.

My pulse quickened, a wild dance of hope and fear. "A clinical trial?"

"Yes, we're seeing promising results, and given your situation, we think you'd be an excellent candidate. Would you like to hear more?"

Nate leaned closer, his breath warm against my ear as I nodded fervently, even though I was on the phone. "Absolutely," I managed to say, my heart racing with a heady mix of curiosity and caution.

Dr. Reynolds launched into a description of the trial, each word painting a vivid picture of potential and possibility. A groundbreaking therapy aimed at tackling the very monster I'd been battling. I tried to absorb every detail, but my mind raced ahead, imagining a future where I could reclaim my life—where I wasn't defined by hospital visits and sterile rooms.

As the call ended, a spark ignited within me, lighting a fire I hadn't realized had dimmed. "Nate," I breathed, "they think I might be able to join the trial. It sounds... promising."

"Wow," he said, his eyes wide with a mix of awe and disbelief. "That's incredible, Ava! You could be part of something groundbreaking."

"Or it could be a disaster," I countered, the sharp edge of reality cutting through my initial excitement. "There are risks, Nate. What if it doesn't work? What if it makes things worse?"

"Or," he replied, his voice steady and sure, "what if it changes everything? What if it's the breakthrough you've been waiting for?"

His unwavering faith in the possibility made my heart swell, a rush of gratitude mingling with the fear that clung like a shadow. I wanted to believe him. I wanted to leap into this unknown, to chase after the flicker of light that promised a way out of the darkness. But the shadows loomed large, whispering doubts that threatened to snuff out my newfound hope.

"Let's do some research," Nate suggested, leaning forward, his intensity igniting a spark within me. "We can weigh the pros and cons together."

Together. The word resonated in my chest, wrapping around my heart like a warm embrace. I felt a surge of determination. Maybe this was the moment we'd been waiting for—the catalyst that could ignite the change we desperately sought.

As we dove into the details of the trial, the weight of uncertainty still hung above us like an ominous cloud, but for the first time in a long while, I felt the flicker of hope grow stronger. The air crackled with possibility, the potential for a new beginning looming just out of reach.

The air was thick with a nervous energy as Nate and I settled into my small apartment, a place that had seen far too many days of isolation and fear. The clutter of books, mismatched mugs, and half-finished art projects created a maze of memories, each item a reminder of the life I'd once lived—a life where spontaneity was an option, not a luxury. But today, a thread of excitement wove through the chaos. We sprawled on the couch, the faint scent of lavender from the candles I kept lit for comfort mixing with the remnants of the hospital's antiseptic haze still clinging to my clothes.

"So, let me get this straight," Nate began, tapping his fingers against his chin like a makeshift metronome. "You could be a guinea pig for a cutting-edge treatment that could either save your life or turn you into a science experiment gone wrong. Sounds fun."

I rolled my eyes, though I couldn't suppress the smile that crept onto my lips. "Thanks for that uplifting summary, Nate. Really helps with the anxiety."

"Hey, I'm just trying to keep it real." He leaned back, arms stretching out on the back of the couch, a casualness that belied the weight of the conversation. "But honestly, we've got to talk about what this means for you. It's not just a decision about treatment; it's a choice about how you want to live your life."

"Right, as if my options haven't been laid out in front of me like a terrible buffet," I shot back, unable to resist the urge to banter. "Do I want the mystery meat of 'let's hope for the best' or the slightly more palatable 'this could ruin everything'?"

"Definitely the mystery meat, obviously," he replied, his expression a mix of mock seriousness and genuine concern. "You know, living dangerously sounds way more exciting."

I took a deep breath, letting the laughter dissolve some of the tension that had crept back in. "What if it doesn't work, though? What if I'm just—what's the phrase?—'kicking the can down the road'? What if this leads to more treatments, more uncertainty?"

Nate turned toward me, the seriousness of his gaze grounding me. "Ava, you're not just kicking a can. You're taking a step. It's like hiking up a steep hill. You can either stay where you are and get comfortable with the view of nothingness, or you can keep climbing, even if you can't see the peak yet."

I looked around the room, each corner echoing my internal struggle, filled with memories of laughter and late-night conversations that often turned to dreams. It was a space that had sheltered my fears, but now it felt suffocating, the weight of my doubts pressing down like an unwelcome blanket.

"Okay, let's talk details." I nodded, trying to summon a resolve I wasn't sure I felt. "What do we know about this trial?"

Nate pulled out his laptop, a sleek silver thing that had seen far more of the world than I had lately. His fingers danced over the keyboard, and within moments, the screen lit up with a flurry of information. "Here we go. 'Breakthrough therapy for advanced conditions.' Sounds promising already, doesn't it?"

"Very optimistic," I said, squinting at the screen. "But tell me, what does 'advanced' actually mean? Like, are we talking 'advanced' as in 'it's been a rough few months' or 'advanced' as in 'grab a shovel and start digging'?"

"Why not both?" he quipped, his grin returning. "In all seriousness, though, it seems like they're targeting patients with conditions like yours, aiming for a significant improvement. The initial trials have shown a 60% success rate in reducing symptoms, and they're doing everything by the book—lots of monitoring, support, the whole shebang."

"60% success rate," I murmured, chewing on the number like it was a piece of taffy. "That's... something."

"Something is better than nothing, right?" He leaned in, excitement flickering in his eyes. "You could be part of a breakthrough! Think of the story we could tell. 'Girl Takes a Leap of Faith; Doctor Becomes Real-Life Hero.'"

"Now you're just making it sound like a bad rom-com," I laughed, imagining my life as a lighthearted movie with overly dramatic music swelling in the background.

"Maybe it is!" He pretended to hold an imaginary microphone. "Tell us, Ava, what's it like being a potential star of your own healing journey?"

"Less glamour, more uncertainty, but I'm getting my hair and makeup done later," I joked, feeling a warmth spread through me, buoyed by his enthusiasm. "But seriously, there's a lot to think about. This isn't just a casual decision."

"True, but every great adventure comes with its risks," he replied, a twinkle in his eye. "What's life without a little unpredictability?"

"Unpredictable is exactly what I'm trying to avoid," I said, letting out a heavy sigh. The room felt charged, as if we were both suspended in a moment where anything could happen.

"Hey," he said, his tone shifting to something softer. "Whatever you choose, I'm in this with you. We can take on whatever comes next, even if it's more hospital visits or paperwork."

I looked at him, seeing the sincerity in his gaze, the way he was rooted beside me, a lighthouse amidst my swirling storm. "You know, it's nice having you here. Sometimes I feel like I'm drowning, and your voice is the life raft I didn't know I needed."

His smile widened, a flash of warmth illuminating his face. "Well, I can't promise to be an expert swimmer, but I'm good at keeping the vibe afloat."

A chuckle escaped me, the laughter weaving through the tension that had gathered around us. "Okay, Captain Positive, let's keep researching. There's got to be more to this than just a catchy title."

We dove back into the sea of information, the glow of the laptop casting a warm light across the room. Each click and scroll unveiled a new layer of hope and fear, a mix that felt both exhilarating and paralyzing. As we sifted through the details, a small part of me began to embrace the uncertainty. Maybe this trial wasn't just a leap into the unknown but a chance to redefine my story.

In the days to come, as I mulled over the options and weighed the risks, I found myself growing more attuned to the idea of change. Hope began to take root, a stubborn weed in the garden of despair. The journey was only beginning, but for the first time in a long while, I felt the stirring of possibility—a new chapter waiting to be written.

The days drifted by in a haze of uncertainty and anticipation, a peculiar blend of hope and fear that felt both exhilarating and exhausting. Nate and I were consumed by the prospect of the clinical trial, each day bringing new layers to peel back and explore. We had transformed my small apartment into an informal war room, papers strewn everywhere like confetti from an overzealous celebration, our laughter mingling with the ever-present hum of possibility.

"So, if I decide to go full 'science experiment,' I want my lab coat to be chic," I joked, tossing a highlighter into the air and watching it land precariously on the edge of my desk. "Maybe something in a deep navy, accessorized with a cute pair of goggles?"

Nate leaned back in his chair, a finger tapping against his lip as if considering my request with the utmost seriousness. "I can see it now. 'Ava the Adventurous: Scientist by Day, Fashionista by Night.'"

"Exactly! If I'm going to be subjected to poking and prodding, I might as well look fabulous while doing it."

He chuckled, but his expression shifted to something more contemplative. "But really, are you ready for this? I mean, it's a big leap, Ava. A clinical trial isn't exactly a spa day."

"Are you kidding? If I have to endure needles, I'd prefer they come with a side of fabulous," I replied, forcing levity into my tone even as I felt the weight of his words. There was a fine line between joking and acknowledging the reality that lay before us, and it felt as if I were walking a tightrope, one misstep away from falling into a chasm of doubt.

"Just promise me you'll think it through." His voice softened, becoming a gentle reminder of the seriousness of our situation. "No one wants to see you hurt, not even for the sake of looking good in a lab coat."

"Trust me, Nate. I'm thinking of this like an adventure. I mean, isn't that what we do? Embrace the chaos and hope for the best?"

"Right, because that worked out so well in the last horror movie we watched together," he replied, raising an eyebrow, his teasing tone breaking through the tension. "Remember when the main character decided to go into the basement?"

I laughed, remembering how we had critiqued the character's poor life choices. "Fair point. If I start hearing creepy noises, I'll reconsider. But right now, it feels like this trial is my best shot at not just surviving but actually living."

His eyes sparkled with understanding, a connection between us that seemed to tighten with every passing moment. "Then let's embrace the chaos. But let's also make a list of questions. The more we know, the better we can navigate this adventure."

I nodded, suddenly energized. "Right! Like, what's the protocol if I start sprouting extra limbs or develop a sudden craving for kale?"

"Do we even know if kale is a side effect?" Nate asked, eyes wide. "Because I can't support that choice. I draw the line at kale."

We made our list, scribbling down questions with a mix of seriousness and humor that felt necessary in the face of what lay ahead. As we continued our brainstorming session, the excitement mingled with dread, a tension that kept my heart racing. It was a strange sort of thrill, a rollercoaster ride through emotions I hadn't expected to feel again.

By the time we finished, I felt both exhausted and exhilarated, as if I'd just run a marathon through my own thoughts. "Okay, we've got the list. Now what?" I leaned back, letting the weight of the world settle momentarily onto Nate's shoulders, a balancing act I was all too familiar with.

"Now we take this to the experts. Let's schedule a meeting with Dr. Reynolds and fire away," he suggested, his tone shifting to a business-like urgency.

"Do you think he'll appreciate our charm and wit?" I asked, smirking. "Or will we just seem like two kids trying to play grown-up?"

"Charm is overrated in a medical setting. It's all about the facts," he replied, crossing his arms and pretending to be serious. "But I think a little humor could go a long way. Who wouldn't want to work with a couple of goofballs?"

We decided to call Dr. Reynolds the next day, the prospect both thrilling and terrifying. Each moment spent researching and planning drew me deeper into the web of this decision. The balance between fear and hope began to tilt more toward the latter, and with Nate by my side, it felt like we could take on anything.

The following afternoon, we walked into the hospital, the sterile smell washing over me like a wave of nostalgia. I could feel the weight of every previous visit pressing against my chest, but today felt different. Today, I was no longer just a patient; I was a contender, someone ready to fight for a brighter future.

As we sat in the waiting room, the silence hung thick with unspoken anxieties. My fingers drummed against my knee as I watched people come and go, their faces reflecting a spectrum of hope, despair, and everything in between. Nate turned to me, a reassuring smile on his lips. "Remember, whatever happens in this meeting, we're a team."

I nodded, inhaling deeply to steady my nerves. "Okay, team. Let's do this."

When Dr. Reynolds entered, his demeanor was calm and professional, but a flicker of warmth danced in his eyes as he greeted us. "Ava, Nate, glad to see you both. I hear you have some questions about the trial?"

"Only a few," I replied, mustering every ounce of confidence I could find. I launched into our list, each question tumbling out in a rapid-fire cadence that mirrored my racing heartbeat. Nate interjected with his own quips, lightening the atmosphere while ensuring the information was relayed clearly.

Dr. Reynolds answered each question thoughtfully, his expertise wrapping around us like a comforting blanket. The more he spoke, the more the excitement bubbled within me, a fizzy sensation that felt almost intoxicating.

But then came the unexpected twist. "Before we proceed," Dr. Reynolds said, pausing as if weighing his words carefully, "I need to inform you that there's an eligibility criterion I hadn't previously mentioned. It's not a disqualifier, but it's something we must discuss."

"Eligibility?" I asked, my stomach dropping slightly. "What do you mean?"

"There's a possibility we might need to conduct additional tests. We want to ensure the treatment aligns with your specific medical history. Given your previous treatments, there could be complications we need to consider."

A silence stretched between us, the air thickening with uncertainty. I could see the concern flickering in Nate's eyes, mirroring my own growing anxiety. "What sort of tests?" I managed to ask, my voice barely above a whisper.

"Genetic testing. It's important to ensure that the trial will be effective for you. But," he continued, "it could lead to some delays in starting the treatment."

I nodded, the implications sinking in. "Delays? How long?"

"Potentially weeks, maybe even months. It depends on how quickly we can process the results."

The room felt as if it were closing in on me, the walls tightening with each passing second. I had come in hopeful, ready to seize my chance, but now I was faced with a new obstacle.

Nate shifted beside me, his voice steady. "We can wait. If this is what it takes for Ava to get the best chance, we'll wait."

The assurance in his words clashed with the swirling doubts in my mind. What if waiting meant missing my opportunity altogether? What if the trial filled up before I could even start? My heart raced, and I could feel panic beginning to creep in.

"Let's not rush this," Dr. Reynolds said gently, his gaze steady. "We'll take this step by step. You deserve the best shot possible, Ava."

As I looked at him, a new realization dawned on me. This wasn't just about a clinical trial or a set of tests. It was about taking control of my narrative, about rewriting the script that had been handed to me.

"Okay," I said slowly, a sense of determination threading through my veins. "I'll do the tests. Whatever it takes."

"Great," Dr. Reynolds replied, the corners of his mouth lifting into a reassuring smile. "I'll have my team set everything up."

We exchanged a few more pleasantries, but as we left the office, a sense of foreboding gnawed at my insides. The uncertainty loomed large, and despite my resolve, I couldn't shake the feeling that this was just the beginning of a much larger battle.

The hallway felt endless, a long stretch of uncertainty ahead of us. Just as we reached the exit, my phone buzzed in my pocket. I fished it out, heart pounding in anticipation, but as I glanced at the screen, the blood drained from my face.

It was a message from the hospital: "URGENT: Please return to the clinic immediately. We need to discuss your recent tests."

Nate turned to me, eyes wide. "What does it say?"

I swallowed hard, the world around me blurring. "I think... I think they might have found something."

As panic twisted in my stomach, the realization hit me: this journey was far from over, and whatever lay ahead could change everything.

Chapter 28: The Tender Goodbye

The garden was alive with color, a riotous display of blooms bursting forth as if they were the very essence of our shared memories. Each flower stood as a testament to our time together, vibrant and full of life, just like the laughter we'd exchanged amidst the petals. I knelt beside the peonies, their fragrance wafting through the air, thick and sweet like the moments we had stolen in this sanctuary from the world. I could still remember the day we planted them, Nate's hands brushing against mine, his laughter mingling with the soft rustle of the leaves. That sound—his laugh—was like a balm to my heart, soothing the frayed edges of my anxiety.

But today, the garden felt different. The air was heavy with anticipation, like the stillness before a storm. My heart raced as I dug my fingers into the moist earth, grounding myself as if I could bury my fears alongside the roots of the flowers. Tomorrow loomed like a shadow, darkening the edges of my thoughts. The trial was not just a date marked on the calendar; it was an impending tidal wave that threatened to sweep away everything we had built. I looked up, and there he was, Nate, standing at the entrance with sunlight framing his silhouette, a living statue of strength and beauty.

He stepped into the garden, the delicate crunch of gravel beneath his boots echoing like a heartbeat, steady and rhythmic. There was a vulnerability in his gaze that pierced through the bravado he usually wore like armor. "Hey," he said, his voice low and soothing, carrying the weight of a thousand unspoken words. I wanted to say something witty, to lighten the heavy air that hung between us, but the words caught in my throat, a tangled mess of fear and longing.

"Hey," I managed, my voice barely a whisper, as I stood and brushed the dirt from my knees. The silence stretched, thick and tangible, until I couldn't bear it any longer. "I was just thinking about the first time we planted these."

His lips curled into that lopsided grin that could make my heart flutter, a small flicker of joy amidst the impending storm. "You mean the time you insisted we plant them in a perfect line, and I—"

"I may have been a little overzealous," I admitted, biting back a smile. "But can you blame me? Look at them now!" I gestured to the peonies, their blossoms unfurling like soft pink silk under the waning sun.

"They're stunning," he agreed, stepping closer, the warmth of his body radiating toward me, an unspoken promise wrapped in the heat of his skin. "Just like you."

My heart soared at the compliment, but with each beat, the reality of tomorrow dragged it back down. "You know, I can't help but think that maybe these flowers are going to be the only thing left after... after everything." The words slipped out before I could stop them, and I hated the quiver in my voice.

Nate's expression shifted, the lightness disappearing as he grasped my hands, his touch sending electric jolts through my fingertips. "Ava, don't say that. We're going to get through this. Together."

Together. The word lingered in the air like the sweet scent of honeysuckle, so intoxicating yet so fragile. "I just—" My voice cracked, and the tears that had been hovering at the edges of my resolve spilled forth. "What if we don't?"

His grip tightened, and he drew me into him, enveloping me in his warmth. I buried my face in his shoulder, inhaling the familiar scent of cedar and something uniquely him, a mix of the outdoors and the promise of adventure. "Listen to me," he murmured, his breath warm against my hair. "No matter what happens, I love you. That doesn't change."

I lifted my head, searching his eyes for the reassurance I desperately needed. "But what if the world tries to pull us apart?" The fear clawed at my insides, a relentless beast threatening to consume me whole.

"Then we fight back," he said, his voice strong and unwavering. "Just like we always have. This isn't the end, Ava. It's just... a bump in the road."

I wanted to believe him. I wanted to cling to the hope that our love could withstand anything. But the uncertainty gnawed at me, a relentless whisper that reminded me of the stakes we faced. "What if I lose you?"

He pulled me closer, the world around us fading into a soft blur. "You won't. I promise you that. I'm not going anywhere."

His words wrapped around me like a cocoon, and for a moment, I felt safe. The sun dipped lower on the horizon, casting a golden hue over the garden, illuminating the flowers in a way that made them appear almost ethereal. It was beautiful and tragic, much like the reality we were facing.

As the vibrant colors of dusk deepened into rich purples and soft blues, I leaned into Nate, letting the warmth of his body chase away the chill of uncertainty. Together, we stood amidst the blooms, the silence only broken by the soft rustling of leaves and the distant call of a night bird. I could feel the weight of our fears, but I also felt the strength of our connection.

"Remember when we talked about traveling the world together?" I asked, a wistful smile breaking through the heaviness.

"Of course," he replied, his eyes sparkling with the remnants of dreams we had spun in this very garden. "And I still think we should go. Just us, with nothing but our backpacks and a map. Adventure awaits."

"Just like in the movies," I said, allowing myself to picture it: us, wandering through bustling markets, laughing over shared meals, dancing under foreign stars. The thought was intoxicating, a fleeting escape from the reality looming on the horizon.

"Exactly like in the movies," he echoed, his gaze locked onto mine, the weight of his promise hanging in the air. "But first, let's make sure we get through this trial. One step at a time, right?"

The sun finally dipped below the horizon, leaving behind a canvas of darkness speckled with stars, each one a reminder of our dreams yet to be fulfilled. I took a deep breath, the crisp evening air filling my lungs, mingling with the scent of the flowers around us.

"Together, then," I said softly, my heart swelling with hope despite the uncertainty that still lingered.

"Always together," he affirmed, his voice steady.

In that moment, as the world fell silent around us, I allowed myself to believe that love could indeed transcend the storms we faced. The garden was our haven, a sanctuary of color and warmth, a reminder that amidst the chaos, beauty could still bloom.

The stars began to twinkle above us like scattered diamonds, shimmering softly against the velvet backdrop of night. The evening air, now cool and fragrant with the scent of night-blooming jasmine, enveloped us in a tender embrace. I could feel the weight of the world outside our garden sanctuary pressing down, yet within these confines, time felt suspended, allowing us to bask in the warmth of our shared moments a little longer. Nate's arms remained around me, sturdy as the oaks that bordered the garden, and I found solace in the rhythm of his heartbeat, a steady reminder that I wasn't alone in this turmoil.

"Do you think we'll ever come back here?" I asked, my voice soft as the breeze that whispered through the leaves. It felt like a ridiculous question, but the thought of the garden, with its blossoming life, made my heart ache.

"Of course we will," Nate replied, his thumb gently stroking the back of my hand. "This place isn't just a garden; it's part of us. Every flower here knows our secrets." He chuckled lightly, and the sound danced around us, easing some of the tension coiled in my chest. "Besides, who else is going to take care of these plants? I can't trust anyone but you not to murder them."

I swatted him playfully on the arm, a smile breaking through my melancholy. "I'll have you know that my peony care is top-notch. It's not my fault they can be a bit temperamental."

"Right, right," he grinned, mischief lighting his eyes. "Just like their gardener."

I leaned into him, the lightness of his teasing a balm to my worries. But the undercurrent of tension was still palpable, each shared laugh tinged with an unspoken dread. "What if things change, Nate? What if we don't come back the same?"

His expression softened, the playful glint replaced by something deeper. "Change is inevitable, Ava. But what matters is how we face it."

I sighed, pulling away just enough to meet his gaze, hoping to decipher the truth within those warm, dark eyes. "You make it sound so simple. But life isn't just a series of choices laid out like a neatly organized toolbox."

Nate chuckled, a low rumble that reverberated through the air. "You know, if it were, I'd have made a 'How to Avoid Life's Messy Situations' handbook by now." He paused, his smile faltering slightly. "But honestly, it's the messiness that makes it all worthwhile. The unpredictability is... well, it's life."

I wanted to believe him, wanted to wrap those words around my heart like a protective shield. But every time I thought of the trial, of the uncertainty hanging over us like a guillotine ready to fall, my insides twisted with fear. "And what if we don't have a happy ending?"

Nate's jaw clenched, a shadow passing over his features as if he could feel the weight of my words. "Hey." He reached up to cup my face, his thumb tracing my cheekbone. "No matter what happens, you need to remember one thing: our story doesn't end here. We've built something beautiful, and that doesn't just vanish because life throws us a curveball."

I wanted to believe him, so desperately that it hurt. "You make it sound so romantic, but life doesn't always follow the script."

"Then we write our own script," he declared, his voice firm, as if the mere act of saying it would conjure the truth into existence. "If the world wants to be dramatic, let it. We'll be the protagonists who find joy in the chaos."

"Protagonists, huh?" I mused, raising an eyebrow. "What do you think our next big adventure will be? Defeating the villain? Finding hidden treasure?"

"Exactly," he said, his eyes twinkling with enthusiasm. "We could be on a treasure hunt for the world's best taco truck."

"Now that sounds like an adventure I can get behind," I laughed, the sound breaking through the clouds of despair hovering over us. "You know, I can picture it now: we'd travel from coast to coast, battling rivals for the last al pastor taco."

"Only to discover that the true treasure was the friends we made along the way," he added, his grin widening. "And the fact that we completely ignored our diets."

We both chuckled, and for a moment, I allowed myself to imagine that future—a life filled with laughter, adventures, and the carefree joy we had once taken for granted. But the gravity of tomorrow soon pulled me back, and I felt my smile falter.

"Seriously, though," I said, my voice dipping into the realm of seriousness again. "What if I lose you in all of this? What if you end up—"

He interrupted, his tone shifting, not harsh but urgent. "Ava, look at me." His fingers found mine again, his grip steady. "I am not going anywhere. No matter what that trial decides, I'm here. I choose you, today and every day after."

His certainty was a balm, and I let it wash over me, saturating the fear with a rush of warmth. "I wish I could be as certain," I admitted, my voice barely above a whisper. "I wish I could see the future and know that it will be okay."

"Maybe we don't have to see the future to know it will be okay," he said, tilting his head as if trying to read my mind. "Maybe it's enough just to take it one day at a time."

I leaned in closer, the comfort of his presence wrapping around me like a favorite blanket. "You're right. That's the key to getting through this: one day, one moment at a time."

As we stood there, the cool breeze rustling the leaves overhead, I felt the boundaries of our small world shift, the weight of possibility expanding within the confines of my heart. "Together?"

"Always together," Nate promised again, his smile infectious and grounding.

We both fell silent, allowing the quiet of the night to envelop us, a shared cocoon of comfort and love. I closed my eyes, letting the sounds of the garden wash over me: the gentle chirp of crickets, the rustle of leaves, the distant hoot of an owl. It felt timeless, suspended between the moments of joy and sorrow, woven together like the vibrant tapestry of our lives.

But as I stood there, nestled against Nate's warmth, I couldn't shake the feeling that we were on the precipice of something monumental, and tomorrow would tip the scales one way or another. The universe seemed to hold its breath, waiting for our next move, and I had to wonder: would we emerge from this trial stronger, or would it fracture us in ways I could only begin to imagine?

The night deepened around us, casting the garden in shades of indigo and shadow, and the air was thick with the heady aroma of jasmine mingling with the lingering scent of the day's warmth. I watched as the stars twinkled to life one by one, like tiny spotlights illuminating the vast stage of our lives, beckoning us into the unknown. Every gentle rustle of the leaves seemed to echo with the questions that hovered just beyond our grasp, the very air vibrating with the electric charge of uncertainty.

Nate, still holding my hands, suddenly broke the silence. "You know, if I had a dollar for every time I thought about running away right now..." He smirked, a lightness in his voice that almost made me forget the gravity of the moment.

"Running away?" I raised an eyebrow, the hint of a smile tugging at my lips. "Where would we even go? I mean, 'No Worries, Australia' sounds nice, but I think they'd prefer tourists who actually pay for their tickets."

"Okay, maybe not Australia," he conceded with a chuckle. "But somewhere far away from courtrooms and lawyers. Picture it: just you and me, a rusty old van, and a playlist of terrible '90s music."

"Now that's a tempting offer," I said, shaking my head. "But we'd probably get lost in the wilderness and wind up as headlines: 'Two Idiots Found Trying to Survive on Granola Bars.'"

He laughed, a deep, rich sound that reverberated through the stillness. "At least it would make for an entertaining read. 'Local couple discovers the magic of nature—after realizing they forgot to pack a tent.'"

"Or we'd set the forest on fire trying to roast marshmallows," I added, picturing our hilarious failure. "What a legacy that would leave!"

"True, but I'd rather be known for our escapades than our misfortunes in a courtroom," he replied, his gaze shifting to the stars above, a hint of longing etched across his features.

The laughter we shared felt like a fragile bubble, shimmering in the night air but threatened to burst at any moment. As the echoes of our humor faded, reality rushed back in, a tidal wave of impending separation that crashed over me. I bit my lip, fighting against the sudden swell of emotion that threatened to choke me.

"What if it goes wrong tomorrow?" I whispered, the words slipping out before I could reel them back in. "What if they decide to make an example of you?"

Nate turned serious, the playful banter evaporating like dew under the rising sun. "Ava, I know the stakes are high, but you have to believe in us. I'm not some random statistic; I'm the guy who's going to fight tooth and nail to prove my worth."

"But you shouldn't have to fight," I replied, frustration bubbling within me. "This shouldn't be happening. It's so unfair!"

He squeezed my hands tighter, his warmth flooding through me. "Life is inherently unfair. I've realized that the only way to navigate it is to grab onto the people we love and hold on for dear life."

The weight of his words sank in, pressing against the hope I still clung to. "It's just... I can't bear the thought of you facing all of this alone."

"You're not alone in this," he said, his eyes steady on mine. "You're part of my team, remember? We'll face whatever comes together."

I inhaled sharply, a lump forming in my throat as the gravity of our situation threatened to overwhelm me. "Together. It sounds so perfect in theory, but what if I'm not strong enough to hold you up?"

Nate released one of my hands and gently brushed a strand of hair behind my ear, his touch sending sparks racing down my spine. "If you ever doubt your strength, just look at these flowers," he said, gesturing around us. "They survive storms, droughts, and harsh winters. They bloom through it all. You're just as resilient."

His words wrapped around me like a warm embrace, but the doubt still clung stubbornly. "I just wish I could protect you from all of this."

"We can't protect each other from everything," he replied softly, "but we can be each other's shield, even if it means taking a few hits along the way."

I looked into his eyes, searching for the reassurance I so desperately needed. There was a quiet determination there, a flicker of the fire that had drawn me to him in the first place. "Promise me one thing," I said, my voice trembling.

"Anything."

"If it gets too heavy... if the weight of it all drags you down, just tell me. I need to know you're okay."

"Only if you promise the same," he shot back, a playful glint returning to his eyes. "No martyrdom allowed. We're in this together, remember?"

"Fine," I conceded, the corners of my mouth lifting in a reluctant smile. "But if you start acting like a lone wolf, I'm showing up with a pack of fierce friends to drag you back."

"Deal."

The tension eased slightly, and for a moment, we stood wrapped in the cocoon of our laughter and whispered promises, but it wasn't long before the night stretched on, bringing with it an uncomfortable stillness.

As I gazed up at the stars, something shifted in the atmosphere, a charged current running through the air. The night felt heavier, the shadows deeper. I glanced sideways at Nate, who had grown uncharacteristically silent, his brow furrowed in thought.

"What is it?" I asked, sensing the change.

He hesitated, eyes darting to the garden gate. "I just... I thought I heard something."

"Something?" My heart raced, the peaceful night morphing into something foreboding.

Nate straightened, his demeanor shifting, alert and tense. "It might be nothing, but..."

Before he could finish, a distant sound pierced the tranquility, like the soft crunch of gravel beneath a heavy boot. My stomach dropped as the shadows around the gate shifted.

"Nate..."

"I know." He stepped in front of me, instinctively shielding me as the figure emerged from the darkness, their features obscured by the veil of night.

"Is that...?" I began, my heart racing, every instinct screaming for us to retreat.

The figure moved closer, and the moonlight caught a glint of something metallic in their hand.

"Stay behind me," Nate whispered, his voice low and steady.

The person stepped into the light, and I gasped, recognition crashing over me like a wave. "No way. It can't be."

But it was. The figure smirked, a familiar but unwelcome presence that shattered the fragile peace we had crafted around ourselves.

"Surprise," they said, voice dripping with mockery, as the realization sank in. This encounter was just the beginning of something far more tumultuous than either of us had ever anticipated.

Chapter 29: The Dawn of Tomorrow

Every step through the hospital's polished corridors felt like navigating a labyrinth woven from threads of dread and hope. The antiseptic scent hung heavy in the air, mingling with the faint aroma of coffee wafting from the café down the hall. I paused to catch my breath, leaning against a wall adorned with pastel artwork depicting serene landscapes. They were a stark contrast to the whirlwind of emotions churning within me. A month ago, the very thought of being here, facing the prospect of a trial, would have sent my mind spiraling into a chasm of despair. But today, there was a flicker of courage lighting my way.

Nate's hand enveloped mine, warm and steady, a lifeline in this sea of uncertainty. His fingers intertwined with mine, each squeeze a silent promise that I wasn't alone in this. He stood beside me, a silent sentinel, his expression a mixture of worry and fierce determination. I could see the tiny lines of stress etching themselves on his forehead, his dark hair tousled yet charmingly unkempt, as if he had run his hands through it a hundred times while waiting for this moment. "You know, if I could, I'd take your place in there," he said, breaking the silence. The lightheartedness in his tone was a feeble attempt to mask the gravity of the situation.

"I wouldn't let you," I retorted, my lips curling into a smile despite the fluttering in my stomach. "You'd probably cry the moment they handed you a needle."

His laugh, deep and infectious, echoed off the walls. "Maybe. But I'd look really good doing it."

Our banter floated like a buoy in turbulent waters, keeping us afloat. There was something undeniably comforting about our exchanges—an anchor amidst the chaos. As I gazed into his warm hazel eyes, I felt the weight of my fears lift, if only for a moment. It was hard to reconcile the Ava who had spent countless nights in anguish with the woman standing here, ready to embrace a future that teetered on the edge of possibility.

"Ready?" Nate's voice was a gentle nudge, a reminder of the reality waiting just beyond those sterile doors. I nodded, though my heart raced like a wild stallion eager to escape. The waiting room was a cacophony of hushed conversations, the occasional blip of medical machinery, and the rustling of papers. Families huddled together, their expressions ranging from hopeful to resigned, each of them battling their own unspoken fears.

We settled into a pair of stiff chairs, the vinyl seats creaking beneath our weight. I leaned back, attempting to steal a moment of calm, but the rhythmic beeping of the monitors played a frantic symphony in my head. I could feel the tension radiating off Nate as he squeezed my hand, and for a fleeting moment, I let my eyes wander. Each face around us told a story—some etched with sorrow, others shining with determination. I couldn't help but wonder what trials they were facing, what burdens they carried. Were they hoping for miracles? Did they feel the weight of their choices, heavy like a stone in their chests?

"Look at us," I said, attempting to lighten the mood. "We're practically a rom-com waiting to happen. Girl with a medical mystery and her handsome, slightly neurotic boyfriend."

Nate smirked, a playful glint in his eyes. "Right. But I bet our story has a few plot twists in store."

I rolled my eyes but couldn't suppress the warmth blooming within me. The corners of my mouth twitched up as I leaned into him, our shoulders brushing. "What if the plot twist is that I wake up from this trial and discover I'm actually a superhero? That would make for an interesting sequel."

"Then I'd have to become your sidekick," he teased, winking at me. "But I'd need a cool outfit. Maybe something with capes? Capes are always a good choice."

Laughter bubbled up, breaking the heaviness in my chest. Our whimsical conversation served as a sanctuary from the reality looming over us. I closed my eyes, envisioning that superhero version of myself—a version unbound by fears or limitations. But as soon as I opened them, the walls around us returned, stark and unyielding, a constant reminder of the momentous event ahead.

The minutes ticked by, each one stretching longer than the last. I could feel the heaviness of anticipation thickening the air. Finally, a doctor entered the waiting area, her presence commanding instant attention. Her crisp white coat contrasted sharply with the soft pastels of the room. She scanned the faces of the anxious families, her expression a blend of empathy and professionalism.

"Ava Bennett?" she called, her voice steady yet soothing.

A shiver ran down my spine at the sound of my name. I felt Nate's grip tighten, a shared understanding passing between us. It was time. The reality of the trial sank in deeper, intertwining with the hope I clung to like a fragile thread.

"I'm here," I said, my voice steadier than I felt. The doctor approached, and her warm smile was a balm to my frayed nerves.

"Are you ready?" she asked gently, her eyes searching mine.

The question hung in the air, pregnant with meaning. I looked at Nate, who nodded, his eyes reflecting unwavering support. I took a deep breath, summoning every ounce of courage I could muster. "Yes. I'm ready."

As I stood, a rush of adrenaline surged through me. I wasn't just walking into a procedure; I was stepping into the unknown, a blank canvas awaiting the brushstrokes of my future. Nate's hand lingered on my back as I moved toward the doorway, a silent pledge of love and strength. Together, we would face whatever came next, and in that moment, I understood that the bond we shared was a fortress, unbreakable and fierce against the storm that lay ahead.

The fluorescent lights buzzed overhead, casting a harsh glow on the stark white walls as I followed the nurse down the corridor. Each step echoed with a blend of uncertainty and anticipation, my heart a restless drumbeat in my chest. As we turned a corner, I caught sight of a window overlooking a small garden, where a single tree stood tall amid patches of colorful blooms. It reminded me of the resilience found in nature, bending but never breaking, and I clung to that image like a lifeline.

"Almost there," the nurse said, glancing back with a smile that didn't quite reach her eyes. I appreciated the effort, though. It felt like an unspoken acknowledgment of our shared anxiety. I could sense Nate's presence behind me, the warmth of his being a constant reminder that I wasn't alone in this. The distance between us felt insurmountable yet comforting, as if the air between us vibrated with our shared fears and hopes.

We reached a door labeled "Preparation Room," and the nurse gestured for me to enter. I hesitated, a sudden wave of doubt crashing over me. "What if I'm not strong enough for this?" The words slipped out before I could stop them. I hadn't expected to voice my fear, but the weight of the moment pulled the truth from my lips.

Nate stepped forward, brushing a strand of hair behind my ear, a gesture so simple yet so profound. "You're the strongest person I know," he said softly, his gaze steady. "You've made it through so much already. You've got this, Ava."

I swallowed hard, his faith in me acting as a shield against my swirling doubts. I nodded, the movement almost imperceptible but resolute. With a deep breath, I stepped inside the room, the cool air tinged with the scent of antiseptic and something else—maybe hope? Or perhaps it was the unmistakable scent of new beginnings.

The room was small, dominated by an examination table in the center, surrounded by various medical instruments that gleamed under the lights like shiny, menacing creatures. I climbed onto the table, the sterile fabric crinkling beneath me. I felt vulnerable, exposed, but I forced myself to focus on the tiny details around me. The framed photos on the wall caught my eye: snapshots of smiling patients, each one embodying triumph over adversity. If they could conquer their fears, so could I.

As the nurse began her preparations, she chatted easily, a practiced distraction. "You know, we've had some amazing stories come out of this trial," she said, her hands deftly organizing equipment. "One patient came in with almost no hope and walked out ready to climb mountains."

"Mountains, huh?" I replied, trying to mirror her lightness. "What kind of mountains are we talking about? The intimidating ones, or the gentle hills?"

She laughed, and for a moment, the tension in the room shifted. "Definitely the intimidating ones. He even sent us pictures from the summit. It was beautiful—just like the view I'm sure you'll have when you're standing on your own mountain someday."

"Good to know I'm in good company," I replied, a flicker of hope igniting within me.

Moments later, the doctor entered, her demeanor professional yet warm. "Ava," she said, offering a reassuring smile. "I'm Dr. Edwards. Are you feeling ready?"

"As ready as I'll ever be," I answered, injecting a hint of bravado into my tone, though my insides still felt like a jumbled mess of nerves.

She reviewed my chart with meticulous care, her brow furrowed slightly as she studied the details. "We're going to do everything we can to ensure your comfort during the trial. You're in great hands, and remember, we'll monitor you closely."

Nate's presence was a comforting weight beside me as the doctor prepared for the procedure. He shifted closer, his shoulder brushing against mine, and I could feel his silent support in the air between

us. I took a deep breath, allowing the steadiness of his energy to seep
into me. I had to believe in this, in us.

"Okay, Ava," Dr. Edwards said, turning her attention back to me.
"Let's begin. Just focus on your breathing, and I'll walk you through
each step."

As the nurse administered the first IV, I felt a prick in my arm
and then the slow trickle of the medicine entering my veins. I closed
my eyes, breathing in deep and slow. With each inhalation, I
visualized that garden outside, the blooms vibrant and alive against
the green, and I imagined the world bursting forth with color after a
long winter.

Nate's voice cut through the silence, a lifeline in this surreal
moment. "You remember our trip to that flower festival last spring?"
he asked, his tone reminiscent, coaxing a smile from my lips.

"Of course! You and that ridiculous hat," I teased, picturing him
in that oversized sun hat, a colorful floral band wrapped around
it. He had insisted it was an essential accessory, but the laughter it
brought made it all worthwhile.

"Hey, it was a statement piece," he defended, his voice
mock-serious. "I was practically a fashion icon."

"Sure, if we're talking about the fashion of the 1990s," I shot
back, grinning at the memory.

Dr. Edwards cleared her throat, suppressing a smile as she
prepared the next step of the procedure. "You two are quite the pair.
I'll bet you keep each other on your toes."

"Oh, you have no idea," Nate replied, a lightness in his tone that
filled the room like sunshine. "Ava's the one who makes life exciting.
I'm just trying to keep up."

The procedure continued, a series of moments interwoven with
laughter and soft words of encouragement. The gentle hum of
machines became a backdrop to our shared banter, and for a while,
I felt weightless, as if I were floating above the anxiety tethering

me to the ground. I could almost convince myself that this wasn't happening—that we were just two friends reminiscing, sharing laughter in a sun-drenched park instead of a sterile room.

But then a sudden jolt of panic pierced through the laughter. I glanced at the IV, the fluid steadily dripping, and my heart raced. What if it didn't work? What if I was making a huge mistake? The fleeting thoughts clawed at me, threatening to unravel the fragile calm I had managed to weave.

Nate must have sensed my shift, for he leaned closer, his voice a low murmur. "Hey, look at me." His eyes were intense, grounding me in a way that felt both comforting and terrifying. "Whatever happens, I'm right here. We're in this together, and I promise you, no matter the outcome, we'll find a way through."

His words, sincere and unwavering, wrapped around me like a warm blanket. In that moment, I allowed myself to lean into his strength, to let go of the spiraling fears. The trial wasn't just a test of my physical strength; it was a testament to the love and support that had carried me thus far. The warmth of our shared memories became a beacon of hope, illuminating the path ahead, however uncertain it may be.

The air was thick with anticipation as I lay on the examination table, my heart beating like a metronome against the backdrop of sterile machinery. Each beep seemed to synchronize with the chaotic rhythm of my thoughts. I could feel Nate's presence beside me, a steadying force, his fingers tracing small circles on my palm—a comforting ritual we had developed during our journey together. The sound of the IV drip, steady and methodical, almost seemed to mock my anxiety. The nurse, still bustling about, had a demeanor that suggested she had been through this many times before, a calm amid the storm.

"You know, I always imagined that when I had my life-changing moment, it would involve a grand adventure, not a hospital gown," I quipped, breaking the silence that had enveloped us. The white fabric clung awkwardly to my body, devoid of any glamor, and I couldn't help but think of the countless movies where the protagonist found themselves transformed through epic quests or romantic gestures.

Nate chuckled, his eyes sparkling with mischief. "Well, maybe this is your grand adventure. Think of it as an extreme sport. You could be the first person to conquer the 'Trial of the Hospital Gown.'"

"Sounds riveting," I shot back, rolling my eyes. "I can already see the highlights reel: 'Ava, battling the IV drip, daringly navigating the maze of hospital furniture!'"

"Don't forget the climactic twist where you accidentally trip over your own feet while trying to look heroic." His laughter filled the room, the kind that warms you from the inside out, igniting a spark of light amidst the sterile surroundings.

The doctor returned, her smile professional but genuine. "All right, Ava, let's get started," she said, her voice steady, bringing me back to the gravity of the moment.

I nodded, summoning my courage. As the doctor began explaining the procedure, my mind drifted momentarily, envisioning a life beyond this moment—sunsets by the beach, laughter spilling into the night as we danced under the stars. I wanted that life; I needed that life.

"Focus on your breathing," the doctor advised, sensing the tension tightening in my shoulders. I inhaled deeply, trying to fill my lungs with courage instead of fear, reminding myself that I was not just here for me, but for Nate too.

The room filled with a soft whir as the machines hummed to life, and the doctor initiated the first phase of the trial. My heart raced as the sensation coursed through me—cold and strangely electric. I squeezed Nate's hand tighter, seeking comfort in the warmth of his skin.

"Hey, you're doing great," he whispered, his voice a soothing balm against my rising anxiety. "Just think of all those ridiculous things you want to do after this."

"Like getting that tattoo of a cat wearing a monocle?" I replied, stifling a nervous laugh.

"Exactly! And maybe a little bow tie for extra flair," he teased, his smile contagious.

The doctor continued her work, occasionally glancing at the monitors, her brows furrowing with focus. The sensation in my arm intensified, and a wave of unease washed over me. "Is it supposed to feel like this?" I asked, trying to mask the tremor in my voice.

"Perfectly normal," she assured me, though I detected a hint of something more serious in her tone. "Just a few more moments."

But as the minutes ticked by, the discomfort shifted from merely strange to alarming. I felt a sudden jolt—sharp, like a bolt of lightning racing up my arm. My breath hitched, and I looked at Nate, panic flooding my veins.

"Something's wrong," I managed to say, my voice barely above a whisper.

Nate's face darkened, concern etched into every feature. "Doctor?" he called, his tone no longer playful. The room's atmosphere shifted dramatically, turning electric with tension.

"Stay calm, Ava," Dr. Edwards said, her voice a mixture of reassurance and urgency. She leaned closer, eyes narrowing as she began to adjust settings on the machines. "Just breathe through it."

But I couldn't. The sensation morphed into something foreign and terrifying, a swirling storm of confusion that swept through my body. I felt like I was unraveling, threads of my reality fraying at the edges.

"Is this supposed to happen?" Nate's voice cut through the chaos, fierce and protective.

"Let's not jump to conclusions," the doctor replied, though the tension in her voice betrayed her certainty. "Ava, can you tell me what you're feeling?"

"I feel... strange," I gasped, my heart pounding like a drum. "Like I'm losing control."

A fleeting moment of fear flickered in Nate's eyes, but he quickly masked it with a reassuring smile, the kind that didn't quite reach his eyes. "You've got this. You've conquered everything that has come your way so far," he said, his voice steady but laced with urgency.

And then it happened—the world around me shifted abruptly, colors bleeding together, sounds warping into a haunting melody that sent my heart racing. I felt weightless, as though I were being pulled in multiple directions at once. It was like being caught in a whirlwind, and the fabric of reality felt thin, like I could reach out and touch another dimension.

"Hold on, Ava," the doctor instructed, her voice distant yet urgent. "We need to stabilize—"

But her words faded, and I was falling, spiraling into darkness. Panic surged, and I grasped desperately at the tendrils of light that flickered just beyond my reach.

"Help! Nate!" I cried out, but the sound was swallowed by the void. Everything blurred, and for a split second, I felt completely and utterly alone.

Just when I thought I was lost, a familiar warmth enveloped me, pulling me back from the abyss. Nate's voice broke through the chaos, fierce and unwavering. "Ava, I'm right here! Focus on me!"

But just as I reached for him, something jolted through me, a pulse of energy that felt like a thunderclap in my veins. My eyes shot open, and I gasped, the world around me snapping back into focus—only, it wasn't the same. The room was eerily quiet, the machines had gone silent, and the air felt heavy with unspoken words.

I blinked, confusion swirling within me. "What just happened?"

Nate's face was pale, eyes wide with a mixture of fear and determination. "You were—something happened. The monitors—"

But before he could finish, the door burst open, and a flurry of medical staff rushed in, faces grave, eyes locking onto me with a mixture of concern and urgency. "Ava, we need you to remain calm," one of them said, but the words felt like a distant echo.

And just as I was about to ask what was happening, I caught a glimpse of something in the corner of my vision—a flicker of movement, a shadow darting across the far wall. The atmosphere shifted again, a tension thick enough to slice through, leaving me teetering on the edge of an uncertainty I had never imagined.

"Stay with me, Ava!" Nate's voice was the last thing I heard before the world around me slipped into a haze, and the flickering shadows began to take form.

Milton Keynes UK
Ingram Content Group UK Ltd.
UKHW040257181024
449757UK00001B/99